SASSY

Other Books Published by Gloria Mallette

Living, Breathing Lies
Weeping Willows Dance

Backlist

Shades of Jade
Promises to Keep
The Honey Well
Distant Lover
What's Done in the Dark
If There Be Pain
When We Practice to Deceive

Gloria Mallette

SASSY

Gemini Press

www.gloriamallette.com

SASSY

Gemini Press
P.O. Box 488
Bartonsville, PA 18321

For Information: gempress@aol.com
Visit website: www.gloriamallette.com

Cover Design: Marion Designs   www.mariondesigns.com

ISBN: 978-0-9678789-3-5

LCCN: 2007936389

First Trade Paperback Printing: May 2009

Printed in Canada

ACKNOWLEDGMENTS

With so much going on in the world today, I must first thank God for allowing me to continue on my literary journey in sound mind and body; and hope for the future.

I also thank my husband Arnold, who continually immerses himself in the world of academics because of his great love for education. Until Sassy, Arnold had never read any of my novels; however, from day one he has traveled this road along with me. I thank Arnold for pushing me to self-publish Shades of Jade nine years ago, and as well for putting down his text books long enough to read Sassy. Much love, respect, and appreciation to my love for believing in me and for marrying me twenty-three years ago.

To my son Jared who wants to be a climatologist or meteorologist when he grows up. Jared, stay the course. You have the foundation, but it is your job to build your future one brick at a time. Focus, determination, hard work, and follow-through will get you the prize. I absolutely adore you.

Who am I without the readers of my books? Thank you all for hanging in there with me. I appreciate your vote of confidence and continued support.

The journey continues.

Prologue

Thursday, 3:38 p.m.

LOUD! The music was loud! The bass thunderous! The singing exhilarating! The catchy, finger-popping, toe-tapping music was heart pounding; but there was no party. There was no dancing. There was no one to enjoy the music that penetrated the blood-splattered egg shell colored walls inside Myra Barrett's statically still apartment, and seeped through plaster and concrete walls out into the adjourning apartments and into the long, narrow hallways of Ellington Tower Apartments. Myra couldn't understand why no one was pounding at her door yelling for her to turn down the music. Her floor, the thirteenth, was one of the quietest floors in the whole twenty-two story building and it was rare for anyone to blast their music so loudly. Maybe that was because most of the tenants of the ten apartments on Myra's floor were over fifty years old. That is except for Myra herself and Alice Reynolds down the hall. Myra was only twenty-seven. She wasn't ready to die.

"God," Myra said feebly with the taste of blood on her tongue, "help me."

Someone had to hear the music. Someone had to be annoyed. The music was deafening. With the right side of her face smashed into the floor, Myra's head was pounding from the roaring bass which made the floor under her pain-racked, blood soaked body vibrate. The walls had to be vibrating, too. They usually did on the rare occasion when the music was especially loud. By now Mrs. Harris next door should have been banging on the door hollering for Myra to turn down her music. Mrs. Harris was diabetic, arthritic, fat, and old. She rarely ever went out except to go to church on Sunday mornings or to see her doctors during the week. Luckily, Mrs. Harris's daughter Barbara did her shopping and squired her to and from her doctors' appointments.

Did Mrs. Harris have a doctor's appointment today? Did she? Where in the world was she? God, please let her come. Please, God.

Myra started to gag. The taste of her own blood seeping into her mouth from her throat reminded Myra that her weak hold on a life she desperately wanted to continue living was slipping away.

Looking back, if Myra could live her life over, there were things she would certainly change, but having Jada would not be one. Sure it had been hard raising Jada alone, but Myra had no regrets. Jada was the reason Myra got out of bed in the morning, and the reason why she hated that she was dying. Thank God Jada was with her grandmother and wasn't there to see her die. Oh, God, Mama. Nita Barrett was not going to be able to handle her death, not after losing her other two children, Russell and Micky, to the cold, well-aimed bullets that snuffed out their worthless lives. Myra grimaced from the intense pain of the stab wounds in her chest and stomach and then from the painful memory of losing her brothers just months apart three years ago. Her mother nearly had a nervous breakdown, but she had been there for her mother to lean on. What about now? Who was her mother going to lean on? How was her mother going to hold herself together to take care of Jada? Oh, God, she had to live. Carrie, her best friend, was lying dead in the back hallway. There was no one else Myra could count on to do right by her baby, especially not Norris. He was the one killing her.

And that was just it. If she had one more chance, what she would most definitely change in her life would be her stupid decision to see Norris outside of the office. He was her boss. For two years she was his executive assistant. She should have left it at that, but when she bumped into him one evening after he asked her out, she didn't say no. Who would? He was so nice, so good-looking, so rich.

"I don't ever mix business with pleasure," he said over dinner, "but I like being with you."

That's how it began. That's how they started seeing each other outside of the office.

"What we do in the office is business," he said. "What we do outside is personal. No one is to know we're seeing each other."

Norris meant what he said. In the office no one had an inkling that they were seeing each other. At times it was disconcerting that she saw the man she sometimes slept with in the office everyday but he acted like he didn't know her beyond her job description. Then she figured if Norris could live his life like that, so could she. He was so worth it, and it was a win-win for her. He was nice to her in the office, he was nice to her outside the office, and he was especially nice to Jada. He never came to visit empty-handed. Jada looked forward to seeing him. He was Santa to them both. Everything was good until now. It was Norris who had savagely plunged the knife into her body more times than she could keep count of. How was she to know when he first kissed her five months ago that he would take her life?

Gagging and then coughing weakly, Myra tried to clear her throat so that she could breathe easier. Even if she was dying, she didn't want to die too soon, but she had to stop thinking about dying. It was life she wanted. Life.

Wow. How funny life was. It was Norris who told her she should not settle for the life she had that she thought was successful. He said she should strive for more. Since she started working for him, she moved out of the Albany Housing

Projects where she was born, and she was only six credits from getting her BA in business administration. She loved working for Yoshito and Braithwaithe. Norris paid her well, but since they started seeing each other outside of the office, he encouraged her to go for her dream of becoming a singer, and she wanted so badly to live to sing again.

How could she be so stupid? She should have known when Norris, out of the blue, wanted to have a personal relationship with her that he meant her no good. He was a great boss but she should have been suspicious of him when he started coming on to her, especially when he had always been about business! Why didn't she see this coming? Hadn't her mother called her naive when it came to trusting people? Yes! Wasn't she warned? Didn't Carrie warn her? The first time she brought Norris home, Carrie had seen right through the warm inviting smile, the calm demeanor, the noble selflessness.

"He reminds me of a cobra waiting for the right moment to strike," Carrie said, but she chalked Carrie's angst up to ignorance of someone different from herself.

Norris was part Japanese and part African-American. His skin was light brown, his black hair was adorably curly, and his eyes were clearly almond shaped. He was born in Japan, but after his mother and father died when he was twelve, he was adopted by an American family and lived the past twenty-three years in America. That made Norris just as American as Carrie, but Carrie labeled Norris an interloper in her country as well as in Myra's life. Carrie kept saying Norris wasn't right but couldn't put her finger exactly on what it was.

"He's playing you, Myra. He latched onto you like a blood sucking leech and you lay back and let him have the run of our apartment. What's up with that? He comes and goes from here like he's the man of the house."

It was a mistake to let Carrie move in with her. She wouldn't be dead now.

"Carrie, lighten up. Norris is a great guy and he's a lot of fun like you used to be. Now, you're so darn serious."

"At least I'm no phony. Myra, wake up! Why can't you see something's wrong! I'm telling you, this guy is smiling in your face for a reason, and it's not because he likes you. No one is that nice and wants nothing in return. He's a psycho. Can't you see it?"

"If that's your assessment of Norris, Carrie, I guess it's too much to ask you to try and get along with him."

"Damn right!"

"So what do we do? I like Norris and he's going to keep coming around as often as I want him to."

After a long bitter glower, Carrie sucked her teeth and stalked out of the apartment, slamming the door hard enough to wake the dead. That was two days ago. Until today, Carrie hadn't been back. Poor, Carrie. Her bloody body lay crumpled up like a rag doll in the back hall. Carrie must have fought hard, blood was every where. She should not have had to die like that. It wasn't right. God, if only she had listened to Carrie. If only she had sensed what Carrie was intuitively sure of, but the truth was, she had been hoping Norris would one day marry her. She never told Carrie, but then she never told Carrie every time Norris made love to her, she felt like she was being raped. In bed, Norris treated her like a hooker he'd picked up from a dark corner up near the Hunt's Point Meat Markets. Two days ago when he choked her, why didn't she see then that he did indeed have another side to him? Was it because he apologized in so many humble, sweet ways she couldn't doubt his sincerity? How then could he turn around a day later and plunge a knife into her body? How could Norris do this to her? *Oh, God!* Footfalls. *He's coming back! Oh, God.*

Myra tried to stop breathing in what little air she was getting. She could feel Norris standing over her. She could feel him looking down upon her with the same evil mask of disdain he wore when he first started stabbing her. She had no idea he hated her so.

Norris laid his hand on Myra's back. She didn't move. She held her breath.

Was he checking to see if she was still alive? What if he realized that she was? Was he going to stab her again? Myra's straining heart barely bleeped while all feelings in her body left her. She was numb. Yet, the nauseating smell of her own warm blood sickened her. She wanted to cough to clear her throat but she made herself hold still although she probably could not have moved if she wanted to.

God, please let this horrible nightmare end.

Norris plunged the knife into Myra's back. Myra screamed—at least she thought she screamed, but her scream was silent to her own ears.

Norris took a moment to look around the apartment. "Two whores down, two bastards to go."

Myra didn't understand what Norris was saying. His voice sounded like a far off whisper on the wind. Although she had not totally surrendered her life, she had no strength to hang on. If she was breathing, Myra didn't know it. The only thing she knew was that she was cold, very cold. Myra felt herself drifting off. Sleep. Yes, she needed to sleep—

#   #   #   #

Norris stood in the center of the room. Slowly he inhaled deeply and just as slowly, he let the air out of his lungs. Several more times he cleared his lungs till he felt clear in his head. That's when he heard the music. It was suddenly too loud. It boomed in his ears. He couldn't take all the bass. He rushed over to the CD player and shut it off. A deadly, ominous silence fell over the entire apartment. Norris stood stark still. His eyes lazily drifted from the CD player up to the smiling portrait of Jada hanging on the wall above the television. He never did like that kid. Her ugly smile always made him want to slap her face, but he never did, he couldn't. It would have ruined everything.

Norris started to rub his hands together but the stickiness stopped him. He looked down at the blood that covered him. He winced. He turned his hands over and saw he'd been scratched on his arm. That was alright. He had nothing to worry about. He held both hands out from his body as he looked down at his clothes. Dark red blood covered him. Without bothering to unbutton his shirt, Norris yanked the shirt up over his head. He couldn't get out of it fast enough, but then he looked down at his chest and saw he had just as much blood on his skin.

"Damn!" He began turning in circles, looking about the room until he saw what he was looking for, a black canvas gym bag next to the window. He went right to the bag and checked it. No blood appeared to be on the outside or the inside of the bag where he had a change of clothes. That is after he showered. Tonight, he had a date with someone very special.

1

Thursday, 7:30 p.m.

Sassy signed her name for what seemed the hundredth time. There was an incredible cramp in two of her fingers that made her grip the pen tighter. She glanced up at the line of people waiting their turn to get their books autographed by her. The E-mail blast to all the Romance Readers Book Club members had worked wonderfully well. She had been signing at Barnes and Noble at Union Square for an hour and a half and there were still at least twenty women waiting to get their books autographed. At this hour many of the women on line had come to the bookstore after their own long workday. All the more reason why she wouldn't dare take a break and alienate a single one of them as her goal was to sell sixty books before she called it quits. And that was at eight, a half an hour away. Cramped fingers or not, grinning and baring it was what she was going to do.

"Sassy, I've read all nine of your previous books," the woman said, "I loved them all, especially *Love Waits.*"

"Thank you." Smiling, Sassy took the opportunity to let her pen slip from her fingers so she could stretch them out. "I hope you'll enjoy *Butterfly* just as much."

"I'm sure I will."

"Thank you," Sassy took the next book from the outstretched hand. "What is—"

"Norris."

That certainly was no woman's name nor was it a woman's voice. Sassy looked up into the handsome face of 'Jason' as she imagined he'd look in her writer's mind.

Norris smiled. Sassy's heart fluttered. Norris had "Jason's" beautiful, weaken-the-knees kind of smile.

Sassy began writing, 'To Norris—"

"Yoshito. Y. .o. .s. .h. .i. .t. .o."

Sassy quickly wrote Norris's name and ended it with, 'Bless you, Sassy Davenport.' Smiling, she handed the closed book back to him.

Taking back his book with one hand, Norris handed Sassy another with the other.

Sassy took the book. "For a friend?"

Norris looked down at the large shopping bag at his side. "For several friends."

Sassy also looked into the shopping bag. It was full of her books. "Well, how nice. Thank you."

"No, thank you. I've always been impressed with your work," Norris said, his voice seductively low.

Sassy smiled as she autographed the second book. "You're a rare breed—a man who reads romance."

"Perhaps, but since we indulge in romance, why not read it?"

"Why not indeed?" Sassy felt heat intensifying on the nape of her neck. She didn't know if she should attribute the rise in her temperature to the flirtatious twinkle in Norris Yoshito's eyes or to his seductive smile.

"I hope you don't mind signing all ten copies?"

Sassy told herself to not focus on how hot she suddenly was. She glanced at the long line and was reminded of her cramped fingers. "Of course not."

The red-headed, frumpy store manager suddenly stepped up to the table. "Excuse me, sir, but the line is rather long. For now, there is a two-autograph per person limit."

Norris glanced down at his shopping bag. "Is that so?

But there is no limit on the number of books any one person may purchase, is there?"

Flustered, the store manager tucked a lock of hair behind her ear. "Well. . .sir. . .we—"

"Mr. Yoshito," Sassy said, speaking up, "If you'll leave the books with me, and give me your name and address, and the names of the people you want the books autographed to, I'll sign them when I'm done here and I'll have them delivered to your home."

"Sir," the store manager said, "we could hold the books here for you for pick up at a more convenient time."

The store manager's suggestion earned her a cool, annoyed look from Norris.

"Let's do this," Sassy said. "Mr. Yoshito, please, leave the books with me. I'll sign them and I'll personally make sure you get them."

"I appreciate that." Norris handed the shopping bag to the silent store manager. "I'll just step over there and write out my list."

"That would be fine," Sassy said.

The store manager sat the shopping bag on the floor next to Sassy's chair. She took Norris's second book and returned it to the bag.

Feeling quite pleased with herself, Sassy reached out to the next person on line.

"Kathy Johnson," the woman said.

"Hi, Kathy." Sassy quickly autographed her book.

Minutes later, a slip of paper was slid on the table in front of Sassy. She knew it was Norris's hand even before she looked up. It was a strong, beautiful hand. His fingers were long; his nails manicured and clean.

"I was thinking," Norris said, "I won't be able to come back here for about a week. Why don't I take a seat in the restaurant across the street and wait until you're done?"

"If you like, but," Sassy said, looking at the line, "it'll be a while."

"I'll wait. Besides, I have nothing better to do."
Sassy arched her brow cynically.

"Of course, I do have a good book to read." Norris tucked his autographed copy of *Butterfly* under his arm. He smiled as he turned to leave. Several women on line smiled as well as they watched him walk away.

Sassy felt like one of her heroines—flustered by the charm and good looks of a dashing stranger. Even her heart was going pitter-patter.

Another book was handed to her. "Hi, Miss Davenport; my name is Lisa Adams."

"Hi Lisa." Sassy eagerly signed the book; funny how the cramping in her fingers seem to no longer bother her.

2

Nita Barrett paced anxiously back and forth in front of the nurse's station. Her cheeks were wet with her tears. Stopping suddenly, she looked up at the ceiling.

"God, who did this to my baby?" Nita began pounding on her chest. "Why? Why? Oh my God. Why?"

A nurse rushed to Nita's side and took hold of her arm to keep her from hurting herself. "Mrs. Barrett, the doctors are doing everything they can to save your daughter life. You must calm yourself before you make yourself sick."

"My baby is in a coma. She's dying," Nita sobbed. "What am I gonna to tell my grand baby? What am I going to do without my baby?"

"Come sit down," the nurse said, taking Nita back to her chair and helping her to sit. She sat down next to Nita, her arm around her shoulders. "Don't think that your daughter will die. Think that she will live."

"You didn't see her! You didn't see all the blood."

"Mrs. Barrett, I understand, but you have to be strong for your daughter. Don't think about how she looked. Think about how beautiful she is in your heart."

"Will you stop telling me how I'm supposed to think! This is my daughter, my baby. I knew something was wrong! My daughter never goes a day without calling me, especially when her child stays with me. If something came up, Myra would have called me! I know my child. I knew something was wrong. And that nasty old super trying to tell me he couldn't let me into her apartment. I'm her mother, dammit! I have a right to go inside my child's apartment. If my baby dies, I want that super locked up!"

The nurse stopped stroking Nita. "She stopped talking altogether."

"Oh, God," Nita cried, clasping her hands together tightly. "Please, God, don't call my baby home to Glory just yet. She got a child of her own to raise, Lord. Please let Myra live. Don't take her like you did my other two babies. Please, Lord." Nita buried her face in her hands and cried.

A young uniformed officer came up and stood in front of the two women. The nurse looked up just as another man, older, his wavy black hair grey at the temples, dressed in a navy blue blazer and jeans came up and stood alongside the officer. In his hand he held a small notepad and pen. He said nothing but the nurse knew who he was. She got up and went back to her station.

The man opened his notepad. He said nothing as he patiently waited for Nita to cry herself out.

Her shoulders shaking, Nita continued to cry.

"Ma'am, I'm Detective Frank Kiefer. I'd like to talk to you about your daughter."

Though she continued to cry, Nita uncovered her face and looked up at Detective Kiefer, who was tired of seeing the tears of mothers hurt by the murder of their children. He sat in the chair the nurse had vacated.

"Ma'am, I know this is a very difficult time for you, but we need to begin the investigation if we are going to catch the perp who did this to your daughter."

Nita began tensely rocking back and forth. She pressed her fingers to her mouth to keep from crying out. Under her breath, she began to moan.

"Mrs. Barrett, do you know of anyone who might have done this? Who might have wanted to harm your daughter?"

Nita's moaning grew louder as she shook her head repeatedly. Tears streamed down her cheeks onto her hands.

"Bear with me, Ma'am. I know it's difficult. Is your daughter married?"

Shaking her head no, Nita moaned pitifully.

"Was your daughter seeing anyone?"

Rocking still, Nita nodded repeatedly.

"Do you know his name?"

Nita lowered her hand to her lap. "Reed Johnson."

Detective Kiefer jotted the name down in his notebook. "Do you know where he lives?"

Nita shook her head.

"Did your daughter ever tell you anything about a disagreement she might have had with Johnson or anyone else she knew?"

Nita said softly, "My daughter had good friends."

"Friends," Detective Kiefer repeated pensively. "Mrs. Barrett, your daughter's apartment was locked from the inside with a key; doubled bolted, in fact."

"I saw that. I was there. I couldn't reach Myra. She wasn't answering her cell phone or her house phone. I knew something was wrong. I just knew."

"Ma'am, when there is no sign of forced entry, chances are the victim knew the assailant."

"Oh, God."

"Who else has a key to your daughter's apartment?"

"Carrie had my key. I was supposed to get another key, but Myra never got around to it."

Detective Keifer glanced at his notepad. "Mrs. Barrett, you told the responding officers that Carrie Kane was your daughter's roommate. How long?"

"About a year. Myra took Carrie in after her and her mother had a falling out."

"Do you know Carrie's mother's name?"

"Betty Kane. She lives on Sterling Avenue in Flatbush. I don't know the exact address."

"We'll find her. What about Carrie Kane? Do you know if she had any enemies?"

"I don't know," Nita said, shaking her head and beginning to cry again. "That poor child. Why?"

"I don't know, ma'am, but I intend to find out. What I need you to do is come up with the names of your daughter's friends. Anything you can tell us may help in this investigation." Detective Kiefer flipped the notepad closed. He beckoned the officer aside. "Stay with her until her family gets here. I'm going back to the apartment. Make sure someone stays with the victim until word comes about her condition. Get it to me right away."

"Yes, sir."

Detective Kiefer, shoving the notepad down inside his jacket pocket, glanced over at Nita Barrett. He shook his head. He had seen this anguish too many times to count. It still left him cold, and it always made him angry. He turned abruptly and walked determinedly out of the hospital.

3

Sassy spotted Norris Yoshito right away among the diners, and again she was impressed. He was really reading her book. The surprise was not that he was reading it, it was a good read, it was that she never see her books in the hands of a man. Women, young and old, made up her fan base, but boy, did it feel good to see her book in the hands of a man. There was something empowering about that. Looking around the restaurant, Sassy wondered how many, if any of the people eating their dinner had ever even heard of her. Her books, although romances, were sprinkled with a strong dose of suspense and were catching on. She had been selling well, and she had gotten great reviews for *Butterfly*, her fourth mainstream novel and her second hard cover, but she was no household name—yet. With each book her readership had grown, but she had yet to have a book turned into a movie. That was her dream—to see her characters come to life on the big screen.

"Table for one?" A waiter asked.

"I'm meeting that gentleman there," she said pointing to Norris who had seen her come in and stood as she was led to the table. He took the shopping bag and held a chair out for her. She stated not to but she sat anyway.

"I'll be back," the waiter said.

"I won't be staying," she said.

The waiter walked off.

"I was hoping you'd have dinner with me." Norris set

the shopping bag next to his chair.

"No, thank you," Sassy said, meaning it. "I hope your friends enjoy my book."

"I have no doubt they will. I'm already enjoying it."

"Good, then I don't have to be embarrassed." Sassy couldn't stop smiling. The man was absolutely divine.

Norris couldn't take his eyes off Sassy. He liked that she was just as attractive as the picture of her on the back of her book. Of course he had known that even before he actually met her. He had seen her in person once before.

The silence was awkward in the midst of so many diners, but Sassy saw only that Norris's gorgeous brown, almond-shaped eyes twinkled when he smiled.

Norris took Sassy's hand and held onto it. "Please, have dinner with me."

It was no surprise to Sassy that Norris's touch was as gentle and as electrifying as it was. She expected that. After all, he was her hero come to life.

"Actually, I have—"

"I won't take no."

"Oh, I have no choice?"

"Of course you do. I hope you choose to join me. I didn't order because I was hoping that you'd honor me by having dinner with me."

"Well, I—"

"Please," Norris said, pulling out the chair for Sassy.

Sassy sat because she really did want to. Never mind that she was supposed to meet Kenneth for dinner. He'd be annoyed with her but so what. Kenneth had stood her up, for business reasons he said, at least three to her never, so he owed her. Right now, she was intrigued by Norris Yoshito. She wanted to know who he was and how is it that he happened to step out of the pages of *Butterfly*.

4

Sassy considered herself a sophisticated woman—at least she saw herself as such. She was not supposed to be easily flustered or flattered by the boyish twinkle in a man's eyes or by the flirtatious curl of his invitingly kissable lips. Hell, she was a writer and a damn good writer at that. She knew every trick in the book and even invented a few for the virile specimen in her books that stole women's hearts, melted their reserve, and unlocked the private vaults of their passion. All the more reason why Sassy was not supposed to get lost in a sultry stare, a seductive smile, a soft chuckle, or a gentle touch. She was not supposed to be hanging onto Norris's every word like it was the gospel, nor was she supposed to be fantasying about what it would be like to have his succulent lips kissing her warm lips instead of the cool rim of his wine glass. Shamefully, Sassy was feeling like she was one of the sex-starved women in the pages of one of her romances. She told herself, *Girl, snap out of it!*

"Yo. .shi. .to," she said, pronouncing Norris's name slowly. "Nice name. Is it Japanese?"

"Yes; my mother's name. My father is Black."

To the point! Not that Sassy hadn't wondered about Norris's slanty eyes, curly hair and tanned skin, being part Cherokee and African-American herself, she was never surprised when it came to the ethnic diversity of her people. On the other hand, she knew, historically, that Japanese people were not known to welcome with open arms the mixing of their bloodline. She was curious about how Norris's parents came to be a couple or if they were indeed a couple since Norris was using his mother's name.

Norris knew well the questioning glint in Sassy's eyes. He'd seen it all of his life. Usually he ignored it but this time, he felt like explaining. "In the early seventies, my father was an enlisted man stationed in Japan."

Sassy questioned, "Okinowa?"

"No, Fuchu which is about 20 kilometers outside of Tokyo. The base is no longer active, but it was called Tachikawa Air Force Base."

"When did the base close down?"

"Middle to late 80's. When I was a kid, I was always curious about that place, so when I went back to Fuchu in '97, I snuck on base and looked around. It was eerie. The base was dilapidated, overgrown, and empty. It was hard to imagine the vibrancy that was once there."

"That's where your mother met your father?"

"Yes. They met, they dated and like most servicemen who dated local girls, when my father's tour of duty was up, he left. By the time my mother found out she was with child, it was too late. I was born several months later."

"Did your mother ever marry?"

"No honorable Japanese man would have her. I am my mother's only child."

Sassy inwardly frowned. "I have to tell you. I have no respect for American soldiers who leave pregnant women behind in foreign countries to weather the disdain of their people. It's disgraceful."

"I won't disagree, but the fault is equally shared with the locals. Whatever their reasons, some locals seek American servicemen despite the possible consequences. My mother never discussed her reason with me, but I'm relatively sure she was looking for a way out of poverty which was not unique to just her. Her story is identifiable to a percentage of women around the globe who happen to live near a military base."

"True, but sadly the children who are left behind grow up without the benefit of their fathers' support or name."

"In Japan, the people are called by their family name, not their given name. Since coming to America, I could have changed my name but I kept my mother's name to honor her. Her family may have disowned her, but I never will. Her name and a picture is all I have left of her. Since coming here, I identify more with my father's heritage although I know well my Japanese heritage."

Sassy was liking this guy more and more. "Yoshito is really a lovely name."

"It wasn't so lovely when I was a kid. A single mother with a brown skin, curly head baby marked me a bastard and my mother a whore."

"That must have been very tough for you."

"Fortunately, I was born with thick skin."

"Did your mother ever hear from your father again?"

"A year after I was born, my father sent a letter but my mother never wrote back."

"Why? Did she never tell him about you?"

"No she didn't. My father didn't know I existed."

"But, Norris, if your father had known about you, he might've gone back."

"My mother didn't want him to feel obligated."

"But he was obligated. You were his son."

"My father was a married man with a son of his own. My mother—"

"Whoa. Your father was no saint, was he?"

"No, but—"

"Your father should have thought about his family waiting for him back in the states before he impregnated your mother. He had some nerve."

A look of sadness clouded Norris's eyes which Sassy saw right away. She had no way of knowing that Norris was remembering saying that very same thing himself when he was ten years old, but his silence made Sassy realize she might have flapped her gums a little too much.

"As you can see, sometimes my mouth operates without the permission of my brain."

"I see, but it's alright. My father, for lack of a better explanation, is a man, but my mother always said the guilt was just as much hers as my father's. She blamed herself for not remaining pure."

"Okay if that's what she believed, but forgive me for being blunt, your father was a dog. He—"

"Perhaps, but being a dog is one of the frailties of being a man, especially a man away from home."

"And that's acceptable?" Sassy wasn't willing to let Norris's father off the hook. "Being away from home is no excuse; a man always has a choice. Would you have cheated on your family, if you had been in your father's shoes?"

Realizing this was a question he had never seriously considered, Norris gave it some thought. He couldn't say he would not have taken a lover if he was away from home for a very long time, but he would not have left a child behind if he had known about it. Back then, was that not his father's situation? Still, he was not his father and hoped to never jeopardize the family he prayed to one day have.

Norris's silence made Sassy realize she was again speaking out of turn, but she continued anyway.

"Look, forgive me for putting my opinionated two cents in your pocket, especially since you don't know me, but I feel so strongly about men not taking care of their children. My father left my mother when I was seven. She raised me without his help. Some men—"

"Actually, my father proved to be a whole like better than some men."

"How? Did he ever support you?"

"Yes."

That surprised Sassy. She was at a lost for words.

"My father is a good man."

"You said 'is'. Do you know your father?"

"Yes."

Sassy's eyes widened. "How?"

"When I was twelve, my mother died."

A feeling of shame rushed through Sassy. "I—"

Norris simply waved off whatever Sassy was about to say. He'd had years to get over his mother's death, but talking about her now was reminding him of the pain of her loss. His throat felt tight, his mouth seemed to dry up. He drank down the rest of his wine.

Sassy couldn't believe how insensitively presumptive she had been. For the first time in her life she felt crass and uneasy. As she straightened the silverware on the napkin in front of her, she reminded herself to close her mouth and open her ears.

Norris raised his wine glass, signaling for the waiter to refill it, which the waiter did right away. Sassy sipped timidly from her wine glass as she watched Norris set his replenished glass down without drinking from it.

"I'm sorry."

"Don't be. Being alone, life was not easy for my mother. I was all she had. I saw her joy whenever she was able to put a smile on my face. Her death was the worse thing to ever happen to me. I wanted to die."

"I'm sorry," Sassy said again.

Norris dismissed Sassy's remorsefulness with a slight wave of his finger. "I got through it because I knew my mother would want me to. After she died, I found letters from my father."

"He wrote more than once?"

"He wrote three times to my mother's family. I don't know how she got the letters or who brought them to her, but I found them. I waited several months until I got up the nerve to write to my father. I told him my mother was dead and that I was on my own on the street. I sent him pictures of me, my mother, and told him the date of my birth."

"Did he believe you right away?"

"He sent for me."

"Just like that?"

"Just like that."

"So you came to America when you were twelve?"

"Actually, I was almost fourteen."

"Why so long?"

"I had no birth certificate, and remember, I didn't write him right away."

"Why didn't you have a birth certificate?"

"It had been stolen with other papers. It took a while to prove who I was, and understand, the bureaucracy in Japan moves just as slowly as it does here in the United States. In the end, my father traveled to Japan to give his blood to prove he was my father."

"Norris, that's great." Sassy said the words but she felt terrible for badmouthing Norris's father. "Your first meeting must have been amazing. Do you remember how you felt when you first saw your father?"

Norris took a sip of his wine, but Sassy could again see the sadness in his eyes. "Why don't we talk about something else?" she said. "Books. Who else do you read besides me?"

Norris chuckled. "Gresham. Patterson. Crichton."

"All the big boys, huh?"

"I'm sure they have nothing on you."

"Yeah, right."

It had been a while since Norris looked back on his life. Surprisingly, the hurt was still there.

"Are you okay?" Sassy asked.

"Old memories, old feelings never lose their sting."

Sassy agreed, "Yeah." Memories of the day her father left her and her mother came to mind. She was seven years old and it was months before she stopped expecting him to come through the door after work with a cherry lollipop for her.

Norris set up his wine glass down. "So, you wanted to know how I felt when I first saw my father."

"Norris, you don't have to keep talking about this."

"I don't mind. I've told very few people about my childhood. I kinda like telling you about it."

Well, he's comfortable with me. "I'm flattered."

"Good. Well, I was amazed. I'd finally met the man I had for so long seen only glimpses of in a mirror."

"That had to have been an awesome feeling."

"It was, but it was also bittersweet."

Sassy understand that. "Because of your mother?"

"Partly. After my mother's death, until my father could claim me, I lived on the streets of Fuchu alongside other children who had no family. To be born Japanese and have white blood or even worse black blood made us outcasts. We were called hiretsukan—bastard. We were ostracized, our mothers shamed and humiliated. Those throw-away children, the street children, became my family. We looked out for each other, we protected each other. We were dirty; we were not welcomed in the schools and many nights we slept with empty stomachs on cardboard boxes; but then, I was rescued from that life, from that uncertain future I was destined for by my father. While for me it was great, for my friend Byron, it was most unfortunate. I left him with a best friend. "

"Did you keep in touch with Byron?"

"Briefly. Soon after I arrived in America, he stopped picking up his letters from the orphanage. I figured he went on with his life in another place."

"What's it like today for mixed race children in Japan?"

"Sassy, Japan is still a purist, insular society. It's one of the few countries that do not allow immigration. Japanese people still do not tolerate or take lightly the so-called weakening or diluting of its blood or culture. Like here in America, Japan has subcultures, minorities, if you will, and Japanese with black blood are considered the lowest of Japanese society."

"Big surprise," Sassy said. "Dark skin, nappy hair, bad blood, huh?"

"My blood is fine by me, but the Japanese people

worship white skin, the whiter the better but it must be pure Japanese blood, not diluted by foreigners. Believe me; a dark-skinned bi-racial child having the nerve to be part Japanese born out of wedlock is as bad as it gets in Japan."

"I can imagine. Their futures must be quite bleak."

"Not for all. Five years ago, I set up a college scholarship fund in my mother's name in Fuchu for the children of the orphanage."

"That's admirable," Sassy said, truly liking the man she had created in her tale of love lost and found. She glimpsed Norris's bare ring finger. A gold band would only make his hand more beautiful.

"I seek no pat on the back, Sassy. These kids need to be given a chance to live, a chance to be educated, a chance to hope. I want them to know that someone cares."

"You said you went back to Japan?"

"About nine years ago. I wanted to see where I came from and I was hoping to find Byron. No one knew anything about him."

Sassy sipped thoughtfully on her wine. Was Norris a figment of her overly active imagination? He was great to look at and he was sensitive and caring, too? How was it that he was walking around unmarried? A man like this could only be this way because of a woman.

"Norris, your mother had to have been a very strong, amazing woman because she had to have known the consequences of having you. Can you tell me about her?"

Memories of his mother made Norris smile. "My mother was incredibly strong. She taught me a great deal about holding my head up and not letting anyone take my dignity."

"How did she support you?"

"She worked in a computer factory on an assembly line. She was on her feet ten hours a day, six days a week."

Thinking about her own sore feet after an afternoon of shopping, Sassy frowned at her own frivolous indulgences.

"Sassy, my mother sacrificed much to make sure that I

was able to go to school, whether I had a pair of shoes on my feet or not. It was the books I had to have. My mother had no other goal, no other purpose. She demanded that I get a good education." Norris felt himself choking up.

"Bless her," Sassy said as she remembered her own mother who had died a year and a half before from a heart attack. "She was so like my mother."

Norris took a hearty gulp of his wine. The glistening of his eyes touched Sassy. When Norris set his glass down, she reached across the table and laid her hand atop his. They held each other's warm gaze. Norris knew in that moment that he would have bought a thousand books if it meant he'd share a moment like this with Sassy.

"My mother would have liked you," he said.

Sassy's cheeks warmed. Her fantasy man would say that? "I'm sure I would have liked her as well, but tell me, how did she die? She had to have been pretty young."

Although Norris knew he was never going to forget how his mother died, he found it unsettling that he could not erase from his mind the bloody sight of his beautiful mother all cut up and mangled like an animal. He didn't mind talking about who his mother was; it was how she died that bothered him. As he looked around the busy restaurant, Norris loosened his tie. Sassy sensed his uneasiness.

She slid her hand off of Norris's. "I did it again."

"That's the writer in you. You're inquisitive and I must say, your question is fair." Norris took a breath and said quickly, "My mother was murdered."

Sassy lay her hand over her sorrowful heart. "My God, Norris. I am so sorry."

Norris nodded. He found a simple, gracious nod worked as well with Americans as it did with the Japanese.

"My mother sent me on an errand. I was gone too long. I returned and found her outside behind our sumai, the little shack we called home. She was dead. She had been stabbed."

"My God. Who would do such a horrific thing?"

"Unfortunately, we never found out. The keisatsu—"

"The who?"

"The keisatsu, the police, believed it was a robbery gone bad. To this day, I still have a problem believing that. We had nothing of value that anyone would want. We were extremely humble people"

"Was anything taken?"

"What little money we had; a few of my mother's personal papers; and my birth certificate."

"Why would anyone take your birth certificate?"

"I don't believe the bastard took the time to sort through what he wanted to take. I believe he simply took whatever he put his filthy hands on. He even took the only piece of jewelry my mother owned, a gold necklace with a heart charm on it. It was the one thing she treasured."

"Was it her mother's?"

"My father gave it to her."

"Thieves, murderers—they're despicable."

"That they are," Norris said sadly, "but there was much to love about my mother. I remember her being very gentle. She was very kind to everyone. She was a humble woman, she had no enemies. My mother never complained about her fate in life, nor did she complain about the people who looked down upon her. She worked hard for me. I wish I could have done more to help her. I wanted to work, I—" Norris choked up. He couldn't go on.

Norris's eyes were again glistening. Sassy again took his hand. "That's not what your mother wanted. Your mother would not have worked one hour less if it meant not giving you a better life. Your education—"

Afraid that his voice would crack if he continued to speak, Norris remained silent. It had been a long time since he'd felt this emotional. He remembered the last morning he was with his mother. She had fixed him breakfast of rice and miso soup, but she had given him extra soup because she said he was a growing boy. To this day, he thought of his mother every time he had a taste for miso soup.

"What is your mother's name?" Sassy quietly asked.

Norris smiled. "Oyuki. Oyuki Yoshito."

"Beautiful name."

"The man who killed her took a beautiful soul. If I ever had one wish, I'd want to come face to face with the man who took my mother's life." Norris lightly pressed his chin into the knuckles of his fist. He closed his eyes as he tried to mentally push the anger he felt rising up from his gut into his chest back down. He was well aware that Sassy, in her quietness, was giving him time to deal with his emotions.

If Sassy had to say specifically what it was about Norris that made her feel a connection to him, it would have to be how he felt about his mother. A man who truly loves his mother, be she dead or alive, has to have a good soul.

Closing his eyes, Norris pressed his fingertips together prayer-like. He took a deep breath and slowly exhaled the tension from his body along with the anger that was always just below the surface for the nameless, faceless man who killed his mother. Somehow, it didn't embarrass him that Sassy was looking at him. He opened his eyes and saw immediately in hers that she was feeling him. If the table wasn't between them, he would wrap her up in his arms.

"As you can see," he said, "I kind of lose it when I talk about how my mother died."

"It's understandable. You lost the most important person in your life."

"Well, fortunately for me, I haven't totally lost my mother. The Japanese part of me believes our ancestors are always with us, watching over us, protecting us, guiding us. I believe this about my mother. She will always be with me."

Those sentiments touched Sassy. "That's beautiful. Do you have a picture of her?"

"Actually, I do." Norris took out his wallet. He showed Sassy first a picture of his mother, a young woman, small of statue, long black hair twisted in a braid over her shoulder, sitting demurely in a white bamboo fan chair.

"She's beautiful," Sassy said.

"Thank you." Norris then showed Sassy a second picture of himself with his mother.

"Aaa. You were adorable. How old were you?"

"Six."

"Your mother was beaming. One would never know how hard a life she was living."

Norris put the pictures back inside his wallet. "I have no memory of that day. I wish I did."

Sassy lay her hand on Norris's. "What you have is the knowledge that you had a wonderful mother who sacrificed all to have you. That kind of love is unequaled."

Norris gently rubbed Sassy's hand. There was no doubt in his mind, he was connecting with Sassy as he had not done with any other woman he'd ever been with, but that didn't surprise him. From the moment she spoke to him, he knew they were going to get along just fine.

Under Norris's intense gaze, Sassy felt like Norris could see right through to the core of her soul, a soul that yearned to experience the sweet, all consuming love she had only written about in her novels. The silence between them was broken only by the thumping of her heart. What was this spell Norris had over her? How is it that he, unlike any other man, made her feel like a teenager meeting the boy of her dreams for the very first time? Whatever it was, as much as she wanted to lose herself in her own fantasy, she couldn't give in to it. Fantasies weren't real. Maybe it was time to call it a night.

5

Sassy laid her napkin on the table. "Well, Mr. Yoshito, it's been a pleasure."

Norris glimpsed Sassy's near-empty wine glass. "Then let's not end it." He reached for her wine glass, but Sassy quickly laid her hand atop it.

"Tempting, but I have to go."

"Oh, come on. I can't believe your writer's mind doesn't have questions of me."

Norris had her there. So many questions were swirling around in her head.

"Come on. You know you want to," Norris teased. "Ask a question before you burst."

Sassy couldn't help but laugh. "Okay. How is it that you came to be at my book signing?"

Norris smiled. "I saw the sign out front that you were in the store. I wanted to meet you, I stepped inside."

"As simple as that, huh? I wouldn't think you'd even know who I was."

"Of course I do, Miss Sassy Davenport."

So he knew her full name, which she never used on her books. Only her true fans knew her last name.

"You seem perplexed."

"I am a bit."

"Then allow me to clarify. The truth is, I have a friend who reads your books. In fact, she has read several select passages to me."

"What passages, from which book?"

"Let's just say she read passages that were guaranteed to put me in the right mood."

"I see," Sassy said, feeling her cheeks warm. Actually, more than her cheeks were warm when she was writing the more sensuous passages. Still, she felt a pang of envy for Norris's friend. If only she had been the one reading to this fabulous man. Soft music, soft rug, no clothes—h'm. Smiling to herself, Sassy picked up her wine glass to keep from openly running her tongue over her lips.

"So," Norris said smiling, "do you ever do readings for special friends?"

The tiny sip of wine Sassy was about to swallow caught in her throat. She began to cough. She quickly put her glass down and coughed into her hand.

"Take a sip." Norris handed Sassy her glass of water.

Sassy took small sips of water. She let the coolness trickle down her throat. She felt like a klutz.

"Are you alright?"

"I'm fine." Maybe she had better keep her mind as pure as a minister's daughter. . .oops, but then again, maybe she had better rethink that. Ministers' daughters have lustful fantasies, too. Didn't Evelyn, her best friend whose late father and uncle were ministers, say there was a time when she couldn't concentrate on her father's sermon because she was fantasying about the tall lanky baritone with the huge feet and big hands who sang in the church choir? Even after Evelyn finally slept with her bigfoot baritone, thoughts of their lovemaking overshadowed the sermons her father preached to her about waiting until she was married before losing her virginity. H'm, maybe she could use that storyline somewhere. Intrigued by the possibility of a new story about a minister's oversexed daughter, Sassy sipped, musingly, from her water glass.

"So, do you ever do readings?" Norris asked again.

"Sure I do—in public. In fact, I will be speaking and doing a read in two weeks on the 21st at The Brooklyn Public

Library at Grand Army Plaza."

"Great. Then it's a date."

This was much too easy. Sassy was going to assume Norris only meant he'd be at the reading.

"Norris, what do you do for a living?"

"I'm an architect."

"Residential or commercial?"

"Both."

"Do I know your work?"

"If you've been inside the Belvedere Hotel in Midtown, or ever seen the Danberry Mansion, you do."

"I've been inside the Belvedere. Really nice detail. I especially like the rotunda up on the ninth floor."

Norris nodded modestly but Sassy didn't miss the proud twinkle in his almond brown eyes. "The recession has been extremely dismal for housing and building markets. Has it affected your company?"

"Somewhat; we're about 10% down. My clients are the ones President Obama will be imposing higher taxes on."

"As he should. You know, one day I'd love to build a house from the ground up. I mean, I can almost see the closets, the kitchen, the bathrooms I'd love to design."

"Perhaps I can help you with your vision."

"Perhaps." The thought of working shoulder to shoulder with Norris was definitely thought provoking. However, since building a house was not in her immediate plans, she hoped to see more of Norris a whole lot sooner than later. Of course, she had to take into consideration that he might be intimately involved with one of the nine women he had books autographed for. Suppose it wasn't just one of the nine? Suppose it was all of the women? Suppose Norris was a Casanova? More importantly, would he be willing to give up all of his women for her? *Whoa! Slow down, girl. You are seriously leaping. This boy might not be for you or really even be interested in you that way.*

"What time are you speaking on the 21st?"

"7:00 p.m."

"I'll pick you up at six. Just tell me where."

Yeah, this was much too easy, but Sassy couldn't be. "I thought you just wanted to attend my reading."

"I do, but I thought we might continue getting to know each other over dinner, since we barely ate tonight."

Where has this man been hiding? He's honorable, he's direct, he's an architect, and he's sexy as hell. What more could a woman ask for? Of course, if Norris topped all that off by being a great lover as well, boy, could he fulfill some fantasies for her!

Norris loved the sexy fullness of Sassy's lips.

If Sassy was right, she could read the victorious glint in Norris's eyes. He was obviously sure he'd worked his magic on her. Okay, so he had her from the minute she looked into his face at the book store, but she was going to have to take a giant step back and slow this dance down. She wrote romance, living it was another thing. As it was, having dinner with Norris tonight had been pretty bold of her, especially when she had a man. At least Kenneth was supposed to be her man. She had been seeing Kenneth exclusively the last two of the four years they'd been seeing each other, but the truth was, she was no closer to thinking about getting married to him than she was two years ago. Besides his family being an issue, it seemed Kenneth would rather be anywhere else than be with her. At times she suspected he was seeing someone else, but she never had the energy or the time to put him through the third degree and often she wondered why. Could it be she didn't want Kenneth to focus all of his attention on her because she no longer wanted him? How ironic. Here she was a romance novelist and in her own life, she couldn't figure out her own feelings.

Of course, she didn't like that Kenneth was no longer interested in attending her book signings or readings. He said he wasn't into standing on the sideline while she kissed ass to sell a book. If smiling and talking to strangers was kissing ass, then so be it. It did her no good if her books sat on the shelf gathering dust or were returned to her publisher by the truckload. Kenneth had been more supportive of her writing career when they first met. Now she felt he was jealous of the attention she got. Lately, more and more, he didn't want to hear about her books, and in turn, admittedly, she had lost interest in his life. Maybe this is why she was so taken with Norris. Norris knew who she was and, from first blush, he seemed interested in her as an author. How nice was that? She could talk about herself for a change, and, of course, it didn't hurt that Norris was so damn good-looking. Just looking at him, she wanted to rip his clothes off and make love to him without first knowing if he was a sloppy wet kisser or a great dry kisser. There was nothing worse than having a man slobber all over her face. God knows, if a man slobbered on her face, surely he'd slobber everywhere else. Yuk. Oh, but looking at Norris's beautiful lips, it would be a sin if he were a sloppy kisser.

Norris locked eyes with Sassy. "I believe I can see what you're thinking."

Sassy didn't look away. She liked the bold flirtatiousness of their game. "Do tell."

Norris glanced at his book on the table and then back at Sassy. "They're saying what Ashley's eyes said to Wyatt on the veranda just before—"

Sassy threw up her hand. "I get the picture, but you are so wrong." *Damn! Am I that obvious?*

Smiling secretly, Norris said, "Please forgive my brashness. I hope I haven't ruined my chance of having dinner with you after your reading."

If she said he had, she'd be lying, but she needed to reclaim a modicum of dignity. Then again, the heck with dignity. She was hot as heck for this man and dinner wasn't all she wanted to share with him.

"Won't a few of your nine friends mind you taking me out to dinner?"

"They're all just friends. I'm sure you have male

friends who are not your lovers, correct?"

"Correct."

"Great. At dinner, I promise," Norris began, holding up two fingers, "on my honor, to be a perfect boy scout. I'll even let my wife chaperone us."

Stunned, Sassy's jaw dropped.

Norris chuckled as he spread his left hand out to Sassy. He wiggled his fingers. "No ring, no ring mark. Not married, never have been, no serious commitment. Okay?"

Not for an instant did Sassy think a joke about a wife chaperoning them funny. She didn't date married men, nor would she ever be a home-wrecker.

"Okay. So, how did you cut yourself?" Sassy asked referring to the cut on the side of Norris's hand.

Norris looked at the thin red mark. "I was cutting open a box with a utility knife. It slipped, just grazed the skin. No big deal."

Sassy checked her watch. "Well, it's late."

"Don't you want to hear the truth about your books?"

Sassy eyed Norris suspiciously. "What truth?"

"The truth is, I do know a few women, but most of the books I bought will go to women who work for me."

Sassy relaxed. "You fraud."

"Yes, but I was quite conspicuous, wasn't I?"

"Actually, you did that by showing up. You were the only male. You could have saved yourself some money."

"The money was well spent. I've been wanting to meet you since I saw you a year ago in LA."

"Really? Where was I in LA?"

"You were speaking at a Delta convention at the Sheraton. I happened by the room you were sitting panel; the door was open. I caught the tail end of the discussion which was quite heated."

"That's because that idiot Lucas Leonard said God knew what he was doing when he created man first; that male characters were inherently stronger than female characters. The discussion was supposed to be about creating and building strong characters, female and male."

"So Lucas asserted that God had a hand in developing literary characters?"

"Norris, the man went off on this tangent that had nothing to do with literature. He said to rule the world, man had to be in control of his emotions, which women were not, and that God gave man control of procreation because women were too fickle. Boy, did he, literally, tick off everyone in that room."

"I saw that."

"The man said fickle. Women aren't the ones who roam the countryside like Johnny Appleseed dropping seeds inside as many women as they can. If men could only get pregnant, they'd cut that crap out." She hoped Norris wasn't thinking she was speaking specifically about his father.

"Sassy, not all men—"

"More than enough do!" Sassy said, assuming she knew what Norris was going to say. "See, Norris, that's what's wrong with most men. They're too proud of that third leg God stuck on you guys as an afterthought to differentiate you from women."

Norris's jaw dropped.

"Seriously. That third leg is the only true physical external thing that sets you apart from women because some men to have breasts bigger than mine; and that's where God messed up. Instead of a third leg, he should have given man a second heart or a third eye or a second brain . . ."

Norris was beginning to feel like a deer caught in the headlights of an oncoming car.

". . . then you men might not start wars, rape women and babies, or steal valuable resources from poor countries. Maybe men might have more feelings or see where women are coming from, and most definitely you guys would have to sit on the toilet like the rest of us to pee, then maybe all those poor trees out there could be spared the indignity of being peed on by you superior beings."

Behind Sassy a woman said, "Amen, sister."

Ignoring the startled look on Norris's face, Sassy turned and lightly high-fived the woman behind her whose own dinner companion, by the frown on his face, wasn't too happy with what Sassy said. She turned back to Norris only to see that he still had a stunned look on his face.

"The point is this, Norris. I'm not saying that men in all their glory can't be who they are, I'm saying men need to embrace at least a smidgen of the emotional substance that give women sensitivity, compassion, understanding, and plain old common sense. Maybe if more men read romance novels, they might better understand why women need honest to God righteous love and not be played with by men who see love as a game of musical chairs."

Norris rubbed his chin. "You certainly don't mince words, do you?"

"I don't have time for games, and please don't confuse who I am with what I write. I am as serious as a heart attack."

Norris liked Sassy's spirit. "I can see that. I tell you what, to show you how sensitive I am, when we next meet, I will have read your entire book and if you like, you can test me over dinner."

The flirty twinkle in Norris's eyes softened Sassy's temperament. Boy was she in trouble, she was liking this man much too much, much too soon and they hadn't even kissed. She pretended to still be annoyed.

"I test very well," Norris said.

"I deduct points for arrogance."

"So how many points have you taken from yourself?"

Norris asked that with such a straight face Sassy didn't presume for one minute he was joking. He didn't look away or crack up laughing. He gazed at her with a look of adoration which made her squeeze her thighs together to quiet the sweet feeling that surged between them. Boy, the man insults her and she's horny as hell for him.

From his inside breast pocket, Norris took a business card. He held it out to Sassy. "My cell phone number is on the back."

Sassy held back from taking the card. "And why do I need your cell phone number?"

"I'll be out of town on business for almost two weeks," Norris said, still holding the card out to Sassy, "but I will be back in time for your reading."

"Okay. And?"

"You might want to tell me something really important, like you can't wait to see me."

"You're impossible." Sassy picked up her pocket-book. "It's been a pleasure."

"If you leave my card, you won't be able to call me if Sasquatch appears at your kitchen window."

Sassy tried to not laugh but the silly smile Norris gave her made the laugh burst softly from her. She took the card and could swear she glimpsed a smug look on Norris's face. How could he know that she was starving for the right man to come along and feed her anemic love life? For too long, Kenneth had not been fulfilling any part of her writer's fantasies or any of her emotional or sexual needs. Kenneth had never made her feel like she would dissolve into nothingness if he simply smiled or touched her. Not even when they first met did she feel the way she was now feeling with Norris—lustfully wanton.

"It just dawned on me," Sassy said. "You never asked if I was married."

Norris flipped his copy of *Butterfly* over and opened it to the back flap. "Sassy lives in New York City with her spoiled Siamese cat, Chester."

Smart ass! Sassy slipped Norris's card inside her pocketbook.

"Arigato," Norris said, bowing his head slightly.

"Which means?"

"Thank you."

The man was smooth. If she didn't watch herself,
Norris could have her calling him before she closed her eyes
tonight, but she couldn't weaken. Norris was a man she had
written as a fantasy. Getting caught up in her own fantasy
could render her vulnerable to being hurt. She couldn't take
that risk, she had been there before.

"Mr. Yoshito," Sassy said, standing. "it has been
interesting."

Norris began to stand also. "I'll walk out with you."

"No, please stay. Finish your wine."

Norris stood anyway while trying to get his money out
of his wallet to pay the bill, but he wasn't fast enough. Sassy
slipped away without a single glance over her shoulder.

6

The blood in Myra Barrett's apartment had long since dried in the week since she was carried out on a stretcher, yet the scent of blood lingered while the cloak of death hovered still in the living room and in the back hallway. Odd shaped specks and irregular smeared lines of dark blood stained the egg-shell-colored-walls, while large and small blotches of deep dark red marred the beauty of the beige carpeting. The living room looked like a slaughter house of gore and broken furniture. The killer had been brutal.

Standing inside the bathroom, for the third time, Frank Kiefer stared up at the torn bits of blue plastic caught in the silver tone metal shower curtain rings that hung loosely on the stainless steel rod above the spotlessly white bathtub. There was little doubt that the curtains had been ripped from the rings and that more than likely the killer had taken the curtains to wrap his bloody clothes up in, but if that was the case, what did the killer wear out of the apartment? It also looked to Frank like the killer may have taken a shower, which was evidenced by the fact that the water had been left running. A bar of hard white soap that had been wet and bloated days before lay in the tub over the drain hole. It had been left there to dry as it had been too soft to pick up the first day. If the killer did shower, this would be the first case Frank had ever been on where the murderer, who didn't live in the residence, took the time to take a shower. The killer was clean and so was the tub. At least to the naked eye. With his latex-gloved hand, Frank picked up the bar of soap and dropped it inside a plastic bag. He prayed that forensics would be able to recover viable DNA off of that soap.

Frank sealed the bag with a firm slide of his fingers.

Joe Lupino stood in the doorway. "What do you think?"

Frank didn't bother to turn around or answer. Joe Lupino, his partner of three and one half years, always, at the start of an investigation, asked that question of him, but the case was a week old and they had no more to go on than they had the first day. The victim's little girl still couldn't tell them much of anything because she wasn't on the scene when her mother was attacked. She did say, "My daddy come see me, and Nored bring me a dolly." Reed Johnson had an alibi and the guy "Nored" they couldn't find. Strangest of all, if he was a friend of the victim's, why wasn't his telephone number anywhere to be found in the victim's possession?

Frank turned his attention to the sink where a blow dryer had been left plugged in. It had been running when the responding officers entered the apartment. Again for the third time, Frank was about to do an inspection of the crime scene with Joe in case they missed something the first two times they were there.

"The blow dryer," Frank said.

"My wife," Joe said, "would never leave a blow dryer plugged in, running, sitting on the bathroom sink."

"I doubt the victim left hers that way. The perp took a shower. He took his time getting himself together. He wasn't worried about being caught. He knew no one would come."

"No forced entry. One set of keys when there were supposed to be two."

"He took the keys with him," Frank said. "Robbery?"

"According to the mother, nothing's missing. There's jewelry on the dresser in the bedroom and there was jewelry on both victims. The pocketbook that was on the floor in the living room was intact. Other than what furniture was overturned or broken, the televisions, the DVD, the stereo are all in place.

There's a brand new computer in a box in the little girl's room."

Frank looked from the empty towel rack next to the tub to the empty one next to the door. All of the towels, including a wet one left on the floor of the bathroom, had been collected by the crime scene investigators.

"Smart ass," Frank said.

"What was that, Frank?"

"I hate killers who think they can outsmart us."

"Yeah. Look, we know his shoe size and the type of shoe," Joe said, hoping that would appease his partner. "There were an awful lot of fingerprints in blood in the front room, and remember, we might get something from the fried chicken bone found in the garbage."

Frank prayed the saliva on the bone belonged to the killer, because the near empty bottle of bleach on the counter in the kitchen told him the killer did some serious cleaning before he left the apartment. They'd be lucky if they found a single hair that didn't belong to either one of the victims or the little girl who couldn't understand why she couldn't come home to the apartment or where her mother was.

"Step back." Frank closed the bathroom door shutting Joe out in the hallway. The only place he hadn't looked was behind the door which was flat against the wall. Surprise, surprise. There it was, another set of fingerprints in blood on the back of the door.

"There is a God," Frank said.

"What you got?"

"Bloody fingerprints."

Joe eased the door open with his rubber-gloved hand. He looked behind the door. "How did we miss that?"

"Cohen won't miss it. He'll be back here today."

"So much blood, Frank. How the heck did the killer get out of this apartment without drawing attention to himself? Those girls had to have done a lot of screaming. Someone around here had to have heard or seen something more than what they've told us."

"Someone probably did." Frank knew full well that most people try to not get involved in police investigations.

"I'll bet my mother's cubic zirconia engagement ring the old man in 13C saw more than he told us."

Frank wondered aloud, "Cubic zirconia?"

"The man is right across the damn hall, Frank. He said he looked out when he heard the door open at 5:45 p.m. I know he saw the perp, and he said the loud music drove him crazy. He said he kept peeking through the peep hole every few minutes. He had to see the perp."

"He said he saw a guy from the back wearing a baseball cap just before he got on the elevator."

"Then why, Frank, didn't he call the police when the music was being blasted? Maybe we could have caught the killer in action. Doesn't he know there's a quality of life law on the books in this city?"

Frank said flatly, "Not in this neighborhood."

"C'mon, Frank. If the cops don't respond here, it's because the people in this neighborhood brought it on themselves; and Frank, before you get on me, you don't live in this neighborhood."

Frank felt that old familiar tightening of his stomach muscles whenever a white cop or detective started talking about how it was black people's fault for how they were perceived or treated. He had been with the New York City police department nineteen years, twelve as a detective and six of those years as a detective with a gold shield. In all of his nineteen years, he had lived acrimoniously with the racism within the department. In fact, within the first month of making detective and wearing plain clothes, he was almost shot by overly zealous blue coats who thought he fit the description of a twenty-two year old, braid wearing African American robbery suspect out in Brownsville, and here he was, a suit and tie wearing, close cut wearing thirty-two year old with a silver badge hanging from his breast pocket. When all the panic died down, that is after he had thrown himself to the ground and thrown his arms out, there were no apologies from the two white cops, nor was there any disciplinary action taken after those same cops remarked, "all niggers look alike" to them.

"These people make it bad for themselves. They—"

"They what, Joe?" Frank asked icily. "What do *these* people do?"

Joe bristled at the cold hard look on Frank's face. "Now, Frank, don't go getting your back up. I just meant that some. . .black. . .ahh, some African Americans make it bad for other good African Americans."

"Which am I, Joe? A bad one or a good one?"

"Frank—"

"Don't be shy, Joe, speak up."

Joe ran his hand nervously through his close cropped hair. "Okay, Frank. We don't need to be getting into discussions about race again. I get your point."

Frank looked unflinchingly into Joe's anxious eyes. "Do you, Joe? When you make comments about *these people*—good or bad—we need to talk about it so I'm clear about your meaning. See, I'm one of *these people*. I was born ten blocks from here. My mother still lives in this neighborhood. So when you talk about *these people*, you're talking about me and my mother."

"No, no, I—"

"How long we been partners, Joe?"

Regretting that he'd said anything about *these people*, Joe answered cautiously, "Three and a half years."

"What are you? Twenty-seven, twenty-eight?"

"Thirty. I've had a few birthdays you missed."

"Well, Joe, I'm forty-two. I was dealing with racism when you were crapping in your diaper, and I'll be dealing with it when I'm crapping in mine forty years from now. For now, I need you to understand one thing, we're partners."

"C'mon, Frank. You're not like the people we pick up on these streets. You don't blast a boom box out of your apartment window; you don't blast your car stereo so loud the car next to you vibrates. I was just trying to say the loud music wasn't so unusual in this neighborhood, in this building. No one lodged a complaint. If someone had, the boys on the beat would have responded and the killings might've been interrupted. Police don't respond to this neighborhood because of how some—not all, Frank—some of these people act."

Although Frank realized he was being a bit sensitive, he wasn't stupid. He knew what Joe said was true. He just didn't like hearing it come from a white man's mouth.

"Just make it clear what you mean, next time."

"Yeah." Joe was relieved.

"What else we got?"

"Nothing. We're still waiting to see if we can get a match on the prints Cohen already lifted. We got nothing from the incinerator, nothing from the trash bins."

Frank scratched the side of his head. "Look, I'm headed over to the hospital. You know how to reach me."

"Likewise. Three o'clock at the precinct?"

"Yep."

Outside the bathroom, Joe bumped into Barry Cohen and his black crime scene case. "Cohen, what's the word?"

Cohen stepped aside. "Vicious. You boys finished in here? This is the last room."

"Frank has something for you." Joe hurried off toward the front of the apartment.

Cohen set his case on the floor just outside the small bathroom. "How's the surviving victim, Frank?"

"Hanging by a thread." Frank was never comfortable around Barry Cohen—the man took death too lightly. Cohen was a twenty-three year veteran and probably would do another twenty before he retired. The man loved his work. He often reminded Frank of a kid with a brand new chemistry set, which was interesting since Cohen had joined the force after being a high school science teacher. He had gone back to school to study forensics he said after watching an episode of Columbo.

That, Frank could understand since Cohen usually wore an old beige London Fog trench coat rain. If Cohen had a head of hair like Columbo, Cohen would have been ecstatic, but Cohen's hair had long since begun creeping away from his forehead.

Cohen looked slowly around the small bathroom. "I've been working ten-hour days on this case just processing the front two rooms and the hallway. Horrific scene. It's a wonder the girl in the hall wasn't completely decapitated."

Frank said nothing. The whole scene boggled his mind. The more crime scenes he saw, the more he realized how demonic people were.

Cohen peered at a stain on the side of the sink. "The defensive wounds on the deceased victim's hands and arms were about the worst I've seen. Two of her fingers on her left hand were severed and one finger on her right hand was left hanging by a sliver of tissue."

Frank considered himself a hardened detective but at times, he felt like a rookie. He felt sick.

Cohen saw the anger in Frank's eyes. "Frank, you're in the wrong business. You're too emotional."

Frank smirked. "I hate murderers." He gave the bathroom over to Cohen. "I bagged that bar of soap for you. I think the killer took a shower."

Cohen looked at the bagged bar of soap on the sink. He then slipped out of his jacket.

"You'll find bloody prints behind the door. Oh, what's happening with the prints you already processed?"

"We should get something back from CODIS any day now." Cohen folded his jacket in half, rolled it up into a tight roll, and slipped it inside a large clear plastic bag which he sat in the hall outside the bathroom door. He unbuttoned his shirt sleeves and expertly rolled them up to his elbows. He laid his case on the floor, unlatched it, and threw the top back. From it he took a small glass jar of colorful jelly beans which he held out to Frank.

As he always did, Frank walked away, but he was

feeling a lot more hopeful about finding his killer. Cohen was one of the best. Once those jellybeans came out, Cohen was going to work. It didn't matter how gruesome a scene he had to work on, Cohen popped those brightly colored jelly beans. After a while, Frank figured it had to be the sweetness of the candy that kept Cohen from tasting the sourness of the death around him. Frank had once tried it himself and almost gagged. The sweetness was too much. He started keeping a small tube of Vicks Vapor Rub and a roll of antacid tablets in his pocket for those awkward moments when he thought his stomach might betray him, but the truth was, he never felt better himself until he could down a shot of vodka. Tonight, as he'd done every night since he'd been on this case, he'd down two shots.

7

There were just as many hustling, bustling people going about their business on the upper lobby level of Grand Central Station as there were outside on 42nd Street in Manhattan. Norris made his way through the hordes of people to the shoe shine stand. He was glad to see there were no other customers. He leaped up onto the high dark wood antique chair.

"Make 'em shine," Norris said to the old black shoeshine man as he put both his leather clad black feet up on the metal foot rests.

The old man whose hands were as black and leathery as the shoes he shined, picked up a flat can of partially used black shoe paste. "Shine is my business. Thirty-two years I been at it. I give the best shine in New York City."

"Then I should be able to see my pearly whites."

"Yes, sir." The shoeshine man went to work smearing black shoe paste on Norris's left shoe.

Norris settled back and opened his newspaper straightaway to page four.

WOMAN STILL IN A COMA!

The Brutal Slashing of two women in their Brooklyn apartment two weeks ago where one woman died, has left the second woman languishing in a coma.

Norris had read the eye-catching headline three times. He had read the article only once. He already knew the details. The police were looking for him, but they didn't know yet it was him they were looking for. They had no motive; they had no eyewitness to the bloody attack. Norris wasn't worried that they would come looking for him. He had left nothing behind for them to even cast a suspicious eye his way. If they happen to get his fingerprints, they would still not have anything. His prints were not on file anywhere. As for Myra, it would be a miracle if she survived, but if she did, he doubted she'd remember anything. Damn. He hated he had to cut Myra up like that. He liked her. If things were different, they could have had a good thing between them. Unfortunately, Myra was only a small part of the picture he had to paint. Besides, Myra was just like his mother. She was a whore.

The shoeshine man was almost finished. Norris checked his watch—6:30 p.m. Huffing his annoyance at the lateness of the hour, he leaned forward and looked searchingly around the lobby. He hated being kept waiting. He tightly rolled up his newspaper. He slammed it into the palm of his left hand.

The shoeshine man, bent over, fleetingly glanced up at Norris, but Norris was unaware of the curious glance the old man gave him. Norris was seeing only Myra as he had last seen her—bloody, mangled. He cut Carrie up even worse. Sloppy. He didn't like being that sloppy but Carrie had fought him like a wild woman. She was so unlike his first kill, the whore was too stunned to fight back.

"Hey, baby!" a shapely blond said as she sauntered up to the shoeshine stand.

"Do you know what time it is?"

"I know, I lost track of time. I'm sorry."

The sparkle in Karen's bright blue eyes and her pouty pink lips told Norris Karen thought she had him wrapped around her little finger. If she only knew how wrong she was. Sure he liked Karen, she was great in bed. Beyond the sex, there was nothing much else she could do for him alive.

The old man slapped the shoe polish stained cotton rag across Norris's right shoe, snapping it and rubbing it quickly across the toe of the shoe in a seesawing motion. When was done, he stepped back and snapped the rag once more, hitting the toe of each of Norris's shoes with a pop.

"The last lick is for good luck," he said.

"Luck is happenstance. I operate by self-conceived design; I leave nothing to chance." Norris stepped down and pulled a twenty dollar bill. He handed it to the shoeshine man. "Keep the change."

"Thank you, sir."

Norris started off.

"Sir, your newspaper," the shoeshine man said.

Norris walked off with his arm around Karen's shoulder. The old man didn't trouble himself running after Norris. He laid the paper back on the seat. Another customer will soon come along and make use of it.

Norris let his hand lay on top of Karen's right breast. "You get what you wanted?"

"I sure did. Wait till you see me in the black teddy I bought just for you, baby."

"I can't wait." Norris began rubbing Karen's breast in search of her nipple.

Karen held onto Norris's hand. "People will see."

"Let them." He slapped Karen's hand away and quickly cupped her whole breast.

"Norris!" Karen again tried to hold Norris's hand, and again, he slapped her away.

A woman walking toward them with her two children in tow glared disapprovingly at Karen and Norris.

"That lady saw you, Norris."

Norris smirked. Karen's now hard nipple was between his two fingers. He squeezed.

"Ouch!" Karen tried to pull away, but Norris tightened his arm around her neck.

He whispered, "Shh! People will hear you." Again he squeezed her nipple.

"Norris, you're hurting me," Karen said in a hushed voice. She tried to loosen Norris's vise-like grip on her nipple but he knocked her hand away and squeezed harder. Karen's eyes watered as Norris kissed her on the side of her head. She stifled her scream by biting down on her own finger. The pain was so paralyzing, she couldn't take another step. Through her tears, she was keenly aware that people, despite their rush to get to their trains glanced her way.

Karen whimpered, "Please stop."

Norris let up on his grip, but he left his hand over Karen's sore nipple. Again, she tried to move his hand, but again he slapped her away although he didn't pinch her.

Karen wiped her face dry on Norris's shoulder. "That was mean, Norris. It was cruel."

Norris squeezed Karen's nipple as hard as he could. Karen gasped in a lung full of air and was about to scream when Norris quickly covered her mouth with his own and kissed her roughly although she was sobbing pitifully.

"You're disgusting!" a middle-age woman said.

"Naw, man. Do your thing," a young man said.

Norris wasn't bothered by the looks he got or by what anyone said. He ended the kiss because he didn't like that Karen had slobbered into his mouth. He let go of Karen's nipple because he had made his point.

"If you ever keep me waiting again, I will feed your nipple to you on a skewer."

Her lips quivering, Karen allowed Norris, with his arm now around her waist to pull her along. Yes, he had made his point. He didn't like waiting for anyone, especially an idiot woman who thought she had him under her thumb. No woman controlled him. No woman.

8

Kenneth was who Sassy was with, but Norris was on her mind. It was two weeks since he gave her his business card. She had taken it out after she got home and looked at it. The gray card announced Norris's firm Yoshito and Braithwaithe in embossed gothic lettering in burgundy and black. Handwritten on the back, Norris's cell phone number area code was nine-one-seven, the same as hers but that didn't necessarily mean he lived in Brooklyn. He could be living any where in the city. Either way, he was close enough to make her want to know where he laid his head at night. Interestingly, he hadn't put his home number down. H'm. Could there be a reason? Okay, stupid. He said he was going to be out of town so why put down his home number? So many questions had been swirling around in Sassy's head about a man she thought was only passing but a minute through her life until she got her first E-mail from him.

"Sassy, I hope you don't mind me emailing you, but I couldn't wait any longer for you to call me. I really enjoyed our brief time together. By the way, the picture on your website does you little justice. I look forward to seeing you on the 21st.   Yours, Norris."

Sassy tried holding off responding to Norris's E-mail as long as she could—two days. The night she E-mailed him back, she had gone to bed but couldn't sleep. At 11:30 she got up, turned her computer back on and went up online.

"Norris, hi.

Nice hearing from you. I agree our brief time together was nice. As for my picture, sir, although I appreciate your kind words, it looks just like me. I hope your business trip is going well and no, I don't mind you emailing me. I like corresponding with interesting people. See you on the 21st. Sassy"

It was hard as heck writing that E-mail and not letting on how badly she wanted to see and speak to him. They started off E-mailing once a day, now they were up to three times a day. The first thing Sassy did every morning now was check her E-mail. Norris must have been doing the same, there was always an early morning E-mail waiting for her. They wrote about their day, they wrote about her book, and they wrote about the little culinary idiosyncrasies that made them each unique. Norris confessed that he liked his peanut butter and jelly creamed together in a bowl before spreading it on whole wheat bread. Sassy had never seen anyone do that before and could only imagine that it must look like cocky on brown bread. Yuk! Sassy gave up one of her own little peculiarities; her love for American cheese. She liked American cheese in white rice, in grits, and in eggs. She also like spinach quiche made with American and Swiss cheese. All of which Norris said would make him barf. In the end, they both agreed they liked steamed broccoli and lobster tail with lots of sweet butter.

While Sassy looked forward to getting E-mail from Norris, she wanted more. She wanted to hear his voice, but dared not call. She had no legitimate reason to call him. If he had her number, he could call and simply say, "I was thinking about you," and everything would be okay. However, at this stage, if she called Norris and said the same thing, she might come off too easy and that wasn't what she wanted him to think. It was an old fashion thought, but that's what she was, old fashion. If her mother was alive, she'd say she was being silly. The truth was she felt like a silly school girl who had yet to be kissed by the boy she fantasized about. What's worse, she had dreamed about Norris nearly every night since she met him—dreams that she consciously started before she even dropped off to sleep. How silly was that? But she couldn't help it. She had never been this close to a fantasy before and tomorrow she was going to see her fantasy in person. She had told no one about meeting Norris, it would have been like exposing her fantasy and that was something oh so very private. The very real problem she was having with her fantasy was it was making her very real relationship with Kenneth pale in comparison. Her evening with him was going terribly. She had been unable to concentrate on anything Kenneth was saying.

"So do you think I should do it?" Kenneth asked while driving Sassy home.

Sassy, looking straight ahead, was lost in thought.

"Sassy! Did you hear what I said?"

Norris's face vanished from Sassy's mind. "What?"

Kenneth shot Sassy an annoyed look. "Did you hear anything I said?"

Why lie? "No, I didn't."

"Sassy, damn. I'd appreciate it if you'd focus on me for a change. You're not the only one who has a life."

"Kenneth, I'm not doing this tonight. You have something to say, say it."

"Do you care that I'm considering investing a lot of money in my brother's restaurant?"

Sassy groaned under her breath. "How much?"

"A hundred and fifty thousand; I can't afford to lose but Burton can't get his restaurant going without me."

Again Sassy groaned. Discussions about Burton never ended on a happy note.

Kenneth went on. "I figure if I invest the money and he runs the restaurant, it should be alright."

"If that's the way it's going to work, then you should do it." She hoped that would be the last word on the subject.

"Yeah, but what do you think?"

Oh, God! Please leave me alone!

"Do you think I should invest?"

Why in the world wasn't she on a ship somewhere far out in the middle of the Atlantic? "Kenneth, if you feel a need to invest in Burton's restaurant then do so."

Kenneth cut his eyes at Sassy. "Do you have to say it like that?"

Lord, help me. "Kenneth, what do you want me to say? This is your decision to make."

"I know. Look, Burton went to that culinary art school in Manhattan. He also took restaurant management at New York City College of Technology. He is certified."

"Okay, so he should be able to make a restaurant work. That's what you're worried about, right?"

Kenneth sighed. "Burton should be able to handle the business end. I can't be hands on with him. I have to trust that he'll be able to make a success of a restaurant."

Sassy mumbled, "For your sake, I hope so."

"What did you say?"

"Kenneth, the country is in a recession. Businesses are closing; people are losing their jobs. Do you think this is a good time to open a new restaurant?"

Kenneth thought about it. "I guess if Burton opens his restaurant, we'll always have a place to eat."

Sassy cringed at the thought. Burton would probably spit in her food. Of more concern to her than that, was Kenneth's indecisiveness and stupidity. He was a flunky for his brother and sister. Why couldn't Kenneth see that his brother was a schemer? Burton was always scheming on something new and Kenneth was always there to finance him. When she first met Kenneth four years ago, Burton was a photographer. That lasted all but five months. Then Burton became a travel agent. That lasted eleven months. Then he became a computer salesman, but seven months later he saw Emeril Lagasse on television and enrolled in cooking school. When Burton found out that Emeril owned a couple of restaurants down in New Orleans, Burton set his mind on doing likewise somewhere on

planet earth. If only Burton's feet were planted on terra firma.
He might see how flighty he was, which reminded Sassy of the
time Burton decided he wanted to become a pilot; another
episodic flight of fancy.

"You don't have much confidence in my brother?"

"Do you?"

"Sassy, why are you—"

"No, Kenneth! Why are you dragging me into this mess
when you already know what you're going to do? You know
your brother. How long do you think he'll stick to this fanciful
venture?"

Kenneth exhaled loudly. "I think he's really serious this
time. He—"

"But Burton has been serious each and every time he
decided he wanted to dive blindly into a new project."

"Yeah, but this time he stuck to the course, he didn't
miss a day."

"Is that supposed to be a big deal?"

"For Burton it is."

"Kenneth, what am I missing here? Burton is supposed
to be a grown man. It shouldn't be a big deal that he stuck to a
course of study or that he didn't miss a day of class. He's
supposed to be responsible, he's almost thirty years old! Are
you planning on being his safety net for the rest of his life?"

When Kenneth didn't answer and his jaw tightened,
Sassy wasn't surprised. Kenneth always got that way when she
didn't agree with him about Burton or anything else. There was
no way she was going to lie to make Kenneth feel better about
supporting a grown rusty ass man who changed jobs and
careers faster than a new mother changed her baby's diapers.
Kenneth was the reason Burton wasn't growing up. Burton was
the youngest of Kenneth and his sister Maureen. Kenneth and
Maureen both felt obliged to honor the promise they made to
their mother before she died fifteen years ago to take care of
Burton. But, damn, how long was that promise supposed to
last? From Sassy's vantage point, Burton, with his spoiled

behind self, was more than taking advantage of Kenneth and Maureen.

"Kenneth, I'm going to say this, and then I'm done. One of these days, you are going to have to pull that safety net you keep in place for Burton and let him wing it on his own."

His jaw tight, Kenneth drove on. Two blocks later he stopped at the traffic light. "You must take me for a fool."

Sassy let her head fall back against the headrest. "Oh, God."

"You talk like I don't know my brother. Sassy, I know Burton's been irresponsible, but this time, I think he's found something he can really sink his teeth into."

Yeah; your bank account.

"And if I'm right, I'm willing to help him this one last time, and it will be the last time, financially. I asked your opinion because I wanted to get your take on it, but obviously that was too much to ask."

Sassy studied Kenneth's tightly clamped jaw as he drove on. He was slick. What he was really asking her to do was tell him to not invest in Burton's restaurant, but she wasn't stepping into that bear trap a third time. A little more than three years ago, she told Kenneth not to give Burton money for flying lessons because it was a waste of time. What major airline was going to hire a man who wanted to be a pilot because he thought the uniforms were cool and he could fly all over the world for free? Surprisingly, Kenneth listened and Burton, on his own, took lessons from some fly-by-night instructor down in Mississippi who lost his license after he almost killed himself and Burton. Seconds after take-off, the plane nose-dived. The official finding by the FTSB was pilot error, but the half smoked blunt found under the instructor's seat got him jail time.

Burton blamed Kenneth for not giving him the money for a more credentialed instructor; Kenneth turned around and blamed her for telling him to not give Burton the money. Kenneth didn't want to give Burton the money then, he does not want to give it to him now. Kenneth needed her to give him a way out, but she wasn't about to, especially after he complained to her after Maureen lost the money he invested in her failed nail salon. What person in her right mind would open up a nail salon in Brooklyn when there were Korean-operated nail salons damn near on every corner? One salon operated by Maureen, a black woman, would not stand a chance if she couldn't offer her services at the same or lower price with just as much variety. Sassy told Kenneth outright, "If it were me, I wouldn't give her a red cent," but Maureen convinced Kenneth that she'd done her research. Maureen was out of business in seven months and Kenneth was out of thirty thousand dollars. When Kenneth complained to her about it, Sassy told him to stop loaning money to his family. That's when he told her, "What I do with my damn money is my business."

Enough said. Sassy was tried of rying to make a blind man see. As far as she was concerned, when it comes to Kenneth and his siblings, she no longer had an opinion. Maureen and Burton used Kenneth way before she came along and would continue to do so long after she was gone. And that was just it, if there was ever a hint she should be taking, this was it. They never agreed on anything when it came to his family and when they fought; it was usually over Kenneth putting his family before her. Okay, so they weren't married, but if this was any indication of how married life was going to be with Kenneth, a band of gold from him was never going to circle her finger or her neck.

"So you don't think I should give Burton the money?"

Sassy peered at Kenneth as if a big black wart popped up on the tip of his nose.

Kenneth glimpsed the "are you stupid?" expression on Sassy's face. "Thanks for nothing."

Sassy coolly turned her head and looked out her window. At this point, she didn't care. Kenneth was going to do what he wanted to do anyway. As an advertising executive, Kenneth was the cream of his crop. He was doing better than any member of his family and brashly boasted about it to them. His ego was huge and so were his pockets. He was certainly ripe for the picking.

Kenneth pulled into the narrow streets of trendy Brooklyn Heights; Sassy put her hand on the door handle even before the car came to a full stop in front of her apartment building on Henry Street. As usual, there were no vacant parking spots as far as the eye could see.

"I'm not prowling for a spot tonight," Kenneth said.

Sassy was relieved. "I have a chapter I have to finish tonight anyway." That wasn't altogether a lie. She did have a chapter to finish; it just didn't have to be tonight.

Sassy barely closed the car door before Kenneth peeled off. She almost shouted, "Good riddance!" but thought better of it. Kenneth would not have heard her anyway. She flipped her hand instead.

Sassy was in her apartment just long enough to feed Chester, turn on her computer, and get to her bedroom when her telephone began ringing. With Chester now curled up in her arms, she answered the telephone.

"Hel—"

"Where have you been? Don't you ever answer your cell phone?"

"Evelyn?"

"Sassy, I've been calling you all afternoon! You—"

"Evelyn, Evelyn. Listen. I'm just getting in. Let me call you after I shower and get under the covers."

"What's wrong with your cell phone? Why didn't you have it on?"

"Because I forgot to charge it last night and it died on me while I was speaking to my agent. Which reminds me, I need to charge my phone." Just as Sassy lowered a discontented Chester to her bed, she heard the familiar call waiting beep.

"Sassy—"

"Hold on a minute." Sassy hurried back to the living

room and picked up her shoulder bag from the sofa. From it, she took her cell phone and headed for her spare bedroom which doubled as her office. She held back from clicking back over to Evelyn until she had set her cell phone up to charge and had brought AOL up on her computer. She couldn't wait to read Norris's response to her last E-mail about what he found most appealing in a woman.

The computer was taking a long time to load. Still she held off from taking Evelyn off of hold. The agitation in Evelyn's voice was clear but that was her norm of late. She and Evelyn Wayne had been friends since they first met more than ten years ago at a writer's conference at the Penta Hotel when they were both only dreaming of becoming writers. While Sassy had stuck to her writing with the tenacity of a pit bull and hounded agents and editors despite them telling her there was no market for her work, Evelyn had given up after the second round of rejections. She shredded her six hundred page manuscript after an agent told her she needed to take some writing courses. Evelyn took that agent's criticism to heart and trashed her own dreams although now she claims to not regret it. Sassy sometimes wondered, especially whenever she had a new title released. Evelyn never asked for a copy of her latest book and although she automatically gave Evelyn a copy, Evelyn admitted to not having read a single one of Sassy's books. Evelyn claimed she was too busy reading proposals and requests for funding for her job as Assistant Director of Programs at the State Counsel on the Arts. Sassy no longer worried about it. She and Evelyn were still friends and reading her books was not a requirement for them being friends.

The computer was ready. Sassy typed in her AOL password and immediately pressed the speaker button on the telephone on her desk before shutting off the cordless phone.

"Sorry about that, Evelyn. I'm trying to—"

"Sassy! Have you spoken to Bernard at all today?"

"No, why?" Sassy hated when she couldn't find something. "Where is that darn charger? I—"

"Sassy!" Evelyn shouted impatiently. "Would you please listen to me?"

"You asked if I'd heard from Bernie. I said I hadn't."

"Did you check your messages?"

Sassy looked for the first time at her answering machine. The red message unit light was flashing, but Sassy also saw that she had 85 messages in her AOL mailbox. Those messages alone were going to keep her busy for hours.

"I'll check the calls when I get off with you."

"Bernard walked out of the hospital earlier today."

Evelyn finally got Sassy's attention. "Walked out? When did he go in? I didn't know he was in the hospital."

"Of course you didn't. You've been too busy signing autographs to know what's going on with the rest of us."

Evelyn's scathingly hurtful words hit Sassy like a zap from a taser. She looked at the telephone as if it were responsible for insulting her.

"FYI, Bernard went into the hospital yesterday!"

"Well, damn! How am I supposed to know that if no one told me?"

"No one could reach you, Miss Author!"

Had she heard right? "Hey, if you have a problem—"

"It's not me who has a problem, it's Bernard. I didn't find out until today that he was in the hospital. He called me around one this afternoon and before I could leave for the hospital, he walked out and came here, probably because he couldn't reach you."

"Evelyn, Bernie knows exactly how to reach me "

"How? On your dead ass cell phone?"

"Evelyn—"

"Unlike you, Sassy, I haven't seen Bernard in over a month."

"That's Bernie's decision, Evelyn, which I don't agree with, but you have to understand what he's going through. Bernie is angry, he's ashamed, and he's suicidal."

Evelyn paused. She said softly, "He's already dying."

"He is not dying. He's gonna be fine."

"This isn't one of your fairytales, Sassy. You can't write a happy ending this time."

"Geez, Evelyn, why don't you come right on out and say you're jealous of my success as writer."

"I don't give a damn about your success! I only care about Bernard. Don't you care how sick he is?"

"What the hell do you think?"

"I don't know what to think. I haven't heard from you since last weekend."

"Wow! Could it be because I've been busy? It's no crime if I don't speak with you every day, Evelyn."

"Hey, you don't ever have to speak to me—"

"Evelyn, what the hell is wrong with you?"

"I keep telling you, it's not me! It's Bernard. He's talking about killing himself. I would think you'd want to know about that or is your so-called career more important."

Sassy took a breath. Evelyn was being viciously nasty and although Sassy had the ammunition to strike back, she didn't see where it was worth it.

"Hold on a minute." Sassy pressed the hold button on the speaker phone before Evelyn had a chance to protest. She needed a time out before she ended up cursing Evelyn out.

Sassy suddenly started. She looked down and saw that Chester was rubbing his body against her leg. Chester was the only constant in her life right now. He loved her no matter what. She used to be able to say the same about Bernard, but of late, she couldn't. He was angry at her, he was angry at Evelyn, he was angry at the world. It had been three years since Bernard first told her he had AIDS, and by that time he already had it two years and didn't know it. The news was devastating for her and Evelyn both. While Evelyn was the mother of Bernard's seven year-old son, Brice, Sassy was Bernard's closest cousin. There was no one else in the world Sassy was closer to than Bernard. When they were kids, Bernard was at her house so much, the other kids on the block thought he was her brother when in fact, he was her first cousin. Bernard's mother was her father's sister. She and Bernard were each only children and although they were three years apart, they bonded early. Bernard took care of her like he was her big brother, but since he got AIDS; at times she had to take care of him like she was his mother. She was the first one Bernard told and even then, it took him months to tell her. He was ashamed that he had AIDS and worse, he was ashamed of how he had contracted it. It wasn't from a man he had gotten AIDS, it was from a woman. A woman he had met at a club; a woman he knew nothing about; a woman he had sex with in the bathroom of the nightclub, without a condom, whose full name he couldn't call to this day. Until that fateful night, Bernard had a clean bill of health, but it was two years before he knew that he had full blown AIDS.

"I just didn't think women could give men AIDS."

Sassy couldn't believe Bernard was that naive. "Bernie, I know you know better than that."

"You don't have to tell me how stupid I am. I know, dammit! I know!"

The pained look on Bernard's face only mirrored the anguish in Sassy's heart. She couldn't say which of them started crying first, she only knew they both cried agonizing tears of disbelief until they were all cried out. Since then, she, Evelyn, and Bernard had been living with his illness, but the illness had changed Bernard. He was always angry and stayed away for months at a time. Often, he grew tired of his three times daily cocktail of pills and would go days without taking them until he'd get so sick he'd have to be hospitalized. Sassy could only guess that was the case again.

Sassy released Evelyn from hold. "Evelyn, if I hear from Bernie, I'll call you."

"Don't put me on hold again!"

"Dammit, Evelyn, stop yelling at me!"

"Well, you don't seem to be hearing what I'm saying! Bernard—"

"Evelyn, I care just as much, if not more, about Bernie. And the fact is, he was inside your apartment. If he was so bad off, why didn't you make him stay there or make him go back to the hospital?"

"I tried! He wouldn't listen to me." Evelyn's voice cracked. "He said he wanted to talk to you."

That was an 'ah ha' moment for Sassy. Evelyn was ticked off because Bernie didn't want to talk to her.

"He's real depressed. He was talking about killing himself. I went upstairs to pick up Brice from the babysitter, but when I came back down, he was gone. Just gone! What are we gonna do?"

Sassy didn't have a clue. As she eased down into the chair behind her desk, she could hear Evelyn crying. Evelyn had every reason to be scared. Bernard had tried to kill himself twice before. First when he learned he had AIDS, and six months later when he thought Evelyn would take their son and move back to Canada where she was from. Both times he had used pills and alcohol, and both times it was Evelyn who found him and got him to the hospital. There was no doubt that Evelyn still loved Bernard despite how he got AIDS.

Sassy introduced Evelyn to Bernard ten years ago when they first met, but back then Bernard was married. When he and Kayla broke up and eventually divorced eight years ago, Bernard and Evelyn got together for what Bernard termed "a little sexercise" every now and then. Evelyn understood that Bernard wasn't interested in getting married again and took him on his terms, and although they never really lived together, they had a pretty steady non-committed relationship that bore them Brice whom Bernard adored. Brice was Bernard's only child.

The night Bernard told Evelyn he had AIDS, Sassy was there to hold both their hands. It was a terrible night. Evelyn pummeled Bernard with her wrathful fists and her blistering words of condemnation and betrayal till her tears and her rage sapped her of her strength. She didn't have the energy to care that Bernard got down on his knees before her and begged for her forgiveness. As was her right, Evelyn wrapped herself up tight in her anger and wouldn't let Bernard near her for almost a year. She allowed him to see his son only if Sassy was with him, but after a while Evelyn's anger couldn't dull the love she still had for Bernard. She cautiously opened herself up to him again but by then Bernard was mad at the world.

Sassy crossed her fingers. "I'm sure one of us will hear from Bernie soon."

"What if we don't? What if he tries to kill himself again? What then?"

Sassy began rubbing her forehead. This was more than she was prepared to deal with tonight. "Evelyn, I need to—"

Chester suddenly ran out of the office just as Sassy's was drawn to the sound of her front door being unlocked.

"Evelyn, hold on." Before Sassy could get up from behind her desk, Bernard stepped into the doorway of her office. Fleetingly, they locked eyes. Bernard hung his tired head but Sassy had already glimpsed the pain and sadness in his dark sunken eyes.

"Oh, God, Bernie."

"He's there?" Evelyn asked. "Let me speak to him!"

Bernard shook his head telling Sassy he didn't want to speak to Evelyn.

"Sassy, let me speak to him!"

"Evelyn, I'll call you back."

"Sassy—"

Sassy never took her eyes off of Bernard as she pressed the speaker button immediately disconnecting Evelyn. This was going to be a long night.

9

As tired as she was, Sassy found herself riding in the back of a squealing, speeding ambulance holding onto Bernard's bony hand as he languished somewhere between lethargy and nightmarish pain. If only he would black out, then he would feel no pain and the ride for Sassy would be a lot less tense. There was an oxygen mask over Bernard's nose and mouth which served to only highlight the anguish and despair ablaze in his eyes. Bernard continually rolled his head from side to side, unable to relax, unable to rid himself of the hopelessness that consumed him.

Bernard said pitifully, "Why don't you just let me die?"

Sassy saw no need to defend what she did to save Bernard's life. She didn't care that he was upset with her for forcing him go back to the hospital. She didn't care that he whined about wanting to die. After he fell in the bathroom while trying to sit down on the toilet, she called 911 despite his feeble objection. He didn't have the strength to stop her. As it was, it was a wonder he made it to her apartment at all.

"Bernie, don't lose faith, you're going to be alright."

Bernard pulled his hand from Sassy. He pulled his oxygen mask down. "I am never going to be alright and you know it. Just look at me. I look nothing like me. I don't feel anything like me. When I look in the mirror, I don't know who I am. Why should I want to live like this?"

Sassy was careful to not look anywhere but into Bernard's eyes. For the past year, his eyes were the only recognizable things on him.

The EMS technician carefully pulled the oxygen mask back up over Bernard's nose and mouth.

"Bernie, I know you're scared and I'm scared for you but you have to take better care of yourself. You don't have to suffer like this."

Again, Bernard removed his oxygen mask. "You try choking down all those damn horse pills; you'd stop taking them too."

The EMS technician again reached for the oxygen mask. Bernard covered it with his shaky hand. "If I stop breathing, let me die."

Sassy looked at the EMS technician who was not the first to look away when their eyes, for an instant, met. She had told the technician Bernard had AIDS, and while he wore latex gloves, he didn't shy away from touching Bernard and appeared not to be bothered by Bernard's emotional outbursts.

A single tear rolled down the side of Bernard's face. "This isn't living. It's a long, slow, painful death."

"Bernie, you can live better than this. I'll help you—"

"You don't give a damn about me!"

"Bernie! What the—"

The EMS technician quickly touched Sassy's arm. He shook his head, but Sassy ignored his admonishment to not argue with Bernard.

"Bernie, this is me. You and I, we know each other better than anyone else in the world. Did you forget the promise we made when we were fourteen years old to always be there for each other no matter what. I'm here, Bernie! I'm here for you and it's killing me to see you like this."

Bernard said flatly. "Then let me die."

"Bernie, you're going to get better. You—"

"Stop lying!" Bernard said breathlessly. "I am never going to get better. I'm never gonna see my son grow up."

While Sassy and the EMS technician avoided looking at each other, both continued to look at Bernard who turned his face to the wall of the ambulance. Sassy steeled herself against crying. What was she to say? She wasn't God. She couldn't give Bernard guarantees.

"Put the mask back on," the EMS technician said.

When Bernard didn't move, Sassy reached for the oxygen mask but Bernard clamped down on it mildly. Sassy got the message. She watched as Bernard put the mask back over his nose and mouth himself. He then closed his eyes.

Bernie's bitterness cut deep. Sassy had no idea he had a problem with her writing career. It was true since the release of *Butterfly* her calendar had been full and she had not been as readily available for Bernard or any of her friends, but that didn't say she didn't care about what happened to him. Yes, he had a deadly disease, but was she not permitted to go on with her life? She wasn't the one who had done something so stupid as to endanger the quality of her health and her life by sleeping around.

Looking at Bernard's tightly knitted brow, Sassy could only imagine he was thinking about how much he hated the woman who had given him AIDS. Sassy's heart ached for Bernard as he gave in to his hopelessness and began to cry tears that didn't flow. Maybe it was a blessing that he didn't know who the woman was. If he did, more than likely the woman would be dead and Bernard would be sick behind bars. When Bernard first found out he was HIV positive and had full blown AIDS, he went back to the club week after week desperately searching for the woman who had stolen his wonderful life. At the club, no one seemed to know of the woman that Bernard only had a first name for. Jonelle had disappeared and Bernard could never reach her on the disconnected telephone number she had given him which angered him so bad he put his fist through a wall in his bedroom. He cursed Jonelle often and looked for her in the face of every woman he passed on the street. After seeing his beguiling viper only once in the low, hypnotic lights of the club, Sassy could only wonder if Bernard would know Jonelle if he actually saw her again. After all, it probably wasn't her face he remembered most about her, it was the pleasure she gave him in those sexually charged moments. Now he damned her to hell for stealing his life, but it was Bernard's anger that kept him from taking better care of himself. He didn't keep to his three times a day regiment of medication and when he was most angry, he wouldn't keep his doctor appointments—he skipped more than he kept. Each and every time Bernard's body started failing him, when painful staph infections and shingles steadily marred his once beautiful skin, Bernard talked only of wanting to die. The gauntness of his once muscular body frightened him just as it frightened the people he used to work with. Seven months ago, Bernard walked out on his management position at Dimensions without telling anyone why.

When his boss, Esra Hawkings, finally caught up with him and asked what was going on, Bernard shouted into the telephone, "None of your damn business!" He slammed the phone down and cried.

Esra wasted no time calling Sassy but she couldn't tell him what was wrong. That was for Bernard to do, but he wouldn't. And it was a shame because, of all people, Esra would have understood—he had a nephew who had died of AIDS early in the nineties. Esra left messages asking Bernard to return to work, but Bernard never did, and that was sad. Bernard had loved his job at Dimensions. Bernard was Dimensions. He made Dimensions the number one best selling men's clothing store in Brooklyn. For seven years Esra depended on Bernard to run Dimensions while he was off, God knows where, involved in so many other ventures that made him as rich as he was. Esra gave Bernard carte blanche to manage Dimensions to the point that Bernard himself went on the buying trips, as well as decided on what designers' line the store would carry. Not to mention it was Bernard who hired and fired employees, and was the catalyst behind the highly touted fashion shows Dimensions held during Fashion Week in

Manhattan's Bryant Park. Dimensions raked in huge profits because of Bernard and his incredible flair for fashion. Two years after Bernard began working for Esra, Esra bought himself a grand old house upstate New York. Bernard didn't go unrewarded, however. He bought himself an expensive condo in Park Slope.

How Dimensions was doing since Bernard left Sassy didn't know, but if Bernard ever got himself together, she had no doubt Esra would gladly take him back; just as Evelyn had. Unfortunately for Esra and Evelyn, the Bernard they knew no longer existed. Not only had AIDS ravaged Bernard's body, AIDS had stolen his light, his joy, his hopes, his dreams, and his lust for life. All he had left was an angry soul.

Sassy reached over to wipe away Bernard's anemic tears but the EMS technician quickly seized her arm in mid-air. Again he shook his head. Sassy didn't have to question why he didn't want her to touch Bernard's tears.

The EMS technician handed Sassy a pair of sterile latex gloves. Before accepting the gloves, she checked to make sure Bernard's eyes were still closed. She took the gloves and pulled one onto her right hand. She then took the tissue the technician handed her and wiped the side of Bernard's face, but Bernard abruptly turned away. Sassy understood. She let him be just as the ambulance pulled up to the emergency room entrance of Long Island College Hospital and came to a stop. Right away the technician opened the back doors.

"I don't want you to come inside," Bernard said as Sassy stepped down out of the ambulance.

"Now you're being ridiculous."

Bernard snatched the oxygen mask completely off. "Dammit, leave! I don't need you! Just leave me alone."

Sassy's nose stung. She was embarrassed. She looked sheepishly at the two EMS technicians lowering Bernard, stretched out on the gurney, to the ground. They appeared to not be paying attention to her or to what Bernard had said as they hurriedly rolled him through the emergency room doors into the hospital, but that didn't make Sassy feel any less humiliated. She dawdled outside the emergency room door unsure of which way to go. She understood Bernard's anger, it was the way he was pushing her away that she didn't understand. When her own tears came, she stopped short of wiping them away when she brought her hand to her face. She was still wearing the latex glove. She pulled it off and tossed it inside a garbage bin just outside the hospital doors. She started to reach inside her shoulder bag for her cell phone but remembered she had left it charging on her desk. From where she stood she could see Bernard being wheeled further away from the door, further away from her. This wasn't right. Bernard was her blood, her family. She had to be with him.

Sassy squared her shoulders and marched inside the hospital. Right away she saw Bernard lying alongside the wall across from the nurse's station. He saw her too. He frowned and covered his face with his raised arm. Sassy got the message. She looked around until she spotted a sign pointing toward a bank of public telephones tucked away in a little out of the way nook. She had to call Evelyn.

"Hey," Sassy said. "It's me."

"Where are you? Where's Bernard?"

"I had him brought to Long Island College Hospital."

"Why didn't you call me back?"

"He asked me not to."

"Oh, so again he's only talking to you?"

"Evelyn, he—"

"I'm nobody, right?"

"Evelyn, he doesn't want me here. He told me to go home."

"So you left him there by himself?" Evelyn shrieked. "You walked out on him?"

Sassy grit her teeth. She squeezed the phone in a grip so tight she hurt her hand.

"I'm coming down there," Evelyn said. "Someone has to be—"

"I'm still at the hospital, Evelyn. If you come and Bernie curses you out, don't say I didn't warn."

Sassy surmised by Evelyn's silence she was having flashbacks about the last time Bernard cursed her out and had her crying like it was her fault he was sick.

"Evelyn, I'll call you as soon as I know how bad it is."

"But I should be there, Sassy. Bernard is my baby's father. I should be there for him."

"I'll call you. I promise." Sassy quickly hung up. She was seconds from losing it. She hid her face in her hands and muted her cries so as not to be heard outside in the emergency room. Her cousin, her best friend, was dying and whether he wanted her there or not, she was staying. Sassy wiped her eyes with the back of her hand before going and standing alongside Bernard. She said nothing. She waited for him to uncover his face but realized he had fallen asleep.

"Are you a relative?" a nurse asked.

"I'm his cousin."

"We need his insurance and medical information."

"I'll get it," Sassy said as the nurse turned to go back to her station.

Mindful to be gentle, Sassy easily rolled Bernard's light body onto his left side and from his hip pocket, took his wallet. She then rolled him again onto his back.

Bernard woke up. "I told you to go home," he said groggily.

"Since when do I take orders from you?"

He crocked, "Get the hell away from me."

Sassy glared at Bernard just as hard as he glared at her, but in his dark lusterless eyes, she saw the cousin she used to know cowering deep inside pleading for her to not desert him. She pinched Bernard on the arm and didn't care that he grimaced and cried out from the painful sting.

"You listen to me you stubborn jerk," she said in a hushed voice. "You better stop acting like you've lost your damn mind up in here."

Bernard stared angrily at Sassy, but said not a word.

"I don't know who the hell you think you're talking to, but you had best shut your mouth and be grateful that I love you. I'm sorry you have AIDS, I wish to God you didn't, but you do. I understand your anger, I understand your hopelessness, but I'm telling you right now, Bernie, I will not take one more second of your nasty, abusive tongue."

Sassy wasn't sure if she was getting through to Bernard or not. He had no expression on his face and his dry, cracked lips were tight.

"Bernie, how you got sick is a damn shame, but dammit, what's done is done. Right now, you have to get to a place in your head that will allow you to live with this disease and go on with your life."

Bernard shot Sassy a smoldering glare.

"Don't look at me like that. I suggest you lay your ass here and cool out, while I go about the business of getting you re-admitted."

"You think—"

Sassy threw up her hand. "Don't wanna hear it."

As soon as Sassy walked away, Bernard again covered his face with his arm. "Mean ass woman," he said.

As she had done many times before, Sassy went about giving information that would admit Bernard into a place he hated to be. When she was done, she kept his wallet. And while she wanted to go over and be with Bernard as doctors poked and prodded his feeble body, she didn't. She couldn't. With every grunt and groan Bernard made, she cringed. In that moment she realized she didn't want to be alone. She went again to the public telephone, this time to call Kenneth.

"Hey," Kenneth said. "I was going to call you tomorrow."

"Kenneth, I'm at the hospital."

"What happened? Are you alright?"

"I'm fine. It's Bernie." Sassy listened to the dead silence in her ear. "Kenneth, I said it's Bernie."

"So what do you want me to do?"

"I want you to come down and keep me company. I'm at Long Island College on Hicks."

Again Kenneth's silence filled Sassy's ears. "Kenneth, I need you."

"Baby, I wanna be there for you, but . . .but you know how I feel about—"

"About what? My cousin?"

"Look, I like your cousin and I'm sorry he got AIDS, but I can't handle—"

"That's just it, Kenneth. There isn't much you can handle, is there?"

"Wait a minute."

"Go to hell!" Sassy slammed the phone down so hard she thought she had broken it. As she had done with Evelyn, Sassy grit her teeth and growled out loud, not caring who heard her. How could she have wasted even a minute of her time on such an ass hole? If it were his idiot brother or sister, Kenneth would be there in the blink of an eye, but for her? No. He couldn't handle being around Bernard, and she could only surmise if it was her suffering with AIDS, Kenneth wouldn't be there for her either.

"Worthless prick." Sassy picked up the telephone again. She dialed her friend Deborah's number, but before Deborah could answer her ringing phone, Sassy hung up. Deborah had enough problems of her own dealing with her two teenage sons, plus Deborah had a manuscript of her own to finish. Again Sassy dialed, then again she hung up. There was no one to call that would understand what she was going through. She didn't want to speak to Evelyn; Evelyn was just as stressed as she was.

Ditching the idea of speaking to anyone, Sassy started away from the telephones but stopped. Norris Yoshido. She remembered how easy it was to talk to him. The E-mail had been fun, but served to enhance her fantasies about him. For the past two weeks she had wanted to hear his voice but there was no legit reason to call him, until now.

Searching the side pocket of her shoulder bag, she found Norris's business card tucked inside a flap in her wallet. She knew he was back in town but as late as it was, he probably was not in his office. Norris's cell phone number was most likely her best bet. Well, nothing beats a failure—

10

Sassy wasn't alone in the hospital waiting room, although she might as well had been. It was so ominously quiet. There were eight other frustrated people waiting as Sassy was, to hear news of their sick family members being seen by doctors who strolled around the emergency room as if they were strolling in the Museum of Natural History, only mildly interested in the animals they had seen so many times before. In the three hours since arriving at the hospital, Sassy had asked nurses several times when Bernard was going to be taken to a room, only to be told they were waiting for test results. They already knew what was wrong with Bernard, why did they need more tests to tell them again?

"Please be patient," an annoyed nurse said to Sassy. "Someone will notify you when your cousin has a bed."

Patient was the last thing Sassy was. She was anxious. She had been on the telephone with Norris only three minutes when he said, "Why don't we do this in person?"

That was two hours and seventeen minutes ago. Did Norris change his mind? Maybe she misunderstood him. Maybe he was playing her. If he was, she would never E-mail or call him again.

A man sitting two chairs away from Sassy got up to leave when his wife was finally released. He left behind his copy of Time Magazine with Barack Obama on the cover. Sassy quickly commandeered the magazine and began to flip through it. She lingered on a story just long enough to get the gist of it before her eyes would again wander to her watch or toward the entrance. Despite the lateness of the hour, traffic in midtown could still be a bottleneck. Maybe Norris was tied up in traffic.

Sassy crossed her legs and immediately re-crossed them. She couldn't believe how antsy she was. It didn't help that she didn't feel exactly just-showered fresh. She was still wearing the same black skirt and lavender blouse she'd put on Wednesday morning and now, here it was 12:55 Thursday morning. She combed through her shoulder length dreadlocks with her fingers as if that would make them look any different. She nonchalantly covered her mouth with her hand and exhaled lightly. Like her clothes, her breath wasn't too fresh. She searched inside her shoulder bag and found a green and white mint which she popped into her mouth. Its sweet freshness perked her up. Maybe she was being a bit self-absorbed about her looks, but that's how Norris made her feel. He probably made a lot of women feel that way. Again she looked at her watch, at the entrance, and then up at the clock on the far wall. One a.m. Norris wasn't coming. She should have never called him. She put herself out there and he showed her. Sassy read another article before tossing the magazine onto the seat next to her.

"Nothing of interest?"

Sassy looked up over her right shoulder. Her heart skipped a beat. When a man smiles as beautiful as Norris, one can only smile back. Lord, Lord, Lord. What a beautiful man.

"I hope I didn't keep you waiting too long."

"Well, I am in a waiting room—waiting."

Norris chuckled as he moved the magazine over to the next chair and sat himself next to Sassy. On top of the magazine, he set the small brown bag he carried.

"You look simply marvelous," he said, mimicking Billy Crystal.

With a sly smile on her lips, Sassy eyed Norris suspiciously. Had he seen her preening? Did he think her vain?

Geez, she didn't check to see if there was any icky stuff in the corner of her eyes.

"How are you holding up?"

"Not too well; can't you tell?"

"Actually, you look great."

"Liar."

"You're right, you look terrible. It hurts my eyes to look at you."

Norris teasingly covered his eyes and Sassy playfully slapped him on the thigh. In less than a minute he had made her smile and his smile made waiting for him worth every eternal minute.

"Thank you for coming."

"Actually, we do have a date this weekend, remember?"

"I do." In the dreariness of the hospital emergency room, the twinkling glint in Norris's eyes brightened the whole room for Sassy.

"I'm glad you called."

Their shoulders were touching. "Thank you for coming, although I apologize for the lateness of the hour."

Norris unbuttoned his sports jacket. "An emergency knows nothing about the lateness of the hour."

Please don't ask.

"Do the doctors know what's wrong yet?"

Didn't I say, don't ask? "They're waiting for test results." Sassy glanced around Norris. "What's in the bag?"

Norris picked up the bag. "Coffee." He opened it. "French vanilla."

Sassy took the white styrofoam coffee cup. "Thank you." She quickly opened the sip flap and began to sip. The coffee was warm and sweet—too sweet.

"It's good," she lied. From the corner of her eye she could see Norris opening the flap of his coffee a bit slower than she had. She waited until he took a sip.

"When did you get back?"

"This afternoon. I sent you an E-mail."

"I didn't get a chance to read my E-mail today. Was your trip successful?"

"I picked up a new client."

"Congrats. What will you be building for him or her?"

"A couple. I'm designing a mansion."

"Nice. How many rooms?"

"Twenty-six, including a theater, a fitness room, and an indoor swimming pool."

"They certainly won't have to ever leave the house. Where is this?"

"Virginia, and it's their third house so they'll skip between states."

"Wow. That's almost sinful. Don't they listen to the news? We're damn near in a depression. How can they be building a third house?"

"Family money and great investments."

"Oh, they must not have invested with Bernard Madoff."

"I'm glad I didn't," Norris audibly breathed a sign of relief.

Sassy was glad to know that Norris had something to invest. "Do you think Madoff will ever get out of jail?"

"Patient Milton!" a nurse called from the door leading to the emergency room.

Sassy stood immediately. "Yes!"

The nurse beckoned for Sassy to follow her inside.

Sassy hurriedly handed Norris her coffee. "I'll be back."

"I'll be here."

Hurrying off, Sassy marveled at how easy it was to be with Norris. "How is he?" Sassy asked of the nurse who was standing at the nurse's station busily scribbling on a chart as if she hadn't heard Sassy. "Did Dr. Wilkshire see him?"

"Mr. Milton is about to go up to his room. He will be on the 9th floor. You can speak to him before he's taken up."

"Is Dr. Wilkshire still here? I'd like to speak to him."

The nurse flipped the chart closed. "The doctor was called away." The nurse walked off without a single word which irked her. Sassy followed anyway but she shot invisible darts into the nurse's back. The nurse stopped at the foot of Bernard's bed. She slipped the chart into a metal pocket.

"Nurse," Sassy said, "if you don't mind, I'd like to know what the doctor said. Is there something I need to know about my cousin?"

The middle-aged West Indian nurse said matter-of-factly, "He has AIDS." She turned on her white rubber-soled heel and walked off, leaving Sassy glaring poison darts at her back. Sassy could never get use to the coldness of some of the nurses she'd encountered since going back and forth to the hospital with Bernard.

"Why are you still here?" Bernard asked.

Sassy moved closer to the head of Bernard's bed. As many times as she'd seen IV needles sticking out of the back of his hands, tubes stuck up his nose, his lips so parched they cracked, by now it shouldn't upset her, but it did. She took a deep breath to keep from welling up.

Bernard groaned. "This is why I don't want you here. You better not cry."

"I will if I want to."

"Smart ass."

Smart ass is what Bernard always called her when she wouldn't do what he wanted her to. No, he never wanted her around when he was this bad off. The nurse didn't have to tell her Bernard's T cell count was excruciatingly low. Right now, his immune system couldn't fight off a nose tickle. Anything could kill him. Again Sassy teared up.

"Bernie, why do you keep doing this to yourself?"

"Ask God why did he let this happen to me?"

"Bernie, you know better than that. You can't blame God."

"Why not? Weren't we taught that God sees all, knows all? Was he too busy to protect me? Was I not one of his favorite children? Why hasn't he answered my prayers? Does he not like me anymore?"

Growing up in a sanctified Baptist church the way she and Bernard did, Sassy almost expected a bolt of lighting to come through the roof of the hospital and strike Bernard dead.

"Bernie, if Grandma was alive, she'd—"

"I'm already being punished."

The sour look on Bernard's face convinced Sassy that anything she said in defense of God would only make him angrier. When he was first diagnosed with AIDS, Bernard went through this incredible "I can lick this" stage. He flooded his body with fresh vegetable and fruit juices which he made himself; downed a multitude of vitamins and minerals; and he went back to church three times a week and stayed in church all day Sunday. Morning and night, Bernard stayed on his knees praying for the miracle he just knew would be bestowed upon him but no miracle ever came. Perhaps it was because Bernard didn't just have the HIV virus, he had full blown AIDS. It wasn't until he was skin and bones and covered with sores and shingles that he gave in to the AIDS treatment Dr. Wilkshire prescribed for him, but that's also when he turned his back on God. At times Bernard blamed God more than he blamed the woman who infected him.

"Sassy, you have got to stop looking so sad around me, you're making me sick." Bernard didn't laugh at his own joke. He licked his dry, chapped lips with a tongue that was thick and white.

"You want some ice?"

He nodded slightly.

Sassy hurried away. She knew exactly where to go. She was back in a flash with a cup of crushed ice. As she had done many times before, she gingerly slipped a piece of ice into Bernard's mouth. He rolled the ice around on his tongue to melt it. He then ran his wet tongue over his lips again.

Sassy gave him another piece of ice. "I'll call Evelyn as soon as I get home."

"I don't wanna see her."

"Bernie, you know—"

"Tell her not to come."

"Patient Milton?" an orderly asked.

Sassy asked, "Are you taking him up now?"

"Yes, ma'am." The orderly began unlocking the wheels of Bernard's bed.

"What room will he be in?"

"923."

Sassy placed the cup of ice in Bernard's right hand. She then kissed him on the cheek. "I'll see you tomorrow. I have your wallet. I'll take care of turning on your phone and television, first thing, okay?"

Closing his eyes, Bernard closed out Sassy and the orderly who, with his foot, released the locks at the base of his bed. Sassy stepped aside as the orderly began wheeling Bernard away from the wall. The tightness in her throat made it difficult to say, "I love you," loud enough for Bernard to hear her. The fact that they'd played this scene out so many times before didn't immune Sassy to the helplessness she felt as Bernard was wheeled out of the emergency room. In her mind she could almost see him being wheeled away to the morgue. She fought hard to not shed a tear but she wasn't strong enough. Before going back out into the waiting room, she dried her eyes and blew her nose. She found Norris reading the magazine she had tossed into the chair.

"Thank you for waiting."

Norris put the magazine back on the chair. "How is your cousin?" He stood.

"He's seen better days." Sassy picked up her coffee from the chair as did Norris. "He's been taken up to his room. Do you mind if I dump this?"

"No problem." Norris took Sassy's cup. On their way to the exit, he dumped both cups into the large trash basket near the door. Together they walked out of the hospital into the cool, crisp early morning air, and together they inhaled its freshness but there was an awkward silence between them.

Sassy wondered, now what? She had gotten him there, but now what was she supposed to do with him? Take him home and screw his brains out, or play it cool and thank him with a handshake?

Norris checked his watch—2:45. Sassy didn't ask about the time, she already knew which is why she felt guilty about calling him.

"I really appreciate you coming to keep me company, but I am so sorry for getting you to come out this late."

Norris showed Sassy his bare left ring finger.

"But you do have to go to work in a few hours, right?"

"Power naps do wonders."

Okay, so he wasn't in a hurry to leave. Should she invite him back to her apartment? She looked down toward Atlantic Avenue. She saw not one car on the usually bumper to bumper avenue that ran the full length of Brooklyn straight into Queens.

"How did you get here?" Norris asked.

"I hitched a ride in the back of the ambulance. Not a great way to travel."

"I imagine not." He was more curious about Sassy's cousin. "Your cousin is going to be okay, isn't he?"

"Well," Sassy said, looking away. "I'm praying."

There was no doubt in Norris's mind that Sassy had no intention of talking about her cousin's illness. That could possibly mean one thing—AIDS. Rarely did anyone ever want to talk about AIDS.

"I'm parked about three blocks west of here. If you want to wait inside, I—"

"This is Brooklyn, not the Left Bank." Sassy boldly wrapped her arm around Norris's arm. He smiled as they sauntered easily down Hicks Street not the least bit concerned about the man who suddenly appeared on the other side of the street walking briskly toward Atlantic Avenue.

"So, Norris, I know what you do for a living, I know

you just 'love' reading romance novels, and . . ."

Norris chuckled.

". . . I know you love E-mailing me."

Norris smiled as he took Sassy's hand and their fingers automatically interlocked. "Did you mind?"

"Not at all." Sassy was enjoying the feel of Norris's hand. "Anyway, I also know that you have a special friend who reads very titillating passages from my books to you."

"Had a special friend. Lately, I've been reading to myself."

That was something to smile at. "That's a good thing. Oh! I know you like to travel, I know you like bike riding, and I even know that you like to play golf."

"All true." Norris stopped walking. He faced Sassy under the glow of a city street lamp. "No games. What do you really want to know?"

In that moment, face to face with Norris, all Sassy really wanted to know was how good a lover he was, but how in the world was she supposed to ask that question?

"That's a devilishly seductive smile if ever I saw one," Norris said. "Don't be chicken."

Sassy laughed. "Okay. First, let me say I'm not a kiss on the first date kind of girl."

"I didn't think you were."

Funny how she wrote her female characters to be bold and adventuresome, and here she was nervous about saying what was on her mind. "Look, I'm a writer of romance and, naturally, I'm curious about you."

"Really?"

"So, I was just wondering, just wondering to myself, how good a lover you are." A wave of heat washed over Sassy's face.

Stepping back, Norris feigned surprise. "I am shocked!"

Sassy slapped her hands on her hips. "You are not! If sexual tension could be measured on a Richter scale, we'd measure seven and all of these buildings would be falling down around us right now, and you know it."

"Only seven?" Norris chuckled. He took Sassy's hands off of her hips and put her arms around his neck.

"The buildings aren't shaking," he said, "but I am." He kissed her at first gently on the lips, and when she kissed him back, he kissed her deeper. It was Sassy who remembered where they were. She ended their kiss.

"I think we should take this inside somewhere," she said.

"I couldn't agree more."

With their arms around each other, they continued on in silence as they both thought about the kiss and the electricity between them.

"This is me." Norris stopped alongside a shiny black Mercedes. The street lamp high overhead shone down brilliantly on the car. What else would he drive, Sassy thought as she got into the car. She watched Norris as he circled the car and got in on the driver's side. He immediately started the car.

"Where to?" he asked.

"Your place," she said without hesitation. The one thing Norris hadn't told her was where he lived. If he was involved with someone, there would be signs in his apartment. Better to find out sooner than later. Just because he doesn't wear a ring meant nothing.

"My place it is. Buckle up. We have a bit of a ride ahead of us." He began to back up.

"Wait, wait," Sassy said, stopping Norris. "Where do you live?"

"Pennsylvania."

"What? I thought you had an apartment or house here in the city."

"At one time I did. I keep a room at the Marriott here in Brooklyn for when I have to stay in the city. No maintenance. My office is in Manhattan which is great because I love the energy of Manhattan when I'm working, but since 911, I'm not comfortable sleeping in Manhattan which is why I stay at the

Marriott here in Brooklyn."

"But you live in Pennsylvania?"

"For six years."

"Where?"

"Blue Mountain. It's not far from the Poconos."

Sassy was amazed. "Were you in Pennsylvania when I called you?"

"I was."

"Did you come all this way because I called you?"

The stunned expression on Sassy's face tickled Norris. "I did."

Sassy looked at Norris with a new appreciation. No man had ever wanted to see her so badly he traveled from two states away to get to her, and this late at night at that.

Norris gently stroked the back of Sassy's hand with his thumb. The heat that crept up Sassy's spine and warmed the nape of her neck could have heated the whole car. As if there was a magnetic pull between their bodies, they leaned toward each other until their lips touched. In a long drawn out minute, they quietly and gently savored the sweetness of their kiss, but the kiss was like a smidgen of delectably sinful chocolate that Sassy wanted more of. Since he met Sassy, Norris had dreamed of making love to her and being so close to her, he was throbbing in anticipation of more than just a kiss, but he dared not show it. Sassy abruptly ended their kiss. She had to. What she increasingly felt made her cross her legs. She lowered the window on her side half way down.

"It's a little hot in here."

"It certainly is," Norris said. "Is it Blue Mountain or the Marriott?"

That was a double entendre if ever she heard one. No matter how it was meant, Sassy was more than willing to come with Norris Yoshito. For once, hopefully, she could experience the passion she labored to infuse in her characters.

"It's a clear night," she said. "What view do you see from your hotel room?"

"The Manhattan skyline."

"Great view."

Norris put his hand on the gear stick to move the car into drive when Sassy suddenly lay her hand on top of his, stopping him.

"What's wrong?"

Sassy took an anxious breath. "We're both safety conscious adults, right?"

Norris knew immediately what Sassy was alluding to. "Have I told you lately how much I like you?"

Okay. So he agrees. Thank God. Sassy lowered her window a bit more.

Norris squeezed Sassy's hand. "I believe in being prepared. I don't believe in leaving anything to chance."

Sassy was relieved but she was nervous. "Now that we've gotten the necessary details out of the way, I think I'm hungry."

"Hungry, as in—"

"Food. I think I'm going to need a lot of energy."

"You just might be right. Food it is."

Norris pulled smoothly out of his tight parking space and headed down to the Marriott Hotel on Adams Street less than a mile away. The lateness of the hour didn't disturb him in the least. In fact, he was wide awake. Earlier, after he had driven a little more than an hour and a half on Interstate 80 to Pennsylvania, he had been exhausted. He had been in bed about two hours when Sassy called and was immediately invigorated. Being with her, whether they made love or not, was well worth a sleepless night; especially a night where there were no nightmares to ruin his waking hour. The tragedy of his mother's death and the sporadic nightmares of brutal murders haunted his sleeping hours. Why that was, Norris never figured out. He was never one to put a hurtful hand on any woman, so dreams of killing women was most disturbing to him. From this minute on, he wanted his dreams to be about the woman he was sitting next to. The night he met Sassy, he sensed she might be the one. When he first E-mailed her twelve days ago and she replied, he found himself falling hard for her. Everyday he eagerly looked forward to her humorous E-mails which were, at the same time, subtly flirtatious. Sassy wasn't alone, however. He flirted with her as well. While not one word or phrase had been untoward in nature, it seemed every word was sexually charged and every E-mail left him feeling like he had engaged in torrid foreplay. As the days wore on, he ached to be with Sassy and couldn't wait to conclude his business and get back to New York. When he first saw her tonight, he wanted to take her into his arms and kiss her immediately, but she hadn't given any sign that this was what she wanted. That wasn't the case now. She was quite clear about what she wanted, and he liked that. He didn't like women who teased and played games with his feelings. What he was looking for in a woman, he just might have found in Sassy.

11

Knock . . . knock . . . knock.

The knocking on the hotel room door pierced the deep sleep Sassy had yet to awaken from on her own. Hazily she opened her eyes and realized she was alone in bed. She heard the unlocking of the door. She heard whispers, but she wasn't curious enough to get out of bed to see to whom Norris was speaking. Besides, the last thing she wanted to do was get out of bed. She pulled the cover up over her head as she was unwilling to let go of the night she'd had with the most incredible lover she'd ever been with. Sassy hugged herself intimately. She squeezed her thighs and her vaginal muscles tight just thinking about being made love to by Norris. Even now, she could all but feel him inside her. It was no dream that she had over and over again reached the peak of ecstasy that for so long she had written about but not personally experienced. And as well, as imaginative as she had been in her romance writings, she had not come close to fully describing how euphoric a feeling it was to have multiple orgasms. There wasn't a part of her body that had not responded to Norris's firm but gentle hands, to his sweet succulent lips, to his tasty nimble tongue, and to every thrust of his body. Lord, Lord, Lord. How wonderful it was that it had not been a dream.

Norris closed the door. He wheeled the service cart to the foot of the bed. While Sassy slept, he had quietly ordered breakfast and showered. He would have still been sleeping himself if Sassy's snoring hadn't awakened him at 7:25. He had a meeting at 10:00, but he was going to reschedule it. As long as Sassy was with him, he wasn't going anywhere. He looked at her invitingly curvaceous form under the covers where he needed to rejoin her. Norris took off his robe and slipped back into bed. He uncovered Sassy's head but she quickly covered her face with her hand.

"Don't look at me!."

He pulled Sassy's hand down from her face.

"I'm not clean. I haven't even brushed my teeth yet."

"I guess I have my work cut out for me. I'll just have to clean you with my tongue—like a cat." Norris began licking Sassy's shoulder.

"You're awful!" Sassy threw her head back and laughed. As Norris licked her breasts, she felt his hardness against her thigh. She quieted down as her body began to respond to the lascivious ache Norris re-ignited within her core.

Norris slowly flicked his tongue across Sassy's nipple. She pressed her breast into his mouth, her pelvis into his hardness, and she moaned from the sheer pleasure she was getting. Norris took his cue solely from the response Sassy's body was giving him. He lifted Sassy's left leg onto his hip, opening her up to receive him, but just as he was about to enter her, Sassy abruptly pulled her hips back and pushed Norris off top of her.

Sassy quickly sat up. "Not without protection!"

Norris groaned as he flopped onto his back. He stared straight up at the ceiling.

Surprised, Sassy asked, "Not one?"

Norris barely shook his head. He had brought just three condoms. No way did he think he'd get to use all three much less run out of them. As badly as he wanted Sassy, he should have known better. She must think him an idiot.

Seeing how annoyed with himself Norris was, Sassy might have laughed if it wasn't for the fact that she was left carnally unquenched and in desperate need of a tall, ice cold glass of sweet lemonade to cool her down. But looking at

Norris, literally in agony yet magnificent in all of his virile splendor, she couldn't be mad at him. Three times he had sent her soaring, why be greedy?

"Poor baby." Sassy began to slowly massage Norris's chest from one side to the other, stopping only to massage his firm, hard pecs. She eased her hand down to his flat, hard stomach. Norris raised his hand to touch her, but she gently pushed his hand back down to his side. Having no problem with that, Norris closed his eyes and let Sassy have her way with him. She began lightly kissing his body which in no way eased the tension in his groin. His whole body tensed when Sassy, at first timid in her touch, began massaging the very thing she had just minutes before retreated from, but Norris wasn't mad at her. He was loving the softness of her hands; the tip of her tongue on his body; and the velvety feel of her body as she climbed atop him and, with great control began sliding up and down his body. Norris moaned as he grinded himself upwards into Sassy until he lifted her and his own body up off the bed as their bodies gyrated as one. Even without entering Sassy, he felt himself building to an incredible climax that had him quivering in his stomach.

Sassy found herself getting lost in the sheer pleasure she herself was getting. She could feel Norris just at the portal of the temple of her orgasmic delight. Her anxious body yearned for Norris to burst in and hit that one delectable spot, but a tiny voice that sounded so much like Bernard's, screamed in her ears, "You better stop! You better stop!" Then Bernard's sad skeletal face flashed before Sassy's eyes and reminded her of the consequential reality of unsafe sex.

"I'm sorry, I'm sorry," Sassy said as she tried to get down off top of Norris just as he abruptly pulled away from her and grabbed his discarded bathrobe and pressed it into his body just in the nick of time.

Angry with herself for being so foolish, Sassy tried to not think about her own lack of orgasmic achievement. She slid over giving Norris room to collapse onto his sweaty back against her. He rested his damp arm atop her thigh.

"The housekeeper is going to hate you," she said referring to the soiled bathrobe.

"I'm sure she's seen worse."

Sassy said flatly, "She probably has."

Norris turned on his side to face Sassy. He took her hand. He kissed it.

"Thank you," she said, knowing that Norris would understand.

"Next time, I'll have an entire box.

"How do you know they'll be a next time?"

"Oh, there'll be a whole lot of next times, and it's your fault."

"My fault?"

"You've spoiled me for anyone else." Norris kissed Sassy on the side of her face.

Sassy smiled. She really hoped it was true.

Norris again kissed Sassy. "I hope I've spoiled you for anyone else."

If Norris only knew. It was going to be hard as heck for her to even think about being with anyone else. Kenneth was already a distant memory and the truth was, he had never made her feel as satisfied as she felt right now, not ever.

"You're especially quiet," Norris said. "Maybe I should ask if you're seeing anyone before I make a fool of myself."

"If I were seeing anyone, I most definitely wouldn't be lying here next to you, and, FYI, I do believe you may have spoiled me for anyone else as well."

Norris remembered Jason's question from Sassy's book. "So, are we in lust or are we in love?"

Sassy's eyes popped but then she remembered her own writings. "Alana would say both."

"So when do you wanna get married?" The second the question rolled off his tongue, Norris froze.

Sassy lay perfectly still. Jason never asked that question.

Norris's heart thumped. He couldn't believe the word 'married' had spurted from his mouth. This was the first time in his life he'd ever uttered the matrimonial word to any woman, playfully or otherwise. He had hoped to one day to get married, but until this moment, he hadn't been with a woman he could see himself spending long rainy days and cold, snow blown nights with. Certainly, no woman had ever made him want to get up out of his comfortable bed at midnight to eagerly drive ninety miles to sit up in a hospital emergency room with her, or more importantly, made him want to postpone an important meeting to lay up in bed with her. How could he be thinking marriage when he'd only known the woman two weeks?

The silence between them was awkward. "Hey," Sassy said, hoping to get them back to where they were. "I heard a really funny joke the other day. Would you like to hear it?"

"I sure do." Norris rolled his head back and closed his eyes. He could kick himself. He probably scared Sassy, but what was weird, he wasn't scared of the idea of marrying her. Maybe the joke was on him.

Sassy sat up in bed and faced Norris. "Okay!" she said a little too cheery. "This man and his wife, for their fiftieth wedding anniversary, arranged a celebratory Sunday evening dinner at their favorite restaurant with their three grown, well-educated, highly successful children. Well, the happy couple arrived on time, 6:00. But it wasn't until 6:45 that their oldest son arrived." She didn't like that Norris was staring up at the ceiling. "Are you listening to me?"

The truth was, Norris was only half listening. His mind was still on what he said. "I'm listening."

Sassy began to speak faster as she got into telling the joke. "Happy anniversary, Mom and Dad!" the oldest son said as he hurriedly sat down at the table. "Sorry I'm running late, I had an emergency at the hospital with a patient. You know how busy I am. I didn't get a chance to get you a gift."

"No problem," said the father. "The important thing is

you made it."

The middle child, a daughter, rushed into the restaurant. "Happy anniversary, Mom and Dad! I missed my scheduled flight in from New York City because I had to meet with my partners on a case we're defending in Federal Court this week. I'll make up for your gift at Christmas."

"No problem," said the father. "The important thing is you made it."

"Uh oh," Norris said, "Not good."

"Nope," Sassy said. "Anyway, here comes the third child, another daughter. "Happy anniversary, Mom and Dad! I was on a buying trip in Paris and didn't get in until three this afternoon. I'm sorry I didn't get a chance to get you anything."

"No problem," said the mother. "The important thing is you made it."

Norris began smiling. He hadn't heard this joke before.

"After they finished dessert, the father said, 'There's something your mother and I have been meaning to tell you kids for a long time'."

"Tell us, Dad," the son urged.

"Well, your mother and I were very poor when you kids were growing up. We worked hard long hours to send you all to college.

"We know that," the middle daughter said.

"Yes, but do you know that we worked so hard over the years, we never found time to get married."

The three children gasped and they all said, "You mean we're bastards?"

"Damn right," said the mother, "and cheap bastards at that!"

Sassy and Norris both cracked up laughing, but Norris studied the way Sassy dropped her head back and opened her mouth wide to allow her laugh to burst forth. He waited for her to stop laughing before he seized the opportunity to catch her off guard and kiss her. He might have made a Freudian slip, but it was a slip he just might want to live with.

"Wow," Sassy said, catching her breath. "I like the benefits of this relationship. Tell a silly joke, get a kiss. Nice."

"I don't give kisses lightly."

Seeing how serious Norris was, Sassy forgot all about her joke. It wasn't hard to guess why he was so solemn, but as curious as she was about his offhanded proposal of marriage, it wasn't something she wanted to talk about.

"So, what time do you have to be at work?" she asked.

"When I get there."

"Ah. Spoken like the big man in charge."

"Being in charge has its privileges. How about you?"

"When I sit down in front of my computer, I'll be at work, and believe me; I have a lot of work to do."

"What can I do to convince you to play hooky with me?"

"Bad boy; shame on you."

"Shame on me, indeed, if I can't get you to stay with me. Besides, you'd be helping me out."

Sassy eyed Norris skeptically. "And how is that?"

"I need you to be my first."

"First what?"

"I'm a hooky virgin," Norris said.

Sassy laughed. "You're certifiable."

"I have never played hooky from work or school a day in my life, so if you make it too hard for me to convince you, I might run like a mad man back to my office. Surely you don't want me to spend the rest of this beautiful day chained to my drafting table with only my memories of you, do you?"

Sassy rolled her eyes upward. "You are such a ham."

Norris smiled his most innocent smile as Sassy continued to pretend to not be convinced.

"Pretty please." Norris slowly ran his hand up and down Sassy's back.

"Okay, I'll let you corrupt me this one time, but you had better make it worth my while."

"I'll do my best to—"

"Wait!" Sassy suddenly remembered Bernard. "I have to get over to the hospital this morning. I have to get Bernie's services turned on; I have to go over to his condo to make sure everything is okay there; then I have to—"

"I'll go with you."

Sassy pulled back and looked quizzically at Norris. She didn't know if she was ready to introduce him to Bernard.

"Tell me about your cousin. You seem to be very close to him."

"We're more like brother and sister," she said, still not wanting to reveal anything more. "I need a shower." Sassy scooted over to the side of the bed and got up. "I'm starving, how about you?"

"Our breakfast is probably cold."

"Cold will suffice." Sassy kept her back to Norris. She wrapped herself up in one of the extra towels they'd ordered last night.

Norris swung his legs over the side of the bed and sat. "Tell me about your cousin," he said again.

Pretending to be busy tucking the end of the towel, Sassy didn't turn around. "Do you think they'll reheat our breakfast?"

Norris's silence said more to Sassy than his words. It was obvious he felt he had a right to know everything about her. Talking to Norris through E-mail was the way she had gotten to know him, but it was also the way she had been able to keep Bernard's illness from him. There was no question about how Kenneth felt about AIDS. If Norris felt the same, their relationship would end before it ever had a chance. She slowly turned to face him. She wasn't surprised to see an expectant look on his face.

"If I can be your lover," he said, "why can't I be your friend?"

No better sentiment had ever been expressed to Sassy, and not one excuse she could think of had the power to override it. She went around the bed and sat next to Norris.

This time, she took his hand. It was hard to believe he was real. Outside of her books, men like Norris were a rarity.

Norris saw that Sassy's eyes were drowning in a pool of tears. He put his arm around her. "I'm right here."

With her exhaling breath, Sassy let out her burden. "He has AIDS. He's dying."

As Sassy began to cry, Norris wrapped her up in his arms. He now understood Sassy's reluctance to talk about her cousin's illness and as well, why she was so emphatic about him not coming inside her. He was always careful himself but with Sassy, he bent his own rule of never going bareback with anyone.

Minutes later Sassy had cried herself out. "I'm sorry."

"There's nothing to be sorry for. You love your cousin. Tell me about him."

That Sassy did. The more she talked, the better she felt. Other than Evelyn, she hadn't told anyone about Bernard. He never wanted her to. Since learning about Bernard's illness, in her own sex life, until now, she had only been intimate with Kenneth. And with Kenneth, she had always been insistent that he use condoms despite him saying that he was seeing no one else. She didn't care that he didn't like wearing condoms; she only cared that she not get infected with HIV or get pregnant. As far as Sassy was concerned, unless she drew the blood and tested it herself, not even the pope was clean, which is why she was surprised she dared to go as far as she did with Norris this last time.

"I haven't personally dealt with anyone with AIDS, but I'd like to go to the hospital with you. If there's anything I can do, just tell me."

As much as Sassy hated being weepy, she couldn't help herself. For the first time in her life she was with a man who wanted to be there for her. It was such an overwhelming feeling she couldn't stop crying. She clung to Norris as if he were that special gift she prayed for for Christmas. When Sassy finally quieted down, Norris kissed her on the forehead.

Sassy reluctantly let go of Norris. "Thank you," she said, standing. "I'm going to take my shower now."

"We could save time and water if we shower together."

Sassy boldly took in every inch of Norris's well-toned, well-endowed body. As tempted as she was to get wet and slippery with him, she needed to put a wall between them—quick, fast, and in a hurry.

"We could also save time if we showered separately." Sassy hurried into the bathroom and locked the door.

At the door, Norris asked, "What if I keep my hands to myself?"

"It's not your hands I'm worried about."

Norris looked down at himself. He had to admit, "Point well taken." He covered himself with his hands. "I'm going to reorder breakfast. What do you want?"

Sassy called through the door, "Bacon—crisp. Scrambled eggs, cantaloupe, and orange juice.."

"Yes, ma'am."

"Oh, and turn on the news, okay?"

"Will do." Norris quickly reordered breakfast. He turned on the television to Channel 4, The Today Show, the show he listened to and half watched every morning whether he was in the city or in Pennsylvania. For a minute he stood in front of the television listening to the news about a robbery in the Bronx and was about to turn away when the image of a young blond woman popped up on the screen snatched him back. Her face was familiar. He turned up the sound.

"The three-day old murder of twenty-four year-old Karen Markowitz of Brooklyn is still unsolved. Miss Markowitz was found in her bedroom by her mother who had not heard from her in several days. The police are looking for a man, possibly of Hispanic, Polynesian, or Asian descent who was last seen with the victim. If you have any information, please contact the police at (800) 555-0911."

The name Karen Markowitz was somehow familiar to Norris, as was her face. For the life of him, Norris couldn't say where he knew her from, or if he knew her at all. He started to turn away from the television when the name and face connected. Two years ago he met Karen Markowitz at a housewarming dinner party after his firm designed and built her parents' new house up in Eastchester, New York. Back then, Karen was twenty-two, perky, full of life, and quite a vixen. More than once she came onto him. Karen was a pretty girl but she wasn't what he was looking for. Now she's dead. How? Why? So much senseless crime was going on in New York. Just two weeks ago, he called into his office and learned that his executive assistant, Myra Barrett, was one of two women attacked by some maniac. That news hit him like a fast ball thrown by Roger Clements. He was hard-pressed to believe it true about Myra until detectives showed up and questioned everyone in the office.

For the past two weeks, Norris was using his partner's assistant while his office manager interviewed a new assistant for him. He prayed that Myra recuperated fully. For six years, she had been an excellent assistant and from the little he knew about her personally, she had been an excellent mother. For the life of him, he couldn't figure out why anyone would want to kill her. Shaking his head, Norris turned away from the television.

From his jacket hanging in the closet, Norris retrieved his long-silent BlackBerry. He had turned it off last night to keep from being disturbed. Checking it, he saw that he had nine messages. He listened to them all. Four he deleted, five he saved. He checked his E-mail. All twenty-three were important, but only four demanded his immediate attention. He sat at the desk and took his time typing his responses all the while not believing that he wasn't going to work. If anyone had ever told him he would take a day off to be with a woman, he would not have believed it. Whatever spell Sassy had on him, he hoped it was a good one, because he didn't have time for games. He really liked her, and if what he was feeling was real, he might just be in love with her. Why else would marriage pop into his head? His father was going to get a big kick out of this. When he was nineteen, his father told him when the right girl came along, he'd do things he thought he'd never do. Well, his father was right and he couldn't wait to tell him.

12

While all around him other detectives went about their business interviewing witnesses, victims, and alleged perpetrators, Frank Kiefer was keenly aware he had no one to interview on the one case that bothered him the most. He sat at his desk quietly reading, for the third time, the forensics report on the murder of 28 year-old Carrie Kane and the attempted murder of 32 year-old Myra Barrett. Thus far, in all that blood, only that one smear in the bathroom belonged to someone other than the two victims. To Frank that could only mean they were dealing with a perp who thought he was smarter than the average gumshoe. Sure enough, the perp had wiped down many of the surfaces including the doorknobs, and had apparently stepped out of his shoes once outside of the apartment because the blood didn't track outside of Apartment 13C. It might be harder to catch this bastard, but it was going to be all the more satisfying once he did. With new cases sliding across his desk every day, Frank prayed that this case wouldn't end up in the cold case file. After four weeks, there had been no hits in the national DNA data bank, CODIS, or in the Automated Fingerprint Identification System, AFIS. That small DNA sample revealed the blood type, A+, and markers for the ethnicity of the perpetrator—African American and Asian. Myra Barrett's boss fit that profile but so far, Norris Yoshito had an airtight alibi. Frank needed Myra Barrett to wake up and point her finger at the man who did this to her, but her doctors were not optimistic. They said it would be a miracle if Myra Barrett ever regained consciousness. And if she did, whether she'd ever be able to tell them anything of merit was up in the air. All they could do now was play the wait and see game, which Frank wasn't too good at.

In the past month, ten additional cases had been added to Frank's case load, but the Kane/Barrett file still sat on top of his desk in his own open files tray. At times Frank felt as if he were up against a brick wall with no way of scaling it or knocking it down, that is until he heard about the murder of Karen Markowitz. Two days after news of the Markowitz murder broke, Frank contacted the detective over at the 66th Precinct in Midwood assigned the case. He had a disturbing inkling that his case might be remotely connected to the Markowitz case. He compared notes with Detective Robert Morano and learned that a shoeshine man in Grand Central Station had called in and said he'd seen Karen Markowitz a few weeks before with a mixed-race Asian man whose shoes he had shined. That information had Frank's gut talking to him, and if his gut was right, the two murders were committed by the same guy. Never mind that the modus operandi was no where near similar. The Cane and Barrett women were viciously stabbed, whereas the Markowitz woman was strangled in bed. Still, what are the odds that both cases would have a male of African American and Asian decent as a possible perpetrator?

"Frank!" Joe called before he was half way across the room. He hurried to Frank's desk and slammed a sheet of paper on his desk. "This came in on the fax. It's addressed to you."

Frank noted right off that Morano had faxed a copy of a business card. He picked up the paper.

"Norris Yoshito. That's the architect we questioned in the Barrett/Kane case," Joe said as if he had to interpret for Frank what he was reading. "The card was found under the victim's sofa."

Remembering the DNA profile and his face-to-face with Norris Yoshito, Frank wondered if it was really that easy to connect the dots between the two cases.

"This is no coincidence, Frank. This Yoshito fellow is the Barrett woman's boss and remember, her little girl said her mother's friend's name was Nored. Maybe it isn't Nored, Frank. Maybe it's Norris."

"Could be," Frank said flatly. He didn't want to get excited just yet.

"Frank, Yoshito lied. He said he didn't see Barrett outside of the office, but I think he did. The DNA points to him. And why would his card be in the Markowitz apartment?"

"See what else you can pull up on Yoshito."

"I'm on it." Joe slipped behind his own desk across from Frank's. He immediately began pecking out letters on his computer keyboard as he began his cyber hunt for any and everything about a possible killer.

Frank stared at the name—Norris Yoshito. His gut was barking loud. He reached for the bottle of Tums in his top desk drawer. He finally had a name. The question was, did he have a legitimate suspect? Morano was sharing what evidence he found that might link their cases, but he made it clear that he got first shot at questioning any witnesses or possible perpetrators he found. If this Norris Yoshito was his guy, there wasn't going to be a T left uncrossed or a loop left too big for some slick lawyer to slither through.

"If this guy ever spit on the sidewalk, I want to know when and where."

13

Sassy's eyes were closed, not because she was tired, and she was tired, it was almost 10:00 p.m. and she had been at her computer since 8:30 that morning. Although her butt was sore, her back ached, and her eyes were strained, she was determined to finish the last chapter before she allowed herself the luxury of slipping between the sheets and blacking out. She was physically exhausted but her mind was soaring with literary imagery and her fingers were jitterbugging across her keyboard as if they were dancing in front of a live audience. It wasn't music she was hearing in her head, it was her characters' voices and they were channeling through her the story they wanted her to tell, but in Sassy's mind, it was herself and Norris she saw making love. Their bodies melded as one, him deep and full inside her as she got caught up in the ecstasy of the intense sweetness that began at first as just a tiny impulse but surged into an energy charged orgasm that brought tears to her eyes and a scream to her throat. As their bodies rejoiced in the pure rapture of their coupling, Sassy's fingers danced faster and faster over the keyboard. Over the clicking of the keys she could hear the sound of her own breathlessness as the sensation of every stroke and every impassioned word drove her. As she typed, Sassy grinded herself into the seat of her chair as her body responded to the memory of being made love to.

Sassy stopped typing. She couldn't believe how horny she was. Never had her sensuous prose so ignited her erogenous zone like this before. Although she was alone in her apartment, she looked around the room as if to make sure no prying eyes would see what she was about to do. Self-consciously, she slipped her hand down the front of her loose fitting warm-ups into her panties. This was the first time she ever got the urge to touch herself while writing and surprise, surprise, just thinking about her nights with Norris brought her to a very speedy and somewhat satisfying release.

"The man has turned me into a pervert," Sassy said aloud as she hurried to the bathroom to wash her hands. She started to laugh as she dried her hands on her towel. She felt absolutely wonderful. H'm, obviously something had been missing from her past relationships, for no other man in his absence had been able to make love to her mind and body as Norris had. As aware as she was of her body and her sexuality, Sassy had never been one to do herself, and if things continued to go as well as they had been with Norris, she won't have to make it a habit. Since waking this morning, she had been counting the hours and minutes till Norris returned tomorrow from his three-day business trip to Connecticut.

With a secretive smile on her lips, Sassy began reading through what she had typed so quickly and so passionately. She was impressed. She had probably written her best love scenes yet. Again, she had to credit Norris. Until now, she had only been screwed. Being made love to by Norris was sweet yet intense, tender yet passionate, exploratory yet familiar, and most definitely satisfying. Norris didn't just satisfy her carnal need, he satisfied her mentally and emotionally. Every day of the past seven weeks with him had been what romance novels were made of. Tomorrow couldn't come soon enough for her. She began to type again.

Buzzzz!

"Aaaaa!" Sassy hated being interrupted when she was writing. This late at night, who the heck would be ringing her bell anyway.

Buzzzz!

"I'm coming!" Whoever it is, was going to get a piece of her mind. She hurried to the door, quickly unlocked it and yanked it open.

"Kenneth!" Sassy said in a hushed voice so as to not disturb her neighbors. "What the heck are you doing here?"

"That's a stupid question, unless I've been banned from seeing you."

Kenneth spoke clear enough, but it was obvious to Sassy that he'd had one drink too many. His eyes were glassy and his breath was howling.

"I hope you didn't drive over here on your own."

Kenneth snorted, "Are you inferring that I'm drunk?"

Sassy turned her head slightly to avoid the downdraft of fowl breath. "Okay so you're not drunk. What do you want?"

"I wanna talk to you."

"Do you know what time it is?"

"The hell with the time! I wanna talk to you."

From down the hall came the clicking of a lock being opened.

"Come in, but you're not staying." As much as she didn't want to, Sassy stepped aside. "You have five minutes and that's it." Sassy closed the door but she didn't lock it. Nor did she lead Kenneth into the livingroom. She stayed in the entry hallway. Kenneth looked into the livingroom as if he were looking for someone.

"Kenneth, I'm writing. What do you want?"

Kenneth fell back against the wall. "You by yourself?"

Sassy didn't have time for this. Her and Kenneth's time had passed, which is why they stood on opposite sides of her entry way as if they were twelve-year olds not yet socially savvy to carry on a conversation with the opposite sex.

"What do you want, Kenneth?"

"You. I want you back. Why haven't you called me?"

"Actually, I did call you, seven weeks ago; the night Bernie went into the hospital."

"Is he still in the hospital?"

"What do you care? You didn't show up."

"Did that Asian looking guy show up? Is that who you're screwing now?"

Sassy was cool. She took one step to the door and opened it. "Leave."

"Who is the hell is he?" Kenneth belched.

The rancidness of his breath, even from ten feet, hit Sassy in the face. She frowned. "Kenneth, do us both a favor. Stop drinking and don't come back."

"I'm not drunk."

Go home anyway."

Kenneth waved Sassy off. "You never said a damn thing about us breaking up."

"I think not speaking to each other or seeing each other for almost two full months is a real serious clue that we're not together. Now can I get back to my writing? I'm on deadline."

"Oh, yeah, let me let the 'writer' get back to 'writing' her great American novel."

Sassy opened the door wider. "Bye, Kenneth."

Kenneth still made no move to get off the wall that was holding him up.

"Hey. Has any one of your books ever made the New York Times Best Sellers List?"

Sassy smirked. "You know, Kenneth, if I gave a damn about you, that jab might've hurt but since I don't, screw you."

"Isn't that what you've been doing?"

"Kenneth, get the hell out of my apartment!"

"Why, you expecting your new man? What is he anyway? I couldn't tell his pedigree. He must be a mutt. Just your type."

Sassy could just see herself smashing Kenneth in the face with a frying pan. Her grip on the doorknob tightened. "You know, Kenneth, I'm trying to remember what it was about you that I liked, but nothing readily comes to mind."

"I can remind you."

"That would be two seconds I'd rather not waste on a stupid drunk."

Kenneth slowly pulled himself off the wall but in two quick steps, he was right up on Sassy. He grabbed her arm before she could even react.

Sassy tried to pry Kenneth's hand off of her. "What the hell are you doing? Get the—"

Kenneth planted a rough, hard kiss on Sassy's mouth. The putrid taste of his tongue repelled her. With her own tongue, she tried to push his tongue out of her mouth while trying to get free of his hold, but couldn't. With one arm around her waist, Kenneth pressed Sassy back up against the door as he grabbed her jaw to keep her face still while he tried to force his tongue down her throat. Sassy was hurting from the pain in her lips, her jaw, and her back until she realized she wasn't defending herself. She took hold of Kenneth's thumb and snapped it back toward his wrist sending a sharp, jarring pain through his right hand. Kenneth abruptly let go of Sassy, but Sassy didn't let go of his thumb. She immediately switched holds. With both hands, she gripped Kenneth's hand in a disabling wrist lock. She then raised her arms, twisted Kenneth's arm up behind his back which dropped him down onto one knee. Debilitating pain shot through Kenneth's hand and traveled up his arm into his right shoulder. He was at once amazed and amused. The pain was very real and while he grimaced and his eyes watered, he didn't cry, he laughed.

"You're out of your damn mind!" Sassy jerked Kenneth's arm higher which made him almost fall to the floor on his face. He caught himself with his elbow but he was mad.

"Let me up, dammit! This isn't funny anymore!"

"It never was funny to me." She abruptly let go of Kenneth's hand and quickly moved more than an arm's length away from him. She never wanted to have to touch him again. "Get out of my apartment!"

Grimacing in pain, Kenneth slowly got to his feet.

"I want you to leave, Kenneth, before you disturb my

neighbors."

Kenneth slowly rotated his sore shoulder. "I see you learned a little something in that jujitsu class after all."

"I learned enough to protect myself from idiots who try to force themselves on me."

"I didn't force myself on you!"

"Just leave!"

Still rotating his shoulder to ease the pain, Kenneth glowered at Sassy. "If I leave, I won't be coming back."

"Do you see tears in my eyes?"

"I mean it, Sassy. I won't be back."

Sassy extended her arm toward the door to show Kenneth the way out.

"Just like that, you're done with me?"

The dangerous look in Kenneth eyes made Sassy realize her mistake. She should have gone back to the door when she let go of him.

"You're just as done as I am, Kenneth. Since the last time we saw each other, if I made you swear that you weren't with someone else, you'd have to lie."

"I've been with someone; just as you have."

"Fine. Let's not look back. Leave. Please."

Still not making any moves to leave, Kenneth stared fiercely at Sassy which was really pricking her last nerve.

"Kenneth, if I have to call the police, I will."

"All I'm trying to do is talk to you. Is that a crime?"

"Hell yes it is if I don't wanna talk to you!"

Kenneth stepped one step closer to Sassy which made her feel uneasy. She backed up two steps and positioned herself in a ready stance—her feet apart and planted, her arms up in front blocking her torso, her fists ready—which surprised Kenneth.

"What do you think you're gonna do, kick my ass?"

If he only knew how much she wanted to, he'd leave her alone. She was tired of talking and if her Sansei was right, if she had to, she should be able to lay Kenneth's six foot, 195 pound body out in three moves.

"You're a joke," Kenneth said contemptuously. "You must be out of your damn mind if you think you can take me on. I let you take me down before, but you're stupid if you think you can do it again."

Still Sassy said nothing. Her Sansei said if she ever had to fight, don't waste her energy talking.

"Why am I wasting my time with you? I have plenty of women who—"

"Then go to them, Kenneth! Go with my blessing!"

"I don't need your damn permission, you stupid bitch."

Sassy cringed, she tightened her fists. She hated being called a bitch by any man much less by a man she used to sleep with. Kenneth was a fool and she was so glad he was showing who he really was. At the same time, she wished he'd fall through the floor and break his face. Her heart was thumping!

"Bitch, you can't write real literature no matter how hard you try. No one of any intelligence read your crap."

As harsh as Kenneth's words were, and although they stung bitterly, Sassy didn't flutter an eyelash or utter a word in retort. She stayed focused on Kenneth's eyes because she needed to know if he was going to charge at her; and peripherally, she watched his hands and his feet. As angry as he was, no telling what he would do and she had to be ready.

Kenneth turned his back to Sassy. He grabbed the doorknob and yanked the door open but before Sassy could release the tense breath she was holding, Kenneth turned back. He pushed the door closed only half way. Just one big step and he would have been through that open door and out of her apartment. Then she wouldn't have to look at the nauseatingly contrite look on his face.

"Sassy, I'm sorry," he said. "I can't believe I said those things to you. Look at us. Me calling you names and you ready to fight. This is crazy. Baby, I love you. That was the alcohol talking. I'm sorry. I take back everything I said. Baby, you know I respect you. I got mad when I saw you with another man. I didn't mean to say those things to you. I'm sorry. I don't wanna lose you."

Sassy wasn't in a forgiving or a forgetting mood. Her expression of disgust didn't change, nor did her ready-to-kick-his-ass stance.

"Sassy, let me talk to you a minute. It's been rough. Burton stole some money from me, and—"

"He should have stolen every damn penny you got. Now get the hell outta here, I'm tired of looking at you!"

"Bitch! I'll—

Bang!

The door suddenly shot open and hit Kenneth full force in his back, knocking him against the wall. The framed book jacket on the wall next to his head crashed to the floor. Kenneth would have fallen into Sassy had she not jumped out of the way in the split second she realized he was being propelled her way. In her astonishment, Sassy, with her hands covering her mouth, looked from a stunned and dazed Kenneth to the door to see Norris standing there scowling angrily at Kenneth.

Sassy started toward Norris, but he put his hand out, stopping her. He was not yet done with Kenneth.

Kenneth regained his balance. "What the—"

Norris slammed his fist into Kenneth's face. His head hit the wall with a dull thud. Kenneth threw his arms up and whether he was about to try to defend himself Sassy didn't know, but when Norris twice more punched him in the face and Kenneth didn't fight back, Sassy hurriedly grabbed Norris's arm when she saw blood spurt from Kenneth's nose.

"Stop! That's enough! Stop!"

Norris shoved Kenneth to the floor. "Who is this guy?"

"Kenneth. I told you about him."

"You didn't tell me he was a coward. Look at him."

It wasn't the blood or Kenneth's swelling left eye that Norris was telling Sassy to look at, it was the huge wet stain on his pants.

"Not on my floor!"

Kenneth was humiliated. He wouldn't look at Sassy as he pushed himself up off the floor.

"If he ever comes near you again, I'll kill him."

Those threatening words coming from Norris surprised Sassy. "Norris, just let him leave."

"He has to apologize first!" Norris made a grab for Kenneth but Sassy quickly sandwiched herself between them.

"I said let him leave!"

"I heard him disrespect you all the way down the hall."

"Norris, I don't care if he never apologizes. I just want him to leave." Sassy went to the door and held it open. "Kenneth leave, please, before my neighbors call the police."

Just as Kenneth started out the door, Norris kicked him in the seat of his pants and sent him stumbling out into the hallway where he slammed into the far wall. Norris then closed the door with a firm shove.

"I am so glad you came when—"

"You slept with him, didn't you?"

Sassy stiffened. "What?"

"You weren't expecting me until tomorrow. Is that why you had him over today?"

"Do you hear yourself? Or better still, didn't you say you heard Kenneth disrespecting me? Didn't you also hear me telling him to leave? And if I had slept with him, do you think he would have been calling me a bitch?"

Norris paused to consider Sassy's questions. Maybe he was wrong. He reached for Sassy's hand, but she dropped her hand down to her side. She was totally baffled. She had never seen this nasty side of Norris. In the seven weeks they'd been together, she had come to know a loving, sensitive, caring man who had an air of spirituality about him that she in no way sensed around him now. This man had cold eyes and had been almost sadistic in the way he beat on Kenneth.

"I was wrong to speak to you like that," Norris said. He again reached for Sassy but she slapped his hand away.

"Damn right you were. How could you question my fidelity?"

"I saw him—"

"I told you we were over."

"I know, but seeing him here—"

"Meant what? That I had him over for wild, unbridled sex?"

"No, I—"

"Norris, if you can't trust me, we—"

Norris grabbed Sassy and rammed his tongue into her mouth so fast she almost choked. The kiss was hard, it was brutal, it kept her from screaming stop! Her lips hurt. She felt like Norris was raping her mouth. She tried to push his away, she tried to push his tongue out of her mouth. It was just as bad as it had been with Kenneth. She thought about biting Norris's tongue but also thought about the blood that might spill into her mouth. Norris's hold on the back of her head and waist was like a vice. She started to dig her nails into Norris's arm but he abruptly pushed her away.

Sassy stumbled backwards. "Are you crazy?" She rubbed the spit off of her mouth with the back of her hand.

Unfazed, Norris said, "I thought you liked it that way."

"What the hell are you on? Why would you say such a thing to me?"

"Oh. Baby, I'm sorry."

"Baby my ass! Sorry don't do it."

Norris suddenly took Sassy's hand despite her reluctance. "If I was rough, I'm sorry. I saw red when I heard him speak to you so disrespectfully."

"Do you know how scary you are when you're upset?"

"I have an idea."

Sassy pulled her hand from Norris. Sorry wasn't doing it for her. Norris's Jekyll and Hyde personality was unsettling. That kiss was scary. She couldn't shake the feeling that something was off. Something in Norris's eyes said he wasn't sorry and although he apologized, his words felt insincere.

"Norris, you seemed so different. You scared me."

"Of course I'm different when I'm angry. Isn't everyone? Aren't you?"

"Yeah, but—"

"Were you sweet and kind when that idiot was calling you names? If that guy had hit you, would you have not been different from the way you usually are?"

Remembering how she was ready to kick Kenneth's behind, Sassy had to concede that she, too, had morphed into a woman who was unlike the nonviolent woman she normally was. She had taken jujitsu, ironically, at Kenneth's suggestion, to protect herself when she traveled alone on her book tours. Until today, she never had to execute anything she had learned in the two years she studied the art. How ironic it would be Kenneth when she used jujitsu on for the first time.

"Okay, you're right. I guess I wasn't too pretty, but I hope I don't ever have to see you angry again."

"That's unrealistic, but I tell you what, I'd like to put this distasteful little episode behind us. It didn't happen. Let's not ever talk about it."

"What if Kenneth goes to the police?"

"I doubt he will. I'm sure you'd tell the police I was defending you, and besides, he could be brought up on charges for assaulting you."

"But he never hit me."

"You could say that he did."

Sassy was taken aback. "Are you suggesting I lie?"

"Would it be a lie? Didn't he touch you?"

That might have been true, but Sassy wasn't comfortable with lying on Kenneth or anyone.

"Don't look so serious," Norris said. "We won't have any trouble out of that idiot." He swallowed Sassy up in an overly tight embrace. "I'll kill him if he comes near you again."

"Norris!" Sassy tried to pull herself free of Norris's stifling embrace.

"I was joking." He finally let go of Sassy.

"Well I'm not laughing! Between you and Kenneth, I feel like I've stepped into the twilight zone."

"Maybe it was a bad idea for me to come here tonight. I'll leave."

Sassy was torn. A part of her wanted Norris to leave, but "No! I don't want you to leave. I've been waiting for you to get back."

Norris went to the door anyway. "I have some work I need to get to. I'll call you in a few days."

"What?" Sassy was totally baffled. "Aren't we supposed to have dinner with your father and his wife tomorrow? Did you change your mind?"

Norris opened the door. "The hell with that black bastard. I'd rather eat out of a toilet than sit at a table with either him or you."

Sassy's jaw dropped!

Norris walked out of the apartment as cool as a glacier and left Sassy with her mouth open and a startling chill in her mind and body. For a second she couldn't move, she couldn't think, she couldn't believe what came out of Norris's mouth. She kept staring at the door thinking that any minute he was going to come back and say, "April fool!" He didn't and that shocked her even more.

She turned in circles. She didn't know where to go in her own apartment. "He must be on drugs!" She rushed into her office to call Norris on his BlackBerry. With the third ring, Norris's phone switched over to voice mail.

"Norris Yoshito. Please—"

Sassy jabbed the speaker key and disconnected the call. "How could he say that to me?"

Long after Sassy went to bed, between talking to herself and crying, for the life of her, she couldn't vanquish Norris's cruel words from her mind. "I'd rather eat out of a toilet than sit at a table with either him or you."

How could Norris say that to her? How could he do

such a drastic about-face and she not even have a clue that something was wrong? Over the phone just hours ago he said he loved her, and when Kenneth was there, he fought for her. What happened?

14

As she did every morning, Sassy woke up squinting across the room at the illuminated greenish blue numbers on her DVD clock. As usual the time didn't come into focus right away, but once it did she couldn't believe what time it was—8:47 a.m. Uttering a disquieting groan, she lay back and stared up at the ceiling. It was rare that she slept this late but she didn't fall asleep until after four in the morning. She must have picked up the telephone to call Norris at least ten times throughout the night but she never went through with actually placing the calls. The fact that Norris didn't call to apologize or explain himself was as strong a statement as his viciously callous remark. She thought he loved his father. Hell, she thought he loved her.

Knock. . .knock. . .knock! "Sassy!"

Sassy sat straight up in bed. The knock at the door as well as the male voice calling her sounded more like it was inside her apartment than out. She jumped out of bed and grabbed her bathrobe.

"Sassy, are you in here!"

Walking and pulling on her bathrobe, Sassy hurried out of her bedroom and almost screamed when she saw her neighbor, Malcolm, inside her apartment. "Malcolm! How did you get in here?"

"Your door was open."

"No!" Sassy rushed to the open door. "It wasn't open!" She stepped out into the hallway and looked from one end to the other before going back inside. She closed the door, locked it, unlocked it, and locked it again. For the life of her, she couldn't wrap her mind around her door being open while she was in the back sleeping.

"Malcolm, are you sure it was open?"

"I didn't use a key to get in," Malcolm said. "Did you have company last night?"

"Briefly, but neither one of them has a key. How wide open was it?"

"About a foot."

Sassy gasped. She felt her heart quiver as she stared at Malcolm. If it was anyone else, she might have been suspicious but Malcolm, who lived two apartments away with his wife Jenna, was a Jehovah Witness who was so honest, he once went all the way back to the supermarket when he discovered the cashier had given him back five dollars more than she was supposed to.

"Did you lock it last night?"

"Malcolm, I don't make a habit of going to bed and leaving my door unlocked or wide open. I'm not stupid."

"I know that, Sassy, but you have to be careful." Malcolm went back to the door. He checked it. "The lock works fine. Just make sure you check it every night, last thing."

"I always do. I did last night."

Riiiiing!

"I gotta go," Malcolm said. "I'll check in on you later."

Riiiiiiig!

"Thank you! Please do." Sassy firmly closed the door and locked it before grabbing the ringing telephone from the kitchen counter. "Hello!"

"Damn! What are you shouting for?"

Sassy's heart sank. It wasn't Norris, it was Bernard. "Bernie, I'm not in the best of moods this morning so please, let's be real cordial to each other. How are you doing? Is this a good morning for you?"

"Hell no. There ain't a damn thing good about this

morning."

Sassy slumped back against the counter. "Bernie, please try to be more positive. A better attitude might make you feel better as well."

"Sassy, if you're gonna talk crap, I'm hanging up."

Sassy slapped her hand to her forehead in anticipation of Bernard's tirade. As upset as she was about Norris, she was scared out of her mind about her door being open and someone, God knows who, being inside her apartment while she was asleep. It could not have been Norris or Kenneth because neither had a key to her apartment. It just didn't make sense when she definitely locked the door after Norris left.

"Sassy, did you hear me?"

"Actually, I didn't. What's going on? What's wrong?"

"What a dumb ass question!"

"Bernie, don't—"

"I have AIDS, remember? My whole damn life was stolen by a bitch I hope is rotting in hell and you ask me what's wrong? Don't ask me a stupid ass question like that again!"

SLAM!

The earsplitting crack in her ear made Sassy jerk the telephone away. This time it wasn't sleep that blurred her vision, it was her tears. She pressed the off button on her handset and set it back in its cradle on the kitchen counter. Bernard's tirades were getting worse. He was becoming more difficult to talk to, and ever since she put his condo on the market, he'd become more angry. Bernard loved his condo. He had it professionally decorated and showed it off often with his lavish parties. Now she had to sell it because he needed the money to cover his hospital bills; and if he ever left the hospital, he was never going to be able to live alone again. It wasn't that Sassy didn't understand Bernard's rage, she darn near felt his pain but there was nothing she could do to turn back the clock to a time before he was told he was HIV positive and had so much that was right in his life. It angered him that all of his friends were gone. And Evelyn, he shut her out himself but it hurt him just the same. There was no doubt in Sassy's mind that she was Bernard's lifeline, the only person he would talk to and she kept saying the wrong thing. What was she suppose to say? What was she suppose to do to make Bernard see that his life wasn't over. God knows she didn't know. The one time Norris went with her Bernard didn't want him in the room so they never got to meet. Now they never will.

Sassy went to the door to make sure it was locked before going into her bathroom to shower. A long day of work awaited her. No matter how tense, how miserable she felt, she still had to finish her manuscript and get it out, but first she had to get her head right. Lazily, she threw herself onto her bed and curled up with her pillow. Just four days ago it was Norris she was hugging instead.

Riiiiing!

Sassy snatched up the telephone. "Bernie, you have to pull yourself together. I can't help you if you keep tearing me down. I can't take it."

"I see your day hasn't started out too well."

Sassy recognized Norris's voice right away. "What the hell do you want?"

Norris paused. Sassy waited.

"Sassy, is there something I should know?"

"You tell me. What the hell was last night about?"

"Sassy, what happened last night?"

"Oh, you're going to pretend like you don't remember what you said?"

"What did I say?"

"You said you'd rather eat out of a toilet than eat with me or your father!"

"What! Sassy, I didn't talk to you last night!"

"I don't ever have to meet your father or see you again in life." She disconnected Norris. She then tossed the telephone onto the bed. "The hell with you!"

She got up off the bed and headed toward the bathroom.

Riiiiiing! Sassy stopped outside of her office. She let the telephone ring twice when she knew the answering machine would pick up.

"Sassy, I'm still in Connecticut. We need to talk."

Sassy rushed into her office and snatched up the telephone. "You are a liar! You were here last night!"

"Okay, I'm not dealing with it on the phone. I have one more meeting. . ."

"I don't care."

". . . in about an hour before I can leave out of here. If the traffic is right, I should be back in the city around two-thirty, maybe three the latest."

"I don't care."

"Sassy, listen to me. I will come straight to your apartment. I—"

"Don't come here! We're done." The words were said, but that truly wasn't what Sassy wanted.

"Sassy, you say you don't like games, neither do I. On my word, I was not with you last night."

"Norris, you're lying! You burst into my apartment and beat the heck out of Kenneth last night."

"Kenneth? Your old boyfriend?"

"You beat Kenneth to a pulp and then you accused me of sleeping with him behind your back. But worse than that, you said you'd rather eat out of a toilet than—"

"Sassy! How does that make sense when I've eaten you?"

Whatever Sassy was about to say got stuck in her throat. In her anger, she hadn't thought about that. "Then tell me what happened last night."

She waited for Norris to say something that would explain why he was denying being in her apartment, but there were no words from his mouth pouring into her ears. There was only silence, the kind of silence that only a dead telephone echoes.

"Norris? Norris?"

Sassy jabbed the off button as hard as she could. She threw the cordless handset on her desk so hard it bounced and crashed to the floor. The back of the handset popped off and landed two feet away which infuriated her. She grabbed her locks with both hands and clutched them in her fists. She grit her teeth and squealed like a scalded pig. She didn't stop until a tickle in her throat made her cough. She let go of her locks and looked at the handset. The battery was hanging out by a short wire. How so much like her life that handset was. She felt like she was holding on by a thread, a very short thread. She picked up the handset and tried to shove the battery back inside its slot. It seemed to not want to fit neatly back in place, but she wasn't in the mood to fiddle with it.

"You couldn't land on the damn rug! You had to land on the freaking hardwood floor and disembowel your stupid self." It dawned on Sassy that she was cursing out her telephone.

"I'm losing my freaking mind, but then again, with what just happened with Norris and earlier Bernard, who else has the right? It's not my damn fault Bernie has AIDS? Why do I have to take the brunt of all his anger? And Norris, how can he deny he was here when he was?"

Sassy sat behind her desk. "Kenneth saw Norris." She called Kenneth on her crippled handset. She purposely did not unblock her phone number. She didn't want Kenneth to see that it was her calling.

"Yeah?" Kenneth answered gruffly.

"Kenneth, last night—"

He hung up.

That didn't surprise her. He was pathetic anyway but then again, so was she. In twenty minutes three men had hung up on her. At least Kenneth hanging up on her verified that he was in her apartment last night. Why else would he reject her? The problem was Norris. What game was he playing and why?

15

No smile curved Sassy's lips, no frown creased her brow as she waited patiently for the new Staples cashier to finish keying in her shipping information. This was the first time she was late with a manuscript and her editor wanted it shipped UPS overnight. The whole morning and early afternoon had been spent reading her entire manuscript. The changes and corrections she made she prayed was enough to satisfy herself and her editor. She didn't give this manuscript anywhere near as much attention as her previous books because she had spent a lot of time with Norris since meeting him, in addition to running daily back and forth to the hospital to visit Bernard. She was the only one Bernard would see which was terrible for Evelyn and Brice. It wasn't fair to either one, but it was Bernard's call. He didn't want anyone to see him wasting away.

It was 4:15 by the time Sassy walked out of Staples with her purchase of two black ink cartridges for her printer and her UPS receipt tucked down in the side of her shoulder bag. Many of the people who hurried by paid her no mind as she stood outside of Staples on busy Court Street with her back up against the glass wall watching them eagerly leave their work day behind. Going home herself was out of the question. If Norris showed up, she did not want to be there. She kept her cell phone off so she wouldn't be tempted to answer it, but she kept turning it on anyway to see if Norris had called. He hadn't. She felt like crying when she should be glad he wasn't bothering her. God, she really liked him and if she was honest with herself, she was in love with Norris. They had only just begun and that quickly, she had lost him. She should have known it was too good to be true. She couldn't be that lucky. She turned her cell phone off and started walking up Court Street in the direction of the hospital. She might as well get her visit with Bernard over with.

# # # #

Sassy donned a shapeless white hospital gown and over her nose and mouth she pulled a breathing mask as was required before entering Bernard's private room. It wasn't herself she was protecting from infection, it was Bernard. His immune system wasn't much improved from the night he was admitted. At Bernard's closed door she tapped lightly before entering and was floored at what she saw. The mask did little to hide Norris's face. He was sitting at the small table across from Bernard, playing a game of chess. Sassy would not have been more surprised if it was Michael Jackson sitting there instead.

"It's about time you got here," Bernard said. "If it wasn't for Norris, I would think no one cared."

Norris moved his knight. "That's stretching it a bit." He didn't look Sassy's way.

"Why are you standing over there?" Bernard asked. "Are you afraid you might catch something over here."

Mindful to not look at Norris, Sassy retorted, "If I catch anything, it won't be from you."

Bernard captured Norris's knight. "Come closer, Sassy. You're a great distraction for Norris."

Sassy didn't move an inch, but she looked at Norris.

Norris sat back from the table. He deliberately looked at Sassy. "I see I'm going to have to brush up on my game."

"Yeah, you better," Bernard said. "I'm beating you too easily."

"Actually, I'm a little tired from driving down from Connecticut after three straight days of meetings."

Sassy said, "Yeah right," under her breath.

"See that hateful look she's giving you?" Bernard asked. "I wouldn't eat anything she cooked unless it was still in an unopened can."

"Shut up, Bernie!"

"See, she's pissed."

Sassy dropped her shoulder bag and bag from Staples on the foot of Bernard's bed. "Bernie, I've had a rough day which you are partly responsible for."

"Only partly?" Bernard quipped. "Is that because I'm now only half a man?"

Sassy casually walked over to Bernard and poked him in the upper arm. "Boy, I am not doing 'oh, woe is me' today."

Norris quietly watched Sassy with an inquisitive eye.

"Boy?" Bernard asked.

"Bernie, you don't wanna keep messing with me, and neither does your chess partner who shoulders a rather large part of the blame for ruining my day and night."

"Sassy, I've been away for the last three days. I had nothing to do with ruining your day, but I believe I can explain—"

"Excuse me. Do I deaf, dumb, blind and stupid? You were in my apartment, I saw you, I heard you, I felt you."

Norris shot up out of his chair in front of Sassy which made her heart skip a beat. "What do I stand to gain by lying to you about whether I was in your apartment or not? "

"Good question," Bernard said.

Sassy sat on the arm of Bernard's chair. If there was an answer to Norris's question that made sense, she didn't know it. "I see you're in a better mood," she said to Bernard.

"Don't talk to me, talk to him."

She couldn't. She reached over to move Bernard's knight. He slapped her hand. "She's always been so stubborn and closed-minded."

"So have you. I—"

"Talk to me," Norris said. He pulled Sassy up by her arm. "Talk to me."

"Wow!" Bernard was impressed with Norris's no-nonsense attitude.

"Do you mind letting go of my arm?"

Norris let go but he said again, "Talk to me."

Sassy and Norris stood looking into each other's eyes—he seeing anger in hers, she seeing his determination to not back down from her.

"I'm not letting you dismiss me," he said.

"I don't have time for this." Sassy started to turn away but when she saw Norris about to reach for her, she quickly pointed a warning finger at him to match the warning glint in her eyes. Norris got the message. He lowered his arm and Sassy walked away unchallenged.

"What you're seeing, Norris, is the stubborn, childish side of Sassy."

"Shut up, Bernie!" Sassy picked up her shoulder bag.

"See? Childish." Bernard said.

"Bernie, what the hell are you doing? You don't even know what happened."

"Actually I do. Maybe if you stopped pouting and throwing fits like you're a two-year-old, you might be enlightened as well."

"Just hear me out," Norris said.

Sassy snatched up her purchase from Staples bag and her shoulder bag. "I don't know how you got him on your side!" She started for the door.

Norris rushed to the door and blocked Sassy before she could touch the doorknob. "You're not leaving like this."

"I know how to scream."

"All this damn drama," Bernard said as he started preparing himself to get up out of his chair. He rolled his intravenous drip pole to the other side of his chair. "Big baby."

"Listen to me." Norris took both Sassy's shoulder bag

and her Staples bag out of her hands. "I can explain everything."

"How? With another lie? Don't bother. I don't do ignorance, and I will never abide a liar."

Norris despised liars as much as Sassy did and didn't appreciate being called one. "Then you'll listen to me."

Bernard coughed to clear his dry throat. "Norris, I like you. Do you have a good pair of knee pads?"

Sassy tried to pull away. "Are you going to keep manhandling me?"

"Are you going to listen?"

"She will," Bernard said.

"I will not."

"Then I swear on the soul of my mother, I was not in your apartment or in New York City last night. It was not me."

If Sassy could believe the earnest look in Norris's eyes, then she'd have to believe he was telling the truth but what would that say about her? "Are you saying I'm delusional?"

"I'm sick of this damn merry-go-round." Bernard held onto his intravenous drip poll as he got up out of the chair. "You two gotta go. You're making me sick."

Sassy hurried back to Bernard to help him to his bed, but he didn't need or want her help. "Go away!"

"Bernie!"

"Stop fussing over me."

"Would you stop being so grouchy?"

"Get me some ice and I'll think about it."

"Oh really?" Sassy watched Bernard with some difficulty try to up onto his bed and hold on to the intravenous drip poll at the same time. She started to help him but Norris beat her to it. He took hold of Bernard's elbow and hefted him up onto the bed. He then adjusted Bernard's pillows. Sassy would never say it out loud, but felt a tiny pang of jealousy that Bernard let Norris help him.

"When did you two become such fast friends?"

"Are you gonna get the ice?"

"I'm leaving. Ask him."

"Hey! I thought I was your favorite cousin," Bernard said seriously which stopped Sassy from leaving. They looked at each other. Sassy sucked her teeth as she brushed past Norris to get to the plastic water pitcher on the night stand. She snatched it and stomped out of the room.

"She's pissed," Bernard said again.

Rubbing his neck, Norris went over to the window and looked out across the East River into Manhattan. He had hoped what had happened to him months ago was behind him. Having to retell it was to relive it and he hated that.

"Sassy really hates liars," Bernard said.

"Good, because that's not what I am."

"Okay, so I sort of believe you, but are you sure you don't know who that guy was?"

"His name, why he looks so much like me, why he's latched on to my life, I don't know."

"Could he be a long lost brother, a cousin?"

Norris shook his head. He turned away from the window. "I have one brother with whom I do not share my mother. My mother only had me, and I only had her."

"Does your half brother look like you?" Bernard reached for his oxygen mask dangling from the side railing of his bed. He switched on the flow of oxygen and inhaled from his mask.

"My half brother Clarence is my father's son with his wife, who is not Japanese. Clarence looks nothing like me."

Bernard removed his mask. He set it on top of his sunken chest. "You have a serious problem on your hands."

Certainly Norris could not dispute that. He musingly scratched his neck just under the edge of his face mask. He was in love with Sassy. He'd known almost from the start that he'd fallen hard for her.

"Here's the deal," Bernard said. "I won't tell Sassy that she can wrap you around her little finger, if you promise you'll be here for her when I die."

Although he chuckled, Norris sensed the earnestness of Bernard's bribe. "I hope you live. . ."

"Nope, not like this."

". . .but I intend to be here either way."

"Good, then lie."

"I'm confused. Didn't you just say Sassy hated liars?"

"Lie this one time about last night. Sassy thinks she saw you. Agree with her. Apologize for whatever and move on."

"Sassy hates liars remember?"

"Sassy hates broccoli and she hates bean spouts but she eats them anyway because they're healthy for her. This is one of those healthy lies that—"

The door opened. Sassy came back into the room. She didn't notice Bernard's conspiratorial glance at Norris, or Norris's perplexed gaze of uncertainty. She filled Bernard's cup with ice and handed it to him. Then without looking Norris's way, she picked up her things.

"I'll see you tomorrow," she said to Bernard.

"Norris, you're coming with her, right?"

Before Norris could answer for himself, Sassy said, "I don't need an escort."

"I'll be here."

"No you won't. I'm not—"

"Sassy!" Bernard exclaimed. "In case you forgot, I'm dying here. All this negative energy is stressing my extremely weak, almost non-existent immune system. You wanna fight with Norris, take it outside. Go to a bar or to a gym somewhere, but get the hell out of here."

Behind her mask, Sassy's mouth was open, but Norris smiled behind his. He could take lessons in handling Sassy from Bernard. "We'll see you tomorrow," Norris said.

"Please don't let her come back if she's in a bad mood."

Sassy leaned in over Bernard. "You know you have some damn nerve! If you weren't sick in this damn bed, I'd—"

"If doesn't apply to me. I am sick." More than his proclamation, Bernard silenced Sassy with the tormented look in his eyes. "Go home, Sassy. Talk to Norris, but do something really innovative, listen to him."

That hurt. Whatever the reason, Bernard wasn't pulling any punches with her. "Why are you so angry with me?"

"Because you finally found someone you can be happy with and you're telling him to kiss your ass without first hearing him out."

"But he—"

"I need for you to be happy, Sassy, for me. Please, hear him out."

As always, Bernard knew what to say to steal her thunder. He made her look self-absorbed and irrational when she wasn't. Still, she was embarrassed. She left the room.

"Better catch her," Bernard said to Norris.

"Thank you. I'll see you tomorrow." Norris hurried out of the room.

Bernard chuckled to himself as he put his oxygen mask back on. He then turned onto his side and curled himself up into the fetal position he had come to be most comfortable in. He was exhausted. He prayed he would sleep well into the night. He had little energy for much else, but at least asleep, he could dream. He could again see himself as he was before his death sentence. He could again play with his son and make love to the woman he should have never given up. In his dreams he was strong, he was healthy, he was happy. He welcomed sleep because of his dreams.

16

Norris dropped his jacket across the back of Sassy's living room chair. Without giving it a thought, he rolled his sleeves up to his elbows as he often did when he was about to tackle a difficult assignment at work. He took from his wallet several pieces of paper. For five minutes now, Sassy had been hiding back in her bedroom probably hoping that he'd go away, but he wasn't. If he hadn't stayed close on her heel as she raced up the stairs to the third floor, she would have made it into her apartment and slammed the door in his face, but she wasn't getting rid of him that easily. For years, while he established himself, he had no trouble steering clear of serious relationships because he hadn't come across anyone who peaked his interest beyond an occasional night out. Not to say that the women weren't worthy, so many might have been, but rarely, if ever, did he wonder what he might have missed out on. That is until now. He didn't know what it was about Sassy, he just knew she was the one and if he lost her, he just might miss out on something special. However, if Sassy had been thinking she was going to be the sole driver in their relationship, it was time he showed her he was just as good a driver.

Norris entered Sassy's bedroom where he found her sitting on the side of the bed stroking Chester. "Let's talk."

Chester lazily raised his head and looked up at Sassy. Whatever he saw on her face, he didn't want any part of it. He slowly rose up, jumped down off the bed and sauntered past

Norris out of the room.

"You said I was here last night, I say I wasn't. You said I was cruel to you, I say it wasn't me. I said I was in Connecticut until this afternoon, you say I wasn't."

Sassy began impatiently shaking her foot. She wanted so badly to be lying in bed with Norris instead of waiting to hear what fantastical story he was preparing to tell to camouflage what he'd actually done. Maybe he had some kind of mental disorder.

"Okay, look. I have no doubt that something went on here, but before I can express my thoughts on it, look at these." One by one, Norris methodically laid out on the bed next to Sassy, ten restaurant receipts and an invoice from the Marriott hotel. He then watched her face as she looked at the receipts.

"Look at the dates and times."

Sassy was skeptical as she began to read the dates and times on each printed receipt she grew more puzzled.

"May 6 through today, May 9th," Norris said. "Last night I dined with my clients at Daiko, a Japanese restaurant. We arrived at 7:00 p.m., we finished at 9:45 p.m. I returned to my hotel around 10:30 p.m. This afternoon, I checked out of the hotel at 12:45. Sassy, you are more than welcome to speak to my clients, the nakai at the restaurant, and with the staff at the hotel."

Sassy checked the paper the receipts were printed on. It was legitimate receipt paper. She then picked up the hotel receipt which showed that Norris had breakfast at 7:30 a.m., and that he checked out at 12:15 p.m.

"Swear to me," she said, "these are not forged."

Norris raised his hand. "I swear."

Sassy began shaking her head. "I don't know how they're real when you were here."

Norris took out his wallet. "Check my American Express card number against the receipts."

"I don't need to see your card." Sassy still wasn't completely convinced. She stood. She began to pace with her hands on her hips. "I know what I saw. I saw you. I talked to you. I pulled you off of Kenneth. My God, Norris, you even kissed me!"

The kiss still bothered Norris but his concern was split. "Why was Kenneth here?"

"The hell with Kenneth! This isn't about Kenneth. It's about you!"

"Then tell me about the kiss."

"I didn't like it!" Sassy moved away from Norris to the other side of the bed. "Norris, I refuse to let you make me think I'm crazy."

"You're not—"

"I can't be in a relationship that makes me second guess my man. I have to have the truth and nothing less!"

It was clear to Norris he was on the path to losing Sassy if he didn't tell her everything he knew about the man she came face to face with. "Sit down."

Sassy brashly stuck her leg out and boldly folded her arms high across her chest. She wasn't going to set because he said so.

"Please," Norris said quietly. All day he had been tempering his own anger in order to pacify Sassy. He was getting tired.

Sassy sat on the edge of her bed. "Well?"

"Eighteen months ago, I received a call from my bank about rather large purchases on my MasterCard and my AMEX card. Over a three week period, someone charged a total of $37,000 to my account in the form of merchandise and cash advances. At the same time, charges of $13,000 were put on my corporate Diners Club Card."

"Oh, come on. Fifty thousand dollars! You didn't notice and the bank didn't call when the charges first started appearing?"

"I'm a businessman, Sassy. I have a company. I have employees. I have clients. I have expenses. Yes, I have an accountant, but he would not have been concerned, as I wasn't, until a statement came in. However, when I'm especially busy, I can be a bit lax in reviewing my personal statements. Not to mention, at times, I have charged as much as $50,000, if not more myself, in a shorter period of time. The banks initially had no cause to be concerned."

"So what finally triggered their concern?"

"There was a request for the change of my telephone number and mailing address. Thankfully, before the representative would make the change, she asked the security question on file, and the person, after giving incorrect answers, claimed he just couldn't remember but he did have my current address, my driver's license, my date of birth, my place of birth, and the names of my mother and father."

"He had your mother's name? How—"

"I don't know how any of my personal information, especially my mother's name, was acquired. To this day, I don't know who this man is, or—"

"Wait a minute. This person was never caught? You've never seen him?"

"Not once."

"Norris, if what you're saying is true and I pray that it is, the man I saw last night is literally a clone of you. He can step in and out of your life anytime he wants and no one will be the wiser."

Norris felt a chill on the nape of his neck. "Except you."

Remembering how she ached for Norris yesterday, Sassy had not doubt she would have gone to bed with his impostor if he had stayed the night. "If what you say is true, this is scary."

"It's said everyone has a twin."

"I don't know how this guy could look so much like you and not be you. It's spooky."

Norris began collecting his receipts. "It's quite disconcerting, but there was an extensive investigation by the banks. On top of their investigation, I hired a private investigator. Everyone he questioned in the stores where the cards were used said it was me. He showed them my picture. The banks wanted to hold me liable for the charges, but I was able to prove, irrefutably, that I was elsewhere at the time the charges were made." He went around to the side of the bed and Sassy sat next to Sassy.

"Every card I own is now registered with a fraud detector service. All of my bank accounts are secured and can't be touched without a series of check points being engaged. I get a call even if I charge a single dollar to my cards, unless I initiate contact that I will be spending X amount of dollars, as I did the last three days in Connecticut. When I spoke to you this morning and realized what you were saying, I knew I wasn't going to be able to explain this over the telephone."

"Ergo, you hung up on me?"

"I wasn't getting through to you. I immediately called my investigator Cyrus Woodale to get him back on the case full time. The fact that the guy was here is in your apartment, angers me. No telling what he could have done."

Sassy remembered her opened door. She remembered that awful kiss. She began rubbing her lips with the back of her hand.

"I'm sorry," Norris said. "I thought he was done with me and although I don't wish him on anyone else, I hoped he had moved on. I should have told you about him."

"Yes you should have! He followed you to me."

"You said he kiss you. Did you—"

"No!" Sassy got up and moved away from Norris. "I didn't sleep with him! He kissed me and I hated it!" Sassy again wiped her hand across her mouth.

Norris was relieved, but Sassy was fired up. "That man walked straight into my apartment as if he'd been here before. Do you know what could have happened to me if he had come back here; or even if he had stayed? He could have raped me, killed me, anything." Sassy began pacing and nervously shaking her hands. "Oh my God."

Norris tried to take Sassy into his arms to calm her, but

she wouldn't let him. She pulled away from him.

"Do you know I could be dead right now? When I got up this morning, my apartment door was open—wide open!"

"While you were asleep it was open?"

"Isn't that what I said? He could have slit my throat!" Sassy began wringing her hands.

"That bastard! Is anything missing, or was anything disturbed?"

"I don't know. I really didn't check." Sassy stood back as Norris looked around the bedroom. She followed him as he went throughout her apartment checking out every room. Nothing appeared to be taken.

Sassy hadn't thought about it before. "Suppose he put something in here?"

"I don't like it," Norris said from the closed apartment door. He took out his BlackBerry and made a call. "Cyrus, I need you to do a sweep of an apartment." He looked at Sassy. "No, it's my. . .my woman's apartment."

Neither sassy nor Norris felt strange about Norris claiming Sassy as his woman. It felt right. Sassy left Norris to his call and went back into her bedroom where he found her minutes later taking off her shoes.

"Cyrus will check all the rooms for any kind of video or listening devices."

"When?"

"He's sending someone over right away. He'll also change locks."

Sassy sat on her bed. "This is like a murder mystery without the murder."

"Let's just hope it stays that way. He'll never get near you again."

"You can't guarantee me that. You're not with me twenty-four-seven. This guy is dangerous. I saw what he did to Kenneth with his bare hands." Sassy looked at Norris's hands. He knew what she was thinking. He showed her the backs of both his hands. There wasn't a scratch or bruise any where.

"It wasn't me."

Now Sassy really was scared. "Norris, he can reach out and touch me, and obviously you, too, anytime he wants. I'm a private person, Norris, but when I'm out signing books, I'm very much in the public eye, just as you are."

"I'm not a public figure."

"Oh, no? You've been written up in major, high profile newspapers, architectural magazines, house and home magazines, you on the internet, and you've been on television twice since I've been with you."

Riiiiing!

Norris checked his BlackBerry to see who was calling before he answered. "Hey, Dad."

Sassy glanced at her watch. It was 6:45. She had totally forgotten about dinner with Norris's father.

"Hold on." Norris muted the call. "Are we still doing dinner?"

Sassy shrugged. She really wasn't in the mood to meet anyone tonight.

Norris said to his father, "We'll be there in an hour." He ended the call.

"Why did you do that? I don't feel like—"

"We won't stay long but when you move in with me this weekend . . ."

"What?"

". . . my father should know who you are."

Sassy stared at Norris as if he had spoken in a language she didn't understand. "Move in as in cohabit?"

"You'd be a lot safer and there is a lot more room in my house than here in this apartment."

"More room doesn't make it any safer, Norris. Who's to say this guy hasn't already followed us to your house?"

"If he has, he's never gotten inside and he never will. If he finds his way up to Blue Mountain, he'll be spotted immediately. Blue Mountain is a gated community."

"I know that, Norris, but still I don't know."

"Sassy, there are no corners to stand on, no hallways or dark alleys to hide in. If anyone parked on the roads linger to long, someone will be alerted and I guarantee you, the police will be called. I will personally talk to the security company so they will be ready. Unless this guy knows someone, he'll stand out like Bozo the Clown at a debutante ball."

"What happens when you have to stay in the city?"

"You'll stay in the city with me either here or at the hotel."

Sassy looked around her bedroom. "Norris, I don't know about this. I don't like moving around too much."

"Then we'll stay at the house. You're safest there. My alarm system is hooked up to the police. It will be activated whether you're in the house or not. My house is on lakefront property and you can—"

"Norris, you don't have to sell me on your house. I just don't like changing my life because of some maniac."

"Sassy, we've been going back and forth between here and the house for the past three months anyway. The only difference is you'll stay there."

"True. "Okay, after this guy is caught, I'm coming back to my apartment. Plus, I will be coming back to the city to visit Bernard, and if he gets to leave the hospital, he will be staying here. He no longer has his condo."

"We'll deal with that when the time comes. If you like, you can come to the city everyday with me. If you wish to work here during the day, you can. I'm having an alarm installed here as well."

If Sassy didn't know better, she could swear she was being set up, but why?

"I drive my own car to Pennsylvania."

"You don't have to. I have a second car in the garage."

"I like having my own." Sassy felt as if she'd been through a negotiations meeting with her publishing house. "Oh, and Chester comes with me."

"Not a problem." Norris drew Sassy into his arms but

Sassy wasn't feeling romantic. She couldn't help but wonder if fate was playing a trick on her. In one hour, she and Norris went from dating to moving in together. What fate had in store for them, she couldn't wait to find out.

17

The first thing Sassy noticed about Mr. Norris Wilson was his beautiful bright white smile. Whether he bought those teeth or whether he was lucky enough to be born with them, Sassy couldn't tell, but Mr. Wilson flashed his perfect teeth every time he smiled, which was interesting because once she got past his smile, Sassy saw that Mr. Wilson was not an especially good-looking man. His caramel-colored face was pockmarked on both his cheeks, and his nostrils were so wide Sassy could swear she could see the back of his throat. What Mr. Wilson had going for him besides his beautiful smile, was his beautiful wife Alicia who insisted that Sassy call her by her first name. No one would believe Alicia was sixty-four years old when she looked fifty. Her shoulder length gray hair was stylishly flipped on the ends and framed her taut, unlined face as if it were a picture. Alicia wasn't a slim woman, she was rather plump and shorter than her taller slim husband probably by a foot. Mr. Wilson and Alicia were definitely opposites in looks, but by the time dinner was finished and they all were sitting on the sun porch finishing off the most delicious key lime pie Sassy had ever eaten, she saw that Alicia and Mr. Wilson were perfectly paired. They not only finished each other's sentences, they seemed to know what the other would say before words were even spoken. After forty-two years of marriage, they still smiled at each other and touched each other as if they had only been married a year. Sassy, however, wasn't naive. No marriage could go forty-two years without its ups and downs and surely, when Alicia found out about Norris and his mother in Japan, she had to come undone.

"Norris, before I forget," Alicia said. "Mr. Lewis couldn't come for dinner. He said he'll see you next time."

"The last time I saw him he said he wanted to be in Charleston when his first great grand baby was born."

"Any day now," Alicia said.

Sassy gave Norris an inquisitive look.

"Mr. Lewis lives next door," Norris explained. "When I was a kid, Mr. Lewis and his late wife sort of adopted me."

"They tried to steal you," Mr. Wilson said.

"They were great." Norris smiled at the memory of Mr. and Mrs. Lewis taking him all the way up to the Bronx Zoo without his father's knowledge after they'd found him sulking out on the back porch after another run-in with Clarence.

"I miss Cara," Alicia said. "She was special."

Norris said softly, "She made the best chocolate chip and oatmeal cookies."

"I lost fifteen pounds after Cara died," Alicia said not too happily."

"Sassy," Mr. Wilson said, "did Norris tell you Alicia is a big fan of yours?"

"He didn't."

"Well, I am. I love your books. I—"

"She loves the sex in your books," Mr. Wilson said.

"Look who's talking. You should thank Sassy for writing those books." Alicia winked at Sassy.

Norris smiled but he looked away. Sassy, on the other hand, got a kick from hearing that her books were responsible for some sexually intimate moments between couples.

"Alicia," Mr. Wilson said, "you don't need to be telling people our business."

"Norris, grow up. Your son knows he wasn't born of an immaculate conception."

Mr. Wilson stared pointedly at Alicia who flipped her hand good-naturedly at him.

"Norris," Alicia said, "your father is forever a prude."

Norris barely smiled. His thoughts were of his mother. He wondered as he used to as a boy, what kind of relationship his mother and father might have had.

"Sassy, I love your books. I like that there enough sex to get the juices flowing."

"Oh, brother!" Mr. Wilson said.

Alicia again flipped her hand at her husband. "Ignore him. Sassy, you know what else I like? I like that you don't just write about young girls. You write older women in love too."

"I never thought love for only for the young."

"Good, because I intend on being in love and making love all over this house as long as I can before father time sneaks up on me and shut down my equipment."

"Woman, you're crazy!" Mr. Wilson said.

Laughing, Sassy glimpsed Norris trying to not laugh, while Alicia had an audaciously smug look on her face.

"Woman, you need to stop reading those books cause you act like you sex crazed."

"No, honey. I'm a woman who appreciates good sex and lots of it. I know you can testify to that."

"Okay," Norris said. "Alicia, that's too much information even for me."

"That's for damn sure!" Mr. Wilson seconded. "Sassy didn't come to hear all that mess."

"Honey, Sassy isn't writing books for the pope. Sassy writes romance books for real people with real sex scenes in them. She—"

"That doesn't mean she wants to hear an over-sexed woman talk about sex when she just finished eating."

"It's alright, Mr. Wilson. I love Alicia's candor."

"Don't pay him any mind, Sassy. He loves my candor, too. I'm just glad he finally got his doctor—"

"Alicia! Why are you telling my business?"

"My goodness, Norris. There's no secret about Viagra."

"Alicia!"

Alicia and Sassy laughed, and although Norris felt sorry for his father, he laughed as well. His father had always been shy about discussing sex. When Norris was sixteen, their one and only talk about sex lasted less than five minutes which was just enough time for his father to give him a box of condoms, a pat on the back, and advice to always respect the girl.

Staring hard at his wife, Mr. Wilson wasn't amused.

Sassy whispered, "Your father is really mad."

"Dad, you let Alicia get you every time."

"Oh, Norris," Alicia said to her husband. "Stop being so thin-skinned. More men than you can imagine have problems getting it up—"

"And keeping it up," Sassy interjected which made Norris and his father raise a brow at her. "It's the truth."

"It certainly is," Alicia agreed.

Norris asked Sassy, "How do you know a lot of men have a problem keeping it up?"

"Can we please talk about something else?" Mr. Wilson shifted uncomfortably in his chair.

"I asked them," Sassy said. "For three years I worked on a survey for the University of Michigan which had to do with men and sexuality."

"That must have been interesting!" Alicia said excitedly.

"It was. So many men admitted on that survey that they embellished or exaggerated their sexual prowess. They told us interviewers more than they tell the boys in the bar or in the locker room."

"Did any of them admit to liking their women fingering—"

"For Christ sake, Alicia! Change the damn subject!"

Sassy and Norris fell against each other laughing. It was obvious to everyone except Mr. Wilson that Alicia was teasing him. The sly look on Alicia's face said she was enjoying the reaction she was getting from her husband.

"Goodness, Norris," Alicia said, "we're just talking.

Sex keeps people young and beautiful. In fact, I'm due for my beauty treatment tonight."

Again, Sassy couldn't contain her laughter. Norris coughed to keep from laughing at his father who couldn't hide his embarrassment. Mr. Wilson snatched up the remote control, turned on the television and began rapidly channel surfing.

Alicia winked at Sassy. "Honey, can I get you something?"

Mr. Wilson grumbled as he continually changed channels so quickly he had no way of knowing what was on any given channel.

"Okay!" Norris said as he stood. He began collecting the dessert dishes. "I think I'll take these into the kitchen. Can I bring anyone anything?"

Mr. Wilson slammed the remote down on the side table and zipped out of the room ahead of Norris.

With the men out of the room, Alicia smiled broadly. "I love doing that to him."

"No kidding."

"He's such a prude. He's always been a prude and at times, it can be quite frustrating."

"I'm sure, but it's so rare to see a man so bashful," Sassy said, "especially at his age."

"Yes, but as shy as my husband is about discussing sex, once the lights are off, he really is a wonderful lover. He—"

"Alicia." Sassy brushed her locks off of her shoulder. "I don't think I need to hear anymore."

"Fine," Alicia said, her tone serious. "Let's talk about Norris. He's a good man, he's like his father. Be good to him."

"Of course I—"

"My marriage almost ended when we got that first letter years ago. It took me a long time to forgive my husband for sleeping with another woman, and even longer to forgive him for making a baby with her."

"That's understandable."

"Is it? I didn't want another woman's child with my

husband in my house. I didn't care that Norris was an orphan or that he scrounged for his food on the street. I hated that his presence reminded me everyday of my husband's infidelity while I was here at home worrying about him, missing him."

"What changed your mind? I mean you're still married and Norris seems to love and respect you."

Alicia shrugged. "God, prayers, and truthfully," Alicia lowered her voice, "the whore was dead."

That was the last thing Sassy expected to hear. She wondered if Norris had any idea Alicia felt that way about his mother. He had never mentioned anything negative about Alicia. In fact, he was always so complementary of her.

"It sounds cruel," Alicia said, "but I was grateful I didn't have to compete with her for my husband's—"

"So, what are we talking about now?" Norris asked as he and his father came back onto the sun porch. Mr. Wilson sat down and picked up his television remote.

"Sassy's books," Alicia said. "I want her to sign some of them for me."

"I'd love to."

"I'll get them." Alicia went for her books.

"She tells all of her friends Norris is dating you," Mr. Wilson said.

Norris slipped his arm around Sassy's shoulders. "You're a celebrity."

Sassy gently nudged Norris in the side. "Very funny."

Alicia returned with an armful of books. "I think I have them all."

Sassy took three of the books that were about to fall. "This is great, thank you."

"I heard from Clarence earlier," Mr. Wilson said.

Not that he was really interested, Norris asked, "How's he doing?"

"You know your brother. The Drug Enforcement Agency is his life. He said he's been held over in Thailand another six months. He's headed to Columbia from there."

Norris ached to tell his father he didn't care to hear about Clarence or whatever Clarence was up to. In fact, the best part of the evening was not having Clarence's name mentioned.

"That job keeps Clarence on foreign soil," Mr. Wilson said. "I bet when he finally settles down, it'll be overseas somewhere. Did I tell you he went to Japan again?"

Norris's interest was peaked. "Wasn't that last year? November?"

"I did tell you. Well, Clarence said he had a few weeks. He said it was just as easy to go to Japan as anywhere else."

"Where did you say he went in Japan?"

"He said Tokyo. This was his third trip."

"You never told me he went to Japan three times."

"You never asked," Mr. Wilson put down his remote control. "I thought Clarence would have told you himself."

Norris didn't know how his father could think that. He and Clarence rarely talked, but it was ironic that Clarence went to Japan at all considering the derogatory names he called him and his mother. Japan should have been the last place on earth Clarence ever wanted to visit.

Half listening to Norris's conversation about his brother with his father, Sassy continued autographing her books. She knew very little about Clarence Wilson except that he was a DEA agent and that he and Norris never got along.

"I really enjoyed this one," Alicia said, indicating *Passions Lost*.

"It was fun writing it," Sassy said.

Mr. Wilson said Norris, "Son, you can't keep holding on to what Clarence did to you when you were kids."

"Dad, let it go." Norris tried to focus on Sassy as she signed her name but he couldn't get Clarence off his mind or his stomach which always soured whenever his father tried to push him to forgive Clarence. From the first day he met his half brother, Clarence made it clear he didn't want him in his house or near his father.

"Son, I believe Clarence regrets—"

"It's about time we started back to Brooklyn," Norris said. He checked his watch.

Sassy's ears perked at Norris's balky tone just as she was about to sign *Butterfly*. She opened the book to her own signature.

"Oh," Alicia said. "Norris gave me that one. It's already signed, but would you personalize it?"

Sassy tapped Norris lightly on the thigh with the pen and tapped the book when he looked. She smiled but he didn't.

"It's getting late." Norris stood.

"She still has another book to sign," Alicia said.

Mr. Wilson also stood. "Sassy, you're the first woman my son's brought home since he was twenty-one."

Sassy beamed, "That's nice to hear." She gave Alicia the last autographed book.

"My first autographed books," Alicia said proudly.

"We have to get going." Norris held his hand out to Sassy and helped her up. Sassy tried to signal Norris with her eyes that this was the opportune moment for him to tell his father and Alicia that she would be staying with him, but obviously he didn't think so because he ignored her.

At the door Norris hugged Alicia. "Dinner was great as usual." He hugged his father.

While Sassy went through the motion of thanking Alicia for having her over for dinner and, as well, for reading her books, she hoped she could get away without having to hug Alicia. What little Alicia said about Norris and his mother spoke volumes. It's no wonder Norris had problems with Clarence. Clarence had to know from the start how his mother felt about his father's infidelity. Alicia hugged Sassy before Sassy had a chance to escape. Mr. Wilson, too, she hugged but he was well worth hugging. Within minutes they were headed east on the Brooklyn Queens Expressway heading back to Brooklyn. As late as it was, the traffic on the expressway was bustling. Norris didn't relax behind the wheel until he was moving at the same speed as the cars in front and back of him.

"Why didn't you tell your father I would be staying with you?"

"Timing; it never seemed right."

"O-kay."

Norris moved smoothly into the middle lane. He glanced at Sassy. "You want to know about Clarence."

"You never spoke at length about him."

"We never got along. I usurped his position as the favorite son."

"Jealousy?"

"If Clarence had taken a moment to get to know me, he might have understood my joy and my father's joy had everything to do with discovering that I had a father and my father had another son. Our coming together was not ordained to separate him from his father."

"Your father alluded to something Clarence did to you when you were younger."

Through his rearview and left side view mirrors, Norris saw the way was clear for him to again change lanes. He felt Sassy's eyes on him as he sped up and moved into the third lane. By now she had to know talking about Clarence set his teeth on edge, but he could tell by Sassy's unrelenting stare that she wasn't backing down until he told her something.

"Is it that important to you?"

"Yes." She wasn't ready to tell him that Clarence's attitude toward him might have been influenced by Alicia's anger that his father had an affair that produced a baby.

"When I was fifteen, my father insisted I go on a ski trip up to Lake Placid with my brother and several of his buddies from his high school football team. I didn't want to go and Clarence definitely didn't want me tagging along but my father pushed it because he thought the trip would bring us closer."

"Apparently it didn't."

"By the end of the first day, I thought maybe my father

was right. Clarence treated me well. He and his friends taught me enough about skiing to keep me up on my feet. Even dinner went well. Neither Clarence nor his friends taunted me. Second day same thing, except this time after dinner, they took me off trail skiing. I should have known something was up when they raced far ahead me. They left me in the woods."

"No they didn't!"

"I took off the skis to avoid slamming into trees, but walking in deep snow was exhausting. My feet were freezing. It got dark really fast but thank God for white snow. I was able to see pretty well but I still walked in circles for hours. The short of it, I didn't enjoy my sleep-over in the woods."

"No one came looking for you?"

"Not my brother."

"What a bastard! How did you get through the night?"

For a brief moment Norris realized he was about to reveal something he had never spoken about before. He took his eyes off the road just long enough to see both anticipation and anger on Sassy's face.

"The ski outfit I had on was warm for a while, but then it wasn't enough. I walked until I couldn't feel my feet or my legs. I was so tired; all I wanted to do was lie down and sleep."

"They say that's the last thing a person should do."

"It is, but when one is in that situation all knowledge goes out the window. I fell against this giant of a tree. That tree was huge. Sassy, I laughed as I slid down this tree to the ground. I laughed so hard I cried and when I stopped I heard my mother say, 'It's okay. Go to sleep, baby,' but she said it in Japanese."

"She's your guardian angel."

"Sassy, I huddled against that tree like I was huddling against my mother. I felt like she was holding me, keeping me warm because I stopped feeling so cold. When I woke up in the morning, I walked right out of the woods. I didn't get turned around one time. I got back to the resort in time to get breakfast. I didn't even have frostbite."

"No one asked what happened to you?"

"Other than Clarence and his friends, no one knew I was missing. I called my father and he lost it. We were supposed to stay one more day, but my father flew up to Lake Placid to get me and Clarence. He gave Clarence such a brutal tongue lashing I almost felt sorry for him."

"I'm glad you said almost, because you should have jacked his behind up."

Norris laughed. "I going to start calling you champ."

"I don't care. What Clarence did was vicious. You could have died. You could have frozen to death or gotten mauled by some wild animal. That bastard! I hope I never meet him."

"Okay, champ." Norris kept his eyes on the road ahead as he pat Sassy on her thigh. "I made it. I'm okay."

"I don't know how people can be so mean."

"Easy. For some people being mean is easy. Being nice is what's hard."

"I guess you're right."

"That day is behind me. Clarence went away to college, he started his career soon after, we never lived under the same roof again. I rarely see him and when I do, we don't talk about that weekend. In fact, we don't talk. Clarence is a nonentity in my life."

18

From Norris's screened-in deck high above Blue Mountain Lake, Sassy sat transfixed by the bright reflective beauty of the early morning sun bouncing off of the water below. The expansive deck running the full length along the back of the house was Sassy's favorite place to sit morning, noon, and night. Her twelve-day-long stay in Norris's house had done little to prod her into completing the editorial revisions in her manuscript. Most mornings after she worked out in Norris's well-equipped exercise room in the basement, she sat wrapped up in a light throw sipping a cup of cinnamon tea while dreamily gazing out across the lake at trees whose leaves and branches scarcely moved in the gentle early morning breeze.

Up until three days ago, going for long walks around the estate grounds was part of Sassy's early morning ritual after she'd seen Norris off at the crack of dawn. The crisp, fresh mountain air was physically invigorating, while the sight of the rising sun exalted her mind and soul. Never had she felt so alive. That is until she rounded a curve in the road and came up on a black bear just about to cross the road about fifty feet in front of her. She froze in mid stride. Her eyes bugged and she stopped breathing. Her heart was pounded. The bear, which wasn't especially big or especially small but was blacker than tar, looked at her gawking at him and seemed to be trying to decide if he should continue on his way or come up to her. His head and shoulders swayed toward her and then back again in the direction he had been going. Each time he looked back at her, with his mouth hanging open, Sassy's legs shook, her hands trembled, and she swore her heart stopped.

To herself Sassy kept saying, "Please go, please go, please go." The bear wasn't going and she wasn't about to move. She prayed for a car to come, but none came. She wracked her brain for what to do but came up with nothing but, "Don't move." There was a long stick about ten feet from her, but she was no stranger to Animal Planet. She knew if she made an unexpected move, the bear would be on top of her before she took one step.

After about a minute and not knowing what else to do, she said, at first timidly, "Shoo." When the bear didn't move, she said louder, "Shoo!" The bear must have thought she was stupid because he gave her the funniest look that seem to say, "And . . .what now?" Then as if he remembered he had an appointment with his buddies, the bear lumbered on across the street like a big black shadow and disappeared into the woods. Sassy didn't waste one second backing away from the spot she almost wet herself in. Once she was around the bend, she about-faced and sprinted back to the house.

That was Monday. That was the last time she dared venture out of the house for a walk alone. She was quite comfortable sitting on the deck watching geese alight onto the lake, and was entranced with their antics of dunking their heads, cleaning their bodies, and catching their food in their bills. The geese seemed oblivious to the deer that came early in the morning and at dusk to drink their fill of water. The whole scene was idyllic. The only other time Sassy had been this relaxed was when she was in Cancun and again in Aruba on vacation, which is what being at Norris's house felt like. She blamed the deck and the lake for lulling her into a state of lethargy. Not a thing got done the first two days she was there. That is until Norris came up with the idea of setting his alarm clock to go off at 9:00 a.m. When it went off, it pealed like a school bell and effectively snapped Sassy out of her inert trance. To shut it off, she had to get up and go inside to the kitchen where the clock sat on the counter. Then she would lock the deck door, set the house alarm, and officially begin her work day in the dining room where she had her computer set up. Until she developed immunity to the mesmerizing allure of the deck, she was not going to be able to write out there.

Three times Sassy had been back to the city to see Bernard and to collect more of her clothes. On days like today when she didn't drive in to New York with Norris, she felt sorry for him. Norris left the house as early as 5:30 in the morning to get to work in Manhattan, and before coming home, he went into Brooklyn to visit Bernard at the hospital, which was really too much, but Norris wouldn't hear her concerns.

"I'm in the city anyway. I can visit Bernard and save you the trip. You'll have more time to write."

"This is true but then you should save your car and yourself the wear and tear. Stay in my apartment. Go to work from there."

"No."

"But Norris, you could get at least four more hours of sleep. You're getting up at four in the morning, getting to the city at seven, seven-thirty in the morning, just to make sure I'm safe. You're making me feel guilty about being here."

"I'd feel guilty if you weren't here. Besides, if you weren't here, I would have the displeasure of waking up without you by my side."

What could she say to that? Only once had she slept alone in the bedroom Norris gave her. As much as Sassy hated to admit it, waking up next to Norris with his arms around her made her feel like the heroines she wrote about. She fell asleep in his arms; she woke up in his arms. The truth was that quick, she was beginning to feel like they were a married couple. She sent Norris off to work with a kiss; she greeted him at night with a hug and a kiss; she cooked his dinner, she fixed his plate, and the strangest thing was, she didn't mind. She was starting to become a better cook. With Kenneth, she had a problem getting him a soda from the refrigerator.

The loud jangle of the alarm clock plucked Sassy from her contemplative trance. She got up immediately and went back into the house. While the alarm continued its assault on her ears, she took her time locking the heavy glass sliding door.

Riiiiing!

At the same time Sassy silenced the alarm clock, she quickly answered her cell phone, which she kept in a leather pouch around her waist during the day.

"Good morning, Evelyn."

"Brice and I went to the hospital yesterday. They wouldn't let us see Bernard. He's still telling them he doesn't want to see us."

"I know."

"Sassy, my baby wants to see his father! I can't keep telling him his father is away when Brice knows that Bernard use to call him every day no matter where he was."

"I know you can't."

"Brice is seven years old, Sassy. He knows his father. He's been crying almost every night. This is hurting him!"

"I know it is, Evelyn, I'll—"

"Bernard can't just disappear from Brice's life without saying something to him. This can scar him for life. Sassy, Bernard has to explain to Brice what happened to him. I've already told Brice how sick his father is, but Brice wants to see him anyway. I'm telling you, Sassy, if Bernard doesn't let Brice see him soon, I am going to tell Brice that his father is dead!"

That tranquil feeling Sassy had only minutes before enjoyed vanished. Memories of her own mother's unexpected death and the thought of Bernard dying sobered her right up. There were ten short hours between the time she last spoke to her mother and the time she died. Like Norris, she didn't get a chance to hold her mother's hand one last time; to tell her how much she really loved her; or to say that final good-bye with a kiss on her soft sweet cheek. Evelyn was right.

"Sassy, will you talk to him again?"

"I will, Evelyn, but I think Bernie is ashamed of how he looks, and—"

"He can't look that bad, Sassy, he was always slim anyway."

"Evelyn, slim and skeletal are two complete animals."

"I don't care. Brice isn't afraid to see his father."

"Okay, fine. I will talk to Bernie—"

Another in coming call beeped in Sassy's ear. "Evelyn, I have to take this call. I'll call you later."

"What time?"

"I don't know; as soon after I talk to Bernie."

Beep. Sassy switched over.

"Hello?" Sassy said irritably.

"What's wrong?" Norris asked.

"I was just talking to Evelyn. Brice is having a hard time not seeing his father."

"I can imagine."

"I have to talk to Bernie. I'm coming into the city today."

"You stay put."

"Excuse me?" Sassy asked incredulously.

"I don't want you to come into the city alone."

Sassy told herself to stay calm. Maybe Norris didn't realize what he saying. "Norris, I have to talk to Bernard in person. I will be driving into the city today."

"Not today, Sassy, it—"

"Honey, as much as I appreciate your concern for me, I am not your prisoner."

"No you're not, but—"

"There is no but. I am coming to the city today to visit with my cousin and as well, to take care of some business. You have a good day."

Sassy firmly set her closed cell phone down on the granite counter top and let out one long frustrated scream! Just because she was in Norris's house didn't give him the power to tell her what to do.

"He can't tell me what to do! He's not my husband, but even if he was, he can't tell me what to do." Sassy started out of the kitchen.

Riiiiiiing!

Sassy looked at her cell phone, but she didn't touch it.

Riiiiiiing!

She snatched the phone. "You can't tell me what to do."

"I don't want to fight" Norris said calmly.

"Then don't. I'm heading to the city."

"I can't stop you. I'm sorry if you thought I was telling you what to do. Obviously I was wrong to say it the way I did, but I don't want you hurt."

"I know that, Norris, but—"

"I don't know who this guy is, Sassy, and until I do, I intend on making sure that you stay safe."

"Norris, I love you for that, but I can't stay sequestered away in this house for ever. I have a life."

"Baby, I know. I respect who you are and what your needs are, but if it comes down to me losing you because of some psycho, I will insist, no, I will demand . . ."

Sassy's jaw dropped.

". . .that you stay your stubborn behind up in blue mountain until I get there."

Sassy should have been outraged but oddly, she started laughing.

"I'd come and get you right now except I have a very important meeting I cannot cancel. So, as I said, I will see Bernard this evening. I will convince him to see his son."

"Oh, so you think you can convince Bernie to see his son when I haven't had any luck in weeks?"

"I can."

"And why is that?"

"I'm not you; I'm not Evelyn. I'm a new friend who has no emotional history with Bernard."

That Sassy hadn't thought about. "Okay, you might

have a point, but you still can't tell me what to do. By the way, I've been meaning to ask, how did you get Bernie to let you in to see him when he wouldn't see anyone but me?"

"I walked into his room; he thought I was a doctor."

"And once you said you weren't?"

"I told him we might as well get to know each other; I was in love with you."

"That's all?"

"That's all that's important. Besides, he said you talked about me all the time."

"Big mouth. Look, I'll give you a chance to talk to him about seeing his son. However, I might still go to the city."

"That's completely up to you, but when I see you, I'm going to put you across my knee and spank you."

Sassy smiled. "Promise?"

"Absolutely. I love you."

It wasn't the first time he said he loved her, but it was the first time he told her what she couldn't do. Wow. She started to call Norris back but remembered how busy he was. God, she was loving this man more and more every day. She could only pray that there were no surprises and that he was everything he appeared to be.

19

It was late. It was close to eleven p.m. Sassy sat curled up on a chaise lounge out on the Norris's deck with Chester snoozing on her lap. Throughout the day despite calls from her anxious agent; an impatient, heart-broken Evelyn; and a hostile Bernard, Sassy stayed focused and determined to finish her manuscript. Only after the last page was corrected and the entire manuscript E-mailed to her agent, did Sassy allow herself the luxury of going back out onto the deck where the stress of the day slowly slid off of her tense shoulders like cool syrup over the sides of a stack of hot pancakes. By then a bright full moon had risen high in the star-filled northeastern sky. The deck lanterns were not on, Sassy didn't need their light. She was beginning to enjoy sitting in the dark with only the moon lighting the night.

Far across the lake Sassy could see several houses, even those with no lights on. For about twenty minutes all was quiet until the tree frogs started making their eerie croaking sound that was so much louder than the occasional cricket she heard. Norris told her the tree frogs came out only at night—as well they should. They'd probably scare her to death if she saw them in the light of day. Besides, who knew that frogs lived up in trees or that they made so much darn noise? Still, Sassy had to admit, the frog orchestra didn't much bother her anymore. It certainly was no where near as bad as the blaring horns and sirens of New York City. She could get use to living up in the mountains of northeast Pennsylvania.

Sassy tuned out the tree frogs and idly began searching the star-filled sky for constellations she could identify. After identifying seven, she closed her eyes but a rustling sound in the thickets beneath the deck made her quickly open them. She and Chester both were as still as statues listening for any indication of the sound they thought they may have heard.

There; the soft crackle of dry brush. Sassy eased upright; Chester got up on all fours. He hunched his back. Sassy clutched Chester to her chest as she got quietly up off the chaise lounge and crept over to the railing. She couldn't look down over the railing immediately beneath her because of the screen, but she strained her eyes trying to see what she could anyway.

Again! Louder! The sound of something or someone in the bushes. Whether it was man or animal, Sassy wasn't waiting to find out. She bolted inside the house; tossed Chester to the floor; and slammed and locked the sliding deck door. The glass was supposed to be unbreakable. She prayed it was, but with no curtains or shades she had no shield to hide behind. She hurriedly reset the house alarm and made a beeline for the family room and turned on the television to drown out any noise that might filter through the glass door, but nothing she turned to interested her until she got to MSNBC and saw that Rachel Maddow was on. During the presidential campaign, Rachel Maddow and Keith Oberman single-handedly kept her glued to the television. Rachel had a wicked sense of humor but nothing she was speaking about kept Sassy from looking repeatedly at the clock on the cable box. It was 11:51 p.m. It was 5:30 p.m. when she last spoke to Norris.

"I'm running late," he said. "I'm still with a client but I'll make it out to the hospital before visiting hours are over."

Norris was off the phone before she could say, "Call me after you see Bernie."

At this hour, visiting hours were definitely over. She wanted to call Bernie but didn't want to wake him if he was sleep. Where in the world was Norris? He should have been home by now. He could—

Thump! Chester jumped off the sofa and loped away.

Sassy quickly muted the television. She sat perfectly still. She listened. Then the muffled, motorized sound of the garage door opening told her that Norris was home. She hurried to the pantry closet where the security alarm box was but waited for Norris to stick his key into the lock of the inner garage door before disarming it. She could hear the outer garage door closing, but there was no sound of the key turning inside the lock. She waited, just as Chester did near the door. A long minute passed. The wait was heart-pounding. What if it wasn't Norris?

Finally the sound of the inner garage door being unlocked allayed Sassy's fear that someone other than Norris had gotten into the garage. She disarmed the alarm. The door opened. She expected to see Norris enter but he didn't. Curious, but apprehensive, she went to the door. Norris was helping Bernard out of the back seat of his car. Bernard had pants on, but he also still had on his hospital gown.

"What happened?"

"He checked himself out," Norris said.

Sassy hurried into the garage. She slipped her arm around Bernard's horridly emaciated body. "Oh, Bernie," was all Sassy was able to say. She was inwardly repulsed by the feel of his skeletal frame against her, but she willed herself to not show it on her face. What showed on Bernard's almost unrecognizably bony face was his agony. He made a wheezing sound as he struggled to breathe.

"I can walk," Bernard said.

Chester saw what he needed to see. He walked off, not the least bit interested.

"I know you're glad to see me."

Sassy's nose immediately starting stinging. She fought against crying as she slowly climbed the two steps with Bernard into the house. Behind them, Norris locked the door.

"Let's take him up to the third bedroom down the hall," Norris said as he walked on the other side of Bernard.

At the bottom of the stairs to the second floor, Sassy said, "Wait." There had to be at least fourteen steps to climb. "Bernie, I don't think you can make it up these stairs."

"I'll carry him." Norris started to bend to pick up Bernard, but Bernard pulled back.

"I'm not that damn weak!"

"Bernie, you can't—"

"Sassy, just give me your damn arm and let's get up these damn stairs."

There was no use arguing. Sassy crooked her arm for Bernard take hold. They began their slow, steady climb.

"I'll stay behind you, just in case," Norris volunteered.

Sassy said, "We have to get some surgical masks."

"I picked up some," Norris said.

"I swear," Bernard said, "if anyone wears those things around me, I will leave."

"Bernie, they're for your protection."

"I'll leave." Bernard said. He was beginning to sound winded.

"No surgical masks," Norris said. "Do you want to rest a minute?"

Bernard didn't answer as he held tighter to Sassy. To her surprise, Bernard, although breathing heavily, walked up the stairs a lot faster than she expected. In the bedroom, he headed straight for the bed and sat.

"Bernie, you tired yourself out. That was too much."

Norris agreed. "Let's get him in bed."

Bernard held up his hand telling Sassy to wait while he caught his breath. Sassy quickly turned down the bed. She then started to unbuckle Bernard's belt. He hit her hand.

"Don't even think about it."

"I'll take care of it," Norris said. Bernard didn't resist as Norris unlaced and took off his shoes. Tears Sassy did not want to shed emptied from her anyway. She turned her back.

She couldn't watch as Norris patiently worked to take Bernard's pants off without dislodging the catheter and urine sack he still wore. All the while Bernard looked straight ahead.

"Sassy." Norris held Bernard's pants out to her. "Hang these up."

Sassy didn't move as she stared at Bernard's bony knees and legs. They looked nothing like the strong muscular legs Bernard developed over years of biking upstate New York in the Catskill Mountains.

Norris put Bernard's pants in Sassy's hand. "Sassy. Baby, hang these up." He nudged Sassy toward the closet before turning back to Bernard. He helped Bernard lay down sideways onto the high bed, and when Bernard moaned in pain, he carefully lifted Bernard's legs onto the bed.

"Sorry," Norris said as he drew the covers up over Bernard.

"I'm the one who's sorry," Bernard said.

The woefully anguished look in Bernard's eyes overwhelmed Sassy. She dropped his pants to the floor and ran from the room. Minutes later Norris found her lying on his bed crying. He sat on the bed next to her and rubbed her back until her crying waned.

"He's dying," she said. "He's really dying."

Norris pulled Sassy up and took her into his arms. For a moment they were silent.

"I don't know what to do for him," Sassy said.

"Just be here for him."

Sassy eased out of Norris's embrace. "He looks worse than he did five days ago. He should have stayed in the hospital."

"Sassy, the hospital wasn't doing him any good. You talked to him on the telephone every day. You know his disposition was getting worse. You said so yourself. He wasn't listening to anyone; he was quick to curse out the nurses, the doctors, and I know I heard him curse God."

"He's angry, Norris. Can you blame him?"

"No, but he's not helping himself by not taking his medications and speaking badly to those who have to take care of him."

Sassy knew Norris was right, but still, "You should have called me. Why didn't you call me or take my calls?"

"Because it would have been a waste of time. Bernard said he'd jump out of the window and die on the sidewalk before he left this earth in a hospital bed. And I tell you, he was so determined to leave the hospital, he was trying to wheel himself out in a wheelchair. I don't know where he got the strength. The nurses and doctors couldn't do anything with him. He told them if they didn't let him go, he'd throw himself down the stairs."

Sassy knew well how determined Bernard was when he wanted something. "I wish he was equally resolute about wanting to live."

"Well, he isn't. The doctor on duty threw up his hands. He wrote several prescriptions, and ordered the nurse to have Bernard sign a waiver. Now he's here."

"Why didn't you take him to my apartment?"

"He wanted to be with you and that's here."

"Are you sure it's okay?"

"Do you really need to ask?"

The loving look in Norris's eyes said she didn't. "Thank you." She kissed him lightly on the lips. "I'll get his prescriptions filled tomorrow."

"They're already filled. I went to that all-night pharmacy on 5th Avenue in Park Slope. It took a while but they had everything."

"You didn't have to do that. I have his prescription card. Give me the receipt, I'll—"

"It's not up for discussion. The medication and a portable oxygen tank are out in my car." Norris started to stand but Sassy held onto him as if she feared letting him out of her sight.

"You are so amazing."

"You finally noticed."

"I'm serious. You barely know Bernie, yet you took care of him as if you'd known all your life. How do you do it?"

Norris said simply, "My mother. My mother taught me to not turn my back on any man in need. My father taught me the meaning of 'there but by the grace of God go I'. Ultimately, we all hope someone will do right by us in our time of need."

"I will always do right by you." This time Sassy kissed Norris passionately, appreciatively, and sincerely. Norris returned Sassy's kiss just as fervently and although words were unsaid, for every day he spent with Sassy, he knew he was truly falling in love with her.

Two rooms away Bernard's hacking dry cough broke the spell of their kiss.

"I'll get his medications and oxygen tank," Norris said.

Together they set about preparing to take care of Bernard. From Norris she took Bernard's medication and quickly shooed him away as he had already done so much and had to get back to the city in less than six hours. Once Bernard was set up with all that he needed, he fell into a deep sleep and was unaware that Sassy was standing over him quietly praying that if God had a spare miracle, she hoped he'd send it Bernard's way.

20

Seventy-two hours later Sassy lay wide awake. At 2:30 in the morning she couldn't get back to sleep for worrying. Her mind was tired, her body was tired, yet every time she dropped off to deep sleep she was awakened by Bernard. Last night if she got more than twenty straight minutes of sleep, she didn't know a thing about it. If Bernard wasn't coughing, wheezing, or moaning, he was feebly calling out, "Nurse." Weak and exhausted, in his confusion Bernard seemed to have forgotten where he was and when he saw Sassy the third time she went in to check on him, he was genuinely surprised to see her. It was a wonder that Bernard could rest at all, he had no intravenous drip to keep him hydrated and no morphine to quiet the constant pain that tortured him from within. The substitutes the doctor prescribed were too weak and didn't last very long. Frequently, Bernard needed water or ice and didn't have the strength to get it for himself. As hard as she tried, not a thing Sassy did gave him relief. Yet Bernard refused to go back to the hospital and she got tired of arguing with him.

On this, the third night, Sassy worried about Norris. Every time he heard her stir or get up out of bed, he'd awaken.

Half asleep, he'd say, "I'll go."

Each time she'd softly shush him, "Go back to sleep," and often he did.

Just as Sassy began to get that drowsy, about to black out feeling, she heard Bernard moan. She waited. He moaned again, this time longer. It was 2:37 a.m. It was the fifth time tonight she had to slip out of bed. She'd be lying if she said she wasn't terribly annoyed—she wanted desperately to sleep; but the minute she set tired eyes on Bernard, she counted her blessings and wished to God that lack of sleep could be the very least of Bernard's worries.

Bernard touched his throat to indicate to Sassy that his throat was dry. She removed his oxygen mask; propped his pillows higher and held the bottle of water from which he sipped through a straw she held to his dry, chapped lips. Bernard drank less than a quarter of cup of water and could drink no more. Sassy went to put his oxygen mask back on, Bernard shook his head no. She let him have his way. She turned to leave but before she could take one step toward the door, Bernard groaned again. She stopped. What was the use of going back to bed when she'd only have to get up again?

From the linen closet in the hallway Sassy took down a blanket. She went back into Bernard's room and sat in the large stuffed chair near the window with her bare feet tucked under her body. She wrapped herself up in the blanket; and with only the light from the hall casting a ray of light across Bernard's morbidly thin face, she stared at him. Bernard was wasting away right before her eyes and there was nothing she could do about it. It pained her to know that Bernard would never see his son become a man, or see the grandchildren his son might one day give him. It was so much to lose because of one night of unbridled sex with a selfish woman who had to know she was HIV positive. Damn her!

Bernard said softly, "Cremate me."

"Try to get some sleep."

"Promise."

The last thing she wanted to talk about was burning him up. "Fine. Now put the oxygen mask back on."

"If I have anything left, take care of Brice."

"Bernie, that's your job. In fact, you need to see—"

"Stop!" Bernard brought his hand to his forehead. "Stop."

Because of the lateness of the hour, Sassy didn't push. Neither one of them wanted to talk about what bothered them most. God knows she did not want to talk about burning Bernard up. Back when they were teenagers, when they were both healthy and strong, it was so easy to talk about cremation because death and dying was such an intangible. Now that death was inevitable for Bernard, the reality of it all was too painful.

Wrapped still in the blanket, Sassy went and sat on the side of the bed within arm's length of Bernard's face. She gently placed the oxygen mask back over his nose and mouth, but again he removed it.

"Come on, Bernie."

"Promise me."

Sassy turned on the lamp. "Bernie, remember when Mommy died?"

"Of course I do."

"Well, do you remember how I didn't want to go to her funeral because if I went I'd have to face the reality of her death?"

Bernard put the oxygen mask back on himself. He then looked at Sassy as if to say, "and?"

"Do you remember telling me if I didn't go, if I didn't say that final goodbye, I'd always be looking for my mother to walk through the door?"

Bernard laid his hand on Sassy's hand and it struck her how cold and bony his hand was.

"Bernie, your illness has put me back in the same place." Sassy began tearing. "In all my life, no one has ever been a closer friend to me than you. Since our mothers died, we haven't dealt with the rest of our crazy family, what little there is. It really has been you and me. Bernie, I'm not dealing too well with the reality of losing you. I want you to go back to the hospital. I need you to fight for your life."

"Can't."

"Just like that, you can't?"

"Don't want to."

Sassy exhaled a gush of air. "You're not being fair, Bernie. I'm not ready to say goodbye. I still want to see you walk through the door; I still want to hear your voice; I still want to laugh at your stupid jokes. You wanna talk about your death; I don't." Sassy wiped at her cheek.

Bernard removed his oxygen mask. "You've always been my best friend, but you're really my sister. I love you, Sassy."

Sassy gently held Bernard's frail hand to her cheek while she cried the saddest tears she'd ever cried beyond the tears she cried for her mother.

"Be careful," Bernard said, "you might catch something from me."

"Oh, Bernie," Sassy said as she lowered his hand. "If I caught anything from you, I caught it years ago and I plan on treasuring it the rest of my life."

Although he could not shed a tear, Bernard cried as well. What Sassy didn't know was that her crying awakened Norris. For a minute he stood in the doorway watching them and feeling their pain. He then entered the room and sat on the bed close up behind Sassy.

"Is this a private party?"

"It's a pity party," Sassy said. "It's open to the public."

"Norris, shouldn't there be a law against pretty girls crying ugly?" Bernard asked.

"Thanks a lot." Sassy wiped at her eyes with the back of her hand.

Norris got up and pulled the chair Sassy had sat in earlier closer to the bed and sat in it himself. He looked at Sassy. "She's pretty even when she cries."

"Bless you my child," Sassy said although she didn't feel like joking.

"Spoken like a man in love," Bernard said."

"Okay," Sassy said. "Let's not—"

"I am in love with her, but she already knows that."

Norris sat back.

Sassy was a mite embarrassed. "Can we not talk about me like I'm not here?"

"Do you love her enough to marry her?"

"Bernie!" Sassy flung the blanket off of her shoulders and quickly stood. "Stop it!"

Bernard frowned. "Don't shout."

"Then don't you start any mess. Norris, ignore him."

Norris was amused. "Actually, Sassy, I do love you enough to marry you, which you already know."

Yes, she did know; they'd talked casually about marriage a number of times.

"Norris, I love you, too, but—"

"I don't have time for buts," Bernard said. "You either love the man enough to marry him or you don't."

No one could get under Sassy's skin and irritate her like Bernard. "Bernie, this is something we have to discuss at 3:00 in the morning."

"It is if there is a possibility that I might die before 9:00 in the morning."

"Dammit, Bernie, stop it! I am not going to let you manipulate me or Norris into making a commitment neither one of us is prepared to make. So cut it out!"

If Bernard was bothered by her rebuke, Sassy saw no signs of it. Bernard took his time filling his lungs with oxygen. Norris, on the other hand, was looking at her like he was waiting for her to deliver the punch line to some joke she'd just flubbed which irked the crap out of her.

"Why are you looking at me like that?" Sassy asked.

"Because I'm wondering why you've chosen to speak for me."

"But I—"

"Sassy, how do you know that I'm not prepared to make a commitment to you?"

"Well, I assume—"

"Your assumption is wrong," Norris said. "I am

prepared."

"Can you marry her before I die?" Bernard chimed in.

Sassy fell into stunned silence. This discussion didn't seem off-the-cuff. Bernard and Norris had talked, but as far as she was concerned, they were both out of their damn minds.

"I'm going back to bed." Sassy headed for the door.

"You're a coward!" Bernard said. "You're a punk.

Sassy turned back.

"Leave her alone," Norris said.

"No! She's scared out of her damn mind to live the life she writes about. She's a coward."

"You're pushing me, Bernard."

"Not hard enough, Sassafina!"

Sassy visibly shuttered. She detested the name her grandmother gave her and Bernard knew well how much. She was seventeen when her grandmother died; two weeks later, with her mother's blessing, she legally changed her name to Sassy which she revealed to Norris since he promised to never let that name roll off of his tongue. Maybe he didn't say the name but he was getting a good snicker at her expense which was Bernard's fault.

"Let me tell you something, Bernard! You are a—"

"Okay!" Norris jumped up between Sassy and Bernard. "Look, we're all tired. Let's—"

"She's a phony!" Bernard refused to let up.

"You're a manipulator!"

Norris stepped back out of the line of fire!

"Sassy, you write romance. You create romantic situations for your heroines all the time but you're too scared to live a life of romance yourself."

"Dah! That's because I write fantasy, Bernard! My God! Catch a clue. My stories are not my reality."

"They could be. Sassy, Norris loves you. He can give you the romance you write about."

"Bernie, stop this! Why are you riding me like this?"

"Before I die I'd like to know you're with someone

who really loves you."

Bernard's sentiment took the fight out of Sassy. She looked at Norris but it was obvious he in agreement with Bernard. "Okay, let me say this," she said. "I do love you, Norris, but marriage is a huge leap I think should be taken incrementally over time in small steps."

"Translation," Bernard said. "She's scared."

Norris was too tired to go another round. "This is where I take my leave."

"No!" Bernard said. "You have to stay."

"Bernie, he has to get up in less than an hour."

"He's lucky. In a little while, I won't ever to able to get up again."

There was no question what Bernard meant. "Bernie, you can't keep manipulating us."

"You'll thank me one day."

"I'll just take a seat." Norris sat and looking at Sassy, he pat his lap. "You wanna join me?"

Sassy huffed. She rolled her eyes at Bernard but she sat on Norris's lap.

"Thank you," Bernard said. "Now let's get down to business."

21

Not for one minute did Sassy like that Norris was so willing to appease Bernard when Bernard was obviously trying to control them; or if she should be grateful that Norris was so understanding of Bernard and his illness. Not many men would be. As tired as Norris was, if he was willing to sit and hear Bernard out, then she could try a little harder to tolerate him herself.

"Sassy, you once told me you wrote romance because it made you feel good."

"Big revelation, Bernie, fantasies makes everyone feel good, but we don't all get lost in them."

"For once in your life, maybe it's time you did."

"Are you listening to this?" Sassy asked Norris who had begun to nod out. "Are we supposed to stay up for this? Bernie, I don't think so. I've had enough." She started to get up but Norris held her down. The truth was, Norris was feeling pretty tortured himself but he was curious.

"Let's hear him out."

"What for? Norris, we haven't known each other long enough for either one of us to stand in the bathroom brushing our teeth while the other sits on the toilet reading a magazine."

Norris was so tired, he couldn't laugh. "Is that your benchmark for a strong, long lasting marriage?"

"It's one of them. Isn't it yours?"

"Not really. A second bathroom eliminates that problem; besides, we've been practically living together for months and I think I can handle being in the house when you're in the bathroom."

Bernard chuckled behind his oxygen mask which heightened Sassy's irritation.

"Norris, you don't get it!"

Bernard took off his oxygen mask. "That's because no one goes to the bathroom in your books except to take a bath or to screw in the bathtub or shower."

Sassy pushed herself up off of Norris. "Bernie, what is wrong with you!"

"I'm disgusted with you; I'm tired of your excuses. Norris, this isn't about the bathroom. Sassy is just plain old scared to get married—period.."

"That's not true!"

"Hey!" Norris said, "I have a solution. Let's not get married."

Sassy could see that Norris was hurt, but she couldn't believe he seriously wanted to get married. "Norris—"

"Sassy, I don't want you marrying me when you're being pressured, or feel like you've been manipulated, or if you just don't want to. Yes, I love you and to be honest, I'd marry you in a heartbeat but if that's not what you want, I understand."

Sassy was speechless. With both Norris and Bernard looking at her, she felt like a deer caught in the headlights. She shook her head and left the room but she heard Norris say, "I need to go to her." She went back to their bedroom and threw herself into the bed. Here it was 3:42 in the morning and she was as ticked off as if she had been tailgated by an aggressive New York City cab driver. Bernard was that aggressive driver and she wanted so badly to backup hard and ram him off the damn street. How could he embarrass her and put her on the spot like that. Yes, she loved Norris, but marriage? So soon? Honestly, she couldn't hate Bernard for caring about her, but he didn't have to make her sound like a desperate old maid who needed to be set up. And Norris, why was he so willing to go along with Bernard? In fact, was he still in there?

Sassy threw the covers back and hustled back to Bernard's room just as Bernard was saying, "...she has always been fiercely independent."

"Since when is being independent a sin? I believe strongly that God blesses the woman who can stand on her own two feet without leaning herself up against some man, which is what I've been doing staying here in this house."

"Oh, no," Bernard said. "Now she's preaching."

"Bernie—"

"Sassy, you're here with me but you haven't been doing much leaning up against me. You're holding your own, but if you have to lean up against me, by all means do so with the knowledge that you won't lose an ounce of who you are."

"How magnanimous of you."

"It is, isn't it?" Norris smiled to show Sassy that he wasn't offended although she was.

"Finally," Bernard said. "A man you can't intimidate."

"Damn, Bernie, if I were dying to marry Norris. . ."

Norris laughed to himself.

". . .you would have ruined it for me."

"You're doing that all by yourself," Bernard said.

"Bernie, I don't know what else to say to you. Maybe you haven't noticed; I already like Norris. I practically live with him. You can stop trying to push me off on him."

"Do you love me?"

"Yeah, do you love him?"

"Geez! I already said I did! What do you guys want from me?" Sassy was at her breaking point.

"Well," Bernard began, "if you decide to marry Norris in six months or twelve months or even in three days, I won't be here to walk you down the aisle like I promised." Bernard held his oxygen mask to his nose more to hide behind than to breathe through. He was overwhelmed with emotions.

In that moment Sassy understood. She had walked right smack dab into that one. She had stood up for Bernard that long ago weekend when he married Kayla Greene in a ceremony that almost didn't happen. Despite the fact that she and Kayla never became the best of friends because Kayla didn't like that she and Bernard were so close, Bernard asked Kayla to include her in her bridal party. Kayla said, "Hell no." Bernard stood his ground and argued there would be no wedding unless Sassy was included, but Sassy didn't want to be a bride's maid for someone who didn't want her. With so much money spent on the wedding, Kayla kept her mouth shut when Sassy showed up at the church wearing a fabulous black tuxedo and stood up for Bernard as his best man. Kayla absolutely hated her for that and tried to exclude her as much as she could from their lives.

Bernard removed his mask. "We promised our mothers we'd always look out for each other."

Sassy turned to Norris who was half asleep. She tapped him. "He's good, isn't he?"

Norris really didn't know or care. He barely raised a brow as he slumped further down in the chair. Sassy couldn't blame him.

"Bernie, it's late. I tell you what. Norris and I will think about getting married if you think seriously about seeing your son. And by the way, you might want to think about trying to live for him." Sassy could tell by the pain etched on Bernard's face that he didn't like her conditional offer. She waited while he took his time breathing in more oxygen.

"If you took your medicine the way you're supposed to, you'd be breathing a lot easier."

"Maybe I don't want to breathe a lot easier. Even if I lived, I have a death sentence that will never go away."

"But you owe Brice the opportunity to be with you no matter your quality of life."

"Sassy, I suffer no illusion. I'm dying."

"Because you've given up."

"Dammit, I'm dying because I have AIDS! Look at me! You think I haven't noticed that you only look me in the eye because you don't want to see what the rest of my body look like? Just look at me." Bernard snatched his pajama shirt open and exposed his skeletal chest. He didn't concern himself with the buttons that popped off.

Although Sassy had already seen Bernard's emaciated body she had no desire to see it now. She looked him dead in the eye but the anguish she saw there was too much to bear. She welled up. She had to look away.

"Look at me!" Bernard shouted.

The loud noise awakened Norris. Through bleary eyes he quickly determined that nothing had changed. He fell off to sleep again.

Looking at Bernard, tears slipped down Sassy's cheeks. "Close your shirt."

Bernard defiantly opened his shirt wider. "If you think taking medicine will miraculous restore my body to its former physique, you're mistaken. Sassy, this isn't living, this is dying. I refuse to keep forestalling the inevitable. I don't want any more medicine, no more doctors, no more hospitals, and I'm sure as hell tired of you changing my damn diaper! I will not have my son see me like this!"

No matter how much she wiped, Sassy couldn't stop her tears from flowing. It was hard for her to be Bernard's caretaker, but it was drastically harder for him having her change his diaper and wipe his behind Every time she did, Bernard closed his eyes and shut her out completely. Often after she left the room and would hear his crying.

"Sassy, you are the only person who has ever loved me unconditionally. You didn't turn me away when I told you I had AIDS. Evelyn did and took my son with her." Bernard inhaled deeply from the oxygen mask.

"But she forgave you, Bernie. You can't keep her away because for a minute she was confused and hurt."

Norris woke up. Groggily, he listened

"She's still hurt and it's because of me. I hurt my son, too. I can't see them without seeing how much I hurt them."

"But, Bernie, they're hurting more now because they

can't see you. You have to—"

"No."

"Bernie, you have to—"

"No! No! No!" Bernard rolled his head from side to side. He then sucked more oxygen into his lungs.

Norris sat up. "I have never met two more stubborn people in my life."

Sassy's tears began to ebb. "It's him. He's always been that way."

"Sassy, I get what Bernard is trying to do."

"I do too, but—"

"No you don't," Bernard said.

"Sassy, this isn't about whether or not you can take care of yourself, and it's not about me being the man you should marry because I can 'so-called' take care of you. It's also not about him trying to manipulate you; or force you to do something you don't want to do. We've danced lightly around the subject so it's not foreign to us. This is about you being with someone who loves you, and that would be me."

"Hallelujah," Bernard said, relieved. He took his time inhaling from his oxygen mask.

"Okay, so I'm in love with you as well, Norris, but the problem I have is, you're letting him push us into getting married within the next forty-eight hours when we've known each other less than six months."

"You can't be worried about that," Bernard said. "Our grandparents got married three weeks after they met, and they were married for nineteen years. Only death ended their marriage."

Sassy could see her one argument vanishing. "Bernie, it's not the length of time one knows a person, it's the sum total of who they are together."

Norris asked Sassy, "Do you like who we are together?"

There was no use lying. "Yes, I do."

Norris took Sassy's hand. "Then, what does length of

time matter? Let's get married."

Unexpectedly, Sassy started yawning and couldn't stop herself. She fell against Norris. "I'm so sorry!" She yawned again and this time so did Norris. Their infectious yawning didn't affect Bernard. If anything, it irritated him to watch them yawning and laughing as they tried to kiss but couldn't because they couldn't keep their mouths closed together long enough.

"Okay, Okay!" Bernard said, irritably. "Can you get married tomorrow?"

Sassy instantly stopped yawning. "Tomorrow? Bernie, I haven't even said yes yet."

"It is yes, isn't it?" Norris asked.

Sassy started to answer—

"It's yes," Bernard said, "and it's tomorrow."

"Here we go," Sassy said. "Bernie, it is impossible for Norris and me to get married tomorrow. I have to—"

"Sassy, a big wedding with a ten tier cake takes time to arrange. Time isn't what I have. You have to get married tomorrow."

"Tomorrow is impossible!"

"Get the hell out of my room!"

"Hey! You've gotten what you've strong-armed and badgered me for for the past two and a half hours. Norris lost sleep while bending over backwards trying to pacify your cantankerous behind. You better be glad Norris is here because I've lost all patience with you. So dammit, be nice!"

Bernard took a last full drag of oxygen. "I don't have time to be nice," he said flatly. "The hell with both of you."

"No you didn't! Bernie!"

"I have to get ready for work," Norris said.

"All you two can say is tomorrow is impossible. At least you have tomorrow and a bucket load of tomorrows after that. I can probably pinpoint the day down to the hour and second that I will die, and you know what's disgustingly terrible about it, I can't wait for that second to come."

Norris stopped at the door. Until he met Sassy, he had

never lived in the moment. He had stepped into her book signing on a whim; on impulse, he asked her to move in with him; and likewise, he asked her marry him. As tired as he was, he was the happiest he'd been in years.

"Sassy, we can get married at City Hall in New York."

Surprised, Sassy asked, "When?"

"I'm not going back," Bernard said. "It has to be here."

Sassy held her achy head. "Oh, God. Bernie, I—"

"I'm not going back to New York."

"Okay," Norris said. "We have to find out what the waiting period is here in Pennsylvania. In New York I know it's twenty-four hours."

"Get the license in New York today, get married here tomorrow," Bernard said.

"I'll see what I can do," Norris said, "but I can't promise it'll be tomorrow."

"Bernie, you're not being reasonable!"

"I don't have to be reasonable; I don't have to be nice; and I don't have to worry about you being mad at me. When I leave this room, I'll be leaving feet first with no knowledge of whether my bare ass is exposed or not." Bernard put the oxygen mask back on. He closed his eyes.

"Bernie—"

"We'll talk." Norris started to pull Sassy toward the door, but she had more to say.

"Bernie, you've been calling all the shots, now I'm calling one. If Norris and I get married tomorrow, Evelyn and Brice have to be here, and you have to talk to both of them."

Bernard didn't open his eyes.

"Do you hear me, Bernie? You have to see your son. You owe him his goodbye." The minute Sassy said the word goodbye; she realized she had accepted the inevitable.

Still, Bernard didn't open his eyes.

Norris firmly pulled Sassy outside of the room. "It's up to him. Right now, I have to get ready for work."

"Norris, you can't drive to the city. You're exhausted."

"I'll be fine. Besides, I have to stop by my father's on the way to work."

"Why so early?"

"Let's talk while I get ready." Norris glanced in at Bernard who seemed to be asleep. "He should sleep all day."

"I'll see them," Bernard said.

Both Sassy and Norris looked at Bernard. His eyes were still closed. He had begun to sink into a deep comatose-like sleep. He welcomed it.

22

With a little more than half of his day over, Norris felt like he could fall asleep on the backs of ten porcupines and not feel a single quill prick. He was bone tired. He had one more meeting before he could call it a day and leave the office. Every spare moment he could grab, he called Sassy just to hear her voice, to see how she was doing, to see if caring for Bernard was overwhelming her. It was.

"Bernard needs to be hydrated at the hospital, but his stubborn behind won't go. He's outright killing himself."

"I know," Norris yawned.

"Norris, how are you holding up?"

"As long as I keep busy and don't think about how tired I am, I'm fine."

"I'm so sorry."

"Don't be. We're in this together."

"Oh, honey, thank you. How is your father and Alicia?"

"They're both well."

"Did you tell them what we were planning to do?"

"I told them."

Thinking Norris would say more, Sassy waited. "And? What did your father say?"

"He thinks we're moving too fast, but in the end, he's fine with whatever decision I make."

Sassy groaned. "Norris, are you sure about this?"

"I'm sure."

"But your father didn't give us a ringing endorsement."

"Do we need one?"

"Well, I guess not." She would have preferred Mr. Wilson's approval since he was so important in Norris's life, but life goes on.

"Will you still be able to make it to Brooklyn to meet up with Evelyn?"

"I'm planning to leave here by 2:30. I should meet up with her at 3:15 in front of the Municipal Building."

"I'm keeping my fingers crossed."

"Pray," Norris said. He didn't know how Evelyn was going to pull it off, but Sassy swore that Evelyn could pass for her. He couldn't imagine, although Sassy's own driver's license photo did her little justice and didn't look much as she did in person. Sassy's dreadlocks were at least six inches longer since the photograph was taken three years ago. Now they touched her shoulders and framed her beautiful face like an exquisite portrait. He had been in Evelyn's company a handful of times and no way, no how did he see any resemblance to Sassy. For the life of him, he didn't see how Evelyn was going to be able to fool anyone, but Sassy assured him Evelyn knew what to do. He certainly hoped so. Seeing the inside of a jail for fraud or any reason was not on his 'things to do' list. He'd be lying if he said he wasn't nervous about perpetrating a fraud, but he had no choice since Sassy wouldn't leave Bernard's side for fear that he'd die while she was in New York. They couldn't get the license to marry in Pennsylvania; the wait was too long—three days. In New York, it was only one.

Buzzzz!

Norris pressed the intercom button. "Yes, Kimberly," he said to his new secretary.

"Mr. Yoshito, a Detective Kiefer and a Detective Lupino are here to see you."

Norris looked questioningly at the telephone. He had been kept apprised of Myra's condition by his office manager; and he and his partner had opted to keep Myra on payroll to keep her medical insurance active. Why would the detectives be back to see him?

"Tell them I have only a few minutes to spare. Send them in."

Norris stood behind his desk as the detectives were shown into his office. "Gentlemen, I have only a few minutes."

"Mr. Yoshito, that's all we need," Frank Keifer said. He shook Norris's hand only because Norris extended it, but it repulsed him to shake the hand of a man he suspected of being a killer.

"Have a seat." Norris sat along with the detectives. "How can I help you?"

"Mr. Yoshito," Frank said. "We have information that strongly suggests you were seeing your secretary, Myra Barrett, outside of the office."

Norris sat back. "Your information is incorrect."

"When was the last time you were with the victim in her apartment?"

"Detective, your information is incorrect. Myra Barrett is my secretary. We had no relationship outside of this office."

"Mr. Yoshito," Joe said, "Are you willing to submit a sample of your blood for DNA testing?"

While Norris didn't bat an eye, a strong feeling of apprehension surged through his veins. He buzzed his secretary.

"Yes?" Kimberly asked.

"Get attorney Edwin Patterson on the line."

"Right away."

"Why do you need a lawyer?" Joe Lupino asked.

"Why are you asking questions that strongly suggest that a lawyer might be warranted?"

"Mr. Yoshito," Frank said, "we are investigating any and all possible leads to solve this case. Is there a reason why you might be concerned about being charged?"

Norris calmly interlocked his fingers on top of his desk. "Detective, the fact that you're intimating I had a personal relationship, which I did not, with my secretary who is barely out of a coma after almost being killed, as her roommate was, then I would be an idiot to not be concerned."

"Perhaps, but—"

Buzzzz!

Norris pressed the intercom button. "Yes?"

"Mr. Patterson is in court. His assistant will have him call you as soon as he's available."

Norris clicked off his intercom. He stood. "Gentlemen, if you're citing me for jaywalking or for spitting in the subway, please do so. If you need to speak with me regarding a murder or attempted murder, please do so in the presence of my attorney who is obviously not in attendance. Now, if you'll excuse me—"

"Karen Markowitz," Frank quickly said. "How well did you know Karen Markowitz?"

Norris could feel a rush of blood spurt from his heart. The face of the pretty young blond flashed before his eyes.

Frank couldn't read the look on Norris's face and hoped Norris didn't catch on that they were casting a line without real bait. Beyond finding his business card in the dead woman's apartment; a connection with a woman who happened to be his secretary; and an old shoeshine man's statement that he saw an Asian looking man with Karen Markowitz, as yet, they had nothing solid to charge him with.

"Karen Markowitz, Mr. Yoshito. How well—"

"I met Karen only once two years ago. I attended a dinner at her parents' home which I designed and built."

This was not news to Frank. They'd already gotten that information from the victim's parents, but what parents ever knows everything about their child?

"Mr. Yoshito, have you ever been inside Karen Markowitz's apartment?"

That feeling of dread within Norris intensified. This wasn't about him. This was about the bastard whom he couldn't talk about until he knew exactly who he was.

"I have not."

"Were you intimately involved with the victim?"

Norris leveled a *I can't believe you asked me that stupid ass question* look on Detective Keifer. Didn't he know this wasn't about him? This was about the lowlife who dared to insinuate himself into his business and personal life and was now trying to set him up for two murders.

"Detective, this meeting is over." Norris moved to the side of his desk.

Both detectives stood.

Buzzzz!

Norris answered his intercom, "Yes?"

"Mr. George Jeroski is here for his appointment."

"One minute; send him in." To the detectives he said, "I was never intimately involved with Karen Markowitz or Myra Barrett. I suggest you look elsewhere for your murderer. Now if—"

"Mr. Yoshito, what size shoe do you wear?"

Norris shot Joe a hateful glare. "We're done."

"Mr. Yoshito," Frank said, "Myra Barrett was almost killed. Carrie Kane and Karen Markowitz were killed. Would you say it's a strange coincidence that these victims share a connection to you?"

"If you believe in six degrees of separation, then it's no coincidence." Norris went directly to the door and opened it. He purposely squared his shoulders and held his head high in the hope that his angst didn't show in his face or in his demeanor.

Joe held a business card out to Norris. "Have your lawyer call us."

Norris took the card. He didn't have a second to gather his thoughts or calm his anxiety as his client and the detectives passed right in front of him. He needed to call Cyrus, but that would have to wait.

"Mr. Jeroski," Norris said as he shook his client's hand, "I see you have your blueprints."

"Yes. My wife couldn't make it but she has enough sticky notes on the blueprints to make her presence felt."

"That's perfectly fine."

Norris spread the blueprints out on his oversized drafting table. Although he tried, he could not fully focus on the plans before him. It was bad enough when his credit identity had been stolen, but the possibility of being erroneously charged with murder was gnawing at him. If it was the same guy who'd stolen from him, he needed to find him fast. Why this guy chose him as his target was unfathomable.

Buzzzz!

"Excuse me." Norris pressed the intercom on the telephone on his drafting table. "Yes, Kimberly."

"Mr. Patterson is on one."

"I'll take it in the conference room. And see if you can reach Cyrus Woodale."

"Yes, sir."

"Mr. Jeroski," Norris said, "if you will excuse me, I have to take this call. I'll be right back."

Norris hurried to the privacy of his conference room. He had to legally arm and protect himself and at the same time, find and disarm the guy who seemed hell bent on snatching his life from him.

23

Despite the lateness of the hour, The City Clerk's office in Brooklyn was still teeming with eager brides to be and quite a number of laid back grooms perhaps not as eager. The few who fidgeted most likely wished they were elsewhere, but Norris couldn't say that was his reason for feeling restless. He had no fear of marrying Sassy. In fact, he looked forward to sharing his life with her. No, the reasons for his angst were two-fold. He couldn't stop thinking about the detectives who showed up in his office and all but accused him of killing Karen Markowitz, assaulting his secretary, and of killing her roommate. Although his attorney said he had nothing to worry about, Norris felt he did. Someone out there was hell bent on destroying him and he didn't have a clue as to why. If he had made an enemy, he couldn't recall who, where or when. In his business, he never had to meet with or do business with his competitors, so it didn't surprise him that Cyrus had come up empty after checking out all of his business associates and clients who had nothing but praise for his work. So who?

Evelyn tugged at Norris's arm.

Norris snapped out of his intensive pondering and saw that the couples ahead of him and Evelyn had moved up. He quickly moved up as well.

"Sorry, I have a lot on my mind."

"Apparently." Evelyn put on her reading glasses. She whispered, "How's this?"

Norris studied Evelyn's face with her glasses on. He

still saw no resemblance to Sassy with or without the reading glasses; and he didn't see how Evelyn was going to fool the clerk. Admittedly, Evelyn was about the same size and height as Sassy, but in the face, Evelyn looked nothing like Sassy. Evelyn's skin color was lighter, her eyes were smaller, her lips thinner, and her hair was straight which is why she was wearing a black dreadlock wig.

Maybe it was because Evelyn was standing on line in front of Norris and he was looking down on top of her head, but it was quite obvious to him that Evelyn's dreadlocks were not growing out of her scalp. In fact, he couldn't see Evelyn's scalp at all through the thick black dreadlocks covering her head. Until he met Sassy, he had never been out with a woman who wore dreadlocks; not that dreadlocks were a deterrent. In fact, he thought most women who wore dreadlocks intriguingly exotic. He loved Sassy's dreadlocks and often found himself touching them. On the occasion that she sat and re-twisted her dreadlocks, he loved watching her. It was a turn-on and often when she was done, they made love.

Making love isn't what he felt like doing with Evelyn. The only thing her fake dreadlocks did was miraculously somehow change the look of her face. The front of the wig swept across Evelyn's forehead over her left eye, so unlike how Sassy wore her own dreadlocks, which were usually pulled back off of her face. Of course Evelyn was covering up as much of her face as allowable to hopefully fool the beholder of her face and Sassy's driver's license.

"Next."

"Oh God." Evelyn was suddenly nervous.

Norris took Evelyn's hand. He squeezed it.

"Good afternoon," Norris said to the fifty-something strawberry blond female clerk.

The clerk did not respond in kind. She glanced at her wrist watch but did not look up at Norris or Evelyn, and barely moved her hand to accept the marriage license application Norris slid across the counter to her. Any other time, the bored look on the clerk's flushed face might have irritated Norris, not this time. He welcomed her indifference. He was glad she wasn't giving him or Evelyn much eye contact. Still, they both waited with bated breath while the clerk first reviewed the application and then began typing the information into the computer. Unlike Norris who barely twitched a muscle, Evelyn shifted from foot to foot.

"Birth certificates, passports, drivers' licenses," the clerk said flatly.

Norris slid his birth passport and driver's license across the counter to the clerk, while Evelyn, with her hand flat on top of Sassy's birth certificate and driver's license, timidly slid them to the center of the counter. Evelyn didn't pull her hand back. Norris gently took her hand and drew it to his lips, and while she stared up at him, he kissed the back of her hand.

"You're definitely a keeper," Evelyn said as the clerk picked up Sassy's birth certificate and driver's license. Evelyn kept her profile to the clerk. Out of the corner of her eye, she saw the clerk enter Sassy's information into the computer."

"What the hell do you mean, you changed your mind?" A woman suddenly said aloud.

"I said, let's talk about it outside."

Like everyone else in the City Clerk's office, Norris and Evelyn looked at the young African American woman trying to keep her man, who was at least two decades older than her, from walking out on her which he did anyway.

Evelyn said in a low voice to Norris, "That's embarrassing," but Norris's focus was back on the clerk as she retrieved his marriage license from her printer.

The clerk gave Sassy's and Norris's documents back to them. "Are there any reasons why you cannot be legally wed?"

"No," Norris answered for himself and Evelyn. He couldn't believe how lax the clerk was. The scrutiny he half expected didn't happen.

"Please check to make sure all the information is correct," the clerk said.

Norris and Evelyn both reviewed the marriage license. "It's correct," Norris said.

"Sign here." The clerk pointed to the signature line.

"Sassy, you sign first," Norris said more as a reminder to Evelyn what name she was supposed to be signing. Evelyn signed Sassy's full name just as she had practiced it since early that morning.

Norris signed and the clerk handed him a booklet. "There is a mandatory twenty-four hour waiting period before your marriage ceremony can be performed. The information in this booklet will answer any questions you have pertaining to name changes and who is permitted to perform the marriage ceremony. That will be $35.00. Money order or credit card?"

Norris handed over his credit card. Minutes later with his receipt and marriage license in hand, he and Evelyn hurried out of the Clerk's Office before the clerk woke up and thought twice about how she could better do her job.

Outside on Joralemon Street with a horde of people milling about, Evelyn reached up to snatch off her wig.

"No!" Norris said. "Not in front of the Municipal Building. There are people, there are cameras."

"Oops."

"Were do we go from here?" Norris asked.

"To my apartment to pick up my son. I told my Uncle Morgan that you would send a limo for him tomorrow."

"It's already scheduled for 2:00 p.m." They started walking toward the parking lot on Livingston Street three blocks away.

"What denomination is your uncle?"

"Baptist."

"Does he know everything about Bernard?"

"He knows. He doesn't like the circumstances, but he's willing to perform the wedding because he likes Sassy. He used to like Bernard."

"He doesn't anymore?"

"He was very angry with Bernard when he first got

AIDS, but then he said only God was pure enough to judge man. Personally, I think he feels Bernard is getting his punishment here on earth, especially since he's dying of AIDS."

"That's one man's opinion. Are you going to be able to handle seeing Bernard?"

Evelyn considered the question. "I have to be strong for my son. Brice hasn't seen his father in almost six months. He may have a hard time but I've been preparing him as best I could."

Norris chivalrously held onto Evelyn's arm as they crossed busy Adams Street with quick long strides.

"Evelyn, if you don't mind me asking, why is it that you and Bernard never married?"

Briefly pensive, Evelyn said, "I'm not Sassy."

"You don't mean that."

"I mean every word. Sassy is the only woman Bernard has ever really loved. Me, his ex-wife, we're flawed, so unlike Sassy. She's perfect."

Whether it was jealousy of Sassy and Bernard's relationship or anger at Bernard for not marrying her and maybe even comparing her to Sassy, whatever the reason, it was clear to Norris that Evelyn harbored a great deal of animosity toward Sassy. He wondered if Sassy was aware of it?

"No one is quite perfect." Norris thought about how surprisingly bad a cook Sassy was. She made the worst fried chicken he had ever eaten.

"I don't think Bernard will agree with you. Do you know he has criticized every man Sassy has ever been with? Not one man was ever good enough for her to marry, except you. Aren't you the lucky one?"

Norris wasn't about to say it aloud but he did feel lucky. Just across the street he could see the valet parking lot where he left his car. "By the way, I read online if Sassy and I get married in Pennsylvania with our New York marriage license, it can't be filed in New York State. Does your uncle know this?"

"He mentioned it. He said if you and Sassy were serious and wanted to get married again in New York, he'd perform the ceremony again."

"Good."

Arriving at the parking lot, Norris handed the attendant his parking ticket. "It's a black Mercedes."

The attendant hurried off through the full parking lot. Norris glanced at his watch. It was 4:56 p.m. He calculated with traffic, by the time he drove into Crown Heights to pick up Brice and head back into Manhattan, it could be as late as 7:00 p.m. when he finally exit the city. Norris was tired and just thinking about the crawling traffic on Canal Street leading to the Holland Tunnel and the long drive afterwards exhausted him more. On a more positive note, this time tomorrow, he and Sassy will be married.

Off in the distance, Norris spotted the parking lot attendant he had given his ticket to scratching his head. The attendant looked again at the ticket he held.

"Excuse me." Norris met up with the attendant at the parking lot booth. "Is there a problem with my car?"

"Just a minute, sir."

The attendant entered the booth. He closed the door behind him and began talking with the manager. Norris could see that both men were searching the key board on the wall. As they checked every key, their discussion became more animated which made Norris's level of concern grow.

Evelyn joined Norris. "What's going on?"

"That's what I'm about to find out."

Norris opened the door just as the attendant said, "It's not here!"

"I hope you're not talking about my car."

"Sir," the manager said, "if you'll give us a minute, we'll bring your car around."

"Don't!" Norris said firmly.

"Sir?"

"Don't waste my time, and don't lie to me. Where is my car? Where are the keys to my car?"

Unsure as to what to say, the two men looked at the key board on the wall, and then at each other.

Norris took out his cell phone.

"Sir," the manager said. "The attendant who parked your car is on break. He—"

"He's back!" the attendant said. "Ralph! Hurry up!"

All eyes were on a slim, youthful looking East Indian man who hurried to them at a jog. The manager quickly pulled Ralph aside. "The black Mercedes, where is it?"

"I gave the car to him," Ralph said, pointing to Norris.

Norris snatched his ticket from the first attendant's hand and held it up. "Would I have this ticket if I had my car?"

"He gave your car to someone else?" Evelyn asked.

Ralph looked from Norris to his manager. "I. . .I gave it to him."

"Then why do I still have my ticket, and why am I standing here asking for my damn car?"

Neither man answered.

"Isn't it your practice to take the customer's ticket?"

Not one of the men was willing to admit it was their practice to collect and keep the ticket once the customer picked up his car.

Evelyn took out her cell phone. "I'll call the police."

Norris glared at Ralph. "You do that."

Tapping 911 into her cell phone, Evelyn moved away from the men.

"Sir," Ralph said. "I gave the car to you thirty minutes ago. It had Pennsylvania plates on it. You gave me a forty dollar tip because you lost the ticket."

Norris held up his ticket. "What the hell is this?"

The manager punched Ralph in the arm. "You are not supposed to release a car without a ticket!"

"He said he lost it," Ralph said.

"Thirty minutes ago I was in the City Clerk's Office. I

was not out here paying you off and stealing my own car."

Under Norris's accusatory glare and his co-workers' condemnatory stare, Ralph's confusion as to whom he gave the car to made him jittery. He began scratching the back of his hands and talking to himself. He was sure he gave the car to the man standing in front of him.

"Sue them," Evelyn said, coming back to Norris.

Norris turned on the attendant. "You gave my car to a man who didn't have this receipt. How could you just hand my car over? How could you mistake him for me?"

"I thought it was you."

"What was he wearing? Was he wearing what I'm wearing; a medium gray suit, a white shirt, a blue, gray and white tie? Can you say definitively he had on this very same suit?" Norris stretched his arms out for Ralph to get a good look at him.

Ralph's eyes flitted about as he looked Norris over.

The manager asked, "Ralph, did the man have on these same clothes?"

"I don't remember, but I thought it was him."

"Dammit, we don't all look alike!" Norris held the ticket tight in his fist. "I have the only legitimate proof that my car was parked in this lot on this date. You gave my car to a man without demanding his ticket or proof that he owned my car! You idiot!" Norris turned his back to the men. He needed to put distance between them before he punched one of them out.

"Sir, the man knew your license plate number. He had identification," Ralph said.

Norris whirled around. "It wasn't my identification! What did he have, a driver's license?"

"Yes, a driver's license."

"If he had a driver's license, then he had a name on it? What was his name?"

Ralph scratched his head. "Ah...ah. I don't remember."

"Dammit!" Norris wanted so badly to shove his fist in

the attendant's face. Instead, he stepped several paces back and shook his fist not at the attendant, but at the man who, for some godforsaken reason, wore his face and was determined to make his life a living hell. But why? In God's name, why?

"The police should be here in a minute," Evelyn said. "I told them they stole your car."

"We did not steal his car!" the manager said. "The attendant said he gave him the car. He had to have given him his ticket. No car is released without a ticket."

Norris again held up his ticket. "Do you produce duplicate tickets?"

"No, no; one ticket per car, one ticket."

Norris looked closely at the identification card pinned to the manager's white shirt. "Listen to me, Alvin Garrick. I have more important things to do than stand in this parking lot accusing employees of Edison Parking of stealing my car. All I want is my car. Get it now!"

"Norris," Evelyn said, "The police are here."

Norris noted the police car pulling into the parking lot. "Call Sassy. Tell her what happened. Then call Enterprise. See if I can pick up a rental."

Evelyn quickly checked her watch. "It's pretty late to call in for a rental. What if I can't get one?"

"Then get a limo that will take us to Pennsylvania."

"I'll see what I can do."

While the parking lot attendants and the manager huddled together, Norris went straight to the policemen getting out of their car. Whomever it was that had set his mind to destroying his life had better have a real close relationship with God, because only God was going to be able to save his miserable life.

24

Sassy entered Bernard's room carrying two whole wheat peanut butter and jelly sandwiches and two small glasses of milk on a serving tray. Bernard was drawn up in a tight fetal position on his right side. His eyes were closed. He seemed to be breathing easy without his oxygen mask; and that was because the minute he knew, in fact, that Evelyn and Brice were coming, he started taking his cocktail of medication.

From one of the open back windows facing the lake, a soft tepid breeze gently winnowed the powder blue curtains that hung there. Sassy quietly set the tray on the standing tray next to the bed. She sat in the chair next to the open window. She pulled the curtain aside and didn't mind that it fell lightly onto her back as she rested her elbows on the window's ledge and looked out over the water.

Far out on the lake, a lone man, his features indistinguishable to Sassy, slowly rowed his little boat upstream seemingly without a care in the world, so unlike herself. She should be writing but her mind wasn't on creating new characters. Bernard was dying and Norris was being stalked by someone who obviously had nothing better to do than be a pain in the ass. What did he want from Norris? Could Norris have done something to this man and not realized it? Or does he know and won't tell her?

"What are you looking at?" Bernard asked in a lowly hoarse voice.

Sassy pulled the curtain around her body to the back of

the chair. "Playing possum on me, huh?"

"No, I was just too tired to keep my eyes open."

"Big surprise. You need to eat something so I can give you your medications." Sassy got up and went to Bernard. She slipped her arm under his thin body. "Come on. Try to sit up."

It was a strain, but with three pillows behind him, Bernard was able to sit upright. "I've become what I've always dreaded."

"Keep taking your medication and you won't be an invalid."

"You're delusional. No amount of medication is going to save me."

"Bernie, you don't know that. You—"

"Sassy!"

Sassy put up her hands in surrender. She was lucky Bernard was taking any medication at all. Three steps back was what she was going to have to do but she wasn't completely giving up. She pulled the tray closer to Bernard. She picked up half of his sandwich.

"It's your favorite."

Bernard squinted at the sandwich. When he realized what it was, he lay his head back against the pillow and smiled. Often enough they had reminisced about the first year they shared their first two bedroom apartment in Brooklyn. Between the two of them they didn't make enough money to live like the successful college graduates they envisioned they were. The rent was too high and there were times when they had to count all of their loose change to come up with enough to buy something to eat. Every two weeks when they got paid no matter what else they bought, they always bought three loaves of whole wheat bread which they kept in the refrigerator; ten cans of chicken noodle soup, ten cans of tomato soup, a two-pound jar of peanut butter, and a two-pound jar of grape jelly.

"Bernie, remember how we use to go to work and pretend like we had plenty of money to spend on restaurants at lunchtime when we didn't, and then every night at home, we were eating peanut butter and jelly sandwiches with tomato soup or chicken noodle soup?"

"We were too proud to tell our folks how bad off we were."

"Yeah, but they knew. Remember how Mama always talked about how much weight I was losing? She knew I wasn't dieting." Sassy laughed. "She knew I was starving."

Bernard started to laugh but his laugh quickly turned into a woeful little cry. Sassy put the sandwich down. She sat on the bed and pulled Bernard close to heart. She held him while he cried his dry-eyed tears. She knew well why he was crying. As broke as they were, those long ago days were some of the happiest years of their lives. They laughed all the time; they partied with the best of them; they had big dreams; and they came out on top when it came to learning how to manage their meager salaries. In the end, they never asked for help from their parents. They showed them they could make it on their own and they did quite well.

Sassy was careful to not hold Bernard to tightly. "It was always the two of us, huh?"

"Till the end."

"Definitely, but let's not hurry it, okay? Please try to eat at least half of a sandwich."

Bernard frowned. He had no appetite for food of any kind. "You're not gonna let up, are you?"

"Nope." Sassy eased Bernard back against his pillow. She handed him half of his sandwich and watched as he timidly bit into a corner of it. A four-year-old might have taken a bigger bite, but for Bernard, that was the most solid food he'd had in his mouth in days. He chewed slowly.

"See, it's not that bad. You can't keep eating pea soup."

"It tastes better than this; this taste like cardboard."

"You always said that. Take another bite."

Although he didn't have the appetite for it, Bernard took another small bite. He again chewed slowly while Sassy closely watched over him in case she had to thrust the small garbage container on the floor next to the bed under his chin.

"Did Norris call?" Bernard asked. "Shouldn't they be here by now?"

"Actually, Evelyn called about an hour ago. You were asleep. She said the parking lot attendants gave Norris's car to someone else."

"What?"

"That's what she said. They'll try to rent a car or take a limo if they have to."

"They're gonna get Norris's car back, aren't they?"

"I think they better. Norris is really upset."

"I bet."

"Keep eating. You're going to need your strength when they do get here."

Bernard handed the remainder of the sandwich to Sassy. He then gestured for her to give him a napkin which she did right away. Bernard deposited what was in his mouth into the napkin. He squeezed the napkin up into a tight ball and handed it to Sassy. She was disappointed but she dumped the napkin without lecturing him.

"Do you wanna try a little milk?"

"Water."

Sassy pulled the tray back from the bed before giving Bernard his bottled water. Through a straw he sipped a little water and handed it back to her. For the briefest of moments they locked eyes, but it was Bernard who lowered his.

"What's wrong?" Sassy asked.

Bernard laid his head back on the pillow. With his bony arm, he covered his eyes.

"Whatever it is, Bernie, just say it."

His arm still covered his eyes. "I lied."

Sassy had no idea what he was referring to. "About?"

Bernard lowered his arm. "I know who gave me AIDS."

Sassy wasn't too surprised. A part of her had always known that Bernard knew a whole lot more than he was admitting to. She never pushed him to tell more because she wanted to believe he'd never lie to her.

"If you're thinking I got it from a man, I didn't. I did get it from a woman."

Sassy folded her arms and like a disapproving mother, she scowled down at Bernard. "Who?"

"She wasn't a stranger."

As much as Sassy wanted to know from whom Bernard contracted the HIV virus from, she wasn't sure if she could handle it. She went to the window and looked out at the lake. Funny, the water always looked calm, yet branches and debris belched up from the water lay along its banks. Sassy felt that she was just like that water on the surface, but her insides were churning. All these years she had been angry right along with Bernard that some woman, out of no where, had given him AIDS and stolen his life. She had conjured up a hate so strong for the nameless, faceless woman that at times she just knew the woman could feel it.

"You have to know the truth."

"Then tell it if it'll make you feel better."

Before Bernard could say anything, he belched. He then said softly, "Kayla."

Sassy arms flopped to her side. She slowly faced Bernard. "Did you say Kayla as in your ex-wife Kayla?"

Bernard's silence spoke as loud as any response he could have uttered.

Sassy clasped her hands to her mouth. She grunted as if she was in pain. Bernard couldn't look at Sassy. He waited for her rebuke, but Sassy was having trouble wrapping her mind around Kayla being the one who gave Bernard AIDS. Maybe it was because she couldn't believe Kayla had AIDS at all. Kayla had been such a fastidiously uptight woman; Sassy couldn't imagine her being with anyone without first checking his medical history. Even when she cheated on Bernard, she carried her own condoms which is how Bernard discovered she had been cheating in the first place.

"Kayla! Are you kidding me? Kayla!"

Sassy stormed out of the room to keep from putting her hands on Bernard. At the top of the stairs, she dropped down onto her butt and started to scream. She screamed! She screamed! She screamed until her throat got irritated and scratchy. She started coughing hard and loud till she almost threw up. When she stopped gagging, she started crying, but crying only made her angrier. She jumped up and charged back into the room.

"You know it's bad enough you cheated on Evelyn with Kayla, but to cheat and not use protection is the stupidest thing in the world! My God, Bernie! Don't you know how to protect your damn self? Don't you know how to use a damn condom?"

Bernard lay still and closed to the sight of Sassy's rage.

"Look at me!" Sassy grabbed Bernard's bony chin and turned his head toward her. "Look at me!"

Bernard reluctantly opened his eyes and despite the anguish Sassy saw there, she didn't let up.

"Was it worth it; the cheating, the lying?" She let go of Bernard's chin. "Was being with Kayla worth your life? She never gave a damn about you! When you married her I told you she was wrong for you, but I didn't try to stop you. Maybe it's my fault. I should have knocked your ass out and locked you up in an outhouse, which would have been safer than sleeping with Kayla! Is she suffering as much as you, Bernie? God forgive me but I hope she's suffering worse than any man, woman, or child ever suffered."

Bernard said sadly, "She died three years ago."

Sassy was stunned. "Bernie, you've known all along it was Kayla. How could you keep that from me? How could you keep me in the dark about your life? And Kayla, how in the hell did you get back with her? You hated her. How in the world could you?"

Bernard said in a low voice, "You hated Kayla."

"What?"

"You hated Kayla, Sassy! I never hated her. I married her because I loved her."

"But you also divorced her after she cheated on you. If you loved her so damn much, why did you leave her?"

With a bitter smile, Bernard looked pointedly at Sassy.

"No! Uh uh." She stood over Bernard. "Don't you dare put the failure of your marriage on me. I didn't sleep in the bed you and Kayla made. Your marriage ended because she cheated on you not once, not twice, but seven times that you know of. Her cheating had nothing to do with me!"

"Kayla said it did."

Sassy was so angry and tense, her neck and shoulders hurt. "She was a liar!"

"Kayla said I loved you more than I loved her."

"That's because she was stupid!"

"Sassy, Kayla was right when she said I looked to you for everything and nothing she did ever measured up to you."

"How the hell is that my fault? That was Kayla's insecurity, not mine. I never shoved my resume down her throat. Nor did I ever belittle or insult the bartending career she chose to pursue. I gave Kayla nothing but respect in her house, and if I'm guilty of anything, I ignored her, I didn't talk to her. I didn't like her."

"That was glaringly obvious."

"I didn't marry her, Bernie, you did. She didn't have to please me and I didn't have to kiss her ass."

"No, but I begged you to be friends with her."

"Friends?" Sassy laughed bitterly. "I tried talking to Kayla but it was like rubbing my face on a cactus. It was painful. The woman had no conversation."

"She wasn't that bad."

"Not to you. You were in love with her, which I never understood, but then, hey, that's the mystery of love. The chemistry was between you and Kayla, not me. For me, Kayla had no conversation or friendship. For me, she had snide remarks and nasty looks. If jealousy was driving her, there was no way we could have ever been friends."

Bernard dropped his head back on the pillow. He stared

up at the ceiling. "What about Evelyn? Isn't she a little jealous of you being an author?"

"If she is, she's handling it a whole lot better than Kayla ever did. At least we talk."

"Sassy, you didn't give Kayla a chance."

Sassy jabbed her finger at Bernard. "No you don't! You don't blame me for the failure of your marriage or Kayla's undoing. I told you Kayla was bad for you from the start but I didn't stop you from marrying her. All Kayla wanted to do was spend your money and suck you dry of any ambition. She was the one who convinced you to not go back to school, which you later regretted. Whatever Kayla did for you in bed made you stupid for her and negligent of yourself."

"That's not true."

"Hell yes it is and she was very jealous of me."

Bernard rubbed a dry, itchy spot on his chest. "Kayla said that about you. She said you hated her because you couldn't sleep with me."

Sassy gasped. That was like a slap in the face. "Do me a favor. Don't tell me another ignorant thing that bitch said."

Bernard grimaced. He reached for his oxygen tank.

"And yes, I said bitch, because that was an ugly thing for her to say. If she wasn't already dead, I'd kill her."

For the first time in hours, Bernard turned on his oxygen machine. His hands were trembling as he tried to pull on his mask. Sassy snatched the mask out of Bernard's hands and none too gently placed it over his nose and mouth. In a huff, she put her hands on her hips and waited impatiently for Bernard to breathe easy again.

"God forgive me for speaking ill of the dead, but I still don't like Kayla. In fact, now I hate her."

"You don't have to hate her. I've been hating enough for both of us."

Sassy paced at the foot of the bed. "Bernie, we were close since we were babies. Were we supposed to stop being friends or stop being related just to make Kayla happy? She didn't like me, I didn't like her. And again, as much as I didn't like her, I didn't stop you from marrying her and I didn't tell you to leave her. You did that all on your own."

Bernard slid the mask off. "It was either you or Kayla."

"No, it was either your pride or all the men she was sleeping with."

Remembering the arguments, the lies, the hurt, Bernard said thoughtfully, "I couldn't deal with it anymore."

"You should not have hung around after the first one."

Bernard couldn't dispute that. He thought about all the what ifs that would have made all the difference in world in his life. Sassy went back to the window and sat. Maybe it was her fault. Maybe if she had tried to stop Bernard from marrying Kayla, maybe he wouldn't have AIDS.

"I talked to Kayla before she died. She—"

"No! I don't want to know what Kayla had to say."

Bernard went on anyway. "She couldn't understand why you were so important to me. She hated when you called, she hated when I needed to talk to you. She hated that she and I didn't have that chemistry."

"Bernie, I will not take the blame for you and Kayla's inability to mesh seamlessly as a couple. The fact that you and Kayla never became the best of friends and lovers had nothing to do with me. And when the hell did you start seeing her again anyway?"

Bernard took a minute to think. "I went to a party with Esra. Kayla was there. That was almost six years ago."

"My God, Bernie, how could you not tell me?" Again the tears came. She felt betrayed.

"I promised Kayla I wouldn't tell you unless we decided to get back together. And the truth is I didn't wanna have to deal with you telling me I was making a mistake."

"Well, seeing as how things turned out—"

"I don't need to be reminded!" Bernard quickly took in some oxygen. "I live my mistake every day. Don't you think I know—"

"That's just it, Bernie. I don't think you know a damn thing! You obviously didn't know you could get HIV from an infected person, man or woman; you didn't know that you had to protect yourself by wearing a damn condom; and apparently, you didn't know you were doing a stupid thing sleeping with Kayla, in the first place, when she was angry with you for having a baby with Evelyn! Of course you didn't know any of those things. How dare I assume you would use the head on your shoulders to make the right choices about your life."

Bernard's teeth were clenched so tight his jaw hurt. As his chest visibly rose and fell, he could feel the raised veins in his neck and forehead pulse as he squeezed his eyes shut.

"You're a thief, Bernie!" Tears rolled down Sassy's cheeks. "You're a thief."

Bernard's chin quivered.

"You robbed me of you. You've taken away my best friend. If you were so worried about leaving me alone on this earth, you would have been a hell of a lot more discerning about who you slept with and how you slept with them. The one you should be angry with is Kayla. That's who you've been angry with all along, but you couldn't say that, could you? That's because you were living a lie, Bernie, and you know it. You need to keep on being angry at Kayla. She's the one who stole your life. And what about Evelyn? Did you even think about her? Suppose you had infected her or Brice?"

The tightness in Bernard's body began to ease. He relaxed his jaw. The thought of the possibility of infecting his son or Evelyn still haunted him. Everyday he thanked God he had not infected either one, but all the credit belonged to Evelyn. It was Evelyn who made him wear a condom because she didn't want to get pregnant again. The subject of HIV or AIDS wasn't one they ever had to discuss because they both were supposed to be smart enough to protect themselves. Sassy had every right to be angry with him.

Sassy couldn't stop crying. "Bernie, why didn't you just leave Kayla alone? I bet my last dollar in the world she didn't even tell you she had AIDS. She didn't did she? I know she didn't. When did she tell you she had AIDS, Bernie? When?"

Bernard lowered his head. He couldn't say the words.

Sobbing, Sassy turned and looked out the window.

"Her mother called me to come to the hospital. That's when I found out. That's when I went and got tested."

"Selfish!" Sassy said disgustedly.

"She said it was payback. She said if I had loved her as much as I loved you, she would not have had to cheat. She blamed me."

"So it's your fault and indirectly my fault, too? Great."

Bernard didn't deny it. "When she died, I wanted to be glad but I wasn't. I was angry, I was sad, I was mad, and I was scared. I knew I would be following her to her grave and I hated her for infecting me. I hate her now. I'm dying and I'm looking forward to dying just to end this misery. I hate living like this. I hate it!"

Despite not wanting to live, Bernard took more of his life's breath from his oxygen mask. He was breathing a lot easier now that he told Sassy the truth. He didn't look her way, but he knew she was back to looking out at the lake. When he heard her sniffle, he also knew that she was crying for him. He let her cry, because he couldn't cry for himself.

25

If Sassy had to say so herself, she probably made the best spaghetti and meat sauce she'd ever made in her life, but if she had to judge how good her spaghetti was by the sad, troubled faces around the table, she would have to give herself a thumb down. The only one eating with any pleasurable enthusiasm was Brice. He sucked in long strings of spaghetti until the red tomato sauce coated his lips and dripped back into his plate. Brice always liked spaghetti which is why Sassy made it in the first place, but she was always afraid he'd suck a string of spaghetti straight down his throat and choke. So far he hadn't, thank God.

On the other hand, Norris, with a slow steady twirling of his fork, tightly wound his spaghetti till not a string was left dangling. When he did finally put the fork into his barely opened mouth, he had to use his teeth to pull the spaghetti off the fork. Earlier while she was making the spaghetti, Sassy had fantasized that Norris would literarily go gaga over her first home cooked spaghetti meal in his house. She even made meatballs, though she could have given him canned spaghetti and he would not have noticed. Still she wasn't mad at him. Norris had every right to be uptight. She would be too if some maniac was stalking her, screwing up her life. The questions she and Norris both pondered was what did the stalker ultimately want from him, and why was Norris his target? Until the man was found, the answers would remain elusive.

Sassy glanced furtively in Evelyn's direction. Evelyn

liked spaghetti as well, but she was jabbing her fork into her spaghetti like she was angry with it for being stringy. She'd quickly twirl a plump fork full knowing that it wouldn't fit inside her mouth and then annoyed, she'd shake the spaghetti off the fork and start all over again. In the twenty minutes since they'd been sitting at the table, Evelyn had eaten only one fork full of spaghetti but that didn't surprise Sassy. Evelyn rarely had an appetite for anything she cooked.

"How come everybody's so quiet?" Brice asked.

Norris surmised from the closed look on Sassy's face and the sullen look on Evelyn's that neither was going to answer Brice's question, so he did. "Sometimes, it's good to eat in silence. The food goes down easier and digests better."

Brice momentarily thought about what Norris said. "Oh," he finally said. "That makes sense." He went back to twirling his fork in the small mound of spaghetti he had left.

As loquacious as Sassy was, like everyone else at the table, she didn't have an appetite for meaningless chitchat. She was still upset with Bernard, whom they had heard not a peep from since Evelyn's startled gasp at the sight of him sent him cowering under his covers into his fetal cocoon of condemnation and despair.

Sassy promptly ushered Evelyn out of Bernard's room into the third bedroom where Evelyn started crying which disturbed Brice. Thankfully, Norris, despite his own annoyance over his lost car, took Brice, who had yet to see his father, down to the lake while Sassy impatiently waited for Evelyn to stop crying.

Evelyn blew her nose. "You said he looked a 'little' different." She tossed her snotty balled up tissue into the garbage container next to the bed. "Well, he looks like death!"

"Lower your voice! He's only two rooms away."

"I'm not going back in there," Evelyn said, her voice just a smidgen lower. "I can't look at him."

As long as she'd known Evelyn, how was it that she never saw how shallow the woman was? "Why are you here,

Evelyn? You insisted on coming. Now that you're here, your only focus is on how Bernie looks. I thought this visit was about Brice."

"It is about Brice! He's Bernard's sole heir."

Sassy tapped herself on the forehead. "Ah! It's about money. I should have known."

"Whatever Bernard has goes to Brice, not you."

Sassy got up and moved far enough away from Evelyn that she couldn't reach out and smack her in the face. Actually, being in the same room was too close. She went to the door. She was about to open it—

"Sassy, I know you don't have a problem with my son getting what's due him."

A dry laugh and, "Humph, humph, humph," was all Sassy could say.

"I be-damn!" Evelyn said. "You're planning to keep all the money for yourself!"

Sassy faced Evelyn. "This is so like you, Evelyn. Your reason for begging me to get Bernie to see you had nothing to do with your love for him or his love for his son. It was only about the money he doesn't even have."

"Bernard has plenty of money. He's always had money."

"Always isn't now, Evelyn. Bernie doesn't have a penny. He's been sick for a very long time. His health insurance doesn't cover all of his expenses. Oh, and just in case you can't connect the dots, Bernie has no income." Sassy could see the confusion and uncertainty in Evelyn's face. This was news she definitely wasn't expecting to hear.

"Well, then. . .how can Bernard still deposit a thousand dollars into my checking account every month? He must have some money."

"My money," Sassy said, noting the deflated look on Evelyn's face. It was priceless. "Bernie no longer has a bank account. For now, that money you get comes from little old me. So it's me you can thank."

Evelyn wasn't convinced. "I don't believe you. Bernard always had money, and he has that condo in Park Slope."

"That condo was sold to pay Bernie's hospital and physicians' bills. Accounts payable didn't extend him gratis because he has AIDS. "

Evelyn still wasn't convinced. "But he had—"

"Savings? Gone bye-bye a long time ago."

Evelyn got to her feet. "My son has to get something. Bernard owes—"

"Owes?" Sassy rushed at Evelyn. She stopped two feet shy of slamming into her.

"Back off of me, Sassy!"

Sassy didn't give an inch. "As long as Bernie was healthy and working, Brice wanted for nothing; you never had to ask for a damn thing for him." Evelyn moved several feet away, but Sassy dogged her. "Whether I want to accept it or not, Bernie is dying. Any remaining financial obligations left afterwards will be expunged. Other than Social Security payments for Brice, whatever you didn't get from Bernie in life, you won't get from him in death because other than some personal items which I will hold onto until Brice is old enough to appreciate them, there is nothing left for you to get your hands on."

"What about his furniture? What did you do with it?"

It should not have surprised Sassy that Evelyn was this petty but it did. "For your information, the very well-to-do man who bought the condo happened to have moved to New York City from Houston sans furniture as he was newly divorced and newly employed. Hence, he took Bernie's apartment as is—furniture, plates, toilet paper, toothpicks, everything. Bernie's clothes and personal items are in storage, for now. Any more questions about money?"

"Damn!" Evelyn snatched her overnight bag off the floor. "I could have stayed my ass in Brooklyn."

"You know, Evelyn, you probably should have. I don't need you here picking Bernie's bones."

"I wish you had said that before I went down to the City Clerk's Office and lied for you."

"Hey. It would have gotten done with or without you."

"That's what you say now," Evelyn began stuffing her clothes back into her overnight bag, "but you damn near begged me to pretend to be you so you could marry a man you barely know."

It was disturbing that they came so easily to this ugly, contentious place but Sassy wasn't about to let Evelyn have the last word. "That man I barely know has selflessly taken care of the man you do know who, by the way, chose to not marry you even though you have a child with him."

"I don't give a damn." Evelyn stuffed her bedroom slippers into her bag. "I'm getting the hell out of here."

"You know where the front door is." Sassy went back to the bedroom door. She felt bad but she wasn't about to let Evelyn know it. "I hope you brought sneakers."

"Bitch," Evelyn said under her breath but loud enough that Sassy heard her before she could get completely out of the room. Sassy turned back.

"Ditto, and I'm sure Bernie can attest to that."

"At least I don't write pabulum puke and call it literature."

Mustering all the control she could, Sassy closed the door without a sound. "Well, the mask comes off. Wow. Hera is that you? Oh, or are you Ajax?"

"What the heck are you talking about?"

"Oh, I thought I was arguing with an educated woman."

"Screw you, Sassy!"

"Greek mythology, Evelyn. Jealousy; isn't that the origin of your insult about my writing?"

"If I were jealous, it wouldn't be of you."

"H'm, I think I know now why you threw away your manuscript." Sassy was feeling sadistically vicious. "It wasn't written well enough to reach the level of pabulum puke which I happen to be well paid for."

"Go to hell!"

"Oh. Poor unimaginative thing, you never had enough of a creative thought to fit inside the head of a tick."

"You think you're so much better than me? You're not."

"Apparently, that's what you think, Evelyn. I've never looked down on you."

"You do it all the time. You've never been a friend of mine. You knew Bernard was cheating on me, but you never said a damn thing."

"That's because I didn't know, and if I did, it would have been none of my business."

"Then neither is my son. Brice isn't staying here; he's leaving with me."

Sassy's hands went to her hips. "Brice will be staying here with his father."

"Brice is my son! He came out of me, not you."

If Evelyn had stabbed Sassy in the heart with eight inches of cold steel, she would not have bled any worse. The one time she had been pregnant, she had lost the baby before it had a chance to develop human features. Her Gyn assured her she could carry a baby to term when she was ready.

"Brice may not be my son, but he is Bernard Milton's son as well as my godson which you asked me to be."

"My mistake."

"It wasn't a mistake four years ago when you had back surgery and couldn't get your ass up off the bed for two months. I took care of Brice while Bernie looked after you although he was dealing with his own illness."

"So what! His illness is his own damn fault!"

"You don't have an ounce of empathy in you, Evelyn, but that's alright. This isn't about you. This is about Brice. If you dropped dead this minute, Brice has a home with me."

"Not unless I say so. You nor Bernard have any blood ties to my son, so you have no say where he lives."

Not for one minute was Sassy stumped by Evelyn's

statement, especially when Evelyn looked back at her with a self-satisfied smirk on her lips. So now she was supposed to believe that Brice wasn't Bernard's son? Did the woman think she was stupid?

"Have nothing to say *writer*?"

Sassy could literarily see herself slapping Evelyn's face. "You're not only a small, jealous-minded person, Evelyn; you're a vicious bitter witch to sink this low."

"I don't give a damn what you say about me. I get the last laugh. Bernard isn't Brice's father. Lawrence Noland is my son's father. So like I said, you have no say."

Sassy knew Lawrence Noland and knew well how much of a horn-dog he was. Lawrence was a studio musician she and Evelyn, together, met eight years ago when he was playing down in Soho. There was no disputing how sexy Lawrence was when he caressed his sax with his big hands and thrust his pelvis against it while he sucked on its mouthpiece with his succulently moist lips. There wasn't a dry woman in the room when Lawrence finished his set. It was Evelyn who got Lawrence to come over to their table, and although Evelyn denied it at first, she and Lawrence did get together on and off for a while. However, it never crossed Sassy's mind that Lawrence could be Brice's father. If it were true, it would devastate Bernard, but it couldn't be true. She tried to remember every detail of Lawrence's face which wasn't so easy since it had been at least three years since she last saw him. As faint an image as she had in her head, she couldn't see a resemblance. Nope, she didn't think so.

As if she regretted exposing her secret, Evelyn sat on the edge of the bed and held her head as if the weight of the world was on her shoulders.

"Are you so small, Evelyn, you'd let the lack of money deprive your son of his father?"

"Leave me alone."

"Evelyn, if you say to Bernie what you said to me about Lawrence, I swear before God, I will make your life a living hell. And if you ever so much as hint to Brice that Bernie isn't his father, I hope God slaps you to your knees."

Evelyn and Sassy challenged each other in their unrelenting gaze.

"You don't scare me," Evelyn said.

"That's funny because you do scare me. We've been closer than some sisters, yet all along you've hated me. You've never been happy for whatever I've accomplished, yet I've been nothing but supportive of you. What went on between you and Bernie never had anything to do with me. I never slept between the two of you. If it's true what you said about Lawrence, unless you have a DNA test to back you up, I'm not buying it."

Evelyn stared hatefully at Sassy, which Sassy took to mean that Evelyn didn't have a DNA test to back up her claim.

"I won't let you hurt Bernie."

"I would not have said a damn thing if you hadn't been riding me."

"Yeah, blame me." Sassy felt sick to her stomach. "Look, Brice is here. I'm sure seeing Bernie one last time won't scar him for life."

"I don't want—"

"It's not about what you want, Evelyn, or what I want. It's about Brice and Bernie and what they each need. Brice doesn't need to grow up thinking he never had a chance to say good-bye to the man he knew as his father. Being such a 'good' mother, I'm sure you want to do right by your son."

Evelyn folded her arms. "Fine. But if Brice gets upset, it's on you."

"I'll deal with it." Sassy turned to leave.

"I hope you don't think I'm letting Bernard see Brice because I'm afraid of you." Evelyn began pulling her clothes from her overnight bag. "Because I'm not."

"Evelyn, grow up." Sassy left the room before things could get any worse.

# # # #

Until they all sat down for her spaghetti dinner, Sassy had said nothing more to Evelyn.

"Sassy?"

"Yes, Brice."

"Is my daddy really here?"

Evelyn stopped twirling her fork. She didn't raise her eyes which Sassy took to mean that Evelyn was leaving it to her to answer Brice's questions about Bernard.

Sassy eased her plate away. "Yes, your daddy is here."

Riiiiiiing!

"Excuse me." Norris whipped his BlackBerry from his belt as he rose from the table. "Hello?" he said as he left the dining room. "What have you found out?" Norris went out onto the deck and firmly slid the glass door closed behind him.

"Where is my daddy?" Brice asked.

From her place at the dining room table, Sassy caught glimpses of Norris as he spoke heatedly into his BlackBerry out on the deck. She wanted so badly to know to whom Norris was speaking.

"Sassy!"

"Yes, Brice," Sassy said refocusing her attention back onto him.

"Where is my daddy?"

Again Sassy looked to Evelyn, and wasn't surprised to see Evelyn arch her brow as if to say, "Go ahead, smarty."

"Brice, your father is asleep upstairs is in his bedroom."

Brice looked up at the ceiling and then again at Sassy. "How come he got a bedroom upstairs? He don't live here."

"Explain that," Evelyn said under her breath.

"Brice, you know your dad's been sick, right?"

"Yeah, but he's not sick anymore. That's how come he's not in the hospital."

Sassy cut her eyes at Evelyn. "Actually, Brice, your dad is still sick. He's very sick and I'm taking care of him."

Brice looked at Evelyn. "Mommy, did you know Daddy is still sick?"

Evelyn sat back from the table. She nodded.

Confused, Brice said, "Oh."

Under the table Sassy pushed her foot into Evelyn's. She couldn't believe Evelyn hadn't told Brice the truth. Evelyn sucked her teeth and shifted her body sideways away from Sassy.

"Brice, do you like the lake?" Sassy asked, hoping to change the subject.

"Mr. Norris said he got a row boat and tomorrow we can go row boating."

"If the weather's good, you sure can."

"Yay!"

Sassy again looked out at the deck. Norris was still on his BlackBerry but he was no longer pacing. He was looking out across the lake.

"Evelyn, don't you think Brice looks a little sleepy?"

"I'm not sleepy."

"Well, you're going to bed anyway." Sassy ignored the sour look on Evelyn's face.

From upstairs in Bernard's room: Thump, thump!

"What's that?" Brice looked up at the ceiling.

Evelyn never took her eye off of Sassy. "Yeah, what is that, Sassy?"

"The window is open upstairs. The wind probably blew the blinds and knocked something over. I'll go check." Sassy ignored Evelyn's cynical smirk. She hurried up to Bernard's room.

After closing the door Sassy asked, "What's wrong? Are you alright?"

"Did you forget about me?"

"Oh, like you're easy to forget. Bernie, I'm downstairs trying to explain to a little boy, whose mother did not tell him that his father was gravely ill."

"I should not have let him come." Bernard sucked in

some oxygen.

"Look, don't you start."

"I don't wanna see in Brice's eyes what I saw in Evelyn's."

"You won't. Brice's love for you is pure. He won't care how you look."

"He won't know it's me."

In that instant, Sassy got an idea. "I'll be right back." She rushed from the room to Norris's den on the first floor. Norris was at his desk typing rapidly into his computer. He gave no sign that he noticed Sassy or heard her when she said his name.

Sassy tapped on the desk to get Norris's attention. "What's going on?"

Unable to pull his eyes from the monitor, Norris said, "That was Cyrus. My car was found on Metropolitan Avenue in Queens."

"Thank God. What condition is it in?"

Norris kept his fingers on the keyboard, but he looked at Sassy. "It seems to be okay. Cyrus used his connections to get a friend to put the prints he lifted from the car through the law enforcement AFIS system. They got a hit. Byron Satoshi."

"Good news, right?"

Norris was uncertain. "H'm. . .don't know."

"What are you thinking?"

"When I was a kid on the streets in Fuchu, my best friend was a boy my age who also had no family. His name was Byron Satoshi."

"You mentioned him before."

"It may not necessarily be the same Byron, and Satoshi isn't that uncommon a name in Japan. When I went back to Japan nine years ago, I looked for Byron. I looked everywhere. I found several Byron Satoshis but not the Byron I knew."

"Do you know if this Byron is from Fuchu?"

"Cyrus is checking."

"From what you remember, does your friend Byron

Satoshi look anything like you?"

"We didn't have the same mother, and his father was Caucasian."

"Then maybe the name is a coincidence."

"Coincidence or not, this Byron Satoshi has it in for me and I need to know why." Norris focused again on his monitor as his fingers went to clicking the keys.

Sassy wanted to stay and look over Norris's shoulder but she had something more pressing to do as well. She quietly took one of Norris's digital cameras from his desk drawer. She slipped through the kitchen and into the family room to avoid having to explain what she was doing to Brice. She trotted back up to Bernard's room. The minute Bernard saw the camera; he pulled the sheet up over his face.

"Bernie." Sassy easily pulled the sheet down. "A picture, an explanation, and time to digest the information will greatly prepare Brice to see you in person. Don't give into your fear."

"You saw Evelyn's face. She couldn't hide her disgust. I should not have listened to you."

"Bernie, for Brice's sake, you have to dig deep. For him to be this close and not see you would be a shame."

"He's a kid. He won't understand."

"Don't underestimate your son. Because he loves you for you, he'll be more understanding and more accepting of how you now look than most adults."

"I can't do it." Bernard went back to breathing through his oxygen mask.

Sassy sat on the bed. She took Bernard's bony hand. "I believe it'll work. What can we lose?"

"My son," Bernard said, his voice cracking.

"No. Brice is a lot smarter than you realize. He'll ask questions as he should, but he'll still want to see you."

"Are you sure, Sassy? Are you sure? I'll just die if I scare him."

"How can you scare him when you don't scare me?"

Sassy was close to crying. "Bernie, I promise. You'll hold Brice in your arms, just like I'm holding you."

Bernard shook as he cried his dry tears. Sassy prayed hard that God would see it her way and let Bernard hold his son one last time.

"Sassy."

"Yes?"

"Can you forgive me?"

Fresh tears flowed. "Bernie, you're so silly. When have I ever not forgiven you? So, how about that picture? Let's get you your son."

26

Sunrise over Blue Mountain Lake brought no more answers than Sassy and Norris had before they fell off to sleep a little after two in the morning. Norris now knew the name of the man who took his car, which was now parked in the police impound lot out in Queens—but still it made no sense. Cyrus compiled a list of thirty-eight Byron Satoshis in the Northeast. Eleven of them had international driver's license photographs on file and not one of them showed any definitive resemblance to Norris. Yet the parking lot attendant said the man who took Norris's car looked like Norris, used Norris's name and could, in fact, pass for Norris's twin. Norris was left with more questions than answers. No other Byron Satoshi would know him but the one he knew as a child. Cyrus was having no luck getting answers because he couldn't find Byron Satoshi.

Now that it was morning, the day of her impromptu marriage ceremony, Sassy stood at the window in Bernard's room looking out on the lake just as Norris and Brice slowly rowed past the house. Last night, well after Brice was put to bed, she and Evelyn couldn't agree on whether or not Brice should be shown the pictures she had taken of Bernard. Sassy couldn't deny the gaunt ashen man with the thin hair, sad sunken eyes and hollow cheeks might well frighten a little boy who had an older, healthier image in his head of how his father use to look. She had planned on explaining to Brice what to expect before showing him pictures, but Evelyn, in a huff, took Brice off to bed without giving Sassy a chance to begin. The argument she and Evelyn had afterwards made sleeping for Sassy nearly impossible. When she and Norris did finally fall off to sleep, twenty minutes later they were startled awake by the loud explosive ringing of the house alarm which Evelyn set off when she opened the sliding glass door to the deck.

Norris bolted out of bed. He ran headlong down the stairs not knowing what he'd find on the first floor. He shut off the alarm amid screams from Brice, and frantic apologies from Evelyn. Sassy's own heart pounding fear that Norris's stalker had broken into the house sent her racing into the room Brice shared with Evelyn. He wasn't there. Sassy dashed into Bernard's room, flicked on the light, and found Bernard hiding under the cover balled up tight. Although silent in his fear, Bernard was shaking so hard the whole bed shook.

Riiiiiiing!

Downstairs, Norris answered the telephone on the first ring. Sassy knew from the first time she set the alarm off that the security company would be calling to see if everything was alright.

Sassy dropped her knees. She put her face close to Bernard's. His eyes were squeezed shut.

"Bernie, it's okay," she said softly. "It was just the house alarm."

Bernard continued shaking. His breathing was becoming more labored. Nothing Sassy said calmed him. He was scaring her more than the alarm had. She quickly put his oxygen mask on and began rubbing his back.

"Bernie, you have to calm down. Please." Still, Bernard shook. Any minute Sassy knew she was going to have to call 911. She tried as best she could to wrap her arms around Bernard to quiet his shaking body. His shaking continued. She hugged Bernard tighter.

"Daddy, don't be scared."

Sassy looked and saw that Brice had climbed up onto the bed and laid his hand on his back. Brice's cherub of a face was the most beautiful sight ever. "Hey," Sassy said softly.

"You wanna help me make your daddy feel better?"

"Yes."

Sassy let go of her hold on Bernard. "I want you to hug him, so come a little closer." Brice did. Sassy showed him how to lie against Bernard's back with his arms around him. "Okay?" She put her arm around Brice. "Are you alright?"

"Uh-huh."

"Can you talk to him?"

"Uh-huh. Daddy, don't be scared. I'll stay with you."

"Bernie. Bernie, Brice is here. Bernie, your son is hugging you."

"Daddy, I'll take care of you, okay?"

Sassy knew she was witnessing the miracle she had prayed for. She saw the shaking in Bernard's body subside until he stopped shaking altogether. The tightness around his eyes eased and his eyelids began to flutter. This time it wasn't Bernard's back Sassy gently rubbed, it was Brice's as he continued to hold his own father as if he were the child. Bernard's breathing began to normalize.

"See, Sassy," Brice said, "he's alright. He's not scared no more."

"No he's not. He just needed you to be with him."

"I'm gonna stay with him. He'll get better if I stay with him. Oh!" Brice said suddenly. "I'll sing to him. He like when I sing to him."

"Then you should sing to him."

"Okay. ♪Go to sleep, my ba-a-be, my ba-a-be, my ba-a-be. Go to sleep, my ba-a-be, my ba-a-be, my ba-a-be mine.♪"

Never had Sassy been so moved. The irony of Brice singing the song Bernard use to sing to him when he was a baby made her weep.

"Don't cry, Sassy. Daddy's gonna be okay now."

She cried anyway. She put her arms around Brice and Bernard together. "Thank you, Lord," she said. This time when she released Bernard, she looked into his eyes and for the first time in a very long time, she saw tears.

"Bernie, you have your son."

Wanting to get a look at his son, Bernard, with Sassy's help turned onto his back. For an eternal twenty seconds, Sassy waited to see the reaction between them. The look in Bernard's eyes went from fear to pure adoration. In Brice's young eyes, fleetingly, Sassy glimpsed surprise; but then Bernard lovingly touched Brice's head. That familiar touch and recognition of who Bernard was brought a little smile to Brice's lips.

"Hi, big man," Bernard said.

"Hi, Daddy."

Bernard opened his thin arms and Brice, intuitively mindful of how weak his father had to be, lay gently in them.

"Is everything alright?" Norris asked as he entered the room, but then he saw Brice in Bernard's arms and knew that everything was. He put his arm around Sassy. They stood looking at the gift of love before them.

"Where's Evelyn?" Sassy asked.

"I left her down in the family—"

"Brice!" Evelyn called from down the hall. "Brice!"

Brice neither raised his head nor answered Evelyn. Sassy did. "He's in here."

Evelyn came to the doorway but she didn't enter the room. By the tightness of Evelyn's brow, Sassy could see that Evelyn didn't like what she saw.

Sassy went to Evelyn. "Sometimes children are smarter than adults." She didn't wait for Evelyn to respond. "Goodnight."

Evelyn grabbed Sassy's arm. She said in a hushed voice, "You can't leave him in there!"

"Yes I can, and so can you."

"But suppose Bernard dies? What—"

"Leave them alone. Let them have their time."

"We should all go back to bed," Norris said. "We have a long day ahead of us."

"Come on, Brice!" Evelyn said anyway which made Sassy want to strangle her.

"I'm staying with Daddy." Brice got under the covers with Bernard.

"Brice!"

"Are you okay, Brice?" Sassy asked.

"I'm talking to my daddy."

Norris took Evelyn aside. "He's fine."

"But suppose Bernard—"

"No, he won't. Take a look."

Evelyn looked back into the room. Bernard was wearing a surgical mask. Sassy was putting one on Brice who seemed to be enjoying himself.

"If my son gets sick—"

"He won't," Norris assured. "We all, including Bernard, will take care of Brice."

Sassy came into the hallway. "We all love him."

"But he's my son!" Evelyn stormed off to the guest bedroom and slammed the door.

"That woman's crazy," Sassy said.

"Let's leave Evelyn outside of our bedroom." Norris closed their bedroom door. In their bed, Sassy and Norris talked not Evelyn or Bernard, but about themselves and whether their nuptials were just for Bernard's benefit or whether it was going to be the real thing.

"When I built this house," Norris said, "my only thought was of having a place to escape to when I was tired of the city. Other than my father and Alicia, I never bought anyone here."

"Now you have four strangers in your house."

"Three," he said. "Sassy, I don't want a mock marriage. I love you. I want the real thing."

How ironic they came to this juncture in their lives because of Bernard who chose to not live but wanted her to live a happy life with the man of her dreams.

#   #   #   #

After only three hours of sleep, Sassy was wide awake as she watched Norris and Brice row upstream out of sight. Norris was good with Brice, just as he was good with Bernard. How could any woman not fall in love with him?

"He said he loves me," Bernard said.

Sassy turned away from the window. "Who, Norris?"

"Brice, Sassy. Brice said he loves me."

"I already know that. What did y'all talk about?"

"Everything. He wants to be an astronaut."

"He used to want to be a doctor."

Bernard began rubbing his forehead.

"Does your head hurt?"

Bernard stopped rubbing his forehead. "I won't see him grow up. I won't see him become a man."

The only thing Sassy could say was, "Fight for your life, and pray," but Bernard didn't want to hear that.

"I guess we're all born to die; some sooner than later," he said. "Don't let him forget me?"

"Never."

Bernard smiled broadly. He clapped his hands together. He rested them on his lap."

"Share," Sassy said.

"Brice let me hold him. He wasn't scared."

Knock, knock, knock.

Sassy and Bernard both knew it could only be one person. "Can you handle it?" Sassy asked.

"Come in, Evelyn!" Bernard said which surprised Sassy. She almost applauded when Bernard straightened his back and sat up taller.

Evelyn opened the door but she looked at neither Sassy nor Bernard. "My uncle called. He just crossed the Delaware Water Gap."

"Then he'll be here in about twenty minutes. I'll call Norris." Sassy took out her cell phone.

"I'll wait downstairs," Evelyn said.

"Evelyn!" Bernard said, stopping Evelyn just as she

was about to close the door. "I need to talk to you."

Evelyn looked at Bernard as if his head was spinning on his shoulders. She looked to Sassy to say if she should stay or leave, but Sassy wasn't opining about anything regarding Evelyn and Bernard. Just Brice.

"Sassy, do you mind?" Bernard asked.

Sassy didn't mind at all. She didn't look at Evelyn as she passed her because she knew what she'd see—a woman pleading with her eyes to not leave her alone with a man she no longer knew. Sassy heard Bernard tell Evelyn to close the door, which was alright with her. Just as Bernard and Brice had their time, it was now time for Bernard and Evelyn to have theirs. Of course, the nosey part of Sassy wanted to know what they were talking about, but as luck would have it, she didn't have time to hang around and eavesdrop. She had to get Norris and Brice back to the house and she had to change her clothes. She had a decent pair of jeans she could wear to get married in.

27

Reverend Doctor Jessie Bartholomew Morgan was a big, tall, imposing man with a gleaming bald head and a full belly of great food cooked up and served to him by many of the God-fearing sanctified ladies of Holy Alliance Baptist Church. When he went to their homes, he always took his wife of thirty-one years along to protect him from those good sisters who might want to talk about something other than his role as their minister and spiritual advisor. Today, Dr. Morgan didn't bring his wife along. He didn't need protection from his niece or Sassy, although Sassy was beginning to believe she and Norris might need protection from him.

There was no smile on Dr. Morgan's face when he got out of the limousine. When he entered the house with his well-worn black leather bible in hand, the austere, disapproving look on his face sank Sassy's heart. She knew they were in for it. Dr. Morgan was never one to mince his words.

"Thank you for coming, sir," Norris extended his hand.

Dr. Morgan disregarded Norris's outstretched hand. "I am a man of God. I am not in the business of deceiving the Lord or knowingly officiating over a mockery of a marriage. My time is valuable. I'm here because I was asked to come. However, I need someone to speak the truth as to why such a hasty marriage, and don't tell me you're marrying because a sick man asked you to. If this is for financial gain or something illegal, I will not participate. There will be no ceremony."

Norris neither stepped back nor turned away from Dr.

Morgan, but Dr. Morgan stepped away from Norris and sat in one of his large living room chairs. Sassy got a sour taste in her mouth. If Dr. Morgan had concerns about marrying them, why come all this way?

"Dr. Morgan," Norris said, "I respect your candor. I will admit, initially, we were getting married at Bernard's request. However, I love Sassy. I love being with her; I love coming home to her; I love the way she makes me feel; I love her spirit; I love her commitment to family, and most important to me, I love that she trust me."

Under her breath, Evelyn sucked her teeth.

Sassy went and stood at Norris's side. She slipped her arm around his.

"Dr. Morgan, you know me. You know how particular I am. In fact, you told me yourself my standards were too high for most men; that I needed to talk to God about humbling my expectations. Well, I didn't ask God to humble my expectations, I asked him to bless me with a wonderful man. I love Norris. I love that he's moral, principled, and spiritual. I love that I can talk to him all night and never get tired of listening to him or telling him the most inconsequential thought I might have had during my day." She looked at Norris. "He makes me feel special. He's touched me in ways that I've only been able to write about but not personally experience. I feel safe with Norris. I love him because for the first time in my life, I'm in love with a man I really like."

"Wow," Evelyn said softly, as Sassy and Norris gently kissed. She was impressed in spite of being angry at Sassy.

"Certainly, I applaud your passion for each other," Dr. Morgan said. "However, as you've known each other less than a year, I'm concerned—"

Norris started to speak but Sassy quickly said, "Dr. Morgan, I know someone who went with a guy for five years before he proposed to her. They were engaged for seven years before they got married; and a year later, they separated."

"You're talking about Eric and Joan," Evelyn said.

"Yes."

"They're divorced now."

"That's my point," Sassy said. "Relationship longevity does not guarantee a successful marriage."

Dr. Morgan wasn't impressed. He held up his bible. "Proverbs 5:20," he said, sanctimoniously. "'Why wilt thou, my son, be ravished with a strange woman, and embrace the bosom of a stranger?'"

Sassy let go of Norris. "So now I'm supposed to be a *strange* woman who violates or devours Norris? Please, correct me if I'm wrong, Dr. Morgan. Am I to interpret *strange woman* to mean a woman of ill-repute?"

"Sassy," Evelyn said, "I don't know if that's right." She looked to her uncle for clarification.

"The verse speaks to a man who gives himself to a woman he does not know," Dr. Morgan said.

"Then this verse does not refer to me or Sassy," Norris said. "I know Sassy quite well, and whether we're together fifty years or eighty, I look forward to learning something new about her every day."

"That is quite admirable of you, son. However, I believe extensive knowledge of oneself and of one's mate is essential before taking the vows of matrimony."

Sassy was getting more upset. "Am I to understand that you're saying only couples who know each other really, really, really well should get married, and only they can live happily ever after?"

"They stand a better chance of making their marriage work. Marriage is—"

"But, Uncle Morgan," Evelyn chimed in, "what if someone is truly in love? Doesn't that count for something?"

"If their love is real, time will only strengthen it."

"Oh, forget it!" Sassy had had enough. "He doesn't want to marry us. Let's just forget it!" She started to walk away but Norris wouldn't let her go. He pulled Sassy back.

"Dr. Morgan," Norris said, "I believe Ecclesiastes 9:9

says, 'Live joyfully with the wife whom thou lovest all the days of the life of thy vanity, which he hath given thee under the sun, all the days of thy vanity'."

"I know the verse. It means—"

"It means I love Sassy, and I want her to be the wife that I live joyfully with while I have my physical and mental health. I have lived alone for twelve years waiting for the day I'd meet the woman I wanted to marry. I met Sassy. She is that woman."

"H'm," Uncle Morgan said. He forged ahead although he could see that Sassy was angry with him. "Ecclesiastes 4:11 says, 'Again, if two lie together, then they have heat; but how can one be warm alone?' If your love for this woman is physical it won't stand the test of time."

"My love for Sassy transcends the physical. However, she is a beautiful woman and I love loving her."

"Fornication!" Dr. Morgan roared. "Fornication brought down Sampson!"

Sassy couldn't believe she asked this man to marry her and Norris. How could she forget how self-righteous and condescending he was? That's why she stopped going to his church!

"Uncle Morgan," Evelyn said, "I thought Delilah cutting Samson's hair brought him down."

Dr. Morgan looked sternly at Evelyn. "Read your bible! Read between the lines. Delilah was not a virgin; and Samson was not an eunuch. If Samson had not fornicated, he would not have been compromised."

Sassu felt like that was a dig at her and Norris. She tried again to leave but Norris wouldn't let her. He held her hand.

"Dr. Morgan," Norris said. "In this day and time I doubt seriously if very many people consider sexual relations between two consenting adults fornication."

"Most sinners wouldn't," Dr. Morgan said smugly.

All these years Sassy had known Dr. Morgan she never knew him to be this unpleasant. Arrogant, yes; contemptuously mean, no. "Why did you come?" she asked. "Dr. Morgan, if you are opposed to Norris and I getting married, why waste your time and ours coming up here? Why bother?"

"He didn't say he wouldn't marry you," Evelyn said.

"That's how it sounds to me!"

"Sassy," Dr. Morgan began. "You have—"

"Dr. Morgan, if I may interject here," Norris said before Dr. Morgan could answer Sassy's question. "You quoted Proverbs 5:20 when you should have quoted Proverbs 18 and 19. 'Let thy fountain be blessed; and rejoice with the wife of thy youth. Let her be as the loving hind and pleasant roe; let her breasts satisfy thee at all times; and be thou ravished always with her love'."

Dr. Morgan looked down haughtily at Norris to have the nerve to quote the bible to him. Sassy squeezed Norris's hand. Boy was she proud of him!

Norris wasn't finished. "Ecclesiastes 4:9 and 10, Dr. Morgan, says, 'Two are better than one; because they have a good reward for their labour. For if they fall, the one will lift up his fellow; but woe to him that is alone when he falleth; for he hath not another to help him up.' I intend to be here always for Sassy to lift her up and stand tall with her."

"I intend to do the same for you," Sassy said.

"No where in the bible does it say I have to know Sassy a year before marrying her."

If it had been appropriate, Sassy would have high-fived Norris with the loudest slap she could muster. She knew he read the bible, but she had no idea he knew the bible like that, and by the stern expression on Dr. Morgan's face which didn't wilt a bit, the fact that he said nothing probably meant he was amazed as well.

"Dr. Morgan," Sassy said. "I love Norris. This marriage is real for both of us."

"All couples say that. Half of them end up in divorce." Dr. Morgan asked gruffly.

Norris had enough. "Dr. Morgan, you entered my house

with the bearing of a prideful, arrogant man. You wasted no time insulting me and the woman I love; you condemned us before listening to us; and you damned us before blessing us. You say you are a man of God, I question that. I believe you're more like Moab." Norris took out his BlackBerry. "I'll get you a limo back to the city."

"I'm going back with him," Evelyn said.

Sassy glared at Evelyn. "The front door is right there." Sassy started toward the stairs.

Dr. Morgan stood but he didn't head for the door. "Before you place that call, tell what do you know of Moab?"

"I know Moab's loftiness, his arrogance, his pride, his haughtiness brought him God's disfavor. I'll get you that limo."

Norris turned his back to Dr. Morgan. He began to search his BlackBerry address log for the limousine company's telephone number when he was suddenly slapped hard on the back. Startled, Norris turned around just as Dr. Morgan extended his hand to him. This time it was Norris who held back his hand.

A third of the way up the stairs Sassy stopped. She was just as baffled as Evelyn by what Dr. Morgan was doing. He had the look of a sneaky cat that had just eaten the pet canary.

Norris closed his BlackBerry. He studied the gotcha glint in Dr. Morgan's eyes. "You're good," Norris said.

"I'm the best."

"Okay," Sassy said. "What's going on?"

Dr. Morgan continued to hold his hand out to Norris. "Son, don't let your pride keep you from shaking the hand of God's servant."

Sassy finally caught on. "I don't believe this."

"Believe what?" Evelyn asked. "Will someone tell me what just happened?"

Norris firmly shook Dr. Morgan's hand and didn't rebuff Dr. Morgan's powerful embrace.

"He was testing Norris," Sassy said, although she too

was bewildered, and at the same time annoyed.

"I've never seen him do that before," Evelyn said. "He didn't do that to Bernard."

"You and Bernard never got married," Dr. Morgan said. He let go of Norris. "It's good to see you know your bible."

"There was a time when all I had to read was the bible."

"Was that the period when you had to live on the street in Japan?" Sassy asked.

"Yes. The bible is the only thing no one would steal. I still read the bible today, usually at work in the morning."

"Good for you," Dr. Morgan said. "Son, I'd be honored if you could find the time to come to dinner one evening and tell me more about yourself."

"I certainly will."

"I have business back in the city. Where do you want me to perform the ceremony?"

Norris led the way to Bernard's room where Brice was again sitting on the bed close to his father?

"Uncle Morgan!" Brice said. "What are you doing here?"

"I could ask you the same question, boy."

"I came to see my daddy." Brice leaned his head against Bernard's side. "I'm showing him how to use my PSP3 [Play Station Portable3]."

"You're a good son," Dr. Morgan said to Brice, although it was Bernard he was looking at. He went straight to Bernard and laid his hand on his forehead. "'Is any sick among you? Let him call for the elders of the church; and let them pray over him, anointing him with oil in the name of the Lord: And the prayer of faith shall save the sick, and the Lord shall raise him up; and if he have committed sins, they shall be forgiven him'." [James 5:14,15]

Dr. Morgan's back was to Sassy, Evelyn, and Norris. Brice stared wide-eyed up at his great uncle as Dr. Morgan shook Bernard's head with the force of his mighty hand. Bernard held firm his neck and didn't once let on that he was in pain. When Dr. Morgan let go of Bernard and turned back, he had tears in his eyes, and so did Bernard.

"Uncle Morgan," Brice said, "how come you did that to my daddy's head?"

"God told me to."

"Did he tell you to touch my head, too?"

"He didn't tell me yet, but I'll do it anyway." Dr. Morgan laid his hand on Brice's head and said a brief silent prayer over him. "Okay, you're blessed. Now, let's get these two married. If any of you have a cell phone, shut it off. I don't like those things interrupting me."

Norris quickly shut off his BlackBerry. Evelyn did likewise and slipped her cell phone back inside her pant's pockets. Sassy and Norris stood at the foot of Bernard's bed so they were in his direct line of vision.

Dr. Morgan wasted no time. "Dearly beloved, we are gathered here in the sight of God and in the presence of these people to unite Norris Yoshito and Sassy Davenport in holy matrimony. Marriage was ordained by God in Eden and confirmed in Cana of Galilee by the presence of the Lord, and is declared by the Apostle Paul to be honorable among all men. We ask God's blessing on this marriage and pray for love everlasting. Who gives this woman to this man?"

"I do," Bernard said without hesitation.

"I do, too," Brice said, seriously, which made Sassy, Norris, and Bernard smile.

"Shh!" Evelyn admonished.

"Thank you, Brice," Sassy said.

"Do either of you have something you'd like to say?" Dr. Morgan asked, looking at Norris.

Norris shook his head. Dr. Morgan looked at Sassy. She shook her head as well.

"Fine. Do you, Norris take Sassy to be your wife? Do you promise to love, honor, cherish and protect her, forsaking all others and holding only unto her?"

"I do."

"Do you, Sassy, take Norris to be your husband? Do you promise to have and to hold, in sickness and in health, for richer or for poorer, forsaking all others and holding only unto him?"

"I do."

"Do we have rings?" Uncle Morgan asked.

Sassy looked down at her naked ring finger and pretended to pout. Norris lifted her left hand and kissed her ring finger. "Tomorrow," he said.

"That's settled. May I go on?"

"Please do," Norris said.

"I now pronounce you man and wife."

As many times as Sassy had written those words for her characters, hearing them in her own ears for herself seemed somewhat surreal. Unlike her female characters, she wasn't rapturous; she didn't swoon or cry or feel like angels came down and lifted her up to heaven. If she had to put a word to what she was feeling, it would be serene. She almost wanted to ask, "Is this it?" She wondered if Norris was asking himself the same thing. He was still holding her hand, but he was just as quiet, as was Bernard, Evelyn, and Brice. They all seemed to be waiting for Dr. Morgan to tell them what next to do, but Dr. Morgan was flipping through his bible.

Evelyn asked, "Are we gonna stand here all day?"

Bernard quipped, "You don't have to stand. Sit down."

Evelyn shot back, "I wasn't talking to you."

"That's uncalled for," Sassy said in defense of Bernard.

"Well, I wasn't talking to him."

"Evelyn!" Dr. Morgan peered threateningly at Evelyn over the top of his old-fashion aviator glasses as he had done many times before from his pulpit when Evelyn and his daughter couldn't keep their mouths shut during his overly long sermons. When Evelyn said no more, Dr. Morgan was certain she had gotten the message.

"Aren't they supposed to kiss?" Bernard asked. He caught a glimpse of Evelyn as she slipped from the room.

"This isn't a formal ceremony," Dr. Morgan said as he continued turning the pages of his bible. "They can kiss now or later, it's up to them."

"Oh, well," Sassy said. What did she expect? She put her hand out. "Wanna shake on it?"

"Not on your life." Norris wrapped Sassy up tight in his arms and they kissed long and deep. It was electric. It was what Sassy needed.

"Yuk!" Brice covered his eyes.

"That's enough," Dr. Morgan said. "There's plenty of time for that."

"Thank you guys," Bernard said.

"Daddy, where's Mommy going?" Brice asked.

"She'll be back," Bernard said. He raised his hand to Norris who immediately shook his hand. "Thank you."

"Are you happy now?" Sassy asked.

"As long as you are."

"Please, everyone leave," Dr. Morgan said. "I need a moment alone with Bernard." He pulled the chair closer to the bed.

Norris asked, "Would you like something to drink or eat?"

"A glass of water will do fine, before I leave. Brice you leave, too. You can come back when I'm finished."

"Okay." Brice scooted off the bed and scampered out of the room.

"Bernie, do you want me to stay?"

"No."

"Okay." Sassy blew Bernard a kiss. As she and Norris left the room, a sad feeling of foreboding came over her. She didn't want to leave Bernard. She wanted to hear everything that was said to him. Norris closed the door behind them but Sassy stayed at the door with her ear pressed against the wood, but Norris came back and ushered her down the stairs.

"Suppose he's giving Bernie his last rights?"

"That's a possibility."

"It's too soon. I don't want him to do that."

"That's Bernard's decision to make."

"But—"

Norris quickly touched Sassy's lips with his finger, silencing her. She had to know by now there was nothing she could do to alter the direction of Bernard's fate.

"I need some air." Sassy went out onto the deck. Norris followed her out. They were greeted by a soft, warm breeze. Sassy went to the far corner of the large deck and looked out at the lake. When Norris came up behind her and wrapped his arms around her, she laid her head back against his shoulder. He lightly rubbed his cheek against hers. She closed her eyes as he lovingly kissed her neck and aroused her senses. She savored the subtle, yet masculine scent of Norris's cologne.

Sassy turned around to face Norris. "What if we wake up tomorrow and regret—"

"No regrets."

She wrapped her arms around Norris. "Then you owe me a ring."

Norris chuckled. "Not for long. Tomorrow we're going shopping."

They kissed tenderly and then passionately. As they pressed into each other, they felt the sexual tension their bodies generated. They hadn't been intimate since the night Bernard moved in and knowing they were not alone now kept them from succumbing to the moment and falling to the deck to consummate their marriage.

"Damn!" Evelyn said as she walked out onto the deck. "How about a hotel?"

Sassy and Norris immediately stopped kissing, but it was Norris who couldn't face Evelyn.

"Is something wrong?" Sassy was neither embarrassed nor glad to see Evelyn.

"Apparently not out here," Evelyn said. "Anyway, Brice and I will be going back with Uncle Morgan. We—"

"You can go back," Sassy said, "but Brice is staying

overnight as we originally planned and agreed to?"

Evelyn folded her arms. "No he's not."

"Wanna bet?" Sassy planted her hands on her hips.

"Okay, ladies!" Norris stepped in front of Sassy but she immediately came around him.

"Brice is my child!"

"Get over yourself, Evelyn. You didn't have an immaculate conception. Brice stays!"

"Over my dead body!"

Sassy started toward Evelyn, but was pulled back by Norris. "Come on, ladies. You don't want Brice to hear you fighting over him."

"I'm taking my son home, and that's final!"

"Evelyn, why don't you think about what Brice needs besides you? That would be his father."

"Sassy is right."

"Of course you'd say that."

"Because she is," Norris said. "The first thirteen years of my life I didn't have a father, and I was consumed with wondering who he was."

"That's not Brice's problem," Evelyn said.

"Not right now it isn't, but years from now he will have questions. At this moment in time, what they're getting from each other, none of us can give them. Let them have what little time Bernard has left. I promise you, you won't regret it."

"She certainly won't," Dr. Morgan said from the deck door. He came out onto the deck next. He put his arm paternally around Evelyn's shoulder. "A man who suffers and learns from the error of his ways, has a lot to pass on to a son who has yet to misstep but will do so inevitably. I sent Brice upstairs where he needs to be."

Evelyn grunted her disapproval but Dr. Morgan squeezed her so tightly she hurt.

"You leave that boy in the counsel of his father, and you stay here to comfort him when the loss of his father bows his head and waters his eyes. The time he'll need you to wipe his nose is soon coming to an end, but the words he'll get from his dying father, even at his tender age, will live with him all of his life. Now show your manners. Walk me to the door. My limo is outside."

What resistance Evelyn had left seeped out of her like the air from a deflating balloon. She didn't look at Sassy or Norris as she turned to go back into the house.

Sassy said, "You don't have your bible. Did you leave it upstairs?"

"I left it for Bernard. Someone should read it to him. He has my number. He can call me anytime, but you call me when the Lord calls him home."

Just the thought of that day saddened Sassy.

"Dr. Morgan," Norris said, "I have an envelope for you in my den."

"Offerings are collected every Sunday morning. I expect to see you two in church real soon."

"You will," Norris and Dr. Morgan shook hands.

Sassy was relieved when Dr. Morgan and Evelyn left them alone. She slumped back against Norris. "Too bad we can't go to a hotel."

Teasingly, Norris pressed himself into Sassy. "We have the deck."

Sassy pulled back. "You have a lascivious mind."

"You have a lascivious body!"

"Ahem!" Evelyn said.

Sassy and Norris quickly pulled apart to see that Evelyn was back at the door. "If y'all wanna go to a hotel, go. I'll look after Bernard."

Sassy smirked. "Dr. Morgan blessed you out, huh?"

"Take it or leave it." Evelyn started to leave the doorway.

Norris nudged Sassy. "We'll take it!" Sassy said.

Evelyn flipped her hand dismissively at Sassy but said to Norris. "Is there a television I can put in that room? I would like something to do besides look at Bernard."

"There is a television already in the room. The remote is in the night stand. There is a second remote and a remote to raise and lower the large picture on the wall across from the bed. The television is behind the picture."

Evelyn again turned to leave.

"Evelyn," Sassy said. "Please see if you can talk Bernie into seeing his doctor."

"Since when has he ever listened to me?" Evelyn went back into the house.

"She is such a—"

"Let it go," Norris said. "At least she's willing to stay with Bernard tonight."

"Oh, please. She probably wants to get rid of us so she can suffocate him."

Norris was taken aback. "You think she'd do that?"

"Do I believe Pope Benedict XVI wears bright red shiny shoes? You bet I do."

Norris chuckled. "Does he really wear red shoes?"

"Yes he does. Norris, I think we should stay home."

"Sassy, Evelyn isn't that desperate, but I am."

"Convince me," Sassy challenged seductively.

Norris lightly pressed himself into Sassy. They began swaying as in a slow dance that gently stoked the embers that flickered in their bodies. Being fully clothed did nothing to prevent Sassy from feeling Norris's hardness or the sweet sensation that pulsed within.

"A hotel it is," she said.

"Let's go."

"Wait. Didn't you promise to call your father after we were married?"

"We can call him after we've relaxed a bit." Norris started pulling Sassy, but she pulled back.

"But he might be waiting to hear from you now."

"We'll get together with him and Alicia later."

"But I think you should call them anyway."

"If it'll make you happy, I'll call my father." Norris

whipped out his trusty BlackBerry and turned it back on. He pushed one button. The call was answered right away.

"Hey, Dad. We—"

"Who is this?" A man asked.

Norris immediately put on his business voice. "You answered my father's phone. Who are you?"

Sassy saw the concern in Norris's face. "What's wrong?" she asked.

Norris pressed the speaker button on his BlackBerry so that Sassy could hear what was being said on the other end.

"This is Detective Natherson. What is your name?"

Norris suddenly got a cold chill. "Norris Yoshito. Detective, why are you answering my father's phone?"

"Who is your father, sir?"

"Norris Wilson. Let me speak to him," Norris asked although he sensed he wasn't going to.

Sassy clutched Norris's free hand and his arm. She braced herself.

"I'm sorry, sir. Your father and mother have been murdered."

Sassy's breath caught in her throat.

A sharp ache gripped Norris's heart. "That can't be."

"The victims, Mr. and Mrs. Norris Wilson, were identified by a neighbor."

Norris looked at his BlackBerry as if it had morphed into a two headed snake he could make no sense of. "That can't be. I saw my father yesterday."

"Oh my God." Sassy saw the gleam in Norris's eyes dull and the sensual potency in his face and body completely drain away. His shoulders slumped. His legs buckled under him as he dropped heavily into the chair closest to him. He still held his BlackBerry as he looked at Sassy with an expression of total disbelief. Having difficulty believing it herself, Sassy found it hard to put Alicia's smiling, good-natured bantering together with the word murder. How could that be? How could anyone violently snuff the life from such a joyous spirit? Sassy put her arms around Norris's shoulders. He clutched her tightly about her waist and buried his face against her stomach.

"Mr. Yoshito," the detective said, "there is nothing specific we can tell you at this time, but I would like to meet with you."

Norris closed his eyes to stay the tears that were about to fall. Sassy took the BlackBerry from his hand.

"Detective," she said, "we're in Pennsylvania. It'll take us about two hours to get to Queens."

"Ma'am, who are you?"

"I'm his wife."

28

A night of lovemaking in a hotel was a thought instantly dashed, as was Sassy's fear that Evelyn would harm Bernard. Oddly, it felt like she and Norris were already in a funeral procession with the stop and go traffic on Interstate 80. Throughout the ride, Norris asked only once, "Why?" He didn't expect an answer and Sassy didn't pretend to have one. All she could do was hold his hand and marvel at the look of stoic determination to not give in to his pain. Norris had the look of a man on a mission that he couldn't talk about. As soon as they crossed the Hudson River into New York City, Norris gave the driver directions to the police impound yard on 56th Road and Laurel Hill Boulevard under the Kosciusko Bridge in Woodside, Queens. The car wasn't damaged and, strangely, not a thing was missing, not the mini camcorder or the E-Z Pass Norris kept in his glove compartment. Norris wasn't saying it, but he assumed Byron Satoshi was behind it all.

They continued Further on into Queens silent in their individual yet similar thoughts about the pain of loss and the agony of trying to understand the evil in the world. An hour and a half later, Norris parked a block down from his father's house because he couldn't get any closer. As they walked toward the house, Norris secretly hoped someone had made a mistake. He gulped in air to keep from crying, but a wayward tear escaped anyway. Sassy didn't allow herself the luxury of crying, she had to stand as strong for Norris as he had been standing for her with Bernard. Norris's urge to cry had been brief, but she knew his anger wouldn't be.

It had been three and a half hours since they'd spoken to Detective Natherson, and still, there were numerous police cars, marked and unmarked, an ambulances, and three television news vans still parked on the block. The atrocity of the crime demanded extensive attention and as far as Sassy could see, many of the neighbors thought so, too. So many were standing outside their homes, some huddled in packs on front lawns talking about the murders that happened so close to their own front doors; while others stood on their front steps somewhat hesitant about getting any closer to the scene of the crime than they had to.

"Norris!" old Mr. Lewis sitting in his wheelchair next door called out as Norris passed his house. "You come see me after you see about your daddy."

Norris responded with a half-hearted raising of his hand as he continued past his parent's neighbor whom he had known since coming to America. Others who knew Norris offered their condolences as he walked hand-in-hand with the new wife they had no knowledge of. At his father's house, out on the sidewalk, Sassy and Norris were stopped by two police officers at the yellow police tape strung around the front yard.

"I'm going in to see my father."

"Sir—"

"Let that boy in to see his daddy!" Mr. Lewis yelled from next door.

"This is a crime scene. My orders are to let no one in."

"I don't give a damn what your orders are—"

Sassy quickly asked, "Is Detective Natherson inside? He's the one we spoke to. He knew we were coming." She held tight to Norris's arm. She could feel his tenseness.

"Wait here," the young officer said. He turned his back and spoke into his two way radio. Within minutes, a bald-headed, thick set man appeared at the front door.

"That's Detective Natherson," the officer said.

Detective Natherson beckoned for Sassy and Norris to

come up the walkway to the house. Norris wasn't interested in introductions. "I would like to see them." Norris started around Detective Natherson who quickly grabbed him by the arm, stopping him.

"I can't let you back there until crime scene investigators finish processing the scene."

Norris yanked his arm free. "How did they die?"

"Actually, Mr. Yoshito, your mother was taken to Jamaica Hospital."

Norris tried to calm the pounding in his chest. "Alicia is alive?"

"Alicia? Mrs. Wilson isn't your mother?"

"She's my step-mother. You said both were killed."

"That was the first report. Mrs. Wilson is in the intensive care trauma."

"What are her chances?"

"My partner is at the hospital. He'll report in as soon as he has definitive information."

"Okay. I'd like to see my father. Where is he?"

"He's in the kitchen. I can't let you go back there yet. Your father put up a fierce fight but who ever it was overpowered him and his wife. Frankly, your folks were butchered."

Norris grunted as if he were punched in the gut. He fell back against the wall. His face went ashen as he struggled to not lose it.

Sassy clutched Norris's hand as tightly as she could. "Detective, do you know who did it? Was it a home invasion?"

"Mrs. Yoshito, our investigation just got under way. We have nothing definitive to disclose at this time. We do know there was no forced entry."

"So you think they knew their killer?"

Detective Natherson looked pointedly at Norris. "That's the way it's looking."

Half expecting to see Mr. Wilson or Alicia's blood splattered everywhere, Sassy's eyes flitted anxiously from the livingroom to the diningroom but she saw not a drop of blood. However, she was beginning to smell something. She sniffed the air and quickly realized it was the unpleasant, addled smell of decay. She quietly covered her mouth and nose with her hand as she tried to remember the smell of fragrant lavender that filled scented the air when she was last in the house last.

"Mr. Yoshito, perhaps you can answer some questions for me."

Norris cleared his throat. "Like what?".

"Let's go in here." Detective Natherson nodded toward the living room, but Norris hesitated. It was as if the wall wouldn't let him go.

"It's alright," Detective Natherson said, "This room was processed this morning."

"This morning?" Norris pulled away from the wall. "What do you mean this morning? When were they killed?"

"Yesterday? And no one called me? I was only a phone call away. My number is in the memory of my father's house phone and cell phone. Why didn't someone call me?"

"Mr. Yoshito, we had no way of knowing that you were related. Your last name—"

"The neighbors know me. They know my name! I spoke to you around 4:35 this afternoon. Why didn't anyone call me this morning? Yesterday? I can't believe this!"

"Mr. Yoshito, after a preliminary inspection, the medical examiner put the time of death at sometime between 8:30 a.m. and twelve noon yesterday."

"But I saw them as late as 8:15 yesterday morning. I was here! They were fine. My father. . .my father. . .Oh, God."

Sassy felt helpless as Norris turned away. He pressed his forehead against his arm high up on the hall wall. He hid his face just as a dam of tears broke through. Sassy put her arm around Norris. "Detective, would you give us a minute?"

"I'll be in the living room."

As soon as Detective Natherson walked off, Sassy began lightly rubbing Norris's back. She had no words that would comfort him. All she could do was be there for him. Although Sassy's mother didn't die such an horrific death, her passing hurt her to her heart. The indescribable pain Norris was feeling had to be greater by far. Through her hand, Sassy could feel Norris's body quake as he sobbed. In her own silence, Sassy kept asking herself, "How could this happen?"

Murder? Yes, murder was real. So many times she had seen the faces of murder victims and their grief-stricken families on television and while she sympathized with them and understood their grief, she never felt their pain, until now. As her own tears eased down her cheeks for the man she loved and for the father he loved, she couldn't understand why such evil existed in the world. Maybe that's why she was so comfortable writing romance. None of her characters were ever murdered and all her heroes and heroine literally galloped into the sunset.

A few minutes passed before Norris could pull himself together. He cleared his throat, he dried his eyes, he faced Sassy. "My father's been dead since yesterday. Yesterday! Maybe if I had come back—"

"No, Norris, please don't do this to yourself. You might not have been able to do anything."

"But I was here yesterday morning! Everything was fine; Alicia, my father. They were both happy. They were teasing me about you. My father said he knew I was a goner by the way I looked at you. He said he thought no one would ever catch me. He thought that was so funny." Norris couldn't laugh; not when he was still crying.

Sassy tried to hold Norris but being comforted was not what he wanted. He eased out of Sassy's arms. "I should have told him someone was after me. I should have warned him."

"Norris, there is no way you could have known he would go after your parents."

"I should have known he'd go after anyone in my life."

Sassy remembered how afraid she had been since the night she had come face to face with the man she thought was

Norris. "Norris, if he killed your father, then he—"

"No. He will never get near you again."

"But why does he have it in for you?"

"As God is my witness, I don't know."

"Who are you talking about?" Detective Natherson asked as he stepped around Norris.

Norris and Sassy both fell silent. Sassy squeezed Norris's hand, strongly hinting to him to tell the detective about the man who had become a great spoiler in his life.

"Mr. Yoshito, do you know who killed your father?"

"That's a question we'd like to hear the answer to as well," Detective Kiefer said from the front doorway. Just behind him was his partner, Joe Lupino.

"Detective Kiefer?" Detective Natherson asked.

Detectives Kiefer and Natherson shook hands. "This is my partner, Joe Lupino."

Sassy and Norris watched as the brotherhood of law enforcement officers shook hands, but Norris didn't let on that he was rattled by the presence of Detectives Kiefer and Lupino. He never told Sassy they had visited him in his office just yesterday.

"Thanks for the courtesy," Detective Kiefer said to Detective Natherson, but he wasn't looking at Detective Natherson, he was looking at Norris. "Where can we talk?"

Detective Natherson lead the way into the living room, but neither Detective Kiefer nor Lupino followed until Sassy and Norris went ahead of them. No one sat except for Sassy. Just knowing that not too far away lay Norris's father whose life had been snuffed out by someone so diabolically evil, weakened her knees, chilled her heart, and made her wonder why God hadn't stepped in and saved him.

"Have a seat, Mr. Yoshito," Detective Natherson said.

Norris couldn't sit. Every muscle in his body was tight to the point of spasm. He went and stood in front of the mantel where Alicia had proudly hung a large family portrait of the four of them. Norris remembered well the day they sat for that portrait—he was fourteen years old. Clarence insisted on standing behind their father who was sitting next to Alicia, but the photographer thought the balance was better if Norris stood behind him instead. He was already taller than Clarence by three inches.

# # # #

"I'm your son!" Clarence said. "He—"

"You're both my sons," Norris Wilson said definitive tone that left no question in Norris's mind about how his father felt about him. "My blood is equally in both of you. Now stand behind your mother."

Clarence stomped out of the studio but Norris Wilson went after him. It was nearly thirty minutes before they both came back. Clarence didn't look Norris's way, but he did stand behind his mother. It was days later when he and Alicia were home alone that Alicia came into his room with his clean laundry that she tried to explain.

"Sometimes it's difficult for an only child to share what he's never had to share before. Not just his toys, but his parents, their love, their time, their very presence."

Norris closed the drawer on his clean tee shirts. He said nothing as he put away the remainder of his clean clothes.

"Norris, until you came, Clarence was the center of his father's world. They did so many things together. I'm sure you can understand, being your mother's only child yourself, what it was like having your mother all to yourself and sharing her with no one."

Memories of his mother overwhelmed Norris. Tears filled his eyes, but he didn't let Alicia see his face. He kept his head down.

"Your father and I did our best to prepare Clarence for the day you would arrive. You boys have been getting along okay, right?"

Norris shrugged and wiped his sleeve across his eyes.

If getting along meant that neither he nor Clarence had thrown a punch, then they were getting along. Most days Clarence either ignored him or when no one was around, taunted him by calling him half breed, but Clarence's words didn't hold a candle to the disparaging way he and other mixed race kids like him were treated on the streets of Fuchu. Clarence's words only bothered him because he was supposed to be his brother.

"Clarence wanted to stand close to his father because that's where he'd always been. You can understand that, can't you? Clarence wasn't trying to hurt you."

# # # #

Norris didn't believe that then, he didn't believe it now. The only bond between him and Clarence was the blood they shared. They never saw eye to eye; they never had each other's back; and now with their father gone, Norris doubted they'd ever see each other again. The timing of his marriage to Sassy couldn't be more perfect.

"Mr. Yoshito," Detective Natherson said. "You indicated you were here yesterday morning. What time did you arrive?"

Norris turned away from the portrait. "Around seven fifteen."

"Why did you come so early?"

"My father wanted to speak to me in person."

"About what?"

"He just learned he had prostate cancer."

Sassy gasped. She started to wonder why Norris had not told her until she realized everything in his life had been about her and Bernard.

"Did you and your father or his wife have a disagreement?"

Norris and Sassy exchanged stunned but confused looks. "Why are you asking him that?"

Detective Keifer ignored Sassy's question. "Mr.

Yoshito, is there a reason why you can't answer that question?"

Norris forced the lump in his throat way down into his gut. "Besides the absurdness of the question, I need more than a moment to deal with the lost of my father and possibly the loss of his wife, the two people who meant the world to me. I'm sure you can find an ounce of compassion behind your badge to extend me the courtesy of consideration."

"Mrs. Wilson is not his mother?" Detective Natherson said to Detective Keifer.

"No, but I've known her since I was thirteen."

"Mr. Yoshito," Detective Natherson said, "time is of the essence in solving any murder. We need to question any and everyone who may have come in contact with the victims within the last forty-eight hours."

"I understand that," Norris said as his voice cracked, "but I need to see my father. I need to—"

Detective Keifer persisted, "Did you have a disagreement with your father?"

"No! My father and I—"

Sassy sprang to her feet. "What the heck are you trying to say?"

Detective Keifer again ignored Sassy. "What time yesterday morning did you last see your father and his wife?"

"He's already told you that!" Sassy rushed to Norris's side. "They're trying to say you killed your father!"

Norris put his arm around Sassy. "Detective, I last saw my father and his wife around 8:15 yesterday morning. I—"

"Mr. Yoshito," Detective Natherson said, "we have a witness who saw you leave out the back door of this house around 9:45 a.m."

Norris knew immediately who Detective Natherson's witness was. Mr. Lewis, the old man whose house was next door to the left. Mr. Lewis could clearly see anyone leaving out the house through the back door. The back door couldn't be seen by the neighbor on the right side of the house.

"Detective, it was not me Mr. Lewis saw. I have several

witnesses who saw me in my office at 9:00 a.m. I didn't leave my office until 2:30."

"My witness says he's known you since you were a boy. He said he'd know you anywhere. He swears he saw you leave here at 9:45 yesterday morning."

"Did I speak to him? Did I stop and talk to him?"

"He said you waved and kept going."

"Detective, I've known Mr. Lewis for years. If he saw me, he would have shouted out to me just as he did today. Mr. Lewis would not have let me get away without speaking to him, and I would not have walked past him without speaking if I had seen him. It was not me Mr. Lewis saw."

"Did you speak to him today? I know he was out front when you got here."

"Thoughts of my father were more important than speaking to Mr. Lewis or anyone else for that matter."

Detective Natherson turned his back to Sassy and Norris to speak privately to Detectives Keifer and Lupino.

Sassy whispered, "They're trying to say you killed your father and Alicia too, if she dies."

"It's Satoshi."

"Tell them about him."

"Not yet. Cyrus hasn't caught up with him yet."

Detective Natherson turned back. All three detectives eyed Norris.

If Sassy had ever wondered what it was like to look into the faces of hungry lions only seconds from pouncing on their prey, she wondered no more. The accusatory glint in all three detectives' eyes, the cynical set of their lips, and the bold display of their guns unnerved her. She anxiously tapping Norris's arm to get his attention but he was totally focused on Detective Keifer.

"Mr. Yoshito," Detective Keifer said, "are you keeping count of the number of people in your life who've tragically lost their lives?"

"And what the hell is that supposed to mean?" Sassy

asked testily before Norris could respond.

An "ah ha" moment flashed for Detective Keifer. "You don't know do you?"

"Detective, why don't you tell me what you think I don't know."

"Apparently, you don't know about the murder of your husband's secretary, who by the way, died earlier today, or the slaughter of her roommate or the murder of his client's granddaughter."

While Sassy's eyes widened and her jaw slackened, Norris said emphatically, "I am not your killer."

"Maybe he told you something about the unsolved murder of Mrs. Agatha Lewis, the wife of his neighbor next door," Detective Keifer said sarcastically. He then looked Norris straight in the eye. "You don't know what happened there either, do you?"

Sassy got a sick feeling in the pit of her stomach. Why had Norris not told her about any of these incidents?

Norris held Sassy by the shoulders. "It is a well known fact that the Lewis's house was burgled. Mrs. Lewis was home alone. She surprised the burglar. He killed her."

"You should have checked before you went over there," Detective Keifer said nastily.

Sassy gasped. "You supercilious son of a—"

"It's okay!" Norris squeezed Sassy's hand. "Don't listen to him. I was out of the city on business when Mrs. Lewis died."

Sassy started to say something to Detective Keifer but Norris took hold of her chin. "Sassy, look at me. I did not kill Mrs. Lewis."

"I bet," Detective Keifer said. "Mrs. Yoshito, in case you haven't connected the dots, the common link between all these victims, is your husband."

Sassy pulled away from Norris. "Why are you trying to frame my husband? You have the wrong man. He said he didn't kill anyone; I believe him. Norris, tell him he's wrong."

Norris glared bitterly at Detective Keifer. He had never had an instant dislike for anyone until now. The accusatory look in the detective's eyes, the snarly way he spoke to Sassy, and the angry frown on his face made Norris want to slam his fist into Detective Keifer's face. There was no way Norris could bring himself to talk to a man who had already made up his mind about him.

"He can't defend himself," Detective Lupino said. "Need we say more?"

"Actually, I think you've said too damn much as it is," Sassy said testily, but the truth was, it bothered her that not a whimper of a dissent leaped from Norris's mouth. For her own sake, she needed to hear him dispute the charges they were spewing against him. Norris's silence worried her. Why won't he tell them about Byron Satoshi? If there was no truth to the allegations of murder, why was he so quiet. What if it's true? What if he had killed someone? What was she going to do? Oh God. She had to stop thinking like that. This was not the time to be struck with doubt when she had just married the man. But still, what if he is a murderer? Wouldn't that be the reason why he didn't tell her about the other murders? Oh God. What had she gotten herself into?

29

"Lady, you've been had," Detective Keifer said. "You're married to a murderer."

Sassy knew her confidence in Norris was shaken, but she fronted anyway. "I know my husband well enough to know he didn't kill anyone. Norris, tell them you had nothing to do with any of those murders."

Sullen, Norris continually glared at Detective Keifer. "Why bother?"

"Norris—"

"That's right," Detective Keifer said. "You and I both know the truth! By the way, don't you care that your secretary died? How often did you visit Myra Barrett, Mr. Yoshito?"

"Detective, I've never had an affair with Myra Barrett. I've never visited her at her home or anywhere else outside of my office."

"Liar!" Detective Keifer sneered.

"Go to hell!" Norris said low in his throat.

By the minute, Sassy was getting more worried. "None of this is true, right?"

Norris looked deep into Sassy's frightened eyes. If no other person in the world believed him, it was important that Sassy did. Again, hoping that it would be enough, he squeezed her hand.

"Mr. Yoshito," Detective Natherson said, "is there anything you can tell us about the murder of your father?"

"Detective, if I knew anything I wouldn't be standing

here wasting time. My father meant everything to me and so did his wife. Killing them would be akin to cutting my own throat."

"Interesting choice of words," Detective Lupino said. "All the victims except one were cut up."

Norris grumbled low in his throat, "Not by me."

"That's not the way I see it," Detective Keifer said. "You're a killer and I'm gonna prove it."

Panic choked Sassy. "Tell them about Byron Satoshi."

"Who is Byron Satoshi?" Detective Natherson asked.

With the glare of condemnation shooting at him from all three detectives, Norris decided this was not the time to talk about Byron Satoshi when he didn't know where he was and if he was, in fact, the man out to destroy his life. Yes, he might have stolen his car, but he had no definitive proof that Satoshi was the man who killed his father or any of the other victims.

Anxiously squeezing Norris's hand, Sassy pleaded, "Tell them or they'll charge you with murder."

"Detective," Norris said to Detective Natherson, "I did not kill my father or any one of the other unfortunate victims. If you're going to charge me, then I need to call my lawyer."

"I bet you would," Detective Keifer said.

"Mr. Yoshito, did you kill Norris Wilson and attempt to kill Alicia Wilson?" Detective Natherson asked.

Norris narrowed his eyes and looked from one detective to the other. "If the measure of a man was in how well he did his job, then each of you is a miserable failure. You've already condemned and convicted me. I've never killed anyone in my life." Norris squeezed Sassy's hand. She squeezed back because she believed him.

"You are our sole suspect," Detective Keifer said.

"What else do we have to tell you?" Sassy let got of Norris's hand. "He didn't do it! You need to go and look else where for your murderer."

"You need to take your own damn advice," Detective Keifer retorted, "and look for another husband because this one is going to jail."

Sassy was astounded that the hawked-eyed detective with the angry snarl was so bullheaded and narrow-minded in his bitter condemnation of Norris. "You're a bastard!"

"He's not worth it!" Norris pulled Sassy back. "Weak men like him hide behind badges."

Detective Keifer baited, "Murderers hide behind the skirts of naive women."

"Detective!" Detective Natherson said. He stepped in-between Norris and Detective Keifer.

Norris pushed forward but Sassy pushed him back and strained to hold him still. There was less than ten feet between the two men, but Sassy could swear that volts of angry energy shot through her body.

"Norris, he's trying to get to you! He's trying to make you react so he can arrest you!"

"You wanna come at me, killer? Get from behind the skirt. Come on!"

"Detective, can I speak to you outside?" Detective Natherson asked.

"Why are you people letting him talk to us like this? We're not criminals!"

"Let's everybody calm down," Detective Natherson said. "This is not the way we do it out here."

"Then let's move it to Brooklyn. I got three dead bodies in Brooklyn. His ass belongs to me!"

"This is my investigation, Detective!" Detective Natherson said.

Sassy couldn't take it. "He's despicable!"

"Lady, the despicable one is the one you've been sleeping with."

Norris said brashly, "Don't ever let me see you without that badge."

"Still threatening me, killer?"

"Dammit!" Detective Natherson exclaimed. "Detective, this is my damn investigation and I'm not letting you screw it up! If there is to be an arrest, it will be my arrest, my collar! You and your partner step down or get out!"

Defiant in his anger, Detective Keifer didn't move. He kept his belligerent glare fixed on Norris just as Norris fixed his on him.

"Why are you people not listening to me?" Sassy asked. "Norris did not kill his father! He—"

"Sassy, if they're arresting me—"

"No one is under arrest!" Detective Natherson shouted.

"Detective," Sassy said. "There is a guy named Byron Satoshi who has been impersonating Norris for months."

"Sassy!"

"He stole Norris's financial identity; he stole his car just yesterday from Brooklyn, and he's been inside my apartment."

"This is crap," Detective Keifer said.

"Your apartment?" Detective Lupino asked. "I thought you said you were married."

"We just got married, but I still have my apartment, but that's not important. Byron—"

"Sassy, we need to first speak to my attorney."

"No, Norris! We need to tell them about Byron Satoshi!"

"But he may not be the right guy."

"Suppose he is? Detective, I've been hiding in the house in Pennsylvania for weeks now because this guy showed up in my apartment in Brooklyn. I've seen him and so have other people."

"What does he look like?" Detective Natherson asked.

Sassy hesitated. She looked back at Norris who wasn't too pleased with her, but she didn't care. If he wasn't going to defend himself, she was. "The guy looks like Norris. He could be his twin."

"This is bull!" Detective Keifer blurted. "She's lying!"

"I'm telling the truth! You're accusing the wrong man!"

The skeptical looks on the faces of all three detectives

told Sassy they didn't believe a word she said. "It is the truth!"

Detective Keifer scoffed, "Does she roll over and play dead for you too?"

"Screw you, you incompetent Cro-Magnon bastard!" Sassy said.

"Sassy!"

"Lady, I'll shove my gun—"

"Detective!"

"Hey!" Norris lurched forward. "You don't talk to her like that!"

"How do you want me to talk to the bitch?"

"That's it!" Detective Natherson said. "Detective, leave!"

Lurching forward with his partner trying to hold him back, Detective Keifer bared his teeth. "Not without him."

"Get him out of here!" Detective Natherson shouted at Detective Lupino while trying to block Detective Keifer but was himself slammed aside.

"Don't get in my way!" Detective Keifer warned.

"Detective, you—"

"He's crazy!" Sassy said. "He—"

Quickly moving Sassy out the way, Norris pointed to Detective Keifer and beckoned him to bring it.

Sassy shrieked, "No!"

Detective Keifer bolted!

"Frank!"

As Detective Keifer charged at him, Norris fluidly sidestepped, backward pivoted as he raised his elbow, and using Detective Keifer's own momentum, knocked him off balance. Detective Keifer slammed into the side of the sofa with a loud grunt! Norris's pulse was racing. He faced Detective Keifer as he coolly raised his hands in surrender. He winked at Sassy but Sassy was aghast at what she'd just seen.

Behind Norris, Detective Lupino shouted, "Grab some floor! Grab some floor!" Detective Lupino had one hand on his holstered revolver and the other pointing menacingly at Norris back. Norris didn't move.

Sassy immediately jumped behind Norris to protect his back! "He didn't hit him! He didn't hit him!"

"Get out of the way!" Detective Lupino shouted at Sassy, but Sassy didn't move even when Norris ordered her to.

"Sassy, get back!"

"Not on your life!"

Detective Keifer glared at Norris. "You bastard!" As angry as he was, his age told on him as he got awkwardly up off the floor while simultaneously trying to draw his revolver, but Detective Natherson was right on top of him. He clamped down on his hand!

"Not here!"

Detective Keifer shouted, "God dammit get off me!"

Norris dared not take his eyes off of Detective Keifer. "Sassy, get out of the way!"

"If either one of them shoot you, they shoot me too."

"This isn't going down in my precinct!" Detective Natherson said. "You pull that revolver and I'll be the first up testifying before the review board."

"He assaulted an officer!"

"You went after him!"

Panting and thinking about the consequences, Detective Keifer gave up on drawing his revolver.

"Lady, move or you're under arrest!" Detective Lupino ordered though he didn't approach Sassy.

"If you touch me, I will E-mail blast MySpace, Facebook, Twitter, the Mayor's office, the Governor's office, CNN, MSNBC, and every other major news station, and newspaper in this country!"

"Sassy, I don't want you in this!" Norris pulled Sassy from behind him and pushed her aside. "Stay there!" he ordered as Detective Keifer came at him. Norris quickly locked his fingers behind his head and stood with feet firmly planted two feet apart.

"Don't touch him!" Sassy shouted.

Growling, Detective Keifer punched Norris square in the stomach which Norris saw coming and tightened his abs which deflected the punch. Detective Keifer then tried to yank Norris's arm down so he could wrench it up behind his back but Norris, showing no strain, no pain, and no intention of allowing himself to be slammed to the floor, channeled throughout his body his Kyokushinkai training. Detective Keifer punched Norris in the side, while Detective Lupino tried kicking Norris's left leg from under him, but staring straight ahead, Norris held his body as rigid as a mighty, unbendable oak. He clamped down on his jaw and set his sight on an invisible mark on the wall. Unless they shot him, he wasn't going down.

"Leave him alone!" Sassy went at Detective Keifer with her fists but was intercepted from the side by Detective Natherson who grabbed her and turned her completely around.

"Do you wanna make it worse?"

"Why don't you stop them?"

Thump! Thump! Thump! "Great question!"

The loud thumping coming from the archway startled everyone. They all immediately turned to see who had banged so thunderously on the wall.

"Is this a private party?"

Sassy knew instantly who the man was and so did Norris although he couldn't see him. The weight of the two detectives on his body kept him from turning around. The two detectives had stopped tussling with Norris, but neither released their hold on him. Detective Natherson, as well, continued to hold on to Sassy's arm.

"This is police business!" Detective Keifer bellowed. "Get the fu—"

"Hey!" Clarence Wilson roared! He came further into the living room. "You better swallow that damn word before you find your tongue sandwiched between your blue balls."

Detectives Keifer and Lupino were both uncertain as to whom they were about to deal with. They eased up, though not completely, on their hold on Norris and their determination to take him down to the floor.

Sassy yanked herself free of Detective Natherson's weakening hold. She scooted away from him in case he was of a mind to again grab onto her. She hastily gave Clarence the once over. He was a few inches shorter than Norris but looked a whole lot like their father.

"What business is this of yours?" Detective Keifer asked.

"A better question," Clarence said. "Why the hell are you manhandling my half brother and his wife?" Clarence took from his breast pocket a shiny black leather wallet. He smoothly flipped it open exposing his gold DEA badge.

Unimpressed, Detective Keifer snarled, "Well, *Agent* Wilson, I got one myself. You wanna see it?"

"If it's not federal with a Harvard law degree behind it, it's not worth looking at."

Detective Keifer tightened his hold on Norris in retaliation for being insulted by Clarence, while Detective Lupino eased up on Norris altogether.

"Agent Wilson," Detective Lupino said, "are you aware your parents were attached here in their home? Your father didn't make it."

Clarence put his badge away. He looked at the family portrait over the fireplace, then back at Detective Lupino. "Detective, I've just flown more than twenty-one hours from Bangkok after getting a disturbing call yesterday afternoon about the murder of my father. I won't bore you with the details of how I took that news, but seeing my half brother assaulted in my parents house by officers of the law makes my homecoming all the more agonizing. I don't believe for one minute Norris killed our father or attempted to kill my mother. Why you suspect him, I can't begin to imagine, but I'm not in the mood to deal with your wild suppositions. Let him go."

"Finally, a voice of reason," Sassy said.

Clarence looked at Sassy but he didn't acknowledge

her.

Detective Keifer was reluctant but when all eyes were on him, he finally let go against his better judgment. He stayed close to Norris which Norris didn't seem bothered by.

"You got a call yesterday?" Norris asked. "Why wasn't I called? Why didn't you call me?"

"Actually, I thought you might have already known. You were already in the city."

"Who called you?" Detective Natherson asked.

"Detective, I'll sit down with you after I've seen about my father. I suppose my father is still in the house since the coroner's van is still sitting out front."

"The crime scene investigators are still working back there. I'd appreciate it if you didn't interfere."

"Collect your evidence, Detective. Norris and I will wait here until they're done."

"Your brother is our prime suspect," Detective Keifer said. "He—"

"Detective," Clarence said, "unless you caught Norris with a weapon in his hand standing over my parents with their blood splattered all over him, you don't have a case against him. However, if you have an arrest warrant, produce it."

"I can haul this man in for questioning without a warrant." Detective Keifer took hold of Norris's arm.

Although Norris didn't resist, he didn't want Sassy to see him arrested.

"He can't do that, can he?" Sassy asked.

"Detective, you can ask my brother to appear at the precinct at his own volition with or without me; or get a warrant to appear if he so declines. Until then, let him go."

Detective Keifer's bullheadedness would not let him take his hands off of Norris Yoshito. "This man killed four people."

"I've killed no one!"

"Detective, beyond your gut feeling," Clarence said sarcastically, "what definitive evidence do you have?"

"I don't care who you are," Detective Keifer said, "I'm not gonna keep taking your crap."

"I got a big shovel. How much more crap you can stomach is up to you."

Norris wasn't impressed with Clarence's bravado. When they were kids, Clarence never stood up for him in school, on the playground, or right there on their block. A lot of the fights he got into were incited by Clarence.

Detective Keifer made a move to step up to Clarence but Detective Natherson, facing Detective Keifer, quickly stepped in-between them. "I've had enough of this! This is a crime scene, not a boxing match! We have a murder to investigate. Detective, if you have something, put it on the table. If not, take your partner and leave."

"We have witnesses!" Detective Lupino quickly volunteered. "Witnesses who can place Yoshito at the scene of each murder, including yesterday morning leaving this house."

"I have never been to Myra Barrett's or Karen Markowitz's apartments, and I have every right to come and go from this house as I damn well please."

"Detective," Clarence said, "if all you have are witnesses whose testimony can be seriously disputed, your charges may never get past a grand jury. Where's your hard evidence; your eyewitnesses to the crime; your prints; your DNA?"

"Not in my pocket, that's for damn sure." Detective Keifer said. "I'm taking this man in for assault on an officer, and there is not a damn thing you can do about it."

"How are your arches?" Clarence pulled out his cell phone. He flipped it open. "South Jamaica, Brownsville, East New York, South Bronx, Harlem?"

The mere reference of his early years as a beat cop in one of the roughest sections of north-central Brooklyn made Detective Keifer wince, but he wasn't about to be bullied by a drug enforcement cop who had no authority to stop him from arresting the murder suspect who had caused him to lose many a night's sleep.

"Make your call," Detective Keifer dared.

"Hold up," Detective Natherson said stopping Clarence. He went to Detective Keifer. "Let me have a word with you and your partner, outside."

He'd never admit it, but Detective Keifer knew he had no other choice but to walk away. He had nothing substantive, nothing that would get him an indictment. Still, he was pissed. He let go of Norris but, spitefully, he elbowed Norris in the rib but was shocked when Norris instinctively struck back with a harder blow to his rib.

Detective Keifer grunted. "You son of a bitch!"

Clarence laughed. Sassy jumped back against the wall out of the way.

Detective Keifer again grabbed for his revolver. This time, both Natherson and Lupino grabbed his arms and pulled him, struggling and bitching out of the room. "You're not getting away from me! I'm gonna get you! I'm gonna lock your ass up for the murder of those girls!"

Sassy went to Norris. "He's crazy! Are you alright?"

"I'm a damn sight far from being alright."

Clarence waited until the sound of Detective Keifer's rant lessened as he was taken outside the house. He turned on Norris. "What did you have to do with this?"

"What the hell are you guys inhaling in this room?" Sassy asked.

"Lady, I wasn't talking to you."

Sassy's eyes widened in surprise.

"Hey! Don't talk to my wife like that!"

Clarence was not intimidated by Norris's rebuke. He didn't even bother to glance in Sassy's direction to see that she was still in shock. She tried to give Clarence the benefit of the doubt—this was a horrible time to meet, but she couldn't help but remember what her mother used to say. "First impressions, no matter the circumstance, are the real deal."

Clarence stepped closer to Norris and Sassy. Norris

firmly but gently pushed Sassy an arm's distance away while locked in a hard stare with Clarence.

"No," Sassy said. "Please don't."

"I don't have time for niceties," Clarence said. "My father—"

"Your father?"

"My father, your father, what damn difference does it make? He's been murdered and *my* mother could die any minute! What you know, I need to know—now!"

Unblinking, unafraid, and still unimpressed with Clarence's bravado, Norris, challengingly matched stares with the man who was once the boy overheard asking God to send him back to Japan because he didn't want him to be his brother.

Sassy felt like she was caught in a pen with two bulls. She started backing away. "Norris, please, let's leave."

"Maybe that detective is right about you," Clarence said.

"That's right, Clarence, peel back the mask. Let the real bastard in you out."

"Norris!" Sassy rushed to see if Detective Natherson was in the hallway. He wasn't. No one was.

Clarence made a grab for Norris's jacket collar but, with lightening speed, Norris knocked Clarence's hand away and immediately they began grappling, hand-to-hand. From their mouths came not a sound, not even a grunt. The scathing flurry of open-handed slaps and wrists blocks fluttered like the wings of two fighting roosters.

Sassy shouted in a hushed voice, "What the heck are you guys eating, the testicles of raging bulls? What's wrong with you all? Norris! Norris!"

Norris's unwavering concentration was on Clarence whose forehead poured beads of sweat.

"Norris! Norris, please!"

The flurry of hands suddenly stopped. Norris and Clarence both stood with the backs of their right hands pressed hard against each other. Neither made a threatening move with their other hand as they, nose flaring, lips tight, glared menacingly at each other.

Clarence sneered, "You think you can take me?"

On the streets of Fuchu, Norris learned a long time ago to never waste energy on words when there was an inevitable fight at hand. His lips didn't move, nor did his hands. He stayed at the ready.

Sassy glimpsed Detective Natherson just outside the living room before he pulled back out of sight. She was sure he was still listening.

"Guys, please, listen," Sassy said. "This is not the time or place to open old wounds. Clarence, before you were defending Norris. Now, you're accusing him."

"It was all for show," Norris said. It had been years since they last fought, and even then, they had not been able to finish it. Their father had pulled them apart and no amount of talking or reasoning had ever brought them together. Norris lowered his hand at the same time as Clarence.

Clarence stepped back. "Did you have anything to do with it?"

"That's insulting," Sassy said.

Norris boldly stepped up to Clarence. "Out of respect for our father, I won't take you down in his house."

"The big outdoors is always out there."

Sassy pulled Norris back but she couldn't pull his eyes off of Clarence. "Don't you guys have something more important to do than kicking each other's behind?"

"You better listen to your *wife* before you get hurt."

"Oh grow up, Clarence!" Sassy snapped. "You and Norris aren't kids anymore fighting for daddy's attention. It's obvious you're a bully, but you're not scaring anyone with your little badge and big mouth."

Clarence looked haughtily at Sassy. "Look who's calling the kettle black."

"Let me tell you—"

"Sassy! This is not your battle."

"But he—"

"Sassy, arguing pointlessly with a man stubborn in his ways, cold in his heart, and vindictive in his mind is a waste of time and energy. It—"

"Man, cut out the bull! Confucius wasn't your daddy. I want to know why my father is dead."

Clarence Wilson, Sassy did not like. She so wanted badly to curse him out for being such a jerk. She walked away to keep from saying anything. She went to the window.

"Look," Norris said, it didn't exactly make my day to call home this afternoon to speak to Dad and have Detective Natherson tell me Dad and Alicia had been murdered. That's all I know."

"Why are you a suspect?"

Sassy blurted, "Because that detective is insane."

"That aside," Norris said with an apologetic glance at Sassy, "it seems I'm the common link in a number of murders. Months ago my assistant's roommate was murdered, and my assistant, Myra Barrett, was stabbed within an inch of her life. Some time after, the granddaughter of one of my clients was murdered, and now Dad and maybe even—" Norris choked up.

"My mother better not die."

At the window, Sassy, without turning around said, "Byron Satoshi."

Clarence waited to see if Sassy would say more. When she didn't he asked Norris, "What do you know about him?"

"Byron Satoshi is the guy my investigator believes has been impersonating me. We thought it was only about identity theft, but now it seems he may be behind these murders. We're still trying to track him down."

"I'm confused," Clarence said. "Don't you know who Byron Satoshi is?"

Sassy turned from the window.

"As a kid in Japan, I had a friend named Byron Satoshi but I don't think this is the same guy. What do you know about

Byron Satoshi?"

Clarence smirked. "In my line of work, I get to know a lot of criminals."

"Byron Satoshi is a drug dealer?"

"According to DEA operatives, that's exactly what your old friend is."

"Are you saying he's the same Byron I knew as a boy?"

"He is."

Norris narrowed his eyes suspiciously. "I never discussed my childhood or anyone I ever knew with you. How do you know I knew a Byron Satoshi at all?"

Clarence scratched the side of his nose. "I happened to be in Japan when Byron Satoshi was brought in. I once worked with the agents who collared him. I sat in on the interrogation and learned that Satoshi was from Fuchu. He came from the same orphanage, and he's the same age as you. I mentioned you were from Fuchu and he said he remembered you."

"Just like that he remembered me?"

"Yep."

Sassy asked, "Does he resemble Norris?"

Clarence studied Norris's face. "Maybe around the eyes, but not much else."

Norris and Sassy exchanged dubious glances. "If he's a drug dealer arrested in Japan," Sassy asked, "how is he now in America?"

"Confidential."

"In other words," Norris said, "he made a deal."

"Something like that."

"Why is he after me?"

"Who says he is? He could be after me. I wasn't so nice to him in lock-up. He swore to one day get even."

"If you were just visiting, how did you happen to have the privilege of abusing someone else's prisoner?"

"If I tell you that, I'd have to kill you."

"Yeah, I bet. How did Byron Satoshi—" Norris caught sight movement in the hallway. "Wait!" He hurried past

Clarence.

Right on Norris's heels, Clarence hurried into the hall as the covered body of their father was about to be wheeled out of the house.

Norris and Clarence both grabbed the side of the gurney. "I'm his son," Clarence said.

The two men from the coroner's office stopped.

"We're his sons," Norris corrected.

Sassy stayed where she was. She didn't have the stomach to see for herself what fear and death did to the face of a man whose light had burned so bright only hours and days ago. When she heard Norris say, "Oh God," she couldn't bring herself to go to the man she had only hours ago married. At this moment she was supposed to be in a hotel two states away up in the mountains nestling serenely in Norris's arms. Instead she was here in the middle of a murder investigation where Norris was the chief suspect, and his old childhood friend was his chief pain in the ass. If this guy was the same person Norris knew when he was a boy, what reason could he have for impersonating Norris?

For the umpteenth time, Sassy told herself she could not have made up this drama if she tried. Looking back into the hallway, she saw that Norris had his hand on his father's forehead, while Clarence stood looking down on his father but wasn't touching him. Clarence was probably use to seeing death and was probably responsible for causing the death of his fair share. Who Clarence was and what he might have done wasn't the uppermost thing on Sassy's mind though. It was Norris. That detective had it in for him. Norris could not have killed his father or any of the women mentioned. It would make him a monster and she could not allow herself to believe that such a beast lived within the man she fell in love with. The murderer had to be Byron Satoshi.

30

For the third time in less than two minutes, Norris glanced up at the wall clock in the lobby of the Queens Hospital Center—10:47 a.m. Having to wait another thirteen minutes was like having to wait thirteen hours. Time was scarcely moving. It seemed hours since he saw Sassy off in a limo back up to Blue Mountain which was little more than an hour ago. He couldn't call to talk to her, her cell phone battery had died on her last night while she was waiting at the precinct for him. Whoever said the dawning of a new day would bring answers to questions unsolvable in the darkness of night, were wrong. After spending damn near half the night at the precinct being questioned by Detective Natherson, Norris still didn't know why his father or any of the women directly or indirectly connected to him were killed. It was only through God's grace that Alicia was still holding on, but it was clear, the killer had intended to kill her as well. Once his father's body was removed from the house, Norris had only a few minutes with Clarence before Detective Natherson asked them both to come down to the precinct for questioning. In those few minutes, Clarence said only that he would have the DEA locate Byron Satoshi, and if Satoshi had anything to do with their father's murder, he would pay for it. The problem was, Norris didn't sense that Clarence was telling him all he knew. It seemed an unlikely coincidence that Clarence would just happen upon Byron Satoshi in Japan. What were the odds of such a meeting?

Norris sipped cautiously from the cup of hot black

coffee he had gotten from the hospital cafeteria. The heat stung his tongue; the bitterness of the coffee jolted his taste buds and made him grimace. Despite that, Norris took another sip; this time bigger. He needed to stay awake, wide awake and alert. He hadn't slept all night. Sassy had fallen asleep at 4:30 a.m. but she awakened an hour later because of his restlessness. It wasn't fair to put her through the confusion of his life and although she did not want to leave him, he convinced her to go back up to Blue Mountain to check on Bernard in person.

Riiiing!

Norris immediately answered his BlackBerry. "Yes!"

"Hi," Sassy said. "I'm at the house."

"Good. How's Bernard?"

"He's holding his own but I think he's weaker. He's back to refusing to take his medicines."

"What are you going to do?"

"What can I do? Evelyn wants to call an ambulance, but Bernard was adamant as usual."

"Honor his wish."

It wasn't difficult for Norris to figure out, by Sassy's silence, what she was thinking.

"Sassy, you're not doing a Kevorkian. You're not giving Bernard anything to help him—"

"But I'm letting him die."

"No, you're honoring his wish to choose where he wants to die. You shouldn't feel guilty about this."

Again Sassy was silent. Norris could hear her sniffle softly. "Look, after I visit Alicia, I'm going to head back up there. You—"

"No! Norris, you can't leave New York. That detective—"

"I wasn't arrested. I wasn't charged. Right after you left, I spoke to my lawyer. He said the accusations are frivolous and until, and if the police get an indictment, I'm free to come and go."

"But you still need to stay in New York to get some

answers. I'll do what I have to do here."

"Alright. I do have to get to the bottom of this. I'll be home as soon as I can."

"Any luck reaching Clarence this morning?"

"Not yet. I've been back to the house but I couldn't get in. I spoke to Mr. Lewis. He said he thought it was strange that I was wearing a red baseball cap with my suit."

"I've never seen you wear a baseball cap."

"Because I've never bought one. Mr. Lewis said he told the police about the cap but they didn't think it was important."

"That's because they've already made up their minds."

"Yeah," Norris said. "We'll see what Cyrus comes up with. His men have a lead on Byron Satoshi in the East Village."

"That's good."

"Keep your fingers crossed." Norris looked up at the clock on the wall. "Okay, it's almost eleven." He dropped his unfinished coffee in the garbage can as he started walking toward the bank of elevators.

"I've been praying for Alicia."

"Thank you," Norris said somberly. "I'll call you after I see her."

"Norris."

"Yeah?"

"Watch your back around Clarence."

"You don't have to tell me that."

"Then I'll just tell you I love you."

"I love you."

A soothing feeling so unlike the hot bitter coffee Norris had been drinking warmed his body. "I love you, too." Just as he ended the call, one of the elevator doors slid open and out stepped Clarence. Norris didn't have to guess where he'd been.

Angry-eyed and tight-lipped, Clarence plowed past Norris as if he didn't see him. "Clarence!" Norris took off after him. "How is Alicia?"

Clarence abruptly halted. "Dead! She's dead. You

succeeded."

"Are you accusing me—" Norris couldn't even finish his own question. It was incredulous a thought to say out loud.

Clarence stalked off, leaving Norris feeling like he had been rammed in the chest, but Norris didn't have time to pout. With his BlackBerry still in his hand, he sped off after Clarence, yet he was mindful and apologetic to the woman and little boy he almost knocked down in his haste to catch up with Clarence who barreled steadily toward the exit. Norris grabbed Clarence's arm to stop him, but Clarence angrily yanked his arm free and continued on out of the hospital bustling headlong for the parking lot. Norris quickly matched Clarence stride for stride.

"You can't possibly believe I had anything to do with killing our father and your mother! Alicia was good to me. She—"

Clarence stopped in his tracks. "Don't you ever speak my mother's name out of your goddamn mouth again." Clarence stormed off but Norris wasn't letting him get away.

"Byron Satoshi isn't after you, it's me. If he's the killer, why is he killing people connected to me?"

Clarence spotted his rental car. He headed for it with Norris still on his heels.

"What do you know, Clarence?"

Breathing heavily not from walking, but from anger, Clarence said gruffly, "You killed them!" He pulled the keys to his rental car from his jacket pocket. "You killed all of them!"

Norris snatched Clarence around to face him. "What did you say?"

Clarence brusquely grabbed Norris up by the lapels of his jacket. "You son of a bitch! You killed my mother, you killed my father, and you killed those girls!"

With an immediate double-fisted underarm outside block maneuver, Norris powerfully broke Clarence's hold on his lapels! They both stood at the ready.

"You know I didn't kill them, but I suspect you know who did."

Through clenched teeth, Clarence snarled, "Put your hands on me again you half breed son of a bitch, I'll kill you!"

Norris didn't blink in the face of Clarence's contemptuously hateful words. He bristled. His triceps tensed, his back stiffened, his shoulders squared, his stomach tightened, his hands, one holding the BlackBerry, snapped into rock hard fists. As close as they stood, Norris had no doubt he could fell Clarence with one deadly blow to the throat, nose, or heart.

They both stood ready to fight, but Norris had more to say. "I'm not fourteen anymore, Clarence."

"I should have killed you then."

"You couldn't."

"Why, because Dad stopped me?"

"No, because I respected Dad."

Clarence stepped dangerously close up on Norris. Less than a foot separated them. "Dad is gone."

"I'm not here to fight you. I—"

"I have never liked you. From the first day you crawled on your belly into my house, I hated your guts."

There was a time when such words would have bothered Norris, not today. "We need never see each other again in life; just tell me what I need to know about Byron Satoshi."

Clarence's conniving smirk confirmed for Norris that Clarence knew a hell of a lot more than he was going to admit. "You are a lowlife," Norris said.

"Yeah!" Clarence challengingly chest bumped Norris, but unlike he did when the detectives tried to take him down, Norris allowed himself be pushed two steps back and, although his eyes were fixed on Clarence, he checked to see, just as Clarence did, if anyone was close enough in the parking lot to see what was happening between them. He glimpsed one of the parking attendants heading in their direction.

"Hey!" the attendant shouted from a distance. "You guys need help finding your car?"

Clarence scoffed, "You're a murderer."

The nape of Norris's neck burned. His fists were so tight he could feel his knuckles pop. The urge to ram Clarence's nose up into his head was growing stronger by the second. Norris stepped back off of Clarence, but Clarence, as if he were engaged in a two step with Norris, immediately stepped right back close up on Norris putting him even more on guard.

"You better get started designing yourself a fancy jail cell. You're a murderer and I intend to help put you away for the rest of your miserable life."

Norris could feel the veins throbbing in his temples and in his fists. "Knowing you, you probably should be on death row along with all the other criminals you likely bedded down with."

Clarence made a move to head butt Norris, but Norris, flinging his BlackBerry to free up his left hand, swiftly threw his right arm up and pushed Clarence back. Clarence came right back at Norris with a right hand jab.

"Hey!" the attendant shouted as he jogged closer to Norris and Clarence.

Norris quickly sidestepped, grabbed Clarence's extended wrist with his right hand, brutally twisted it downward forcing Clarence to lurch toward the ground; and at the same time, rammed the ball of his left hand into Clarence's elbow, dislocating it with a sickening snap! Clarence hollered from the excruciating pain.

"Damn, man!" the attendant shouted. "That move was the bomb!"

Norris shoved Clarence into the side of his car.

"You're finished!" Clarence shouted at Norris's back as Norris walked off in search of his own car. Grimacing, Clarence cradled his dislocated arm as he braced himself against his car.

"You're going to jail! Don't count on that co-called wife of yours being around to visit you! She won't be!"

Norris passed the young Black parking attendant who raised his hand for a victorious high five. Norris went on without acknowledging him.

"That's alright. You still the man!" The attendant went over to Clarence. "Hey, man, you alright?"

"You saw what happened! You saw him break my arm!"

"Yeah, man! I saw the whole thing."

"Then you're my witness!" Clarence grunted from his pain. "Call the police!"

"The hospital is right behind you."

"I need the police, dammit!"

"Man, you call the police. I ain't gettin' in this, besides you threw the first punch. The man defended himself." The attendant started walking away.

"A C-note! I'll give you a C-note if you say he attacked me."

The attendant turned back. "Deuce."

"You got it!"

With his left hand, Clarence awkwardly retrieved his wallet from his right front pants pocket. He fumbled but he finally separated two hundred dollar bills from the copious amount of bills in his wallet. He handed it to the attendant whose eyes widened at the sight of so much money.

"Another deuce, I'll say he had a gun, too."

Clarence didn't have to mull that proposition over for long. He handed the attendant two more bills.

"Want me to call 911 or you gonna do it?"

"You do it," Clarence winced as he sank to the ground against his car.

The attendant whipped his cell phone off of his belt. He flipped it open and was about to press the first button when he looked around and saw the man who had passed him by without high-fiving him.

"Aw, damn!" The attendant re-holstered his cell phone.

"What are you doing?" Clarence asked. "Call the damn police!"

"Check that out."

Clarence looked in the direction the attendant was looking. Thirty feet away, in plain sight, stood Norris looking back at them through a mini palm-sized camcorder. He had taped their entire transaction. Clarence groaned and slammed his head back against the side of his car.

"Damn!" The attendant threw the four bills onto Clarence's chest. "I ain't doing no time." Mumbling to himself, the attendant stalked off.

Norris lowered his camcorder. He fixed a shrewd but disgusted glare on Clarence. He turned smoothly and was about to walk away when he spotted his BlackBerry which had broken apart next to a large van. He retrieved it and hurried away.

Clarence took his cell phone from his inside jacket pocket. He started to call the police but on second thought, decided against it. He would take care of Norris himself. He made another call instead.

As angry as he was, Norris had to remind himself to not peel out and draw unwanted attention to himself. As he drove slowly out of the parking lot, he had a bitter sweet tinge of satisfaction that he followed his instinct to video Clarence just in case Clarence tried to claim he did more harm than he actually did. He was lucky the camcorder was still under the passenger seat and that Satoshi had not taken it. Too bad he didn't have a video camera filming the inside of his car. Then he would know for sure what Satoshi looked like. For now, he had to be satisfied that he had Clarence on video paying that attendant to lie for him. If the police came after him, he would plead self-defense, but right now, he had to get out of New York City before Clarence sicced the police on him and stopped him. He had to get back to Blue Mountain. He had to make sure Sassy was alright. When Clarence said she wouldn't be around to visit him in jail, an alarm went off in his head. With so many people he knew getting killed, he couldn't risk leaving Sassy alone for too long.

31

Sassy was lost in thought as she sat at the kitchen table absentmindedly nursing a cup of warm apple cinnamon tea. She felt drained, emotionally and physically. She was torn between worrying about the unsettling possibility of Norris being charged with murder; and the reality of the imminent death of the only family member who had, throughout her life, been so many things to her—cousin, brother, worst critic, private cheerleader, advisor, best friend. As much as she did not want to leave Norris alone in New York City to defend himself against the nonsensical hatefulness of his brother; she didn't balk when Norris insisted she go back to Blue Mountain to see about Bernard in person. After what she saw, she had no doubt that Norris could defend himself. Throughout the night, from the precinct to the apartment, Evelyn had called every hour on the hour to update her on Bernard's condition, which was dire according to Evelyn. Evelyn was scared. She didn't want Bernard to die on her watch. The truth was, Sassy had no desire to bear witness to Bernard taking his last breath either, but she had no choice. She couldn't let him die alone, but it would be a lot easier handle if Norris had been able to come back with her. Then again, she was being selfish. Norris had just lost his father. He had so much more to deal with.

"We're leaving," Evelyn said from just outside the kitchen. On her shoulder she carried her large overnight bag.

"Does Bernie know—"

"We said our goodbyes." Evelyn gently pulled Brice to

her side and held him against her body.

Sassy got the message. The word goodbye was so final. She fought back tears as she looked at Brice. His little shoulders were slumped and his head was down. His bottom lip was pushed out in the sweetest little pout. Sassy went and crouched in front of him and he instantly fell into her arms. She held him tight as his sadness at leaving his father brought him to tears.

"It's okay, baby. I'll take real good care of your daddy."

Sorrowful tears rolled down Brice's cheeks. He looked so much like Bernard did at his age. Undoubtedly, he was going to look like Bernard as an adult.

"My daddy told me he was dying. How you gonna take care of him?"

"Well, I'm going to sit with him; I'm going to hold him, just like I'm holding you; and I am going tell him how much we will always love him. Do you remember what he told you about going to see God?"

Brice nodded.

"Good. Because when your daddy closes his eyes to go to sleep with God, I'm going to kiss him and tell him we'll see him when our turn comes to go see God. Okay?"

Again Brice nodded.

Toot. . .toot!

Evelyn wiped a tear from her cheek. "The car's here," she said. She held her hand out to Brice, but Sassy stood and took Brice's hand. She led the way to the waiting car from the Pocono Cab Company that would take them back to New York City. At the car she hugged Brice as long as she could. The next time she would see him, it would be on the occasion of his father's funeral.

As the car drove away, Sassy felt herself welling up. The knowledge that Bernard was dying swelled her soul with overwhelming sorrow, while her mind was filled with concern for Norris. What if he was charged with murder? What if he was convicted? Tears rolled down Sassy's cheeks. She gave in to the moment for only an instant. She had to get back to Bernard. She wiped her eyes as she looked up at the late September sky filled with white clouds and the brightness of the mid afternoon sun. Sassy was about to ask God why Bernard had to die but stopped herself. God had to be tired of being asked that question. Surely if God flipped the script and asked instead, "Do you want to go in his place?" The truth was, unless it was her own child, she wouldn't know how to answer. So she just thanked God for allowing Bernard be in her life for so long.

Sassy again wiped away her tears as she looked around at her new neighborhood. The silence was so loud she felt as if her ears were plugged. She loved it. It was so different from being in Brooklyn or Manhattan. Each single family house was big and was beautifully landscaped. Some sat high up on hills, others sat below the road close to the lake. All were quiet, all were distant. Not one soul behind those doors knew that Bernard was dying in the beautiful house she stood in front of, but wasn't that the way of the world? Life and death intermingling; joy and pain, blessings all the same. Looking up again at the sky, her head back, Sassy stretched her arms high and wide to God.

"Thy will be done, Lord, but please ease Bernie's pain, and please keep Norris safe." She slowly lowered her arms, touched her heels to the ground and started back down the long sloping driveway to the house. Her thoughts went to Clarence. Clarence had a mean spirit, no telling what he might try to do to Norris. As she entered the house, she continued to quietly pray, "God, please—"

CRASH!

Sassy's head jerked upward toward the ceiling from whence the crashing sound had come. Hurriedly, she shoved the front door and took off running up the stairs, unaware that the door had not closed all the way. She dashed into the guest bedroom where she saw immediately that Bernard had knocked over his large oxygen tank. His eyes were closed. Bernard lay with his right shoulder part way off the bed; his right arm flopped over the side. His oxygen mask was not on his face.

"Bernie!"

Sassy bustled over to the side of the bed. She heaved the oxygen tank back up right. She checked that it was stable before putting the mask back over Bernard's nose and mouth.

"Bernie! Bernie!"

No response. Sassy put her ear to his sunken chest. Thankfully, his heart wasn't beating as shallow as his breathing.

"Bernie!" Sassy anxiously tapped Bernard's cheek. "Bernie, wake up! Bernie!"

Still, Bernard did not open his eyes. Sassy pulled Bernard's pillow from under his head so his airway would be completely open.

"Bernie, please wake up." Sassy's throat tightened, her eyes watered as she kept tapping on Bernard's shallow cheek hoping to revive him. "Please, Bernie."

"Is he dead?" Norris asked just inches behind Sassy.

"Oh my God!" Sassy threw her arms around Norris's neck. "I'm so glad you're here! Please, help me with Bernie."

Norris wrapped Sassy's arms from around his neck. "He looks pretty bad. He's dying."

Sassy looked down at Bernard and then back at Norris. "But he's not dead yet. He's. . .he's still breathing."

"Hopefully, not for long."

"Norris! Why would you say that? I thought you liked Bernie." Sassy started giving Bernard chest compressions.

Norris folded his arms high across his chest. "This isn't about liking him, this guy is dying."

For the first time since meeting Norris, Sassy felt like cursing him out. "This guy? Why are you being so cold? Bernie is like my brother. He's my heart. Just like your father is yours. I wasn't cold with you last night with your parents."

"You're right." Norris eased Sassy aside. "I'm sorry. Let me do that."

Sassy stepped back to let Norris get closer to Bernard. "Don't let him die yet."

Norris leaned down to listen to Bernard's chest. "How long has he been out?"

"Not long. Maybe five minutes." Sassy began wringing her hands. "I was coming into the house when I heard his oxygen tank fall over. When I got up here he was unconscious."

With one hand atop the over, Norris began pushing forcefully down on Bernard's chest which upset Sassy all the more. "That's too hard! You're going to break his ribs."

"That won't be hard. He's nothing but skin and bones. Norris eased up.

"What?" Sassy peered incomprehensibly at Norris.

In sequences of three, Norris pushed down a bit lighter on Bernard's chest. "Why don't you take him to the hospital?"

Baffled by Norris's attitude, Sassy looked skeptically at him. "Are you okay?"

Again Norris put his ear to Bernard's chest. "He's still with us."

Sassy was struck by the raw scratch marks on the right side of Norris's neck. Sassy froze.

Norris straightened up. "I'm no doctor. You need to get him to the hospital."

Fear suddenly gripped Sassy. Goose bumps popped up on her arms. "You're. . .you're right. I'm going—"

"On second thought, let him die," Norris said. He slipped his free hand down into his pants pocket.

Sassy went weak in knees. Her heart quivered. She looked hard at the man who was supposed to be her husband. Her heart felt like it wanted to burst out of her chest. Goose bumps popped up on her arms. She stared at the raw, red scratch marks on Norris's neck. They started at the side and dropped down inside of his collar hiding their length, hiding their ugliness. Although she feared what she would see, Sassy looked into the eyes of the man she suspected wasn't Norris.

The coldness, the detachment from any connection with her made her heart quiver. She began inching her way to the foot of the bed, but Norris stayed right on top of her, intimidating her with his closeness. She had been slow in realizing that this wasn't her Norris.

"I think I left the tea kettle on. I'll be—"

Norris zipped around Sassy and stood between her and the open door. Sassy backed up against the high wrought iron and wood footboard of the bed to put two more feet between her and the man she was sure was the imposter. If this was Byron Satoshi, he wouldn't be looking so much like Norris. They didn't have the same parents.

"You look scared. Are you afraid of me?"

Afraid was exactly what Sassy was. She told herself, "Be calm." She gripped the top railing of the footboard which hit her just above her waist. She set her feet a foot apart. This was one time she wished she were wearing three inch heels instead of flat soft sole loafers.

Behind him back Norris's imposter eased the door closed with his elbow. "Can't fool you twice, huh?"

"Are you Byron Satoshi?"

From his jacket pocket he took a pair of blue latex gloves. "Yoshito. My name is Norris Yoshito."

"You may look like Norris, but that's about it." Sassy watched with restrained anxiety as Satoshi pulled on the latex gloves. There was no doubt what he intended to do.

"I'm better than your Norris."

"Murderer, liar, thief. Nope. You can't begin to touch the sole of Norris's dirtiest shoes. Satoshi is what I know you as, although that name is questionable."

Satoshi slipped his gloved hand inside his right pants pocket. "Bold talk for a woman who is about to die."

Sassy worried what Satoshi would pull out of his pocket this time. She had to keep him talking. "I'm curious. You look so much like Norris, but he has no brother. Did you have plastic surgery to look like him?"

Satoshi turned his face slightly from side to side. "No scars."

"Oh, you have scars, but those scars are probably scratches from Alicia Wilson."

Satoshi touched his neck. "That was a touch old lady."

"But why would you wanna kill her?"

"Collateral damage. She got in the way."

"Oh God. You have no soul."

"So I've been told."

"You're cold! Why are you killing people in Norris's life? Why do you look like him?"

"Easier to steal his identity if I look like him."

Sassy dead-panned Satoshi. "Identity theft can be done over the internet without ever setting eyes on the victim. What's the real reason you've had plastic surgery or whatever the hell you've done to look like Norris?"

Satoshi laughed cynically. "Maybe I'm Norris's long lost brother from the streets of Fuchu."

"He doesn't have a brother."

"Maybe I'm angry he left me to fend for myself while he lived like a king in this country. Maybe I'm here to get revenge."

"Norris did not desert you! His father—"

"Shut up!" Satoshi pulled his hand out of his pocket and revealed to Sassy the large silver switchblade he intended to use on her. She could hardly catch her breath when Satoshi pressed the side of the knife with his thumb and a shiny, menacing six inch blade sprang out of hiding. He waved it slowly in her face, and got kick out of seeing her cringe.

"Byron, listen to me. Norris told me about you. In fact, nine years ago he went back to Fuchu looking for you."

"Did he find me? Oops, I guess not."

"Norris said it was because of you he survived on the streets at all."

"This thing will cut through raw hide as easily as it will cut through butter." Satoshi menacingly ran his finger across the blade of his knife. He made it obvious he was looking at Bernard. "Should I give you a demonstration?"

"I was never one for show and tell. It's a child's game."

Satoshi abruptly jabbed the knife at Sassy. Startled, Sassy shrieked, which made Satoshi laugh. "Is this something a child will do?" he asked.

"Sure, a crazy child."

Satoshi's eyes narrowed. "Are you calling me crazy?"

Hell yeah! "Are you a child?"

Satoshi wasn't convinced. "You be careful. I am not here to play games with you."

No kidding! Sassy knew well why Satoshi was there, but that wasn't going to stop her from at least trying to save her own life. If she was going out, she was going out either talking or fighting. One of them had to work.

"Byron, you sound like you've been in America a long time. You almost don't have an accent and actually, you sound an awful lot like Norris. If Norris had known you were—"

Satoshi aggressively lurched at Sassy catching her off guard making her scream! He grabbed a fistful of her hair, viciously yanked her head back, and got tight up in her face. He pressed the tip of the knife to her throat.

"Shut your big mouth!" Satoshi sprayed Sassy's face with his spittle. "You talk like a clucking hen. I will kill you slowest of all just to see you suffer."

The icy rush Sassy felt coursing through her veins was driven by her fear. A queasy feeling filled her stomach, a sour taste filled her mouth, and her back ached from bending backwards away from Satoshi. Specks of his spit were on her lips, in her open mouth, and to add insult to injury, she was breathing in his foul peanut smelling breath which nauseated her more. Sassy could barely swallow without feeling the prick of the blade at her throat. She wanted to punch Satoshi in the rib cage; she wanted to knee him in the groin; but she knew his knife would enter her flesh before she could make a move to escape. Not to mention that she was shaking so hard she didn't feel like she had the strength to swat a fly. She held tighter to the footboard to keep from falling over onto the bed onto Bernard's legs. She might lose her life, but if Bernard was still alive, she did not want to harm him, nor did she want him to regain consciousness while Satoshi was there. Surely, Satoshi wouldn't think twice about killing him. She had to do something. In her mind she tried to map out every possible move she could make when and if the opportunity arose. She prayed Satoshi would wait a bit longer before he killed her. As it was, it was a miracle he hadn't killed her already.

Her mouth dry, her neck stinging, her back painfully sore, Sassy whispered, "I'm sorry."

"You better be." Satoshi pulled away from Sassy. "Don't talk to me about what Norris would have done, I know what he and his whore of a mother did. I will make him pay with his life!"

As scared as she was, Sassy knew she had to stay calm and, as well, not speak positive in any way about Norris. That definitely irritated Satoshi. "You're right. Norris was wrong and his mother was a whore. He betrayed you. I would be angry too if I were you."

"You think I'm a fool? You think you can commiserate with me, distract me from what I came here to do?"

"No. No. I'm just now understanding why you hate Norris; but I'm curious. Why did you walk away when you had me alone in my apartment? You could have killed me then."

Satoshi said flatly, "I was feeling charitable."

That really got under Sassy's skin. "How magnanimous of you; you must have been exhausted from killing so many people?"

Satoshi sneered. "Obviously not if I'm here to kill you now." He again stepped dangerously close to Sassy.

Sassy prayed that Satoshi would not close the two foot space between them. "Why do you have to kill me? Why did you have to kill anyone Norris knew? If you had a problem with Norris leaving you, you could have talked to him."

"Talk! Talk!" Satoshi stabbed furiously at the air just inches from Sassy as if he was killing the word talk itself, which made Sassy more uneasy, more jittery. Right now she could use some of Bernard's oxygen.

"Talk won't give me Norris's education, his money, or this house. Talk won't make me forget the nightmare that was my life. I had nothing! I had no one! Norris had his whore of a mother to feed him and his skunk of a father to give him a life I dared not dream about. Talk!" Again, Satoshi stabbed in mid air which made Sassy jump.

"Talk won't pay me back for the hell I lived on the streets of Fuchu, Yokota, and Tokyo like I was rotten discarded trash! For years I stood outside the walls of Tachikawa begging for food but really hoping that one of the soldiers, my father, would recognize me and claim me as his son."

"But how would—"

"Not one of those black bastards was honorable enough to claim me and end my misery. The hell with talk!"

This was definitely not Byron Satoshi! The real Byron would have been looking for a white father, not a black one. "I'm sorry you—"

"Only cowards use the word sorry!" Satoshi spat on the floor.

Sassy tried to not show how disgusted she was. Talking about disrespect; spitting in someone's house was the ultimate, but what did she expect from a homicidal lunatic?

"That's what's wrong with Americans. You are sorry people who talk a lot of empty words. I don't need to talk to Norris, I need to destroy him. When he goes to jail and is put to death, I will have great satisfaction."

"So killing me and anyone else Norris knows gets you your revenge when he's convicted for your crimes?"

Satoshi responded not with his mouth but with his dark, intensely baneful eyes which unnerved Sassy.

"You can't keep blaming Norris for the wrongs of your life. Norris was a child when his mother was killed. Like you, he was a child living on the street. How can you hold him responsible for your life when he couldn't take care of himself. Norris was lucky he was able to get in touch with his father and, miraculously, that his father gave a damn." Seeing that Satoshi appeared to be listening, Sassy dared to keep talking.

"Norris did go back looking for you, but you must have already moved to this country. He had no way of knowing that, so you can't hold Norris, the man, accountable for promises he made as a child. You can not make Norris responsible for your life and how it turned out."

Satoshi promptly backhanded Sassy across the mouth. "Shut up!"

Startled, Sassy brought her trembling hands to her stinging lips. She tasted blood. Angry tears brimmed but she refused to fall down and cry. She used to think if she ever saw the devil, she would know him. Not because of horns or fangs but because someone so evil had to give off evil vibes or reek of the most vile smell in the world. How wrong she had been. There were no evil vibes or vile smells. Until Satoshi got angry, he looked so much like Norris she could understand how everyone who saw him was easily fooled. Satoshi was evil incarnate yet he was using Norris's handsome face to camouflage his wickedness.

Irritated by the defiantly angry look in Sassy's eyes, Satoshi pushed himself up on Sassy again, and again he pressed the blade against her throat. He grabbed a fistful of her locks. She gasped from the pain but refused to let him see how much he was hurting her.

"Don't test me," Satoshi warned. "You can't win."

Unwelcome tears seeped from the corner of Sassy's right eye. She could feel her chest heaving against his.

Satoshi let up on the pressure on Sassy's throat. "How would you like to be married to me instead of him?"

"Is that supposed to be a trick question?" She wondered how he knew she and Norris had gotten married?

"You're a smart ass. I don't know how Norris put up

with your mouth."

"I know why you haven't killed me yet. You're waiting for Norris. You want him to see me die."

Satoshi winked with a devilish smirk on his lips.

"Suppose he can't come home today? I'm sure you know he's under investigation for the murders *you* obviously committed with *his* face."

"Seems he has a problem, but I suggest you get him here or I will spend the night skinning every inch of your flesh off of your body." Satoshi grabbed Sassy and shoved her toward the telephone on the night stand. He picked up the cordless telephone. He held it out to Sassy but she didn't take it.

"Call him now!"

Sassy snatched the telephone from Satoshi. She punched in the speed dial number to Norris's BlackBerry. While the telephone rang, she looked at Bernard. She could have sworn she saw his eyelids flutter, but she couldn't be sure. She didn't want to stare at him, Satoshi might see her.

After several unanswered rings, she said, "He's not answering. He might still be with the police."

Satoshi thought about that. "Leave a message and make it urgent."

Sassy said, "Norris, it's me. Please don't—"

Satoshi snatched the telephone! He stuck out at Sassy's jaw but she dropped against the bed, possibly avoiding getting her jaw broken. Satoshi was so mad threw the telephone against the wall where it shattered on impact.

"You better pray he gets here within the next two hours!"

"If anything, I'm praying you get religion."

Satoshi yanked Sassy up and shoved her into the chair. She sprang right back up.

"You don't need to keep pushing me! I can walk, you vicious bastard!"

Too late Sassy realized what she'd said. She saw

Satoshi's eyes flare with rage, and too late she glimpsed his fist a second before he knocked her out.

32

Slowly Sassy began to come around. Her face hurt, and so did the back of her head. Groggily she touched her tender left cheek. Satoshi had no soul or compassion and he was going to kill her if she didn't do something. Holding her face, Sassy sat up and looked around the room. He wasn't there. He was gone! He was really gone, but then Sassy heard footfalls coming up the stairs. She looked at the open door. She needed to close and lock it, but before she could get up off the floor, Satoshi walked into the room. He had a half eaten banana and a can of root beer in his hand.

"Look who's awake. Did you have a good nap?"

"Screw you, you lowlife—"

The can of root beer sailed toward Sassy at warp speed. She threw up her arms to block it from hitting her face and absorbed the fiery sting of impact on her forearm. Cold root beer splashed all over her. Angrily she wiped at her face and body. Her arm felt like it was smashed by an iron pole.

"You crazy son of a—"

Satoshi grabbed Sassy up off the floor and smashed her backwards into the wall. With one hand he began choking her, while with the other he held his knife at her left side. Gagging and gasping for air, Sassy pulled and clawed at Satoshi's hand and wrist to no avail. His hold didn't loosen. She raised her knee but Satoshi pushed his knife deep into her side and dispelled any thought she had of kneeing him.

"What was it you were about to say?" Satoshi asked

daringly.

Tears ran down Sassy's face. She couldn't shake her head; she couldn't open her mouth to respond.

"Disrespect me again, I will gladly kill you and not give you a second thought. You understand me?"

Sassy felt like she was about to black out. She nodded as best she could.

Satoshi let her go. He shoved her. "Go downstairs."

Sassy was hurting in so many spots she didn't know what to massage first. She began rubbing her neck while holding on to her cheek. Her arm was throbbing as she looked anxiously at Bernard. "I'll behave. I won't cause you any more trouble," she began to cry. "I promise. Just let me stay here with my cousin. Please."

"He looks like a mummified ninety-year-old man. What he got, AIDS?"

"Yes."

The color drained from Satoshi's face. He looked at his hands. Sassy readied herself for the onslaught of punches she would surely get because Satoshi had touched Bernard.

"Nasty disease," Satoshi said. "Is he gay?"

"No."

"How did he get it?"

Sassy was taken aback by Satoshi's calmness. "From his ex-wife." If Sassy wasn't mistaken, she saw a glint of sadness in Satoshi's eyes. "Do you know someone who has AIDS?"

"Someone who had AIDS.; a good friend."

"I'm sorry."

"Keep your pity, I don't need it." Satoshi looked at Bernard. "If he's not dead, he will be soon."

"Then let me just stay with him a little while longer. What will it hurt? Besides, when Norris gets here, he will come straight up to this room. You won't have to keep looking out for him. You'll hear him come up the stairs, whereas downstairs, he could come in three different ways and you won't hear him until he's right on top of you. Please, I'll sit in the chair and be quiet."

Briefly thinking about it, Satoshi shoved Sassy toward the chair. "Disrespect me again; I will cut your tongue out."

Putting on the meekest face she could muster, Sassy sat in the chair. Satoshi was too wound up to sit. He paced back and forth in front of Sassy with the switchblade open in his hand. She thought of tripping him, but again, saw no advantage to overpowering him. He would be on her too fast. Satoshi went to the window but saw that he could only see the lake and not the front access to the house.

"Damn!" He went back to pacing.

Ten minutes of silence seemed like ten hours. Sassy couldn't take it any more. "When it's all said and done, you will kill me. That's what you came here to do, but please, at least allow me to die knowing the truth about you and Norris."

"Who says there is a truth?"

"Norris told me Byron Satoshi had a white father. That's not what I see when I look at you. I see Norris's brown skin, his curly hair, his Afro-Asian features, and his dark eyes. Where is the real Byron Satoshi? Is he still in Japan? Is he still alive?"

A wily little smile was Satoshi's answer. He stopped in front of Sassy. "What do you think?"

Sassy now not only saw the evil in Satoshi's eyes, she felt it. "I think you killed him."

"You might be right."

"But. . .but why?"

"That's my business."

"Okay, but who are you really? You're not Byron Satoshi. You're not Norris's brother, but looking like him is no coincidence. You must be related in some way."

Satoshi kept pacing but Sassy could he was wrestling with whether or not he was going to tell her anything at all. She knew she should stop pushing for answers but she had to know.

"What is your real name?"

Satoshi didn't answer.

"Okay, don't tell me." She rubbed her left arm which was now swollen. She felt like screaming but knew better. "Okay, Byron, and I call you that because that's the only name I know you by. Please tell me your real name. What do you have to lose? I won't be telling anyone anything you tell me. I'll be dead."

Satoshi took Sassy's hand and pulled her to her feet a lot gentler than he had shoved her into the chair. He put his arm around her waist and pulled her close. Sassy stiffened. As much as she hated the feel of his body against hers, she didn't move.

Uttering not a word, Satoshi began tracing a line on Sassy's neck from ear to ear with the tip of his blade. Sassy trembled. At any given moment, she didn't know which would be her last. Satoshi was playing her. He was trying to get her to react. He swung her around and pushed her back up against the high footboard of the bed.

Sassy knew he was trying to distract her from the question she asked. Well, she wanted to distract him too. "Did you see Norris's picture in a magazine? Is that how you knew how he looked? Where did you get the surgery done?"

Satoshi lowered the knife to Sassy's stomach. "Inside the belly of a sow."

"What?"

"The whore, who squeezed me out of her belly, threw me away. She kept the bastard she thought better than me."

Sassy paused. Was Satoshi saying what she thought he was saying? "Are you saying you're Norris's brother; his twin?"

"I am not his brother! I am not his twin! I am his enemy."

"Okay! You're his enemy, but were you born with Norris?"

"That was my curse."

"You were separated at birth? My God, Norris doesn't

know a thing about you. How did you find out about him?"

"It was my destiny to know he existed."

"But how did you find out? When? Was it here? Was it in Fuchu?"

A cold, long stare was Satoshi's answer.

"Dammit! Just tell me!"

Satoshi glared menacingly at Sassy. "Watch yourself," he said. He pressed the point of his knife into her side.

"Okay! I'm sorry." The knife had entered Sassy's flesh and reminded her that Satoshi was talking only because he intended on killing her. Still she wasn't sorry for how she had spoken to him, she wasn't stupid. She lowered her eyes and waited for Satoshi to speak when he was ready. Until he was ready, he pressed himself against her, which turned her stomach. She didn't know which hurt worse, the knife in her side or him molesting her. He pulled the knife back.

"Excuse me, but do you have to do that?"

Satoshi looked Sassy straight in the eye and grinded himself hard into her public. She kept her legs closed tight. This man was a bastard and she hated him. She willed herself to not feel him, to not let him think he was getting to her.

"So, are you gonna tell me how you came to know about Norris?"

"Sure, why not? My first memory was being with all those damn kids in the orphanage. I hated that place. They packed us mixed blood children in like chickens and treated us like dogs. I left the orphanage when I was ten. On the street I learned to survive."

Sassy couldn't help but wonder if this was a coincidence. "You lived on the street in Fuchu?"

"Not for long. There were better spoils in Tokyo, I visited Fuchu on the rare occasion."

"Did you ever see Norris?

"If I had I would have killed him."

"Why? He's your brother! He had nothing—"

Satoshi stuck his knife in Sassy's face. "He shares my

impure blood but he is not my brother! If it were not for him, I would not have had to eat from the floor the leftovers of a fat slob. I would never have been beaten like a dog that no one wanted. I curse the day that whore conceived me."

Satoshi's hatred for Norris and his mother was so ingrained Sassy knew there was nothing she could ever say would stop him from going after Norris. Wherever Norris was, she prayed he stayed. In the meantime, how she was going to save herself, she didn't know.

"What's wrong?" Satoshi drew back his knife. "The author, the writer of garbage has no more questions? Don't you need more material for the great American novel you'll never get a chance to write?" Satoshi laughed at his own joke.

The sound of his laughter grated on Sassy. "How do you know so much about me? About Norris? How did you know I was a writer, or that Norris and I were married? We only just got married yesterday."

"I have my ways."

"Like the listening devices you planted in my telephones, in my bedroom and my living room when you somehow got back inside my apartment while I was asleep?"

"I should have killed you and spared myself your big mouth."

"Aren't you tried of threatening me?"

"Believe me, my threats are as good as it gets for you."

"Yeah, but how good does it get for you? I don't like being dry-humped by a man who plans on killing me."

Satoshi tried to part Sassy's thighs with his knees but she used her muscular strength in her thighs to keep her thighs and legs closed. Satoshi again stuck his knife into Sassy's side. She cried out from the searing pain. She didn't have to look to see if she was bleeding, she knew she was. She could feel the blood ooze from the cut in her skin.

Satoshi whispered in Sassy's ear, "Open your thighs."

Reluctantly, she did. She closed her eyes and willed herself to detach her mind from her body as Satoshi positioned himself between her thighs. He started rubbing himself on her pubic. Unwelcomed tears poured down Sassy's cheeks.

"What I'm doing is not for my pleasure; it's for your disgrace and your husband's humiliation. Whether he is here or not, I am disrespecting him. If you were Japanese, you'd understand what I mean."

"I know I understand this is my body and it's me you're disrespecting."

"If you shut your mouth, I'll tell you how I found out about Norris."

Sassy pressed her sore lips together. God knows she wish she could get this animal off of her.

"I was in Fuchu for the day. This dumb kid who went to school with Norris mistook me for him. I started to walk away but the kid wouldn't leave me alone. He kept following me like I really was this boy Norris. Then I got curious. I got the kid to 'walk home' with me. That kid was so dumb, he didn't catch on that he was leading me to Norris's house. After he left, I broke into the house. I looked around. I saw Norris's picture. It was like looking at myself."

"Did you see Oyuki?"

"I saw the whore. She was an ugly, ignorant sow."

Satoshi and Sassy locked eyes. The truth she had only minutes ago surmised was now, indeed a fact. "You killed her."

"My first kill."

"You say that like you're talking about your first slice of pizza. You killed your mother! You were only twelve years old! How can you sleep at night?"

"Pretty damn well."

"My God. You didn't let Oyuki die thinking that Norris was her killer?"

Satoshi sneered, "She died knowing she had to pay for shaming me; for making me suffer the indignity of this brown skin and nigger hair."

Sassy was appalled. What Oyuki's last thought was at seeing Norris's face had to be devastating. "How can you live with yourself? You killed your mother and your father. My God. Satan must be holding a special spot in hell for you."

Satoshi smiled as if he'd accomplished something grand. "I did the whore and the dog both a favor. I set her worthless soul free and his black heart I sent straight to hell."

"Don't you understand? Oyuki was a young woman alone with two babies. She couldn't raise two babies alone on her own! How could you kill her? She was your mother!"

"That slut was not my mother! Do not say that again."

Sassy lowered her head. Oyuki's death had to be horrific. She nor Mr. Wilson deserved to die at the hands of their own son. "You don't understand. In that place and time, they were in love."

"They were animals in lust! Their deaths were just."

"Then why did you have to kill Alicia? She had nothing to do with you."

"Collateral damage. She got in the way, just like you."

"What about Myra Barrett, Carrie Kane, Karen Markowitz? Why kill them?"

"They all had a purpose, except Carrie. She should have stayed away. Myra fed me information on Norris's business and finances. Karen, she wasn't part of the plan. She saw me on the street and thought I was the architect. I liked Karen, but things could not have turned out better."

Sassy was bowled over by the cold, detached way Satoshi talked about the women whose young, vibrant lives he stole like a cold-hearted thief. Her life meant nothing to him. In fact, he would get the greatest joy from killing her. As soon as Norris stepped through the door, she was done.

"I don't like you," Satoshi said. He stuck the tip of the blade over Sassy's heart. "Right here." He pressed the steel slowly but firmly against her flesh and smiled when Sassy held her breath. He eased the pressure.

"In less than a minute you could be dead?"

For the umpteenth time Sassy psyched herself into being calm. "I thought you wanted Norris to see me die?"

"You're annoying me."

Like you aren't annoying the hell out of me! "I'm sorry but I'm a little stressed, but you know that. Since you want the ultimate revenge, wouldn't killing me, his wife, right before his eyes do it for you?"

Satoshi sneered at Sassy. "I'll tell you what else will do it for me."

By the lewd way Satoshi was looking at her, it was no mystery to Sassy what he had in mind. She tried to pull away, but Satoshi held her firm and began earnestly rubbing himself up against her. The more she stiffened and grimaced, the more Satoshi got off on her. He began grunting and sucking in air through his teeth. God, she hated this man! His sick ass was trying to get off on her. Never had she been so happy to be wearing a pair of denim jeans.

"Look, we both know you have the power, but you don't have to do this."

With one hand, Satoshi held onto Sassy's behind. He grunted, he moaned his pleasure. The more he rubbed himself on her, the more Sassy wanted to bite, scratch and lash out at him. As if he sensed what she was thinking, Satoshi pressed the blade into the flesh of her throat and was satisfied when she relaxed her thighs and let him nestle between them. Then taunting her, he slid the blade down across her left nipple which, on its own, perked up and made itself visible through her lightweight sweater. He flicked her nipple with the tip of the blade not caring that she squirmed because he was hurting her. Sassy turned her head away and tired to think about Norris and what he would do to Satoshi if he were here. She gritted her teeth as Satoshi slobbered on her neck.

"Damn, you feel good!" Satoshi took the knife into his left hand behind Sassy's back. He thrust his right hand up under her sweater and released her breast from the protection of her bra. Mercilessly, he squeezed her breast till she screamed out in pain. She grabbed his hand.

"I'll cut it off!"

Sassy let go. "You're hurting me!"

"I can hurt you a whole lot worse than this." He squeezed Sassy's breast harder but then he slid his hand down between her thighs and there he rubbed and rubbed till Sassy couldn't take it anymore.

"Stop! Please, stop!"

"Take your pants off!"

"No!"

Satoshi grabbed the waistband of Sassy's jeans and was about to stick his knife down into them.

"Wait! Wait! I'll take them off! Just let me do it."

Satoshi tossed his knife onto the bed behind Sassy. He knocked Sassy's hands aside and began tugging at the button on her jeans.

"If you take off my pants and have sex with me, you might get carried away and not hear Norris when he comes into the house or even when he come up the stairs. You'll be at a disadvantage. Norris knows martial arts. He can fight. You—"

"Shut up!" Satoshi pressed himself against Sassy as he pondered what she said.

Sassy bit down on her bottom lip to keep from screaming out loud. Just below her stomach she could feel his disgusting erection. She had hoped he'd lose interest in her. She gripped the footboard railing so tight her wrist hurt. It was bad enough when he wanted to kill her, but molest her, rape her? She couldn't take that. She didn't know if she could beat Satoshi, but now that he didn't have the knife in his hand, she sure as hell was going to try the minute he afforded her the opportunity.

Satoshi unzipped his own pants. He freed himself which disgusted Sassy. "I will tell your husband how much you enjoyed taking me full into your big mouth."

Refusing to give in to his humiliation and her own tears, Sassy focused her mind on trying to find a way out.

Satoshi stepped back off of Sassy. He gave her the three feet of space she desperately needed, though he stood boastfully in front of her holding his flesh out at her.

"On your knees."

Sassy started to bend her knees but then she suddenly kicked out at Satoshi but he quickly blocked her kick. She immediately gripped the footboard rail and threw herself backwards over the footboard and landed on the bed alongside Bernard's legs. Satoshi made a grab for Sassy's legs but straightaway Sassy went to kicking and bucking like a wild horse. She caught Satoshi in the rib cage with a vicious front kick that made him grunt a gush of air and bend forward. Sassy quickly followed up with a powerful blade kick to Satoshi's face which sent him stumbling backwards.

Sassy didn't wait to see the blood that seeped from the gash on Satoshi's chin. She hurtled herself off the side of bed away from Satoshi, but when she saw him quickly zip himself back inside his pants and lunge for his knife which lay at Bernard's side, she grabbed the black bible from the night stand Dr. Morgan left for Bernard. With all the strength she could muster, she threw the bible at Satoshi's head as he bent down. The bible hit its mark. Satoshi yelped and fell sideways. Sassy made a mad dash for the door. She grabbed the knob, yanked open the door and was about to haul ass when Satoshi grabbed her from behind around her waist. She screamed. He lifted her off her feet and threw her like a rag doll across the room. She screamed. She landed hard on her left hip on the floor against the wrought iron leg of the footboard. She started to get up but agonizing pain shot through her tail bone across her behind and down her left thigh. She couldn't get up.

Breathing like a raging bull, Satoshi started toward Sassy but caught sight of himself in the dresser mirror. He went to the mirror and although he kept his eye on Sassy, he inspected his bloody chin and mouth.

"You're dead!"

Despite the severe pain in Sassy's tail bone and left thigh, she pushed herself to get up onto her knees. She broke out in a cold sweat as she forced herself to crawl around to the

304 SASSY § Gloria Mallette

side of the bed closest to where Bernard lay. If she was going to die, she wanted to be near him.

Satoshi tested the firmness of his front teeth with his finger. Two were loose and bloody. "Dammit!" He sucked his own blood down. "You are going to die ugly, you black bitch."

Grimacing and sweating, Sassy lowered herself onto her right hip. She cried out from the jarring pain that shot through her lower back. Still, she sat back against the side of the bed. She cried because she was mad as hell that she could no longer do anything to defend herself. She hit the floor with her fist! Unlike the heros in her romances, Norris was not going to show up in the nick of time and rescue her.

The more Satoshi's teeth bled, the angrier he got. "I'm going to gut you!" He could see the reflection of the top of Sassy's head over the bed. He turned away from the mirror.

"I will squeeze the life from you with my bare hands! I will cut your heart out and shove it down Norris's throat!"

"Go to hell you crazy, malignant bastard!"

Satoshi hastily closed the short space between him and Sassy. Her screams deterred him not the least. He dropped down onto one knee with his murderous hands ready to strangle Sassy into silence, but Sassy wasn't going out without a fight. Ignoring her pain, she punched, she clawed, she bit wildly at anything she could touch on Satoshi to keep his hands away from her throat, but then he rammed his fist into her gut, doubling her over against his arm with an agonizing grunt.

Satoshi shoved Sassy back against the side of the bed. He thrust his murderous hands around her throat and began to squeeze the life from her. Sassy continually clawed at Satoshi's arm with only one thought in mind—get his DNA under her nails. As her throat was being crushed, Sassy gasped for the last bit of air she could steal.

"Aaaaaaa!" Satoshi howled! A sharp, jarring pain exploded in the left side of his back. He jerked his hands off of Sassy who gagged and croaked incessantly as she tried to get air back into her lungs while above her, Satoshi, ranting,

SASSY § Gloria Mallette 305

frantically reached under then over his left shoulder trying to reach the spot where the stabbing pain was coming from.

Sassy, still coughing hoarsely as she tried to quell the soreness in her throat and feed her oxygen starved lungs, didn't know why Satoshi had stopped strangling her and was amazed when he jumped up off of her howling like a tormented dog. He ran back to the mirror. Sassy strained to get up but couldn't. She grabbed hold of the bedspread and pulled herself around to see what Satoshi was so upset about and was astounded. Protruding from Satoshi's back was his own knife!

"Grrrrrrr!" Satoshi flung his arms madly over and under his shoulder trying to reach the knife which was midway between his shoulder blade and the center of his back. "God dammit! Aaaaaaa!"

Satoshi's primal squall pushed Sassy into trying to get up off the floor despite the debilitating pain in her lower back.

"Sassy," Bernard said softly, startling her.

"Bernie?" Sassy strained to pull herself up onto her knees while guardedly watching Satoshi who was desperately trying to pull his knife out of his back. She looked at Bernard. He had removed his oxygen mask.

Sassy said in a hushed voice, "Thank God, Bernie. Are you alright? I thought you were dead."

"Go," he said weakly.

"I can't. I'm hurt and I won't leave you." She looked for something to fight with. A ballpoint pen on the night stand. She grabbed it.

"Close your eyes," she whispered.

Having used every ounce of energy he had left, Bernard could do nothing more to help Sassy. He didn't close his eyes, however. He slowly rolled his head toward Satoshi.

Frustrated that he couldn't reach the knife, Satoshi slammed his fist down on top of the dresser, shaking the mirror. "I'm gonna kill you!" In the shaking mirror he saw Bernard on the bed, eyes open, looking right at him. He jerked around and looked at Bernard in disbelief.

He growled, "I'm gonna kill both of you!" Satoshi was about to take the first step to charge toward the bed when the bedroom door suddenly flew open and hit the wall with a resounding thunderous clap.

Sassy couldn't believe her eyes!

Before Satoshi could turn in the direction of the door, Norris was already stepping into a powerful roundhouse kick that slammed into Satoshi's upper chest and catapulted him backwards into the dresser with an explosive bang that toppled everything on it. It took but a second for Norris to glimpse Sassy's bruised face and swollen lips. Like a raging bull, he charged at his mirror image just as Satoshi regained his footing and came at him with a blood curdling scream! Rapid fire power punches, bone crushing arm and leg blocks punctuated with loud grunts from both Norris and Satoshi made Sassy cringe. She prayed that Norris would win.

Norris wasn't in the mood for a long drawn out fight. He dropped down onto one knee to avoid Satoshi's roundhouse and came up with a two-fisted slam to Satoshi's left side which made Satoshi cry out in excruciating pain. In a flash, Norris sprang up, grabbed Satoshi in a headlock, snatched him up off his feet into a backwards throw and slammed him hard to the floor on his back. The knife was driven deeper into Satoshi's back. For a second, he looked thunderstruck as he starred up at Norris. Then his eyes closed.

Norris asked Sassy, "Are you alright?"

"I'm a damn sight from alright."

"I know, baby. Give me a minute." Thinking that he had only momentarily knocked Satoshi out, Norris stood over him, fists ready. He kicked Satoshi's leg to see if he was going to come to. Then he saw blood oozing from under Satoshi's body which baffled him just as much as the face Satoshi hid behind. The blood was flowing not from Satoshi's head but from his back which Norris didn't understand.

"He's bleeding from his back," Norris said.

"His knife is in his back."

Norris didn't ask. As far as he was concerned, it was just. Still, he didn't want Satoshi to die; he had questions upon questions to ask him. Norris checked Satoshi's pulse. There was none. Norris stared down at the face of the man who killed his father and women who had nothing in common except him.

With her hand at her throat, Sassy said hoarsely, "He's your twin."

Norris started to say it was impossible, but the face at his feet said it wasn't. "My mother never said a word. I don't understand."

"I have so much to tell you."

Sassy hoarse voice pulled Norris's attention. He went and crouched down in front of her. He gently touched her bruised face. "That bastard."

"I've never been so scared in my life."

"I'm sorry I wasn't here to protect you." He started to pull Sassy to him but she cried out in pain.

"My back!"

"I could kill him all over again." Being very careful, Norris gently lifted Sassy to her feet and then carried her to the other side of the large queen size bed and laid her on her back.

Norris picked up the cordless telephone. "Is Bernard alright?" Norris dialed 911.

Sassy looked over at Bernard. "Bernie."

Bernard didn't answer.

Sassy tapped him gently on the thigh.

Bernard didn't respond.

"Norris, check Bernie. Please check him."

Norris gave his address to the 911 operator as he went around the bed. He checked Bernard's pulse. "Hold on a moment please." He checked again. There was no pulse. He looked at Sassy and she, too, knew. She loving took Bernard's hand. He had saved her life before leaving her for good. Until the end, he had taken care of her.

Epilogue

Sassy glanced up at the long line stretching toward the back of the book store. She was signing her first non-fiction, *Rage Within*. There were three television news stations on site and several newspapers. Two and a half years ago the story of how Norris's twin, Anthony Yoshito, had murdered innocent people in his quest to destroy Norris, whom he felt had been more favored, made news around the country. So far there were three movie offers that Sassy and Norris had yet to seriously consider. They were not so sure they were ready to see their lives acted out in living color. They hadn't yet completely gotten over the loss of Norris's father and his wife and as well, Bernie's death.

Sassy smiled when a news photographer snapped her picture as she autographed another book. Bernie would have gotten a kick out of all of this, especially since the book was dedicated in his memory and that of all the victims of a man who saw revenge as his only way of dealing with his disadvantaged childhood. With his exuberant self, Bernie would have been the first person on line to be interviewed but that would have been the Bernie of old, before he got AIDS and lost the joy in his soul. Bernie was right though. He always said her greatest, critically acclaimed book would come when she wrote from deep within. There was no other way to express the psychotic emotions of a man who, because of his abandonment by his mother, killed mercilessly those he held responsible and those who he used for information.

That long ago day that hordes of policemen from New York and Pennsylvania swarmed into the house and saw for themselves the real murderer who was not Norris, still haunted Sassy. While paramedics worked on her and Bernard, Detective Keifer, in his over zealous determination to arrest Norris, slapped cuffs on Norris's wrists the minute he laid eyes on him. Only after he saw Norris's twin did he begrudgingly let Norris go. To this day, Detective Keifer has yet to apologize to Norris.

There were many, many questions of Sassy while she lay in her hospital bed, but there were many unanswered questions she and Norris had about how his twin found him in the first place. That is until Detective Natherson drove up to Blue Mountain five months after Satoshi was cremated and a month after the investigations of all the murders he committed were closed. And yes, despite DNA verification, she and Norris still referred to the twin he never knew about as Satoshi. Norris didn't want his mother's name tainted by such evil.

# # # #

Over coffee at the dining room table, Detective Natherson passed a stack of E-mail to Norris. "These came off of Anthony Yoshito's personal lap top. We finally located his apartment on the Lower East Side. The lease was in the name of Byron Satoshi. In his strong box we found two original birth certificates. This one is in your name." He slid the envelope across the table to Norris.

Norris didn't tough the envelope up as he was nervous about opening it. "He stole this the day he killed my mother. Since I nor my father knew I was a twin, when we went to get a copy of my birth certificate and the clerk kept insisting I was a twin birth, we told him he was mistaken; that he had the wrong Oyuki Yoshito. They finally straightened it out and I got my single birth certificate. My father and I just didn't know."

"But Satoshi knew," Sassy said.

"He did," Detective Natherson agreed. "Anthony Yoshito kept that secret for years until he put feelers out on the popular web sites looking for Norris Wilson. He wasn't looking for you, Norris. He probably had no idea you were in America, and while you never saw the inquiries, Clarence Wilson did. That was the beginning of their conspiracy to get you."

"Hate is worse than a ticking time bomb," Sassy said.

"According to the E-mail, Anthony Yoshito was looking to come to America. Clarence Wilson, on the other hand, was looking to find a way to destroy you. They made a deal. Money and your life."

Sassy practically jumped out of her chair. "I knew Clarence had a hand in this! That was the only way Satoshi could have gotten so much information about you about us."

"H'm," Norris said glumly as he read one of the E-mails. Although he and Clarence had not spoken or seen each other since the day their father was buried, a small part of him had hoped what Sassy had speculated so adamantly about had no basis in fact. He just never imagined Clarence would sanction the death of a single soul just to take him down.

"According to the E-mail that Anthony Yoshito never got rid of, Clarence Wilson came up with the idea to either kill you or destroy your business. Keep in mind, they both hated you. Together they decided to destroy your reputation, your life and eventually take your freedom."

Sassy could see Norris was trying to not let how upset he was show in front of Detective Natherson, but she saw in his face how hurt he was and she felt it in her heart. She laid her hand on Norris's arm.

"Good people died because of me."

"Wrong," Sassy said. "Good people died because of those two jealous-hearted, diabolical maniacs. Still, it's really hard to believe Clarence plotted to kill his own parents."

"Actually, according to the E-mail," Detective Natherson said, "Wilson stressed that his mother was not to be touched. The day his father was killed, Mrs. Wilson was not supposed to be home."

"Oh, God," Norris said.

"You know, Satoshi said Alicia was collateral damage; that she got in the way."

"He was right. So, for the big news," Detective Natherson said.

Norris looked up from the E-mail he was reading. Sassy could see all the color had drained from his face.

"There is a boatload of E-mail and text messages sent between Anthony Yoshito and Clarence Wilson spanning a period of three years."

Norris pushed the stack of the E-mail back to Detective Natherson. "I don't need to see anymore."

"Clarence Wilson has been arrested and charged with five counts of first degree murder and two counts of attempted murder."

"Wow," Sassy said.

Norris could no longer sit. "Excuse me." He went out onto the deck where the air was cold and crisp. From where she sat, Sassy could tell just by the way he bowed his head that he was praying. The deck was Norris's favorite place to be with God and his mother.

# # # #

Sassy got the idea to write the book after Detective Natherson's visit, but it would be a full year for her body and mind to heal from the trauma Satoshi put her through before she could begin to write the first line. And yes, even in the book she called him Satoshi although his real name was Anthony Yoshito. Oyuki had given her second born son Mr. Wilson's middle name which Satoshi hated. In Japanese, Satoshi meant ashes, and since he was cremated, Satoshi seemed to fit him best.

Once Sassy settled into writing the book, it became

very cathartic for her. It took seven months to finish *Rage Within*, the writing of it gave her closure. When she couldn't sleep, she wrote. When she felt like crying, she wrote. The only time she didn't write was when she missed Bernie the most. That's when she either called Brice or had Evelyn bring him up to Blue Mountain. She planned on keeping her promise to Bernie to take care of his son. Bernie would be proud of her, she was six months from bringing her and Norris's first son into the world. How she wished Bernie was there to see how happy she was.

SHH! DON'T TELL

Intrigue, suspense, and a dab of romance.

2011

ORDER FORM

Order Personally Autographed Copies of Gloria Mallette's
Books: Go to **www.GloriaMallette.com**

Available Books:		
	Sassy	$15.00
	Living, Breathing Lies	$15.00
	Weeping Willows Dance	$15.00

Shipping and Handling: $4.00 per book

Please send E-mail to gempress@aol.com for shipping cost of
three books or more. If ordering off-line, send your money
order or bank check to:

> Gemini Press
> P.O. Box 488
> Bartonsville, PA 18321

Please indicate to whom your book is to autographed.

Name: _____

Address: _____

_____

_____

E-mail _____

Telephone # _____

Title of Book(s) _____

_____

_____